JACK HARKAWAY

✗IN AMERICA✗

BY
BRACEBRIDGE HEMYNG

JACK HARKAWAY
IN AMERICA

BY
BRACEBRIDGE HEMYNG

JACK HARKAWAY SEIZED THE RUFFIAN BY THE COLLAR.

JACK HARKAWAY IN AMERICA.

CHAPTER I.

THE MAN WITH THE EVIL EYE.

"ANY more passengers for the Liverpool express?" The bell rang again, the porters ran to and fro, the guard held his whistle to his lips, ready to give the signal for starting to the engine-driver, and all was bustle and confusion at the Euston-square terminus of the London and North-Western Railway.

Jack Harkaway, who was going to America to look for his only son, stolen by a villain, was accompanied by Harvey and Mr. Mole. They had just settled their wives, Emily and Hilda, in a comfortable first-class carriage, the two former having obtained permission from the ladies to go into another compartment and smoke as far as Rugby, which was the first stoppage, nearly a hundred miles down the line.

Monday, the black servant, whom Harkaway had brought from the Malay Archipelago, was in a third-class carriage with his wife Ada, who was still, as formerly, Emily's maid.

Harvey had been Jack's companion and friend all through his life, and was going West with him, and in his search for Hunston and his missing child.

Mr. Mole had an idea of being a professor in America, and did not care to remain in England without his old pupils, Harkaway and Harvey.

"Now, gentlemen," said the guard, "quick, please, if you're going on."

"Smoking-carriage, guard?" said Jack.

"This way, smoking, sir. Jump in, please."

Jack entered, followed by Mr. Mole and Harvey. He threw his rugs down on the seat, and the door was banged to in a forcible manner peculiar to railway guards.

The whistle sounded, and the panting engine steamed out of the station.

Harvey displayed a bundle of papers, which nobody seemed inclined to look at just then, and Jack drew out his cigar-case, offering a weed to each of his companions.

When they had lighted up, they looked round the carriage, which had two occupants besides themselves.

One was a youth about sixteen years of age, with sharp, restless eyes, and intelligent features.

The other was a man of about forty years of age, tall, rather stout, well-made, and apparently extremely muscular.

His features were strikingly handsome, but his face was not an agreeable one to look at.

From his eyes flashed a peculiar fire, like an electric light, which darted straight through anyone he looked at.

It was like being mesmerised to meet this man's fixed stare.

The person upon whom he concentrated his sinister regards, at first felt uncomfortable, and, as a rule, afterwards gave himself up to the evil influence.

What is known as electro-biology was expressed in the glance of this singular individual.

The train had not proceeded far before he turned his gaze full upon Jack, who shivered, he scarcely knew why, and was forced to look up.

Rain was falling in torrents, and the heavy drops, driven by the wind, splashed mournfully against the windows.

"Nice weather for travelling?" exclaimed the stranger.

"Is it?" replied Jack, who felt an instinctive dislike to this man, and resented his addressing him as an impertinence.

"I say it is nice weather," continued the stranger, "and having said so, there is no necessity for you to ask me the question."

"Your opinion about the weather is a matter of the most perfect indifference to me," answered Jack.

"That is scarcely a polite remark, Mr. Harkaway."

Jack started.

"You know my name?" he said.

"I was in Naples a few weeks last Fall, and most people in that city have heard of you."

"Indeed! To whom may I be talking?" said Jack, more coolly.

The stranger handed him a card, upon which Jack read—

MR. MILES FENTON,

The World.

"That is an odd address, Mr. Fenton," said he, with a smile.

"Well, you see, I travel around constantly, and never stop long in one place."

"You are a cosmopolite?"

"Exactly. It would be folly were I to put Naples on my card, when I might be in London the next week, and equally foolish if I wrote London, when the following month I might land in New York, or San Francisco."

"You are a great traveller."

Miles Fenton shrugged his shoulders.

"What s travelling now-a-days?" he replied. "Locomotion is so rapid and easy that distance is done away with. Cook was a traveller, Columbus was a traveller, and so was Mungo Park, but as for me, I am simply a restless mortal, who is as good as an annuity to railways and steamboats."

"How did you know me in Naples?" asked Jack.

"You were pointed out to me in the Café d'Europe as an eccentric Englishman."

"Really?"

"It was said that you were crazy about the extermination of brigands, and there was some talk of asking you to become Chief of the Police, as you evinced such an inclination for thief-taking."

Jack was doubtful whether Mr. Fenton was quietly chaffing him, or if that was his usual way of talking.

A vein of sarcasm ran through his remarks, which was rather irritating.

"I should have cultivated your acquaintance," continued Miles Fenton, "had I not been suddenly obliged to go to Constantinople."

Jack made no reply, and Mr. Fenton taking up a paper behind which he hid his dazzling eyes, the conversation dropped.

Who was this singular man, who talked about the world as his home, and spoke of going to the extreme east or west as if he had been going from the car to his country house?

This was the question that puzzled Jack.

He was roused from the reverie into which he had plunged by Mr. Mole.

"Can I trouble you for a cigar, Harkaway?" he said.

"Very sorry, sir, but my case is empty," replied Jack.

"Are you better off, Harvey?"

"No sir," answered Harvey. "My case is in my great-coat, which I left in the carriage with the ladies."

Mr. Mole drew out some sandwiches and his sherry flask, and applied his lips to the latter.

"Railway travelling excites thirst," he remarked, "in a most remarkable degree."

The youth we have alluded to was sitting opposite the professor, and looking up, he said—

"Don't apologise."

"What for?"

"Drinking. You made an excuse. It isn't necessary. Drinking is a British custom, I guess?"

As he spoke, the youth produced a cigar-case, and drew one out.

"You don't object to smoke?" he asked.

"Thank you. I will take one, as you are so kind," replied Mr. Mole. "Hand them over, please."

"No, sir," was the reply.

"I thought you asked me to have one?"

"No, sirree."

"What! you won't give me one of your cigars?"

"No, sirree, bob," answered the youth, emphatically.

Mr. Mole fell back in his seat and looked disgusted.

"Well," he said, "I will say that I have usually found a little sociability amongst my travelling companions."

"You think me real mean, don't you?" asked the youth.

"I must confess I do."

"Will you tell me any reason why I should give you a twelve-cent Havana?"

"There's no particular reason, certainly."

"Nor do I. Now I'll tell you what I'll do with you. We'll trade on this twelve-cent Havana. I'm a little sick to-day. Give me a sandwich and the weed is yours."

"With pleasure. Will you try some sherry?"

"I'd rather have water; but just a sip of sherry will suit my complaint, I guess."

The flask and the case changed hands, and as Mr. Mole returned the latter, he said, rather stiffly—

"I'm obliged to you, young gentleman."

"You're wrong. I am not a young gentleman. My father keeps a store in New York, and I've been over to London for him on business," replied the youth.

"It does you great credit, at your age."

"Oh, we start early in the States, and learn to get our own living as soon as we can walk."

"I have heard of the precocity of Americans."

"That's a big word, and, as I haven't my 'Webster's Dictionary' with me, perhaps you'd come down a peg or two."

"I will endeavour to adapt my conversation to your limited understanding."

"That's rough on me," laughed the youth.

"I didn't intend—"

"Oh, yes, you did. I saw you were down on me like a beaver. My name's Felix S. Prye, and I can see as far through a six-inch plank in a lumber-yard as most people. All the Pryes are good at that."

"What do you think of London?" asked Mr. Mole.

"It's a tall city—mighty tall; but you're too slow, I guess," returned Prye.

"We make money, though."

"Yes, and it's lucky for you, or you wouldn't have found the 'Alabama' so easy to pay. That was a steep hill for you Britishers to foot up, I guess."

Mr. Mole looked dignified.

"My!" cried Felix S. Prye; "we were kinder tickled at home to think of John Bull parting with that bullion."

He chuckled to himself as if immensely pleased at the thought of the payment of the indemnity.

"You were set on arbitration," he added. "But perhaps you'd better fight next time."

"We look upon you as our brethren," said Mr. Mole, "and a war between two kindred nations ought to be avoided."

"That's so," replied Felix S. Prye. "The Secesh hold the same opinion, I guess, by this time; but if ever you are tired of holding Canada or the West India Islands, I daresay the American nation will help you out of the difficulty."

He laughed again, quietly, to himself.

"Going over the big drink?" he said, looking up.

"I beg your pardon," said Mr. Mole.

"Are you crossing over to the other side?"

"We are."

"What ship?"

"The 'City of Athens.'"

"My! That is my vessel. We travel together. I shall be glad to see you in New York city, if you call at my father's store in Eighth Avenue."

"What does your father sell?"

"He keeps everything but the Ten Commandments, I guess, and there's no call for them in New York city," answered Felix S. Prye.

"I think I shall like New York," replied Mr. Mole, a little sarcastically, "if all the Americans resemble you."

"That's hard," said the youth. "You're fond of hitting out at me."

"It is my way to return favours. Can I offer you my flask again?"

"No, sir. Sherry is an internal application

which is not good to come at too often; thank you all the same. You come to me in Eighth Avenue and I'll take you around."

"I shall be much oblig d."

"You shall taste our oysters—they're real elegant. I'll give you a pan roast and lager beer in Fulton Market."

Mr. Mole expressed himself deeply grateful for this offer.

"What are you going to do over the other side?" continued Mr. Prye.

"That depends upon circumstances."

"Well, I guess there are two things open to you. A man can go into real estate, or keep a lager-shop, if he can't do anything else. They're both a refuge for the destitute."

The train now slackened speed, and presently ran into Rugby.

Jack and Harvey got out to stretch their legs, and have a brief chat with the ladies.

"Are you comfortable?" asked Jack, looking in at Emily and Hilda.

"Perfectly," replied Emily.

"Is there anything you want?"

"Only your society; have you done smoking?'

"Not quite. We stop again at Crewe," replied Jack.

"You want an extension of leave, I suppose?" said Hilda. "Very well; you may go back again, but we shall expect you at Crewe."

Jack smiled, and returned to his carriage with Harvey.

"What the men find to amuse them in smoking alone, I can't imagine," said Emily.

"It's only selfishness," replied Hilda.

"That comes after marriage," said Emily. "They are not like that when they are courting us."

"Heigho!" remarked Hilda, with a slight yawn; "what fools girls are to get married!"

"I won't go so far as that," replied Emily. "Jack and I are very happy. If we could only get our poor, dear child back again—"

"Hush!" interrupted Hilda. "You promised me, dearest, not to fret. We are on the track, you know."

"Oh, my darling! my darling!" cried Emily.

She burst into tears, and hid her face in her hands, weeping bitterly.

CHAPTER II.

THE CRYPTOGRAPH.

At Crewe, Jack, Harvey, and Mr. Mole entered the ladies' carriage, having smoked until they were tired.

"Curious fellow, that young Prye," said Mr. Mole.

"Not half so curious as Mr. Miles Fenton," remarked Jack.

"How that man's eyes go through you!" observed Harvey.

"By Jove! yes. I thought once I should have gone to sleep when he was looking at me."

"That exactly describes my sensation," said Harvey.

"I should not be surprised if he were to turn out some travelling showman in the mesmerist line," said Mr. Mole.

"Perhaps Mole's right," replied Jack. "If he is a professional mesmerist, that would account for his travelling about."

"He's a clever fellow, anyhow," said Harvey.

"And one of the most remarkable men I have met with for some time. Somehow, Dick, I feel as if he was mixed up in some way with my fate."

"How?"

"I can't say how, exactly," replied Jack,

thoughtfully. "But it is so; I've got the feeling."

Mr. Mole produced a piece of paper which, when opened, was an ordinary telegraph sheet, such as messages are sent out on from the office.

"What have you hold of there, sir?" asked Jack.

"That's what I want to know, Harkaway," replied Mr. Mole.

"Where did you pick it up?"

"This Mr. Fenton dropped it as he got out of the carriage to go into the refreshment-room at Crewe."

"Why didn't you give it back to him?'

"I couldn't. We hadn't time, so I intended to return it when we reached Liverpool. It's a telegram, but so strangely worded I cannot make head or tail of it."

"Perhaps it's a confidential communication that ought to be held sacred," said Jack. "Never pry into a man's private affairs. Fold it up."

"I hope, Harkaway, I am as careful about right and wrong in such matters as any other gentleman!" answered Mr. Mole.

"I didn't say you were not, sir."

"But you implied it."

"If I did, I beg your pardon."

"That is settled; say no more about it," said Mr. Mole. "But with regard to this paper, it seems to me to be written in secret characters."

"Really?"

"Look at it yourself. Syriac or Chaldee could not be more difficult to decipher."

Jack took the paper from his hand and cast his eye carelessly over it.

"By Jove!" he said. "It is evidently a cryptograph, or hidden writing. When I was at school, I was rather fond of making out cryptographs."

"You're clever if you read that."

"I can read it. The question is to translate it," answered Jack.

"What is it, dear?" asked Emily, who had partially recovered from her fit of depression.

"We met a most mysterious man in the smoking-carriage," said Jack. "In Italy, the people would have said he had the evil eye."

"The evil eye!" repeated Emily.

"I never saw such an eye before in all my travels. Ugh! It makes me shiver to think of it."

"Does this paper belong to him?"

"Mr. Mole says he dropped it. Now, look here, all of you. Would there be any harm in my trying to make it out?"

"None at all," was the unanimous response.

"I wouldn't do anything mean."

"Forge ahead, old man, and put your squeamishness in your pocket," said Harvey "Perhaps this cryptographic telegram may give us some insight into the mysterious Mr. Fenton's particular line of business."

"I'll bet you a bottle of wine, Harkaway, you don't make sense of it," said Mr. Mole.

"Done with you, sir," replied Jack, looking at his watch. "It is now twelve o'clock," he continued; "we are not due before half-past one in the morning at Liverpool. So we have an hour and a half."

"The midnight hour," remarked Harvey. "Just the time for mystery."

"What a bad light this lamp gives," said Jack, leaning back to see the paper as well as he could.

He pored over it for some time in perplexity.

"It's a lick," he said. "It's nothing but figures. Listen to this—

"13.14 : 18.6.8 : 18.16 : 7.16.13.19 : 6.8.20 : 12 : 2 : 12.8.20 : 2 : 14.11 4 : 4.16.6 : 6 : 19 : 19.6.16. 13.6.6.8.7 : 4.13.13 : 18.12.19 : 12 : 6 : 6.13.11.6.- 20.17.8.19.11 : 21.4.8.2 : 11.4 : 2.8.14.

11.8.12 "

"I should think that those figures correspond to letters in the alphabet," said Harvey.

"No doubt," replied Jack.

"Read that over again, Harkaway," said Mr. Mole.

Jack did so.

"Do you observe," continued Mole, "that twenty-one is the highest figure employed in this cryptograph?"

"Yes."

"In the alphabet there are how many letters?"

"Twenty-six."

"Precisely. And how many vowels?"

"Five."

"Very well," said Mr. Mole. "It is evident, to my mind, that the vowels are left out."

"Bravo, sir!" cried Jack. "That's a discovery."

"Now, if the letters are numbered right off, 21 would draw B."

"So it would."

"Try it that way. 13.14 is the beginning. That would be Q and R."

"Can't make anything of that, sir," replied Jack.

"Nor I," said Mole, puzzled.

Some minutes elapsed, and no one spoke.

"Work it backward, old man," said Harvey.

"You fellows have a monopoly of ideas to-night," replied Jack. "I'm beaten straight out."

He looked at the telegram, and found that, reading it as if the alphabetical letters were numbered up from Z, 13 and 14 would be L and K.

"L. K.," he muttered. "Luck, lick, look. That's it. Look. 18.6.8.: F. T. R. Faster, filter, after. Hurrah! Look after. That will do."

"Bravo!" said Mr. Mole. "We are progressing."

"I think we've got the key, now," remarked Harvey.

"How clever you men are," said Emily.

"I shall cry my bet off," said Mr. Mole. "More especially as I have been instrumental in solving the enigma."

"I'll let you off, sir," answered Jack. "Now, hold on. Let me read this."

He was occupied for some time with a pencil and his pocket-book.

At length he looked up, very gravely.

"What's the matter, Jack dear?" inquired Emily.

"I don't like it," he replied.

"Like what?"

"This cryptographic telegram. It looks ugly."

"Read it! Read it!" cried everybody.

"This is what I make of it—

"Look after ——. If he should trace me to America, you know what to do. Death! Letters will find me at the 'Office,' Houston-street, New York. "ONE ARM."

"You see," cried Jack, "that the name of the person to be looked after is purposely omitted, and the whole thing would not matter much, were it not for the signature."

"One arm means—" began Harvey.

Jack took the word out of his mouth.

"Hunston," he replied.

"Exactly what I was going to say."

"This telegram comes from Naples," Jack went on. "It is dated Naples, and there is 'from One Arm,' in cipher. If Mr. Miles Fenton really dropped this—"

"I saw him do so," said Mr. Mole.

"Then Fenton is a friend of Hunston's, and they have been corresponding. Fenton has received information of my movements, and intends to dog me."

"Oh, dear me!" said Emily, with a sigh. "More intrigues, more danger!"

"It can't be helped, Emmy, dearest," answered Jack. "Fore-warned is fore-armed, you know."

"So it is. But if this dreadful Miles Fenton, the man with the evil eye, should—should—"

She broke off abruptly, and put her handkerchief to her eyes.

"Should kill you, dear, what should I do?"

"He's got to do it first. I carry a six-shoooter, and am not afraid of half a dozen Miles Fentons," said Jack, bravely.

"Hunston must have made a lot of money with Barboni," observed Harvey.

"I expect he has got clear off with a pile," answered Jack. "Miles Fenton does not look like the sort of man to work for nothing."

"Not much," said Harvey.

"Well, if we can get to New York before the 'Santa Maria,' we shall gobble up Mr. Hunston."

"There is every chance of it. In fact, it is Wall-street to a lemon," replied Harvey.

"What a head that fellow Hunston must have!" observed Mr. Mole. "Only fancy his thinking of employing a man to watch you, Harkaway!"

"He means to do something more than watch, I expect," replied Jack.

"It is fortunate I found the cryptograph; but I am always doing something for you boys. What would you be without me?"

"I shall keep this telegram. Don't say a word about it, any of you."

"Not I," replied Harvey.

"If Mr. Fenton misses it, he may find out, if he can, where it has gone to."

"Where shall we stop to-night?" asked Emily.

"At the Great Northern Hotel," replied Jack.

"When do we sail?"

Jack consulted a bill he had in his pocket.

"The Royal mail steamer 'City of Athens,'" he replied, "will sail for New York on Thursday, calling at Queenstown the following day to embark mails and passengers. A steam-tender will leave the north landing stage, Prince's Pier-head, punctually at two o'clock in the afternoon, on Thursday, to convey saloon passengers and their baggage on board."

"That will give us nice time to get everything ready," said Emily.

Soon afterwards the train ran into Lime-street Station, the tickets were collected, and the engine carried the passengers on to Liverpool.

They walked from the terminus into the hotel, and having secured their room, went up in the elevator to bed.

Jack was unusually silent and thoughtful.

While booking his room, he had noticed Mr. Miles Fenton in the hall, talking to the porter.

"Your number, sir, will be 197," he heard the porter say, as he came back from the office.

"And mine," muttered Jack, "is 196. I must look out."

Knowing what he did, Miles Fenton was an awkward man to have for a neighbour.

If his suspicions were correct, and he was really the person indicated in the mysterious telegram, and admitting that the sender, "One Arm," was Hunston, there was danger ahead.

It was not enough for him that he had stolen the child.

He wanted—he hungered for—the life of its father.

CHAPTER III.

A NIGHT OF HORROR.

JACK took the precaution to lock and double-lock his door.

When he retired to rest, his mind was too much disturbed for sleep.

He thought of Hunston, of the grudge he owed him for shooting him in the arm, and the fearful power he would have over his child.

Hunston could ill-treat the boy, could teach him at his tender age to hate his father and mother, and could bring him up in the vilest way.

It was in his power to make him a low blackguard, a thief, and even a murderer.

Jack clenched his hands so tightly that the nails ran into the flesh.

It was gall and wormwood to him to think that Hunston should have the whip-hand of him in this way.

How often had he spared his life, when he might have wiped him out of his track?

His life-long enemy was at work.

"Let me once more have the chance, and I'll show Hunston no pity," he muttered.

If he had had him before his eyes at that moment, he would have shot him.

But his chance had gone by, and it was doubtful when they would meet again.

At length he was inclined for rest.

He took one look out at the night, which was dull and cloudy after the rain.

His window opened upon St. George's Hall, but he great pile was indistinct and misty.

A clock struck the hour of three.

Feeling under his pillow to see if his revolver was ready to his hand, Jack got into bed, and kissing the forehead of his slumbering wife, prepared for sleep.

After a long time he fell into a restless slumber.

How long he slept he did not know, but he awoke fancying that some one was bending over him.

The grey dawn was breaking through the ragged, drifting clouds, and by the imperfect light he saw the dim outline of a human form.

In its shadowy hand was a long, sharp, gleaming knife, upraised, and in the act of descending.

It was too dark to distinguish the features of the intruder, but his eyes glistened like live coals, and thrilled Jack to the marrow of his bones.

For a moment he could not move.

He was fascinated by a strange power, flashed from brain to brain.

Fearful that his last hour had come, Jack made a supreme effort, and, with a wild cry, started up.

The spell was broken.

He turned to search for his revolver, and, in doing so, took up the pillow upon which his head had been lying.

This act proved his salvation.

The descending knife plunged into the pillow, instead of the soft flesh it was intended to penetrate.

Grasping his pistol, Jack fired at random, and the figure slowly retreated.

Again he discharged the weapon, just as the shadowy form disappeared through the doorway.

A deeply muttered curse fell upon Jack's ears, and, as he sprang from the bed, the mysterious being was gone.

Emily was aroused by the shots, and, sitting up in bed, looked wildly around.

"Oh, Jack!" she said. "What is the matter? Are you hurt? I have had such a terrible dream about you."

"I'm all right, thank God!" answered Jack, "though I've had a narrow shave, Emmy."

"From what?"

"Being assassinated in my sleep. It was touch and go, unless I've been dreaming."

He proceeded to light a candle, and as he was thus engaged, the night-porter came up with a lantern.

"What's up, sir?" asked the latter. "Was that you shooting?"

"It was," replied Jack. "Show a light. A man has been in my room."

He first examined the door, the lock of which had been neatly picked, evidently by a professional hand.

One bullet had gone through the door, the other was found imbedded in the wall.

The pillow was slashed open, so that the feathers with which it was padded were streaming out.

"It's no dream, but a terrible reality," said Jack. "Go and get me a cup of coffee, porter, I shall not go to sleep again to-night."

"What do you think it was, sir?—robbery?—have you lost anything?" inquired the porter.

"Nothing," replied Jack.

"What was it, then?" the porter asked, scratching his head with an air of perplexity.

"Murder!" said Jack, curtly.

The porter looked at him with a dazed expression, and, shivering in spite of himself, went away.

"Jack!" whispered Emily, under her breath.

"Go to sleep, my pretty one," he answered.

"I can't. Come here, please."

He approached the bed, and laid his hand on her forehead.

"Who was it tried to kill you, dear?"

"Miles Fenton," replied Jack.

"How do you know?"

"I felt his eyes burning into me through the darkness."

"Oh, Jack, how your hand shakes!" said Emily.

"Enough to make it, my child," answered Jack. "This man is worse than a whole band of brigands. I have never been afraid or any one before, but I do fear Miles Fenton."

"Cannot you have him brought to justice?"

"No, dearest. I cannot prove anything. All I can do is to be on my guard. It was only my luck in waking just in time, and having my Derringer handy, that saved me."

"Do you think that Miles Fenton is sent by Hunston to kill you?" continued Emily.

"I don't think it—I know it," answered Jack.

He paced the room impatiently, and then began to dress, having scarcely finished before the porter returned with the coffee.

Jack slipped some money into his hand, and said—

"You need not mention this in the hotel."

"Very well, sir," replied the porter, who looked as if he had serious doubts as to Jack's sanity.

Jack sat patiently looking out of the window into the wet and muddy streets, listening to the boisterous wind which howled under the eaves and roared in the chimney, and watched the night police walking mechanically along their beats.

Emily fell off to sleep again, and, unable to remain still, Jack put on his hat and went downstairs to take a walk through the city.

The streets were deserted, it being too early for business men to be abroad, and the roysterers of the night having reeled home long before.

In Dale-street he stopped, hesitating whether to go on to the Exchange, or retrace his steps to the hotel.

Just at that moment, he heard the report of a pistol, and felt as if some one had tried to knock his hat off.

Turning round rapidly, he saw a cloaked figure running away rapidly.

Instantly he gave chase, but the man crossed the road, darted down Castle-street, and disappeared through an alley.

"This is getting hot," muttered Jack.

He took off his hat, and found it perforated in two places, just above the crown of his head.

An inch lower, and he would have been a dead man.

Trembling with excitement and nervous apprehension, he returned to the hotel, and proceeded at once to his room.

It was broad daylight now.

Emily appeared to be sleeping placidiy.

He walked to the bedside, and spoke to her.

She returned no answer, and the death-like pallor of her face alarmed him.

"Emily! Emily!" he ejaculated, shaking her by the arm.

She did not move, and he noticed that her breathing was so low as to be scarcely perceptible.

Pulling the bedclothes down a little way, he started back in affright.

The sheets were saturated with blood.

"Good God!" he exclaimed. "She is dead! They have murdered her!"

Running to the bell-rope, ne commenced pulling it furiously.

The night-porter again made his appearance.

"Run for a doctor, quick. My wife is dead or dying!" he cried.

"What!" began the porter.

Jack cut him short, by pushing him out of the room, crying—

"A doctor! a doctor!"

Returning to the bedside, aghast with horror and apprehension, he waited impatiently for the arrival of a surgeon.

The minutes seemed hours, and he thought the man would never come.

"At last! at last!" he muttered, as the door opened, and the porter entered, accompanied by a doctor.

"What is the matter, sir?" he inquired.

"My wife, I fear, is dying, or dead!" answered Jack. "For Heaven's sake, lose no time in ascertaining the extent of her injuries!"

This the doctor did without further parley, and tearing the sheet into strips, proceeded to bandage up a wound in the side.

Jack watched him with the utmost interest depicted on his countenance.

"The lady has had a very narrow escape," said the doctor. "The wound is an incised one, made with a sharp weapon, such as a knife, which has glanced along the ribs without inflicting any more serious injury than that occasioned by loss of blood and the inevitable shock to the nervous system."

"Is her life in danger?"

"Not at all. The injury is superficial."

Jack breathed again, and wrung the doctor's hand in hearty recognition of his good tidings.

"Now, how did this happen?" asked the doctor.

"I cannot tell. All I know is that I have an enemy in this house who has twice attempted my life this night," replied Jack.

The doctor shrugged his shoulders, as if he was not accustomed to solve mysteries.

"Do you stay here long?" he asked.

"No. We were to sail to-day for New York, in the 'City of Athens.' The object of my enemy is to prevent me from sailing. Will my wife be able to travel?"

"She might be carried on board, though I should recommend a week's rest in the hotel," answered the doctor.

Jack gnashed his teeth with rage as he reflected that this delay would probably enable the "Santa Maria" to reach New York before him.

The doctor sent to his house for proper surgical bandages and stimulants, under the influence of which Emily revived.

"Jack, dear, are you near me?" she murmured.

"I am here, dearest," he answered.

She grasped his hand, feebly pressing it.

"I have been ill, have I not? What is this pain in my side?"

"The same hand that tried to kill me has injured you, my child; but the doctor says it is nothing serious "

"Thank Heaven for that!" she replied. "I feel very weak and ill, but I should not like to die, Jack, for your sake. You would miss me so much."

A mist came over Jack's eyes.

"You are a brave little pet," he said, "and you will soon be well. You have had a marvellous escape. My only regret is that we shall have t postpone our journey."

"Not for me, dear. Can't I be carried board?"

"I am afraid you are not strong enough."

"Oh, yes, indeed I am," said Emily. "When I think of our child, Jack, and how important it is we should get to New York before Hunston, I am strong enough for anything."

"What do you say, docter?" asked Jack, turning to the medical man.

"I can permit the removal, though I do not advise it," was the reply. "You will carry a surgeon, and consequently you will have every attention and advice. But, my dear sir, allow me to ask you one thing?"

"What?"

"Do you not intend to do anything to discover and punish the author of this dastardly outrage?"

"In this case, doctor, I mean to be my own police," replied Jack.

"Of course, you know best," said the doctor, with another eloquent shrug of the shoulders.

He remained in the room, attending to Emily, while Jack sought Mr. Mole and Harvey, with whom he descended to the breakfast-room, gravely relating the horrors of that eventful night.

His listeners were much shocked.

"Fenton has lost no time in beginning the campaign," said Harvey.

"The villain," said Mr. Mole. "I should like to punch that man's head, Harkaway. It is not often I use such emphatic language, but the occasion justifies it."

"I'll be upsides with him before long, sir," answered Jack.

They had just taken their seats at a table, and were ordering breakfast, for which Jack had very little appetite, when the very person they were speaking about appeared, and placed himself in a vacant chair.

Jack started, and his face flushed.

"Good morning," said Mr. Miles Fenton, who was perfectly calm and self-possessed. "I trust you slept well, Mr. Harkaway."

Astonished at his cool impertinence, Jack looked sternly at him.

"We have engaged this table for ourselves," h replied.

"I believe this is a public room," answered Fenton, "and that any empty chair is the common property of any one staying in the hotel. If you want private apartments, had you not better engage them? Shall I call the waiter and ask the question?"

Jack's only reply was to get up and walk to another table, being closely followed by Mr. Mole and Harvey.

"What confounded cool cheek!" said Jack.

"Rather," replied Harvey; "that fellow's a caution. If any one can beat him on cool cheek, I'd like to see him."

"The man is the incarnation of self-possessed insolence," remarked Mr. Mole.

Miles Fenton was regarding them from a distance with his basilisk eye.

CHAPTER IV.

ON BOARD THE "CITY OF ATHENS."

HE did not seem in the least put out at their departure. On the contrary, there was a devilish leer on his face, which was supported by an air of triumph. Jack returned his fixed gaze with a look of defiance.

But he was forced to drop his eyelids, as it was impossible to withstand Fenton's unearthly stare.

He trembled all over in spite of himself whenever the evil eye was upon him.

* * * * * *

Faithful to her promise, Emily was carried on board the tender, which was waiting at the pier-head to convey the saloon passengers to the steamer.

Fortunately, there was little or no wind, the weather being hazy, with slight rain, and the passage promised to be a fair one—to Queenstown, at all events.

She could give no account of the injury she had received.

All she knew was that she was roused from her sleep by an acute pain, almost immediately becoming insensible.

She fancied, as she opened her eyes, that she obtained a momentary glance of an indistinct figure by the bedside, which glared at her with fierce, vindictive eyes.

This was all.

Jack had her conveyed to her state-room, and sat by her side till the ship started on its long and dangerous voyage, which was to be broken for a few hours at Queenstown.

She was pleased at the change, and declared that she should be quite as much at ease in her berth as at the hotel.

"I would do anything for you and our child, Jack, dear," she said.

"You're a brick, Emily," replied Jack; "and if you keep up your spirits we shall soon pull you through."

He ordered Monday to remain in the passage, within call, to prevent any repetition of the attack, should Mr. Fenton sail in the same ship.

About this he was not yet sure.

But he had not long to remain in doubt.

Going on deck, he entered the smoking-room, where he saw Miles Fenton composedly smoking a cigar and ordering the deck-steward to bring him a pint of champagne.

"Ah! Mr. Harkaway," he exclaimed, with a bland smile, which he could assume successfully at times, "we are destined to travel together, you see."

"I am sorry for it," replied Jack, bluntly.

"How unpolished you are!" continued Fenton. "Did you never hear the dictum of the polite Frenchman who said that language was given us to conceal our thoughts?"

"I shan't take the trouble to conceal mine when you are the subject of them."

"What have I done?" asked Miles Fenton, innocently.

"Ask yourself."

"I see you are determined not to make friends with me. But I will not quarrel with you," said Fenton.

"You may please yourself about that," replied Jack.

"I like an English bear occasionally; he amuses me. Come, let us be enemies. Shall I say something rude? Just to oblige you!" Fenton exclaimed, with a laugh.

"Find some one else to talk to."

"By Jove! that is not difficult on board ship, and you are not so very entertaining, after all."

"I don't mean to be, when I come in contact with an assassin."

Miles Fenton started, and fixed his terrible gaze upon Jack, who averted his eyes.

These two were alone in the room, the other passengers not having yet settled themselves and their baggage, and the deck-steward having gone below for the wine.

Rising, Fenton strode over to Jack and grasped his shoulder with a force that hurt him.

Angrily, Jack struck his arm and knocked it away.

"Hands off, Mr. Fenton," he said. "I don't allow any one to touch me."

"What do you mean by what you have just said?" demanded Miles Fenton.

"Just what you heard."

"You called me an assassin."

"So you are. Last night you made two attempts on my life, and one on my wife's."

"Oh, you are sure of that? It is as well we should understand one another. Perhaps the next attempt may be more successful. Have you anything else against me?"

"Ask Hunston," replied Jack, incautiously.

"Ah!" cried Fenton; "my telegram! The cryptograph! I was not aware you knew so much. No matter. It is the worse for you."

"Just keep clear of me and mine, that's all," answered Jack, "or—"

He drew his pistol from his pocket.

"Or what, Mr. Harkaway?" asked Fenton, coolly.

"I will shoot you as I would a dog," replied Jack.

"For that matter, two can play at the shooting game," said Fenton; "and if it is done clumsily it becomes a hanging matter. But we have said enough. We need not expose our affairs before all the passengers."

"I have done," replied Jack. "Take a fool's advice, as they say, and steer clear of me, my hearty."

He turned on his heel and went below, leaving Miles Fenton to his own reflections.

On consideration, he was sorry he had lost his temper and been so hasty.

It was foolish to display his hand as he had done.

Perhaps it would have been better if he had not let Fenton know that he knew so much about him.

But his conduct had been so outrageous and cowardly that he could not conceal what was in his mind.

Jack was nothing if he was not straightforward and blunt.

A short time afterwards Felix S. Prye and some other passengers entered the smoking-room, followed by Mr. Mole.

"Well, sir," said Felix, "how do you find the ship?"

"Excellently fitted up," answered Mr. Mole. "I have been to the *comptoir des emigrants*, or deck-bar, and I have found out the saloon-bar."

"That is the first move with you Britishers on board ship, I guess," answered Felix.

"Oh!" exclaimed Mr. Mole; "I did it simply with a view to see how the comfort of the passengers was studied."

"Is that so?" replied Felix, with a quiet smile.

Young as he was, he could gauge character accurately, and he saw that Mole's weakness was a fondness for the bottle.

Everything went on smoothly till after dinner, when the ship began to roll.

The ladies retired to their cabins, and faint calls for the stewardess were heard.

About eleven o'clock the next day, the ship arrived in Queenstown harbour, and a tender took on shore those of the passengers who wished to see a little of Ireland.

In the evening the vessel started again on her voyage across the ocean.

Not many passengers appeared at dinner, but Jack, Harvey, and Mr. Mole, being used to the sea, took their places at the purser's table.

Jack had noticed that the purser was a conceited man, proud of his position, and he determined to have some fun with him.

He had not forgotten how to ventriloquise, and throwing his voice close to Mole, he imitated that gentleman, and made him say, " I was not aware that it was customary for the purser to sit down at the same table with saloon passengers."

The purser grew very red.

Every one was silent, and looked curiously at one another, as if they thought something unpleasant was about to happen.

" I am here by the captain's orders, " he replied, " and if any one objects to me, he can go to another table."

" You are not what I call a regular officer, " said Jack, " and I am told you pursers generally rise from cabin-boys, and, therefore, cannot be gentlemen."

" Really, Sir, this is an insult, " said the purser, who felt the hit more because he actually had risen from a cabin-boy to his present position.

" I can't help it," Jack went on. " I believe my opinion is shared by others on board."

" It's my idea, Mr. Mole, that you are not sober, sir, " said the purser.

" Bless me ! " rejoined Mr. Mole. " What do you mean ? "

Jack was silent, now he had made the mischief, and left the couple to fight it out between them.

" You have insulted me, sir, " rejoined the purser, growing redder.

" I ? "

" Yes, sir ; and you will find that I have the power to resent it. You shan't get drunk on board this ship again. "

" You are a very impertinent person."

" Why did you attack me first ? "

" I did not speak, " replied Mole.

" Nonsense, " said the purser, scornfully.

" I say I didn't."

" I heard you."

" Sir," said Mole, you're a——"

He paused to select a suitable epithet for the occasion.

" Well, sir, what am I ? " asked the purser, standing up.

" Perhaps you would not like to hear what I think of you, " answered Mole.

" You insult me for nothing at all. Then you try to sneak out of it by telling a deliberate falsehood, and I leave the passengers to decide what you are," said the purser, with a withering air.

" Dear me, this is very perplexing." said Mole. " I am not conscious of giving any offence."

" Get sober, sir, " cried the purser, " and sit at another table in future."

Saying this, he threw down his knife and fork, and went in a rage to his own cabin, having spoken in a low tone to the barkeeper in passing.

After dinner, Jack sought the smoking-room, to get up a game at whist with Harvey and anyone else who liked to play.

Mr. Mole presently joined him, looking flushed and annoyed.

" That purser is a very extraordinary person, Harkaway," he said.

" What's he done now, sir ? " asked Jack.

" He has stopped my grog. I went to the deck-

bar to get a cocktail, and the man would not serve me. The same below."

" That's rough on you, I guess," said Felix.

" Very much so. ' Why won't you serve me ? ' said I. ' Purser's orders, sir. Your grog's stopped.' Confound the fellow ! "

" I should see the captain, and make a splurge about it," replied Felix.

" I have done so, and the captain says he can' interfere with the purser. They hang together, you see."

" It is because you attacked him at dinner."

" I did not," replied Mr. Mole. " That is a delusion of his. Somebody else spoke, and he singled me out as the victim of his spite."

" Come, now," said Felix ; " that won't wash. I heard you. My ! wasn't I tickled to hear you ! "

" Harkaway," said Mr. Mole, " it's my firm conviction you're at the bottom of this."

" Not I, sir. Wouldn't do such a thing," answered Jack, innocently.

" Make what reparation is in your power ; order a bottle of brandy and give it to me."

" Couldn't think of it, sir. It's against orders."

Mr. Mole groaned and looked miserable.

" Say, now," said Felix S. Prye, " will you take a hand at euchre ? "

" I am not in the humour to play cards," replied Mole. " I feel more like chastising that rascally purser."

" Go for him ! " added Felix.

" I shall pull his nose, I think," said Mole. " It does not do to trifle with me, as Harkaway knows very well ; let the purser look out for squalls. I'm not the man to stand his nonsense. Stop my grog, indeed ! I'll stop his chant."

" Will you ? " exclaimed a voice at his elbow.

The purser had entered the smoking-room, and overheard the threat.

Mr. Mole drew back, and his valiant air vanished as if by magic.

" What did you stop my grog for ? " he asked, mildly ; " surely there is some mistake."

" None at all. You'll find it hard if you begin with me, and don't you try to pull my nose, or I'll have you locked up in the wheel-house all night, and put you in irons."

" You—you're a very violent man," stammered Mole.

" I'm all right if people let me alone. Be advised, and go to your berth. You're full as a tick now. Come to me and apologise in the morning, and we may be better friends," said the purser.

" I have sailed in many ships," said Mole, " but never did I meet with such a tyrant before. I shall complain to the company's agent at New York."

" You may complain to your grandmother, if you like," answered the purser, contemptuously ; adding, " Now, gentlemen, who's for a game of whist ? "

" Our purser's a smart man, I guess," muttered Felix S. Prye, with a smile.

Jack and Harvey were ready, a fourth was soon discovered, and Mr. Mole, finding no one took any further notice of him, went below, grumbling, to seek Monday, whom he sent for some brandy, with which he solaced himself in his state-room.

Miles Fenton had avoided Jack after their conversation in the smoking-room, and did not seem to wish for any further collision.

But Jack knew his snake-like nature, and was on his guard.

The ship had to contend with a hard wind yet she made good way, running from fourteen to fifteen knots, and averaging something like three hundred and thirty miles a day.

The following day Mr. Mole finished the bottle of brandy, and went on deck with unsteady steps.

As the wind was high and the sea rough, the ship lurched a good deal, and, as it gave a pitch to leeward, Mr. Mole went spinning to the side.

Fortunately, Harkaway, who was taking a morning walk, caught his arm.

"Hold up, sir!" he exclaimed.

"I'm all right." replied Mr. Mole. "It's the confounded ship. How it lurches!"

"You've got to find your sea-legs, sir."

"Bother sea-legs, Harkaway. I hate the sea. Give me *terra-firma*; honest land for me, Harkaway," answered Mr. Mole, with an unsteady motion.

"Seen the purser, sir?" asked Jack, with a twinkle in his eye.

"No, nor do I want to see him. I'm full against that man," answered Mole. "A more unpleasant person I never met."

"He's making preparations for you," said Jack.

"Where?" inquired Mole, uneasily.

"In the wheel-house."

"Is he there? I should like to see him put me in there. You wouldn't allow me—me, Professor Mole—to be locked up in the wheel-house, would you?"

"Not much, sir."

"You are my friend and pupil, Harkaway; protect me."

"I will, sir."

"Thank you, Jack. I call you Jack because you are my best friend. But, look here. Is this purser fellow really in the wheel-house?"

"I saw him there, not a moment ago."

Mr. Mole walked to the wheel-house and peeped in at the open door.

The purser was actually there, arranging some camp-stools which he had ordered to be stowed away, as, owing to the rough weather, there was no demand for them, the passengers preferring their berths, or the saloon. to s tting on deck.

Slamming the door, Mr. Mole quickly turned the key, and, going to a window, looked in.

"Goo' mornin'," he said, in a husky voice. "How do you find yourself, Mr. Purser?"

"Hallo! Up to your tricks, are you?" replied the purser. "What have you done to that door?"

"Locked it. That's all"

"Come, let me out, quick, or it will be the worse for you!"

"How's your family, eh, Mr Purser? Are they all well at home (hic), eh?" asked Mole.

The purser came to the window, and looked through.

"None of your larks, I say," he said, angrily.

"Lock me up in the wheel-house, will you?" said Mole.

"I never said so."

"You're locked up yourself now. How do you like it?"

"Let me out."

"Not till you beg my pardon, and put on my grog again," replied Mole, firmly.

"You're tight now."

"Goo' job, too. No thanks (hic) to you."

"Let me out. I say!"

"Beg my (hic) pardon."

"Well, I do. You shall have what you like. Open the door."

"That's right (hic). Purser not such bad sort of fellow, after all," said Mole.

"Now unlock the door, old boy," said the purser, in a persuasive tone.

"Of course I will. We'll take a drink together. Champagne cock-tails, eh (hic)?"

"Anything you like. Look sharp."

Mole staggered to the door, and turned the key allowing the purser to come out.

"Give me your hand. Like purser. Doosed good fellows, pursers (hic)," said Mole, with a benignant smile on his countenance.

The purser took his proffered hand, but not to shake in a friendly spirit.

He swung Mole round, and threw him on his back in the wheel-house.

"Who—what's this?" cried Mole.

"I shall have to talk Yank to you," said the purser. "I guess you're mighty smart, but I'll bet a dollar to a ten-cent stamp you're not a match for me."

In his turn, he shut the door, and locked it.

Lying on his back, with his head upon a coil of rope, Mole said, "Curi'us fel'ow that purser. Can't make him out. No matter. Think go to sleep now (hic)."

In a short time his eyes closed, and he sank into a state of forgetfulness.

Going away from the wheel-house, the purser met Jack, who had been watching this scene with great amusement.

"I've settled your friend, Mr. Harkaway," he said. "Is he always like that?"

"Sometimes," answered Jack. "I think his head was a little affected by the sun when he was among the Malays."

"It's a pity. You ought to keep him from the drink."

"I do as much as I can, but, you see, Mr. Mole is an old friend of mine, and I have a great regard for him. He doesn't mean any harm."

"He's an insulting old fellow," said the purser. "I can't forget what he said last night; yet, for your sake, I won't be hard on him."

"Take no notice of him," replied Jack.

"I'll do the best I can. What do you say to some oysters? We have a few Americans on board, and that's a secret I don't tell every one."

"Thank you," replied Jack.

"Real blue-points, on the half shell. Come to my cabin," added the purser.

Jack accompanied the purser below, and in the saloon passed Miles Fenton, who was reading a book.

He looked up and favoured Harkaway with one of his peculiar glances, which made his flesh creep, it was so vindictive and searching.

"That fellow's only waiting his opportunity," thought Jack.

Emily was getting gradually stronger and better, though it would be some time before she could leave her bed.

Hilda was constant in her attendance upon her, and Ada (Monday's wife) was the most devoted nurse.

As for the black, he kept an almost sleepless watch upon Fenton, following him from the saloon to the deck and the smoking room.

There was little chance of his being able to repeat the outrage he had committed in the hotel at Liverpool

When Mr. Mole woke up, he found the wheel-house door open, and walked out, declaring to himself that he didn't know "what to make of that purser fellow."

The second bell rang for dinner, and, going into the saloon, he took a seat at the nearest table, close to Felix S. Prye.

"How's your health?" asked Felix.

"I shall feel better when I have dined," replied Mr. Mole.

"Did you have a good time in the wheel-house?"

"Oh, yes. I only retired there because I wanted to be quiet."

"You must take care when you get to New York City," said Felix.

"Why, may I ask?"

"If you get full there, you'll be sent up."

"Sent up where?"

"Up the Island. People who get drunk are sent up to the workhouse on Blackwell's Island for ten days."

"I never get drunk, sir," replied Mr. Mole, with dignity; adding, "Steward, some ox-tail soup, and turbot to follow."

"Say, Mr. Mole, do you teach in England?" asked Felix.

"Such is my vocation," answered Mr. Mole.

"You pay more attention to athletics than we do, I guess?"

"Our boys pride themselves upon rowing, foot-ball, and playing cricket well. Have you no games?"

"We have base-ball, which is something like the English game of rounders," answered Felix; "and we play shinney, which, from what I saw in Europe, is like your hockey."

"Wouldn't you like to row well?" inquired Mole.

"I'd rather help my father to make a pile."

"Dear me! how mercenary you American boys must be!"

"My!" replied Felix; "we don't call it mercenary. Our idea, I guess, is to do something that will bring in some currency. We like to make money and to spend it. Come to where we keep in New York city, and I'll show you that American boys think of using their heads more than their arms."

"Dear me!" replied Mr. Mole. "You will be speculating in gold before you're twenty, and per-haps control the expenditure of the city by the time you're thirty."

"No, sir," answered Felix, with a knowing look. "I don't want to be Boss of a Tammany Ring."

Mr. Mole shook his head.

This sort of thing was new to him, and he thought that Mr. Prye was beginning business life too early.

"May I ask if your studies have been attended to?" he inquired.

"What studies?"

"Latin, for instance. Who was Cæsar?"

"I never paid much attention to the ancients," answered Felix. "I can talk German and French. They're useful in business. We don't trade with Rome and Greece."

"As a matter of historical interest, you ought to know who Cæsar was."

"My uncle out West, in Cincinnati, is a trader in hogs," said Felix S. Prye, "and he had a dog to look after the swine. When he wanted a swine sent his way, he called his dog, and his dog went for the swine and seized him by the ear. He called him Seizer, I guess."

"My dear young friend," said Mr. Mole, with a pitying air, "you have yet much to learn."

"I guess you couldn't teach me all I know."

"We will not discuss the question," replied Mole, waving his hand. "Steward, bring me some saddle of mutton and cranberry sauce."

The dinner being over, Mole retired to the smoking-room, to indulge in a cigar.

During the evening, Jack again played at whist with the purser, and the last game of the rubber being a very close one, he, in a moment of excitement, said, "I'll bet half-a-dozen of champagne on the odd trick."

"I'm not a betting man," said the purser.

"I will take that bet," said a voice.

Jack looked up, and saw Miles Fenton.

"Is it on?" asked Harvey, who was Jack's partner.

"Yes, I offered to make the bet, and I'll stand by it," replied Jack.

The game was played out, and Jack won.

Rising from the table, he said, "Mr. Fenton pays for the wine, gentlemen," and lighting a cigar he strolled out on to the deck.

It was a lovely moonlit night.

The silvery orb shone high and full in the heavens, and Jack stood behind the wheel-house at the stern of the vessel, watching the moonlit foam which marked the track of the swiftly-speeding ship.

For more than a quarter of an hour he remained lost in contemplation.

Then he turned to seek his berth.

As he did so, he was seized by two strong arms.

CHAPTER V.

"MAN OVERBOARD."

AT that time of night, the deck was deserted, and in such a place as the rear of the wheel-house, which was right aft, no one on watch could have seen the two men who were fiercely struggling.

Harkaway took a glance at his assailant.

It was as he thought.

"Miles Fenton!" he ejaculated.

There was no answer. Fenton was exerting himself to the utmost to force Jack over the side of the ship.

It was his devilish purpose to plunge him into the hissing, seething sea.

"Your life, or mine!" said Fenton.

"Then, by Heaven! I'll fight for it!" answered Jack, setting his teeth together.

By surprising him as he had done, Fenton had taken him at a disadvantage.

He was forcing him gradually over the side.

Strong though he was, and struggle though he did with all his might, Jack felt himself being gradually raised higher and higher.

A cold sweat broke out all over his body, the damp gathered on his forehead, and stood there like beads, while every vein came out like a cord.

He was holding on to a rope, from which Fenton was trying to force him.

Already he could see the moonlit ocean beneath him.

For hundreds of miles on every side there was nothing but a vast expanse of sea.

What would his fate be if cast overboard?

His only chance was being picked up by a pass-ing ship, but ships on the broad Atlantic are few and far between.

How long could he keep himself afloat by swim-ming?

Perhaps an hour, and then—well, then, he would sink, to rise no more.

"Help! help!" cried Jack, in an agony of despair.

The wind, which was whistling through the shrouds, and making weird music in the straining cordage, mockingly carried his cry to the fluttering sea-gulls following in the ship's wake.

Fenton's murderous hand crept up to Jack's throat, and tightened on it.

Harkaway thought his last hour had come.

His strength was giving way, and the advantage was so much in his antagonist's favour that it seemed hopeless to struggle longer.

"Die!" hissed Fenton, through his teeth, as he prepared to cast him over.

At that moment the luck changed.

Miles Fenton stumbled over a coil of rope, and, for an instant, was compelled to relax his hold, for fear of falling.

was Jack's opportunity.

did not neglect to seize it.

With a cry like that of a wild beast, in which all the pent-up agony of the last few awful moments was let loose, he sprang upon his enemy.

"Ha! ha!" he laughed, hoarsely. "It is my turn now."

Having fine play for his arms, he caught Fenton by one leg, and gave him a sudden toss in the air, such as wrestlers love.

Before he could offer any resistance, or recover from his astonishment, Fenton was over the side.

One wild, despairing cry broke from him.

Then he fell into the sea, his upturned face wearing a perfectly fiendish expression.

"He said it was his life or mine," muttered Jack.

"Very neatly done, sir," said a voice behind him.

Jack started.

He felt that he was justified in doing what he had done, because it was in self-defence, and the man he had thrown overboard had made three distinct attempts on his life.

In addition to which, he was in league with Hunston, and deserved no mercy at his hands.

But he wasn't aware that he had been spied upon.

A very different construction might be placed upon his act, and one which would put him into an awkward position.

This reflection rather dashed his joy at getting rid of Miles Fenton.

"As putty a chuck as I ever see in my life, sir," continued the voice.

With his usual courage, Jack faced the difficulty.

He saw before him a tall, thin man, poorly dressed, yet wearing a confident smile.

"What have you seen?" asked Jack.

"I saw it all, but I didn't like to spoil sport. That's not me. Oh, no!" replied the man.

"Who are you?"

"I'm a steerage passenger. They call me Handy-Dandy Joe. At night, I take a walk aft. The ropes are up in the day-time."

"You can go about your business," said Jack.

"This is my business, sir. You're a gentleman, and I'm a poor man. But when a gentleman commits a crime he puts himself on a level with the poor man directly," said Handy-Dandy Joe, with a chuckle.

"A crime?" said Jack. "What I did was in self-defence. The man said it was my life or his."

"Certainly," continued Joe. "I could reduce the offence from murder to manslaughter. All depends upon my evidence. Fancy my going out to America to seek my fortune and finding it on board ship."

"How do you mean?"

"Why, you're as good as a fortune to me. You'll say, 'Joe, what do you want to hold your tongue?' 'Thank you, sir,' I shall answer; 'five thousand dollars will do to start with.'"

"You'll get nothing out of me," replied Jack.

"Wait till to-morrow, sir," answered Handy-Dandy Joe. "A night's reflection will make you think better of it. If you come down handsome, I shall say nothing when the gent's disappearance is talked of. Good night, sir. Pleasant dreams."

He walked off with his hands in his pockets, leaving Jack much annoyed.

Feeling cold and nervous after the excitement he had just gone through, he returned to the smoking-room.

It was now about half-past twelve. The lights were not out, as the captain had taken Jack's place at the whist-table.

"Seen Mr. Fenton, sir?" asked the deck-steward.

"Eh?" ejaculated Harkaway, as a shivering sensation crept over him.

"He hasn't paid for that wine he lost," continued the steward.

"I saw him looking over the side of the vessel just now," answered Jack, sitting down and lighting a cigar to calm his nerves.

Scarcely had he settled himself, than the first officer came in.

"Large steamer, sir, to starboard," he said.

"Bound west?" asked the captain.

"Yes, sir."

"That must be the White Star. She started after us, and will get in first."

"Shall I signal her?"

"Yes," replied the captain.

The officers rose and went out, all being much annoyed to think that there was a chance of being beaten by a ship that started from Queenstown after the "City of Athens."

Going to the poop, the first officer directed the signaler.

First a rocket was sent up, and then he burnt a blue light.

The steamer was not far behind them, and was visible easily in the moonlight.

"She seems to be stopping," said the captain.

"Man overboard, perhaps?" suggested the purser. "There are her signals. See! see! she answers us."

"It is the White Star," said the captain. "Eh, Mr. Lipscombe?"

"Yes, sir," answered the first officer. "She's the 'Republic,' White Star Line, and she'll beat us by a day or more. Though what she's stopping for is more than I can tell."

Jack wondered, too, what caused her to pause in her voyage and lose valuable time.

Could Miles Fenton have come in her track, and been picked up?

Now his passion was over, he almost wished it might be so.

Yet the idea was too wild and improbable.

Miles Fenton was dead enough by this time.

No fear of that.

Sadly, Jack went below, and after ascertaining from Ada that Emily was better, and had just fallen off into a quiet sleep, he turned into his berth.

When he thought of his poor, wounded, suffering wife, his pity for her assassin vanished.

"By George!" he said, to himself, "he deserves his fate, and God knows he brought it on himself."

CHAPTER VI.

MR. MOLE HAS AN EASY SHAVE.

It wasn't until the middle of the following day that Miles Fenton was missed.

He did not appear at breakfast, nor was he seen at lunch.

Having no friend on board, it was nobody's business to inquire after him; but at length some one said—

"Where's Mr. Fenton?" and another exclaimed, "Fenton's sick, I guess; he hasn't turned up."

The purser made a search after him, and it was finally decided that he was not on the ship.

Much conversation ensued respecting his mysterious disappearance, the result being that it was agreed, on all hands, he must either have fallen overboard or have committed suicide.

Harvey was much excited when he heard the news, and at once sought Jack, who was standing nearly amidships, watching the steerage passengers, some of whom were helping the sailors to heave the log.

A GROUP OF FRIENDS WELCOMED JACK WHEN HIS FOOT TOUCHED AMERICA.

'I say, Jack," said Harvey, "what do you think Fenton's missing."

'Oh! they have found that out, have they ?" answered Jack, who wore a pre-occupied air.

' Did you know it ?"

' Yes."

' How long ago ?"

' Nearly twelve hours."

' Why didn't you say something about it ?"

'Because it wasn't my game," replied Jack. The fact is, Dick, I threw him overboard. Don't look frightened, old man. It was my life or his; though it looked queer for me at first, the luck went against him."

' Did he try to murder you ?"

'Yes, he did, and no mistake about it. I was all alone, right aft, and he fell upon me like a thief in the night. Oh, Dick! I shall never forget that struggle. At one moment I thought it was all over with me," said Jack.

"Does any one know this ?" asked Harvey.

"Only one fellow, a steerage passenger, and money will keep his mouth shut."

"Give him what he asks. It is best not to let the thing get wind; some might put an ugly construction on it."

"That is just what I was thinking. But look here, Dick."

"What ?"

"Do you blame me ?" continued Jack, anxiously.

"No, I don't—frankly, I don't. Self-preservation is the first law of Nature, and seeing what that has done, and tried to do, you had a right to lynch him."

"Thank you, old boy," said Jack; "you have taken a great weight off my mind."

"Good-morning, sir. Hope you have recovered from the effects of your exertions of last night," exclaimed a man.

It was Handy-Dandy Joe.

"How much do you want?" Jack asked, bluntly.

"Fifty will do for the present, sir. I can't spend much on board ship, and if you will be ready with a thousand before we land, we'll say quits till I want some more," replied Handy-Dandy Joe.

Jack opened his pocket-book, and handed him a fifty-pound bank of England note.

"Can I offer you a cigar?" asked Joe.

"No, thank you."

"Quite a little excitement about the disappearance of Mr. Fenton."

"Isn't there?" cried Joe. "Curious affair. Suicide, I suppose. Ta-ta, Mr. Harkaway; stroll on."

Handy-Dandy Joe favoured Jack with an expressive wink, which he repeated three times, lighted a cigar, nodded his head carelessly, and walked away.

"That fellow's a leech," remarked Harvey.

"Can't be helped," answered Jack. "I had to defy him or pay, and as you advised me to do the latter, I did so, though I would rather have fought the thing out on its merits."

"That's just like you," said Harvey. "Here is a man who three times tries to murder you, and nearly killed your wife, and yet, when you bring him to grief in self-defence, then you are sorry for it."

"I'd have liked better to punch his head and let him live to have it punched again."

"The sea doesn't give up its dead," said Harvey.

"That's so," replied Jack.

"We're making a good passage, but that White Star ship will get in before us," continued Harvey, wishing to change the conversation.

"I suppose so," said Jack, abstractedly.

"Have you seen Mole this morning?" asked Harvey.

"No."

"I have. He's tight, in his berth. Monday took me to him, and he's snoring away, with a bottle of brandy in each hand. Can't we have a lark with him?"

"I should like to do something," answered Jack, brightening up. "Suppose we send for the ship's barber, and have his head shaved?"

"Capital!" exclaimed Harvey, rubbing his hands.

"We could swear the purser did it, and there would be another shindy between them."

"By Jove! that's a brilliant idea. We'll have him made as bald as a coot. Wonder if there are any wigs on board?"

"Mole in a wig would be very fine," said Jack, laughing.

They went to the barber's shop and told the barber that they wanted him to shave the head of a friend of theirs.

The barber was a gentleman of colour, by name Stadia.

"Is he sick?" he asked.

"Very bad indeed," replied Jack.

"Fever case, I guess," said the barber, inquiringly.

"Something of that sort," said Harvey.

Mr. Stadia accompanied them to Mr. Mole's berth. Jack held the professor's head, which was duly lathered, without awakening the recipient of the favour.

In two minutes all the hair was off, and the poll as smooth and shining as a polished cocoa-nut shell

"How much?" inquired Jack.

"One dollar," replied Mr. Stadia, passing his hand over the bald head with an air of professional satisfaction.

Retiring from the cabin, Jack and Harvey went on deck, waiting impatiently till Mole should recover from the effects of his brandy-drinking, and make his appearance.

He did this about an hour before dinner.

On his head he had placed a seal-skin cap, both his bottles of brandy were empty, and all he could think of, in his somewhat confused state of mind, was that something to drink would liven him up.

Going into the smoking-room, the resort of the gentlemen at all hours, he looked round him with a benignant smile.

"Good morning, sir," said Jack. "Have you shown up before?"

"Well, no," replied Mole. "This is my first appearance. I sleep a good deal on board this ship. It is the sea-air, I suppose. By-the-way, is it not rather cold?"

"I don't find it so," said Harvey. "We are in the Gulf Stream, and the air ought to be temperate."

"Then I've got a cold in my head."

"Very likely, sir," said Jack.

"Who is going to ask me to drink? Don't all speak at once. Since that marine autocrat, the purser, has stopped my grog, I am obliged to throw myself on the parish, and trust to the charity of my friends for those moderate potations which my age and the state of my health render absolutely necessary.

Jack ordered the deck-steward to bring some brandy and water.

Then Mole drank with much relish, and took off his cap.

"I don't know when I've felt so cold about the head," he remarked.

A titter ran through the cabin, for his appearance was ludicrous in the extreme.

This swelled into a loud roar of laughter.

The merriment was infectious and irresistible.

Old men and young were convulsed, held their sides, stamped their feet, and behaved as if they were going out of their senses.

"What's the joke?" asked Mole, innocently.

At this query the fun redoubled.

"Harkaway," continued Mr Mole, "you might enlighten me. I like a good laugh as well as anybody."

"It's the fifth of November, sir, and somebody's brought a Guy on board," replied Jack.

"A Guy? Dear me; a veritable Guy Fawkes' Excellent. Let me see the Guy, by all means. Bless me! how cold it is! My head's like a frosted turnip."

Felix S. Prye was laughing in a most alarming manner. The tears ran down his cheeks, and his face was dangerously red.

"Take him away, somebody!" he exclaimed. "Oh! do take him away I guess I shall have a fit. Ha! ha! ha!—he! he! he!"

"Are you speaking of me, young man?" asked Mole, angrily.

"He! he! he!—ho! ho! ho!" roared Felix.

"Harkaway, what does all this mean?" continued Mole.

"Ha! ha! ha!" screamed Jack, bursting with laughter.

"Are you all mad? Harvey, speak to me."

"Ho! ho! ho!—ha! ha! ha!" was Harvey's only reply.

And "Ha! ha! ha!" laughed everyone in full diapason, like a pack of hounds in high cry.

Mr. Mole put his hands to his ears to keep out the noise.

"Steward," said Mr. Mole, "some more brandy, hot, with sugar; and, steward, can you tell me what those maniacs are laughing about?"

"Excuse me, sir," replied the deck-steward, "but—ha! ha!—really sir, if you would cover up your head, sir—ha! ha! ha! ha! Oh, Lord! I shall burst."

"So shall I," said Felix, "if you're going to run this machine much longer."

"Cover up my head," said Mr. Mole, puzzled. "I feel—I feel—I feel—I feel like a—hullo! I feel —I feel—hey, man alive, what's this? I feel—By George! I've got no hair! It's dropped off in my sleep!"

He started to his feet.

His face assumed a wild expression, and he continued to pass his hand over his head.

"What's this, what's this?" he went on saying.

"You've been scalped by those nasty Injuns, I guess," said Felix S. Prye, calming himself a little.

"It seems to me that my head, called *caput* by the Latins, has lost its natural covering," said Mole. "Is that so, Mr. Prye?"

"That's so, sir."

"Am I bald?"

"If you ain't bald, then there's hair on a billiard-ball. Some one's raised your wool."

"That accounts for my feeling so cold. It couldn't have dropped off. It must be that confounded purser. I shall take a high hand with him. What would your course of action be, Mr. Prye?"

"I've got a very firm upper lip," answered Felix, "and when I'm sassy, I am sassy."

"I can scarcely realise the fact," continued Mole. "Am I really bald?"

"You're like Samson when Dalila had done with him, sir," replied Jack.

"Get some thatch, sir," suggested Harvey.

"I must get a wig. I can't appear in society like this; it's too absurd. I will go below, and consult my looking-glass."

He put on his cap.

"If that repulsive man, the purser, should appear," he went on, "tell him to dread my just resentment for this last and crowning outrage."

Waving his arms fiercely, he ran from the cabin, and did not stop till he reached his berth.

A steady look at the glass horrified him.

At all times gaunt and big-boned, he now had a skeleton appearance, and looked very ghostly.

"Vengeance! vengeance!" he muttered.

He reascended to the smoking-room, where he found the purser laughing heartily at some good joke.

"Sir—you, sir—you purser fellow!" roared Mole.

"At your service," was the reply.

"How dare you have my head shaved?"

"I had nothing to do with it."

"Sir," said Mole, "you are adding falsehood to your other vices; but, sir, I shall chastise you. Yes, sir; I will show you that Isaac Mole is not to be made a laughing-stock of. The blood of my race is roused. Yes, sir; a Mole has hot blood, sir; and I shall pull your nose."

He made a sudden dash across the table, and succeeded in seizing the purser by the nose.

With all his might he wrung the unoffending organ.

"Take him off. I don't want to hit him. Take him off. Oh!" said the purser.

But the merriment had broke out again.

It was a treat to see how Mole tugged at the purser's nose.

At last, with a final contemptuous tweak, Mole let go his hold.

"Revenge!" he said. "I care not for the loss of my hair now. Hair will grow again; but an insult can never be wiped out."

"Hang the old fool," said the purser, who was a sensible, good-tempered fellow. "How he did pull away at my snout!"

Fearful that the purser might retaliate, Mole retreated, much pleased with himself at what he had done, for he fully believed that he had to thank the purser for being shaved.

For some time there was nothing but laughter in the smoking-room.

The purser took the affair as a joke.

"Some of you have been getting this up for me," he exclaimed. "The old lunatic has had his knife into me ever since he came on board. Who polished him?"

"I did," replied Jack.

"Hanged if I didn't think it was you, Mr. Harkaway. Of course you can do what you like with him, but keep him off my nose in future, will you, kindly?" laughed the purser.

"All right," replied Jack.

"I once saw six whites lose their hair in Texas," remarked a tall, long-legged frontiersman.

"How was that? Indians?" asked Harvey.

"Yes, sir."

"I thought, from what I have read of them, that Indians were nice fellows if you treated them well."

The frontiersman smiled.

"Indians air nice," he answered, "with these trifling exceptions:—An Indian will lie, will steal, has no sense of gratitude, is a treacherous friend and a relentless foe, is lazy, is dirty, and will kill you if he can. Oh! yes, the story-book Indian is very nice; but you come to meet him on his native peraire, and a snake's a better chum."

The bell rang for dinner, and everyone descended to make a hasty toilet.

Mr. Mole appeared in his cap, apologising to the ladies for keeping it on, alleging a severe cold in excuse.

After dinner there was an inquiry for wigs at Harkaway's table, but everyone denied having such a thing in his or her possession.

Jack had his eye on one old lady, though, and determined to put her to the test at the first opportunity.

In the evening the wind freshened, and the sea ran very high.

Sail was taken in, all was made snug for the night, but it was remarked that the captain did not come as usual for his game of cards.

The officers, when spoken to about the weather, shook their heads ominously.

To old hands, like Jack and Harvey, it was clear that a storm was expected.

CHAPTER VII.

THE STORM-TOSSED WRECK.

DURING the night the wind increased to a hurricane, and the sea ran very high, deluging the forecastle, and giving the steerage passengers and crew a very lively time of it.

Mr. Mole occupied an outside berth, and the sea dashed up against the port-holes as if it would crush them in.

By morning it had calmed a little, though the waves continued to be large, and there was a heavy sea on.

The shrill sound of the boatswain's pipes was heard at intervals, as the watch was called to perform various duties and repair damage done to the rigging during the storm.

"Two bells, sir," exclaimed Jack, looking in at Mr. Mole's berth.

"Ah! thank you," replied Mole. "That's nine o'clock, isn't it? I almost forget my sea-terms."

"It's eight bells every four hours, sir," answered Jack. "Ten o'clock, four bells; eleven, six; half-past eleven, seven; and twelve eight. Then we begin again."

"I'll get up," said Mole. "Time for breakfast. This sea-air gives one an appetite."

He sprang out of his berth, and rolled up on the sofa as the ship gave a tremendous lurch.

"Roughish, isn't it?" he asked.

"We've had an awful night. But we sail in a good ship, with a good skipper, and so long as we keep out of the fogs, we have not got much to fear."

Felix S. Prye was berthed next to Mr. Mole, and he looked in as he came by to breakfast.

"Ah! Good-morning, my young friend," said Mr. Mole. "How does this weather suit you?"

"I guess I don't mind a gentle breeze," answered Felix; adding, "How's your cocoa-nut to-day, sir?"

"Cold, Mr. Prye. Very cold."

"It was what I call real mean, not to leave you a scalp-lock. I was glad to see you fix the purser up, right away."

"I flatter myself that I made an example of him."

"You did."

"Were you satisfied with my conduct? Was it manly?"

"That's so. My! his nose is as long as the Chiany Canyon up Colorado, and not half so pretty. You must try my father's patent Lightning Hair Restorer. It has made old age quite scarce and unfashionable."

"What I want first is a wig," said Mole. "At my age, the hair grows slowly."

"I'm on the look-out, sir," remarked Jack.

"I guess we'll take a walk, Mr. Harkaway," said Felix. "Mr. Mole can go on dressing, and join us when he's through. My! wasn't shaving him that way a waste of wool?"

Jack assented, and they took a tour on deck, admiring the grandeur of the rolling waves, which raised them high on their foaming crests one moment, only to dash they down in the trough of the heaving sea the next.

"I calculate there will be a few wrecks," observed Felix.

"No doubt. Many a ship has gone down and left no sign on the broad Atlantic," replied Jack.

"Ah! it's hard life, that of a sailor. Were you brought up to the sea, Mr. Harkaway?"

"Not exactly. I made a voyage when I was quite young, and got wrecked."

"Is that so?"

"Yes. I was for some time among the Malay savages. Since then I have been in the army, and amusing my leisure moments by hunting brigands in Italy."

"You should go West in the States. We have some elegant Indians."

"I have an important task to accomplish first."

"What is that?"

"A brigand stole my only child. I heard he had gone to America, and I'm after him."

"I hope you may find him. Do you keep your army rank?"

"No. I have sold my commission in the British army, and am only a soldier of fortune now. What may be in front of me, I can only faintly imagine. But mine has been an adventurous career so far, and I suppose it will continue as it began."

"There is more real fighting to be done in every-day life, sometimes, than most soldiers see," answered Felix.

"That's very true," said Jack, thoughtfully.

"Well, I guess I shall be real tickled to see you in New York city, Mr. Harkaway, and if you've got any currency you want to be rid of, our store's the place for notions."

"I shall be very pleased, I may say proud to accept your kind invitation."

"Don't forget. When we reach pier 45 in the North River, we shall be scattered like a handful of chaff; but you get on an Eighth Avenue car, marked Hudson and Vesey, and step just past Fourteenth Street. Prye's big enough to see without glasses."

"Do all your streets number up from the city?" asked Jack.

"It's all the city, from the Battery to Harlem and Manhattanville. The business part is down-town, the fashionable portion up-town. Broadway runs right along to Central Park, which is real elegant. The avenues run laterally with Broadway, and the streets, after you get up-town a little, don't have names."

"Only numbers?" inquired Jack.

"That's so; New York is an island, with the North River on one side, and the East River on the other. Our streets run from side to side, and number over a hundred. The cars go up the avenues, except Fifth, which we keep for carriage driving."

"A very good way to lay out a city," replied Jack.

"Oh, we're miles ahead of the Old World. We go ahead. It isn't in us to stand still and imitate. If an American sees a thing done by hand, he never rests thinking how it can be done by machinery," said Felix S. Prye.

Jack laughed, and they descended to the saloon for breakfast, Felix remarking that he guessed he hadn't missed a meal since he'd been on board.

As a matter of fact, the company did not get much profit out of him, as he eat with a vigorous appetite, commencing dinner with soup, and ending with bananas and coffee.

After breakfast, Jack saw Monday going amidship, and beckoned to him.

"Where are you off to?" he asked.

"On um business for Mist' Mole, sare," replied Monday.

"What is that?"

"Him say me not to tell, sare."

"He wants some more brandy, isn't it, and you're going to say it's for me?"

Monday grinned.

"Don't do it. I'll get him as much as is good for him. Tell Mr. Mole you can't get it," said Jack.

Monday nodded and went back.

Jack spoke to the purser.

"Oh, certainly," said the purser in answer to Jack; "anything you ask I'll do, Mr. Harkaway only keep him within bounds. Nose-pulling is apt to become monotonous by repetition, and I might retaliate."

Jack asked Felix to call Mr. Mole, and, when he arrived from his table, with his cap on, to hide his bald head, he said—

"In what way can I be of service to you, Harkaway?"

"Come and split a soda-and-brandy, sir, at the bar."

"The man will not serve me, I fear."

"Oh, yes. The purser has put your grog on again. He says it will make your hair grow," replied Jack.

"Ah! that is refreshing news. The purser is not such an out-and-out villain as I took him to be. Is it that he has the germ of compassion in his breast, or did my attack on him frighten him into leniency?" said Mr. Mole, with a smile of pleasure.

They went to the bar, accompanied by Felix, who asked for some Santa Cruz and gum.

To his disgust, the bar-keeper had no gum, and he said, as he walked away—

"This is a one-horse ship. If it belonged to American owners, I guess they wouldn't have sailed without gum. May I never fill up an alley at Keno again, if I ever sail in a ship without gum."

Suddenly Jack perceived a diminution in the speed of the vessel, and the next moment the beat of the engines was distinctly slower.

"Anything wrong, I wonder ?" he exclaimed.

"Has the ship stopped ?" cried Mole, in alarm. "I will run to my berth, and put on my life-belt. It saved me the last time I was wrecked."

Jack hurried on deck and saw a little knot of passengers intently regarding an object just visible in the distance.

"What is it ?" said Jack to the purser.

"A wreck."

"Steamer ?"

"No; a merchantman. Brig, I should say by the look of her. She's dismasted, and hull down in the water."

The third officer was looking through a glass.

"Below there ! Pipe up, bo'sun," he exclaimed. "We'll lower a boat and board her."

"Is she abandoned?" asked Jack.

"I don't think there is anyone aboard her," replied the officer. "It seems as if the water went in and out of every seam."

"Where are the crew, poor fellows?"

"Got away in the boats, perhaps, or been taken off by a passing steamer."

"She's right in the track of the Liners."

"The storm did it, I expect," said Jack.

"Maybe she's a coffin-ship," answered the officer. "They don't care how they build merchantmen now, so long as they can effect the insurance. That's what the owners want. A 1 at Lloyd's. Those who own such sieves ought to be A 1 in a hot place I won't mention."

The steamer gradually approached the wreck, which was tossed about like a log upon the water.

When near enough, a boat was lowered to examine her, though no sign appeared of any living soul being left upon her.

The sky was leaden and murky, and at times the sea made a clean breach over the wreck.

"Derelict, you bet," said Jack.

The sails were in rags—splintered to ribbons, in fact—cordage hanging broken from mast and yard, bulwarks broken in and shattered.

She had met with an Atlantic storm, and got the worst of the encounter.

Some deck lumber that had broken loose floated around.

The boat made an examination of the wreck, and returned to report.

"Any one on board?" asked the captain.

"No, sir," replied the officer in command. "She's as rotten as a sieve full of water, and won't hold together much longer."

"What's her name ?"

"The 'Santa Maria,' of Naples."

Jack started with surprise.

The "Santa Maria" was the vessel in which Hunston had sailed from Naples for New York.

In this ill-fated ship he had embarked his child.

What had the fate of the crew and passengers been ?

Was Hunston drowned, and had his boy gone down with him to find a watery grave in the middle of the Atlantic ?

He turned faint with horror at the thought.

Better anything than this.

While there is life, there is hope.

Better, far better, that he should be Hunston's

bond-child and slave, than that he should have met such an untimely end.

The order was given to go ahead, and soon the "City of Athens" was once more steaming towards the New World.

She had run about fifteen hundred miles, or one half of the journey.

Harvey found Jack leaning against the companion, plunged in deep thought, and touched him on the shoulder.

"Oh! is it you, Dick ?" said Jack.

"I'm very sorry for this," said Harvey.

"We shall get in before the 'Santa Maria,' anyhow," replied Jack, with a bitter smile.

"I have been talking to the captain, and he thinks the crew have been rescued."

"Why ?" asked Jack, turning his eyes sharply upon Harvey

"Simply because the White Star ship, 'Republic,' is a little ahead of us, and we both take a specified course."

"What's that ?"

"On the outward passage from Queenstown we cross the meridian of 50 deg. at 43 deg. latitude, or at least nothing to the North of 42 deg."

"I see your chain of reasoning," said Jack. "You think the 'Republic' has met with the wreck, and taken the crew off ?"

"Yes; that's my opinion."

"I hope sincerely you may be right. You don't know, Dick, how I love my boy. It would have been my pride to see him grow up under my eyes, and watch his education. The only reason I forgive Mole's excesses is, that he says he feels so cut up at the loss of the boy, he can't help taking a drop too much sometimes."

"Mole's—well, the truth isn't in him," replied Harvey.

"He is much attached to young Jack."

"So we all are, and we mean to have him back again. If I had a youngster like that, I should be proud of him, I can tell you."

"What alarms me is, that Hunston, having him in his power, may bring him up as a thief, and teach him to hate his father."

"He wouldn't be so bad as that."

"Hunston is bad enough for anything, and you know how firm his unprovoked hatred is to me," said Jack.

"By Jove !" replied Harvey, "it would be a wonderful revenge if he did make a ruffian of him, and in about twenty years time he sprung him on you, and ask you how you felt about your son."

Jack passed his hand over his forehead, which was cold and clammy.

"I might reclaim him even then, and I'd rather chance that, Dick, than know that he went down in the 'Santa Maria,' " he said.

"There is an end to our hope of catching Hunston and the boy on their arrival in New York."

"Yes," said Jack, gloomily.

"If rescued at all," continued Harvey, "they may come in on board a merchantman, and the captain says that all waifs and strays in the shape of emigrants are to be heard of at Castle Garden."

"Where's that ?"

"Sort of home for the emigrants, near the Bowling Green and the Battery."

"We'll go there and look," said Jack, with the wild energy of a drowning man who clutches at a straw.

While they were talking, the rolling wreck grew gradually smaller, and at last was only seen as a speck in the distance.

Soon it was lost to sight.

One more mystery of the deep remained unsolved.

CHAPTER VIII.

ARRIVAL IN NEW YORK.

It was the evening of the twelfth day out from Liverpool.

The passengers were, more or less, uneasy and restless, as they expected to make land shortly.

"Ding! ding! ding!"

"Three bells!" exclaimed Jack.

"Half-past nine," said Felix S. Prye. "We shan't get in to-night."

The purser put his head in at the door of the smoking-room.

"Quarantine, gentlemen!" he exclaimed. "Any messages, letters, or telegrams for the shore?"

"Are you going ashore?" asked Jack.

"I go with the mails."

Many passengers wrote letters, or sent telegrams to their friends, but Jack had no friends in the New World, and had no time in leaving England to obtain letters of introduction.

The next morning he was up early, and was glad to find that Emily, although weak, was so far recovered as to be able to walk.

He gently promenaded the deck with her, as the steamer passed Staten Island.

"I feel so much better," said Emily.

"That is one comfort, darling," he answered.

"The stewardess told me about Mr. Fenton being missing," she continued.

"Did she?" said Jack, abstractedly.

"Do you think he committed suicide in a fit of remorse?"

"No."

This was blurted out in a sullen, defiant manner.

Emily noticed a change in his manner, but did not understand it.

"Of course," she went on, "I was very angry with him for attempting my life, and yours, too, dear; but I felt sorry to think that he should have been hurled into eternity with all his sins on his head, and no chance of repentance."

"Hurled is the word," said Jack.

"What do you mean, dear?" asked Emily. "How strange you look!"

"Look here, Emmy," he answered. "I never had any secrets from you, and I don't mean to begin now."

She gazed at him in surprise.

"It is bad for a man to have secrets which he cannot let his wife know," she said.

"So I think. I should have told you this before, but you were too ill."

"Let me sit down, Jack; I feel so faint," said Emily, who began to have an inkling of the truth.

He led her to a seat, and sat down beside her.

"I killed that man!" he commenced.

"You! Oh! Jack!"

"In self-defence," Jack hastened to add. "It was a near shave for me; he had me on the taffrail, and I thought it was all over with me. The luck changed. His foot slipped, and over he went into the sea."

"That's perfectly true," said a voice he knew well. "I saw the whole thing, and very neatly Mr. Harkaway footed up his account. I couldn't have done it better myself."

Jack looked up and saw Handy-Dandy Joe.

"Take your hook," he said, in a tone of annoyance.

"That will be when I choose," answered Joe, insolently.

"You are a steerage passenger, and have no business here."

"I come aft to speak to my friend Harkaway. I call you Harkaway because you are my best friend."

"Dry up," said Jack; "it will be better for you."

"I can sling my hook," said Joe; "but I shan't lose sight of you. I've got to hold my tongue, and I want to be settled with on the C. O. D principle."

"I'll talk to you presently," rejoined Jack. "Stow your cheek for half an hour."

"Do it now," said Joe. "Give me my little pile, unless you want some more of my lip."

Jack grew purple with rage.

He started up, and, seizing the fellow by the throat, threw him along the deck, and, running after him, kicked him amidships, to the amusement and surprise of the passengers on deck.

Handy-Dandy Joe picked himself up, with a dizzy sensation about the head.

He shook his fist at Jack, and walked quickly to the fore-part of the vessel.

Jack explained to Emily the nature of the hold the man had over him.

"Oh, my darling!" she said. "You have got into fresh trouble already, and I feel that you will have no happiness or peace as long as Hunston lives."

"I wish Hunston was with his friend Old Nick," growled Jack.

They promenaded the deck again.

Coming near the rope which ran across the middle of the ship, they again saw Joe.

He didn't attempt to speak to Jack, but he put his hands in his pockets, and began to sing, with an impudent air—

"If ever there was a young scamp,
I flatter myself I am he."

Jack turned round abruptly, and took Emily below, as she wanted to see that her maid was putting her boxes in order, preparatory to landing.

In half an hour they would be off the pier in the North River.

He amused himself by watching the ferry-boats, which were so splendid in their construction, and vast in their appearance, that he was lost in admiration.

Felix S. Prye joined him.

"Something tall in the boat line, Mr. Harkaway," he exclaimed.

"Yes," replied Jack, "you do things on a big scale."

"I rather guess we do. That ferry-boat would make the Britishers stare on the Thames. Yes, sir."

Jack did not contradict this assertion, for he was obliged to admit that a New York ferry-boat, with its capacity for carrying hundreds of passengers, carriages and horses, was a little ahead of the Old Country.

"I hope you'll have a good time, sir, and keep your health," continued Felix; adding, "where do you stay?"

"At the Gilsey House," replied Jack.

"That's on the Broadway, past Madison-square. They'll treat you well, I guess. I shall call on New Year's, if I don't see you before."

"I hope we may meet earlier," Jack said.

"It depends. We've had a bad scare. Our panic has brought me over rather sudden," answered Felix; "and I may have to travel."

"Far?"

"Oh! no; only to Chicago, about fifteen hundred miles West."

"Only!" repeated Jack.

"That's nothing on our continent. You get into a Pullman car, go to sleep at night, and you're there before you've had time to think about it."

"You're a great nation," said Jack.

"Well, we're some pumpkins. But we've got to

extend the Monroe Doctrine, though the Republican party don't march fast."

"What about Cuba?" asked Jack, with a sly smile.

"We don't want it. We could do with it, but the Spanish butchers are not easy to civilize. I guess we've got the 'Virginius' back, and we'll leave the volunteers to cut their own throats, and wipe themselves out."

"They called the American flag a dirty rag," said Jack.

"But they had to respect it," replied Felix. "I calculate the Spaniards can blow against the world. We got our ships of war ready at Key West and that fetched them. They caved in. If we wanted Cuba, we'd have had it, sir, in less than a month."

"Indeed!" said Jack.

"Yes, sir. Wouldn't you like to say as much about Coomassie, in the Ashantee country?"

"The climate of the Gold Coast is deadly to Europeans," answered Jack.

"That's so. But you knew that before you sent your troops there, and you've been mussing about for over three months and have done nothing to speak of."

Jack made no answer.

"I guess the British lion's forgotten how to kick," continued Felix.

"You daren't pull his tail," said Jack, rather annoyed. "If you did—"

"Don't get riled, Mr. Harkaway," interrupted Felix. "The British are a money-making nation, and I respect them so far. Keep your wool down. You'll have to. The Americans are a high-souled nation, and like rocks as well as you; but our Eagle will flap his wings, and make more stir than your lion, when he growls."

"We won't quarrel about a trifle," said Jack. "Goodness knows that I have enough to think about at present."

"Here's your snowball," said Felix, pointing to Monday.

The black was getting the boxes and portmanteaus on deck, as the time of landing was drawing near.

Soon the Battery was in sight, and shortly afterward the "City of Athens" came to the pier of the company, and prepared to swing alongside.

Handy-Dandy Joe came up again to Jack, and touched him familiarly on the shoulder.

"Now, Mr. Harkaway," he said, "do you mean to settle?"

"No, I don't," replied Jack, boldly. "You've got all you will get out of me."

"Is that so?"

"Yes. It's straight."

"Very well. I will go at once to the captain."

"You may go to the deuce, for what I care," said Jack.

Joe seemed staggered.

It was clear he had not expected this.

"Have you thought of the consequences, sir?" he said. "You were the cause of the death of Mr. Fenton by drowning, and it's a case of—"

"Hullo!" said Jack, as his eye fell upon a figure on the pier.

Handy-Dandy Joe followed his gaze, and appeared equally surprised.

He rubbed his eyes.

Look again.

There could be no mistake.

Among the crowd of custom's officers and others was the form of Miles Fenton.

The man was not drowned, after all, for he waved his hand, and shouted out—

"Glad to meet you, Mr. Harkaway!"

"Eh?" said Jack.

"None the worse for falling overboard, you see."

"How did you fix it?" inquired Jack.

"I swam for two days and nights, and then got on the back of a friendly whale I met. He carried me into New York, and I sold him for blubber. It wasn't gratitude, I admit, but it was some cute."

"You'll do," said Jack, who was pleased to think, after all, that he had not killed the man.

"The fact is, Mr. Harkaway, I was picked up by the 'Republic,' and we made such good way, that we beat you shamefully. I shall be glad to see you at my hotel. I thought I'd let you know I was still in the flesh. Come to the Astor House to-night, and dine with me."

"Thank you, I'd rather not," replied Jack.

"It's down-town, and a little out of the way for swells like you," continued Fenton. "But I'll give you a welcome."

He waved his hand again, and walked away, smoking a cigar with the nonchalance of an accomplished man of the world.

Jack turned round upon Joe.

"You can be off about your business," he said.

"I subside into my boots, sir," answered Joe. "The man deceived me. He ought to have died, and blame me if that 'Republic' isn't the biggest swindle afloat."

"Why?"

"She's robbed me. If she hadn't picked the man up, I should have got a decent living out of you. Now, the pitch is crabbed."

"It is like the little bee in the hive, or the pea under the thimble. The quickness of the hand deceives the eye, my noble sportsman, and if the trick isn't done properly, you're played out."

Jack saw he had triumphed, and walked away.

"Good-night. Who is the next gentleman?" said Joe, humming "Beautiful Spring," as he went to look after the carpet-bag that contained his scanty luggage.

Monday was very busy, and having put the lighter parcels together, was standing guard over them.

An agent of the company saw him, and taking him for someone sent on board to work, thought he was having a lazy fit.

"Now, then, Sambo," he said, "hurry up—hurry up!"

"Who you talking to, sare?" demanded Monday.

"You're a coloured help, ain't you?—hurry up."

"I Mist' Harkaway's man, sare. You get away from insulting me, or I give you something not like. Go 'long, sir—hurry up!" said Monday, holding out a stick, threateningly.

The agent retreated in alarm.

"Hurry up! Hurry up!" cried Monday, imitating him.

The agent tumbled over a box, and lay sprawling on the deck.

When he got up, he said, grumblingly—

"I can't make that darkey out."

But, whatever his opinion might have been, he did not attempt to interfere with Monday again.

Shortly after, the passengers landed, the baggage was examined, and Jack's party started in two coaches for the Gilsey House Hotel.

Being provided with rooms, Jack informed Harvey and Emily of Fenton's reappearance.

"That means more trouble," remarked Harvey.

"Nevertheless," said Emily, "I am glad you did not kill him."

"Perhaps I'll have to do it yet," answered Jack. "But we won't meet worry half-way. I want you to make yourself at home, Emily. Will you see to the ladies, Dick?"

"With pleasure," answered Harvey; "are you going out?"

"Yes, I'm going to take a walk with Mole, to

make a few inquiries. It is important I should know, if possible, whether Hunston and my boy were rescued from the—"

He stopped abruptly as he saw Emily's eye fixed upon him.

She had been kept in ignorance of the wreck of the "Santa Maria," and he did not wish her to know anything about it.

"I mean," he continued, coughing in some confusion, "I must find out if Hunston and the child have yet landed in this city."

He hurried away, and told Mr. Mole what he wanted, and they started together, walking through Madison-square until they reached Union-square, and the busy portion of Broadway.

They looked about them with the admiring eyes of strangers, and while lost in wonder at the size of the stores, the general magnificence of the buildings, and the bustling activity displayed on all sides, they were accosted by a person of genteel appearance.

"Strangers in New York city, I guess," he exclaimed. "From Europe, may I ask?"

Jack saw a well-dressed, somewhat simple-looking individual, who seemed highly respectable, wearing a silk hat, a black frock-coat buttoned up, striped pants, dark gloves, and a pair of spectacles.

"My friend and I arrived this morning," replied Jack.

"Ah! singularly fortunate I should have met you. Please to accept my card."

Taking it with a bow, Jack read on it, "Mr. Sensitive Sheepe."

"Thank you," he said. "My name is Harkaway. Allow me to introduce my friend. Mr. Mole, Mr. Sheepe."

"Proud to know you, sir. It is fortunate I left business early to-day. I am a humanitarian, sir. I run a relief office, supported by voluntary contributions. Everybody in New York city knows Sensitive Sheepe. Household word, my name, sir."

"Indeed!"

"I do a great deal of good, sir, though it isn't for me to say it. I'm going to do you good."

"In what way?"

Mr. Sheepe regarded him with a bland smile, as if pitying his ignorance.

"This is a wicked city, sir. It has been likened to the Cities of the Plains. There are scoundrels, sir, who are always on the look-out to rob strangers."

He paused to see the effect of his communication.

"But," he continued, "I will protect you. Under my guidance you shall explore New York city from the Battery to Harlem, and not be a cent the worse for it. Come and take a drink."

"A very sensible proposition," said Mr. Mole.

"Two blocks from here is an excellent liquor-store. The boss who runs it is a friend of mine," said Mr. Sheepe. "Follow me, gentlemen."

He conducted them a short distance down a side-street, and into an oyster-saloon, through which there was a drinking bar.

"As a Britisher, you will like ale, Mr. Harkaway. What is your liquor, Mr. Mole? Allow me to recommend whisky, sir," said Mr. Sheepe.

"Certainly," replied Mole, smiling with satisfaction at having got into company so much to his liking.

"A toby of ale, boss," continued Mr. Sensitive Sheep. "A drink of bourbon and a pony brandy."

The proprietor put a small jug of ale before Jack, a little glass of brandy before Mr. Sheepe, and a bottle, and two tumblers, one of which contained ice-water, before Mr. Mole.

The latter helped himself, taking half a tumbler-ful of spirit.

"Capital custom this, letting people help themselves," he remarked.

"You're a stranger, I guess?" said the proprietor, "or you'd know this wasn't a wholesale store."

"What do you mean?" asked Mole.

"You've got to have a fifteen-cent drink."

"Well?"

"See here, you fill up your glass as if you wanted to bathe your feet in it."

Mr. Mole looked indignant.

"He means you are only expected to take a little," said Mr. Sheepe.

"It's our custom to pour out in moderation, or the machine wouldn't run. No offence. Very good fellow, the boss."

Mr. Mole held out his hand.

"Where no offence is meant, none shall be taken," he said.

The proprietor took the proffered hand, and shook it amiably.

"Known the Mountain Pecker long?" he asked.

"Who?"

"Mr. Sheepe."

"Ha! ha! How playful he is!" laughed Mr. Sheepe. "He is punning on my name. He will tell you that I graze upon the commons and pastures of society. A sheep pecks the mountains for his living."

"You're not particular to a shade," answered the proprietor. "But I guess you're in good hands. Never a capper in the city will touch you while you're with the Pecker."

"Now, tell me how I can serve you, Mr. Harkaway," said Mr. Sheepe, who seemed tired of the bar-keeper's remarks.

"I want to go to Castle Garden," replied Jack. "My friend requires a wig, and I must change some money."

"That we can do here," said Mr. Sensitive Sheepe. "We reckon the dollar at five shillings, so there will be four to the pound English. Thus highly is the American currency appreciated on the Exchanges of the world. How much do you want?"

"I have twenty sovereigns."

"Hand those rocks over, and receive eighty dollars."

Jack did so unsuspectingly, and did not know that he was being cheated out of about one dollar and fifty cents in each sovereign.

"Have you nothing but paper money?" asked Jack, as he was given a bundle of bills and small stamps.

"Only a few one, two, and five-cent nickel pieces. But you'll get used to that in time. Come along. We will buy the thatch for your friend. How did he lose his hair?" said Mr. Sheepe.

"It was an accident on board ship," replied Mr. Mole.

The Pecker let Jack pay for the drinks, and leaning over the bar whispered—

"I shall call later on for my bit, and mind, I must have a full half this time, or we do no more business together."

An affectionate nod from the boss was the only answer to this.

They sallied forth into Broadway, where Mr. Mole was promptly supplied with an elegant wig.

Then they got into a stage, and were taken as far as the City Hall, which the Pecker pointed out to them as the building containing the courts of justice.

Jack's heart throbbed a little as he thought of Hunston, and wondered whether he and the boy had gone to the bottom of the Atlantic.

But no.

He would not harbour the thought.

There was every chance that the crew of the "Santa Maria" had been rescued by some passing steamer, as she lay right in the track of the Liners.

"Humph!" said Mr. Mole; "rather a bad smell here."

He hurried over a drain, which did not emit essence of magnolia.

"It is not generated in New York city, air," answered the Pecker. "I have studied chemistry, and am able to state that the odour is caused by catahydrosulpnitrothyle of permangacarboplatinum, and is wafted over from China, or thereabouts."

"Cata—what did you say?" said Jack. "I am not used to such jaw-breakers. To pronounce those words, a man ought to cough once, sneeze twice, take a handful of consonants, a twenty-five-cent drink, and, by the aid of a stomach-pump, he might get within half a mile of them."

The Pecker laughed.

"You are not a scientist," he remarked.

"Do you know where Houston-street is?" asked Jack, after a pause.

He was thinking of the cryptograph, and the place of meeting appointed by Hunston for Miles Fenton and himself.

"Oh, yes. Do you want to go there?"

"I do."

"Quite an elegant part of New York city, I assure," said the Pecker; "near Bowery and the Five Points."

"I heard there were bad characters there," observed Jack. "Had we not better go to the captain of the ward and get the services of an armed detective? Of course you are acquainted with the captain of the ward?"

"Oh! dear yes. We are very old friends. My! don't we know one another? I also know Justice Bixby, who sits at the Tombs Police Court. But, unfortunately, I cannot give you an introduction at present, as we have quarrelled."

"Really."

"Only a political difference. I threw my influence in for Greeley at the last election for President. It created an ill-feeling, their platform being Republican, and mine Democratic. It will blow over, I guess."

Jack expressed his regret at this, and hoped they might soon be friends again.

They had now reached the Bowling Green, and Castle Garden was before them.

CHAPTER IX.
NEWS OF YOUNG JACK.

WHEN the party reached the large theatre-like building, which once was the abode of the opera, and has echoed to the thrilling notes of the best singers, Jack paused and looked around him.

The extension of New York city has caused the drama to go up-town.

Castle Garden is now the asylum of refuge for the emigrant, and so great has been the progress of this remarkable city that it is not long since it was the resort of the fashionable. Niblo's was once considered very much up-town; but those who start from the theatre adjoining the vast Metropolitan Hotel will have to go a considerable number of blocks before they get away from bricks and mortar.

Jack thought of Sir Henry Hudson, the enterprising Englishman employed by a Dutch company, who, on the 3rd of September, 1609, first passed Sandy Hook and discovered New York.

What a change had taken place in less than three hundred years!

He was roused from his reverie by Mr. Sheepe.

"Pass this way, sir," said the latter, "and make your inquiries upstairs."

Leaving Mole with the Mountain Pecker, Jack obtained permission from the janitors to go to the office.

This overlooked the large circular theatre, and he met with every attention.

"What is your pleasure?" asked a clerk.

"A ship called the 'Santa Maria' was abandoned in mid-ocean," began Jack.

"Where did she hail from?"

"Naples."

"Captain's name?"

"Antonio Giovanni. What I want to know is this —have you received any of her crew or passengers here?"

"We have," answered the clerk, referring to a book. "The officers, passengers, and crew were taken off by the steamship 'Cuba,' and landed here this morning."

"By Jove!" replied Jack. "That is better than I expected."

"We have several of the rescued here. They have lost their all, and—"

"Never mind that," interrupted Jack. "Who were the passengers?"

"Man and a boy," said the clerk, bluntly, not liking Jack's impetuous manner.

"Had the man any distinctive mark?"

"One arm."

"That will do. Where are they?"

"Gone."

"Where?"

"How should I know?" said the clerk.

"Don't you keep them here?"

"Keep who?"

"People who are landed in that way," said Jack.

"What way?"

"Shipwrecked, or—"

"I guess we do our duty," said the clerk. "Emigrants stay here till they communicate with their friends, or they can stop a reasonable while till they get employment. We've lots on hand now waiting for those in want of help to come and see if they can hire them."

"Do you know where the one-armed man and the boy have gone?" asked Jack.

"No," said the clerk, roughly.

The sudden hope which had sprung up in his breast died away as quickly as it had been kindled into life.

"No idea whatever?"

"I've told you I haven't. If a man's got money or friends, we can't keep him here. He comes, and we do our best for him, take his description, and he is free to depart when he likes."

"Thank you. Much obliged," said Jack, who turned to join his companions.

He had learned something, though not much.

Hunston was in New York.

He had been rescued from the wreck of the "Santa Maria," and with him he had a boy.

Jack didn't think it worth while to inquire what name the one-armed man had given, because he was sure to give a false one, and the description he had received satisfied him that it must be the one he was in search of.

There could not have been two one-armed men on board the "Santa Maria" of Naples.

So Jack argued.

"Have you discovered anything?" asked Mole, as Jack rejoined him.

"Yes," replied Jack. "He's all right."

"Hunston is in New York? Is that so? And the boy, my pupil, Young Jack? Do I imagine a vain thing, or can this news be true, Harkaway?"

"That's so," replied Jack; "and I'm so jolly that I could salute the statue of Washington without feeling that George the Third was a donkey, and the War of Independence one of the worst chapters in English history."

Mr. Sensitive Sheepe was carefully examining a packet of chewing tobacco he had bought coming along.

"You're a generous sort of a cuss, I guess."

he said, as he squirted some tobacco-juice in dangerous proximity to Mr. Mole's nose.

"Why?" asked Jack.

"Britishers don't like to own up they've been whipped."

"That is a highly improper remark," said Mr. Mole, "and I feel called upon to resent it."

Mr. Sheepe turned round, and pointed to the Bowling Green.

"See these railings?" he said.

"I do."

"They've got no tops to them. When the Patriots wanted stuff to put in their guns, they broke it off those. Yes, sir, and not even a Tammany Ring, set on improvements, with fifty per cent. to be made on a contract, would dare to touch that sacred metal. No sir."

"I tell you what it is, I shall have to punch your head!" exclaimed Mr. Mole.

"What for?"

"Abusing Great Britain, which is an empire on which the sun never sets."

"The sun's ashamed of doing so, I guess. He rises your way, and sets ours."

"Sir, you are insolent," said Mr. Mole.

"So are you, I guess. I'll have your wig!" replied Mr. Sheepe.

"Gentlemen," said Jack, "what is the meaning of this? Where have you been during my absence?"

"Went to buy some tobacco. Got some Mayflower," answered the Peeker. "That's all, Mr. Harkaway. There's nothing the matter with me. I'm so sensitive, I can't bear to hear my country abused. Only say one word against the Stars and Stripes, and all the feathers in the tail of the American Eagle stand on end like frills upon the—no, not frills—what is the idea?"

"Quills," suggested Jack.

"Exactly. Like quills upon the fearful peccary." Mr. Mole was very angry.

Laying his hand upon Mr. Sheepe's shoulder, he exclaimed, in a severe voice—

"You corrupt mass of misquotation, may the ghost of Shakespeare haunt you! It's fretful porcupine, not fearful peccary. But the fact is, Harkaway, the man is drunk. I took him to have a liquor."

"Did you?" inquired Jack, with a smile.

"He took advantage of my kindness, and had five straight off."

"You drank fair, and had glass and glass with me," said Mr. Sheepe. "But don't bother me. Shoo-fly! I'm looking for a ten-cent stamp in this 'bacca, and blame me if I can find it."

Jack did not like Mr. Sheepe's conversation as well as he had done formerly.

"Mr. Mole," he said, "come with me, please. I am much obliged to this gentleman for his kindness so far. Now we can dispense with his company."

"Dispense with me!" said Mr. Sheepe. "You ain't riled, Mr. Harkaway, are you? I'm so sensitive, you know, and I guess your friend—But I won't say anything. Come and dine with me?"

"Another time," replied Jack.

"You shall have all the delicacies of the season. Gumbo soup, blue-fish, green corn, tender loin-steak, canvas-back duck."

"The roast beef of old England for me," said Mr. Mole. "Come, Harkaway, let us dine with our new friend. You can enjoy the delicacies. I will have a cut of under-done beef."

"Have it rare, if you like," replied Mr. Sheepe.

"Rare! Do you mean raw?"

"We call it rare. Shake hands. I won't have your wig this time. Be a good boy. Sorry if I

offended. I'm so sensitive, you know, if anything is said about Uncle Sam."

Jack took Mr. Mole on one side, and whispered in his ear.

"I think we ought to give Mr. Sheepe something for his trouble, and leave him."

"Oh, no! It would insult him," hastily replied Mole. "He is a highly reputable man. Knows all the best men in New York."

"It was foolish of you to go and drink with him while I was in Castle Garden; and he is not very complimentary in his remarks about you."

"I forgive him, Harkaway," answered Mr. Mole. "We are in a new country, and must make allowances. I may have provoked him, and his observation about my wig was more playful than malicious, I am sure."

"That does not matter," said Jack, with his usual determination. "I have taken a dislike to the man, and shall go home."

"Home!"

"Certainly. Stay with Mr. Sheepe, if you like. I shall not."

"I won't leave you."

"Come along, then," said Jack.

The Pecker saw them conversing together, and though he did not hear what they said, he could guess the purport of their conversation.

A blind beggar stood near them.

Taking a sum of money out of his pocket he said—

"Excuse me a moment. I see a poor blind man. Always give to blind man. Might be blind some day myself. So sensitive, you know."

He ran away, put something in the blind man's hand, and came back smiling with his usual blandness, and looking benignantly through his spectacles at Mr Mole.

"He has a kind heart," said the professor. "I admire him for his charity."

"You would admire anybody who'd drink with you," replied Jack, angrily.

"Harkaway," said Mr. Mole, in a tone of reproach, "is this kind of you?"

"Think of the weight I have on my mind," answered Jack. "Miles Fenton is in New York; so is Hunston and my boy. How do I know that this fellow is not a spy of Hunston's?"

"A spy?"

"Certainly. My experience has taught me to be cautious. You are like a Yorkshireman, and ought to have his coat-of-arms."

"What's that?"

"A flea, a fly, a magpie, and a flitch of bacon."

"Why a flea?" asked Mr. Mole.

"Because a flea will bite any one; so will a Yorkshireman."

"Why a fly?"

"A fly will drink with any one; so will a Yorkshireman."

"Why a magpie?"

"Because a magpie will break with any one, and so will a Yorkshireman."

"Humph!" said Mr. Mole; "your description is sufficiently forcible; but why a flitch of bacon?"

"A flitch of bacon is never any good till it is well-hung; no more is a Yorkshireman."

This had been overheard by Mr. Sensitive Sheepe, and he rubbed his hands together.

"Very good, Mr. Harkaway. First class," he exclaimed. "I think you have hit Mr. Mole off proper."

"Possibly," replied Jack. "We will not argue the point. I am much obliged to you for your kindness. Will you accept—"

"Money!" interrupted Mr. Sheepe, with a smile. "Do I look as if I wanted money? Nonsense!

All I want is your thanks, if you think I have been fortunate enough to be of service to you."

"You are welcome," said Jack. "I am going home."

"May you be happy!" answered Mr. Sheepe. "I kept house once when my poor wife was alive, and we had only one trouble—insects."

"Musquitoes?" said Mr. Mole.

"No; bed-bugs. Will you believe me, sir? Once I got up in the night and burnt about fifty matches looking for the varmints, and as I burnt the matches and caught the creatures, I threw them both into a basin half full of water."

"Well?" said Jack.

"Well, sir, as I stand here a living sinner, those bed-bugs made a raft of those matches, and standing upon their hind legs, serenaded me."

"Eh!"

"They couldn't bite, but they sang in chorus, 'A Life on the Ocean Wave.'"

"That's coming it a little too strong," said Jack.

"So I thought, but when I remonstrated with them, they changed the tune to 'I'm Afloat'"

Jack smiled, and saying "Good-day, sir!" took Mole's arm, and began to retrace his steps.

The Mountain Pecker returned his salutation, but though he fell behind, he did not for a moment lose sight of them.

"I'll have them again, darned quick," he muttered. "May I be caned and laid out in the next free fight, if I don't!"

A wicked gleam appeared in his eye, the soft, almost simple expression of his face vanished, and gave way to a murderous scowl.

While allowing his viler passions play, Mr. Sensitive Sheepe looked more like a bandit than the chairman of a charitable society.

Instead of going up Broadway, as he intended, Jack turned down Beaver-street, towards the East River, and crossing Wall, found himself in Pearl-street.

He wandered on, looking at the names of the streets on the lamps, passed the City Hall on the left, and pulled up in Baxter-street, satisfied that he had lost his way.

It was only natural that he should feel doubtful about proceeding any further without making inquiries.

He was in a strange city, the appearance of the streets and houses did not prepossess him in their favour.

There was a back-slum sort of look about them.

Loafing around were men with villainous and cut-throat faces, such scum of the world, in fact, as will be found in all large commercial centres.

In spite of his natural courage, Jack turned a shade paler.

His hand involuntarily sought his pocket for his revolver.

It was gone.

Next he felt for his purse, containing the bills he had received up-town.

That, too, was missing.

He uttered a cry of vexation.

"What is the matter?" asked Mr. Mole.

"I've lost my money and revolver. The New York thieves have been at work, though how the deuce they managed it I can't tell, as we have spoken to no one except Mr. Sensitive Sheepe."

"He would be incapable of such a crime!" exclaimed Mr. Mole. "That is an honest man, Harkaway, and I feel we have done him an injustice."

Jack shook his head dubiously.

"If you had been guided by me," continued Mole, "we should have retained his services. It is to be regretted that you are so headstrong."

"I was right."

"It doesn't look like it. Where are we now?"

"How should I know? There is Baxter-street on the lamp."

"Don't you know your way home?"

"Is it likely, when I have never been here before?" replied Jack, testily. "We must go on till we find a policeman, I suppose."

Mole groaned.

"I wish to goodness you had not sent Mr. Sheepe away. Here we are, in a strange city, lost. You have been robbed, and I—why, bless me! my purse is gone, too!"

"Yours!"

"As I am alive, it is gone."

"Somebody has seen us coming, and picked us up. It must be that fellow, Sheepe," cried Jack.

"Impossible!"

"I should like to kick the oily scoundrel. What fools we were to talk to a man we did not know!"

"I was not Mr. Sheepe, of that I am certain. Sensitive Sheepe is a man of mark in the city. We have wronged him. Look at his face! It beams with charity. He is all soul. We have been robbed through your obstinacy."

"Shut up with such rot!" exclaimed Jack.

"It is as I say. With Sensitive Sheepe we should have been as right as the mail."

"Not much."

"You will have your own way. I should like to meet that man, and apologize to him for your rudeness. Our pockets must have been picked while staring around us, like greeneys as we are."

The shades of night were beginning to fall, and crept gloomily along, filling up corners and doorways, seeming more sombre and spectral through the flickering glare of the gas.

"If we don't want to be cornered," said Jack, "we must look out. Unarmed and moneyless, we're in a nice scrape."

"Have you nothing—absolutely nothing?" asked Mr. Mole.

"By Jove! we're in luck," answered Jack. "I thought I was dead-broke, but I'm not quite cleaned out. In my waistcoat I have the change out of a five-dollar bill."

"Let us enter a drinking saloon, refresh ourselves, and inquire the way," replied Mole, brightening up under the more cheering prospect which dawned before him.

For a moment Jack hesitated.

The appearance of the houses on all sides was suspicious, and the various tales he had heard of strangers being robbed and murdered in low dens in New York city flashed across him.

Dead bodies of strangers had been found in the rivers around Manhattan Island.

He had a decided objection, at this stage of his career, to being a body.

CHAPTER X.

THE MOUNTAIN PECKER AGAIN.

SUDDENLY Mr. Mole touched Jack's arm.

"Can't you let me alone?" said Jack, crossly. "Cheese it!"

"Don't you see who that is?" cried Mole.

"No."

"It's Sensitive Sheepe. I could swear to him in a thousand. Call him and ask him to tell us which way to go."

"Not I. Come along, and let him rip," replied Jack. "I've turned him up once, and I'm not going on my knees to him. You talk like an old woman. We're all right, if we have lost ourselves in New York the day of our arrival."

"If you are so pig-headed, I'm not going to be," said Mole. "It's my firm conviction that we have wronged that excellent man, by our injurious suspicions."

"Bosh!"

"I shall go to him and ask his help."

Mr. Mole ran after Mr. Sheepe, who was walking slowly, and did not appear to be trying to get out of sight.

"Come here, sir. Come here," said Mole.

The Pecker stopped and retraced his steps.

"Who hailed?" he asked.

"Mr. Mole and Mr. Harkaway, from London."

"Oh! good-evening Mole and Harkaway, from London," said Mr. Sheepe. "Excuse me, I'm pressed for time."

"We're lost. Put us on the right track," said Mole. "For goodness sake, Mr. Sheepe, don't leave us."

"I never like to obtrude myself upon people who evince disinclination for my society," answered the Pecker, with dignity.

"Of course not."

"I know who I am, and—"

"Don't say another word, sir," interrupted Mole. "Stand our friend once more. Will you take a drink?"

"You bet!" answered the Pecker, whose language was not at all times so refined as he seemed to wish to make it.

"Let us go into the first bar," said Jack, making a virtue of necessity. I am cold, tired, and hungry."

"Follow me," said said Sheepe. "You shall be my guest. Pardon me or not speaking first. So sensitive, you know."

He led the way into a saloon, where drinks and oysters were retailed, ordering them half-shells, to which Mole paid great attention, shevelling them into his mouth with the agility of a practised oyster-eater.

"Look at him putting them away like pie," said the Pecker.

"Very good oysters. I'll have some more. Really excellent bivalves," replied Mole.

"Aren't they bully?" asked the Pecker. "Sit down at the table and have some hot Tom and Jerry."

He walked to a table, and Jack had an opportunity of observing the place they had entered.

It was a long, narrow room, with a bar near the door. Tables and chairs ran along each side. Not much business was being done; only two men were lounging at the bar, and the third occupant of the house was a coloured man, who was sitting at a table, with his head resting on his hands.

"Get up!" said the Pecker, giving him a kick on the leg.

He rose, looking angrily at his disturber, and Jack saw that he was not an African, but one of the aboriginal Red Indians of the plains, well-made, though having a slinking look, and a dirty appearance, while the tattered clothes of civilisation hung loosely and awkwardly round him.

"Is that red swine here?" asked the bar-keeper. "I believe he lives here."

"The red man pays for what he has," answered the Indian. "And if not, his knife can settle the account."

He spoke in good English, and after bestowing a look of intense hatred upon Mr. Sheepe, retired to another table, where he again rested his head on his hands and began apparently to slumber.

The bar-keeper, a shrewd Yank, with a hungry, wolfish look about his lean jaws, seemed to hesitate as to the advisability of kicking the Indian out; and thinking better of it, bestowed a curse upon him instead, and supplied the new-comers with the ordered drinks.

"I didn't know you had Red Indians in New York," said Jack.

"No more we have," replied the bar-keeper. "How in thunder should we, seeing we've driven them so far west? He's a solitary specimen, you may be dead sure."

"How did he get here?"

"He comes down with skins, since the Pacific rail track's been opened up. His name's Par-a-wau, or the Warning Devil, and he loafs around here for three months at a time, more or less drunk, generally more."

Jack thought of the time when the red men were the lords of the soil, and how they had owned in fee-simple the very ground on which New Amsterdam, now New York, stood.

The houses in which lived the descendants of the old Knickerbocker families, and the palatial residences of the shoddy aristocracy, where built on the soil which formally sustained the primitive wigwams of the ancient lords of the land.

What a contrast between our times and the period when the continent was untrodden by the white man's foot did the presence resent of this poor solitary waif of the prairies among the bustling and arrogant pale-faces!

Par-a-wau, or the Warning Devil.

There was an air of romance about the very name.

"Guess you're kinder tickled to see the redskin?" said Mr. Sheepe, observing Jack's looks.

"Yes, I am highly interested."

"He's a poor, lying, drunken thief, and has only just come off the Island, where he was sent up for twelve months for passing some wild cat notes."

"What's that?" inquired Mole.

"Bogus money. There was another in it with him; he hasn't the head to plan, and only got his bit out of it. Well, he shoved the queer on his pal."

"Eh?" said Jack.

"Rounded. Split on his accomplice, who got seven years in Sing Sing, while Par-a-wau was let down easy, and he swears to this day he did not know the paper was bogus; but Indians are tough 'uns to lie."

"Right you are, Pecker," exclaimed the bar-keeper. "I'd shoot the whole lot of them, and could bullet him where he sits, though it's more square to give him the lead face to face, and I shan't be particular about that if he turns nasty with me."

One of the men at the bar asked Mr. Sheepe if he was going to stand a drink at this juncture.

"I guess not," answered Mr. Sheepe. "Mind your own lay, and don't interfere with mine."

"I mean having a drink, anyhow," was the reply; "and if you don't cast up, you old rip, I'll—"

"What will you do?" asked Mr. Sheepe, getting on his legs with a threatening air.

"Oh, you're a bully boy," replied the man. "You can't rope in a greeny. Oh, my, no! You can't stock the cards."

Mr. Sheepe hastily threw down a fifty-cent stamp on the counter.

"Take it out of that, cuss you!" he said.

Resuming his seat, he said to Jack—

"Foolish of me, perhaps, to encourage such a seedy-looking bummer; but I'm so sensitive, you know."

The seedy one replenished his glass with old rye, and began to sing "We'll All Drink Stone Blind," which entertaining ditty he kept up for some minutes, to his own apparent satisfaction, if not to the entire delight of his involuntary audience.

THERE WAS A THIRD PARTY.—A MAN SILENTLY WATCHING THE DEATH STRUGGLE.

"I must be going, Mr. Sheepe," said Jack. "Will you kindly put me in the way of getting home?"

"Where are you hanging out?" inquired the Pecker.

"At the Gilsey House."

"We will walk up Canal-street into West Broadway, and you can take the cars."

"It is time I got home, for I have been robbed of my purse and my six-shooter."

"Indeed!" said the Pecker. "But I am not surprised. A stranger ought to leg it mighty quick in these parts of New York city, unless he wants to get mussed about the head with a slung-shot."

"I shall remember that," said Jack, with a thankful feeling that he had got so well out of danger.

He took out what money he had left, and counted it. Three dollars, fifty cents.

The cents he kept for the cars, the dollars he folded up.

Walking to the Indian, he touched his arm.

"Will you accept this from me?" he asked. "You are a stranger here, and it may be useful. If you want more to get back to your native plains, call at the Gilsey House, and ask for Mr. Harkaway; you shall have what you require."

Par-a-wau looked earnestly at Jack.

He rubbed his eyes, as if scarcely able to believe he was in earnest.

"My white brother mocks Par-a-wau," he said "Ugh! it is not well."

"I assure you I am not chaffing," said Jack, forcing the money into his hand.

Assured of his benefactor's generosity, the Indian's eyes sparkled.

Poor fellow!

He had only just come out of the Penitentiary, and the weary months had come and gone, with them sun and moons, bringing no hope to the chained captive.

Perhaps he was innocent of the crime of passing bad money, and had really been the tool in the hands of a villain.

"The heart of Par-a-wau leaps in his breast," he exclaimed. "My white brother has got a soul, and the Apache chief may some day show that he knows how to kiss the hand that feeds him."

"Are you an Apache chief?"

"Some day know, perhaps," said Par-a-wau, changing his tone; "not now. Bad man listen. See Par-a-wau soon."

Jack shook his proffered hand, and rejoined his companions.

"Well," said Mr. Sensitive Sheepe, "you are like me, so sensitive, you know; but I would rather give to whites than reds or blacks."

"Charity should know no such distinction of race," replied Jack.

"Anyhow, you've made a friend for life of Par-a-wau. I guess he'll be like a leech to you now."

They quitted the saloon, and walked to Canal-street.

"By the way, excuse me," said Mr. Sheepe; "but you said something about wishing to go to the 'office' in Houston-street."

"I've changed my mind."

"Will you not go?"

"Not to-night," replied Jack.

Mr. Sensitive Sheepe said no more. He led them across Broadway, and seeing them into the car, left them, hoping they would meet again soon.

When they were seated, Mr. Mole said—

CHAPTER XI.

A FREE FIGHT IN NEW YORK CITY.

"THOUGH I think I should have gone to the 'Office,' Harkaway. Just to look after Mr. Hunston, Young Jack, and Miles Fenton."

"So I shall."

"But you told Mr. Sheepe—"

"Never mind what I told that fellow," said Jack. "I know my game, and when I have had some dinner you bet I shall be on Hunsten's track."

"Oh! I see. Foxing, eh?"

"It is necessary, with a man like Mr. Sensitive Sheepe, as he calls himself, though I'll wager that's not his real name. I saw through him. Didn't you hear his slang, and how all the bar-keepers knew him?"

"No. I didn't notice that," replied Mole.

"Moles are said to be blind," observed Jack.

"Don't be personal, Harkaway. I object to it," said Mr. Mole. "You may be right, and I may be wrong. No matter. Time will show. Still, you would not forget that I am Professor Mole."

"All right, sir. It shan't occur again," answered

Mr. Mole was pacified, and soon after they reached their hotel, where they found the members of their party as well prepared for dinner as they were themselves.

While Jack was at dinner in the hotel, he was reserved and gloomy.

Emily knew that he did not like being questioned, and forbore to trouble him with any queries as to his success during the day, feeling sure that he

would speak to her if he deemed it advisable to do so.

He was thinking of many things.

Of Hunston and Young Jack being saved from the wreck of the "Santa Maria," of their being probably in New York at that moment, of the lustrous, speaking eyes of the Indian, Par-a-wau, whom he had befriended, and of Mr. Sensitive Sheepe, whom he did not like at all.

After dinner, the party retired to their private sitting-room, when coffee and cigars were served.

Calling Monday on one side, he said—

"Go out, please, and buy me a six-shooter revolver, bullets, powder, and caps. Have it loaded in the shop."

"Yes, sare," replied Monday.

Emily looked wistfully at her husband.

She was much better, but far from strong, and reclined upon the sofa, her coffee standing on a chair by her side.

Beckoning to Harvey, she said—

"Jack will not speak to me. He has something on his mind. Will you be so kind as to ask him if he is going out to-night?"

"Certainly," replied Harvey.

He approached Jack, who was looking out of the window, watching the people passing and re-passing, the brilliantly-lighted shops, the cars with their merrily-tinkling bells.

A few feathery snow-flakes began to fall, the wind having changed, and the sky becoming heavy and laden.

"Looks like a wild night," said Harvey.

"Seasonable," replied Jack. "We're not far off Christmas."

"Going out?"

"Yes."

"Where?"

"I've got some work to do," said Jack. "Hunston's in New York. I didn't tell you before because I had no chance, and I don't want to frighten the women."

"Is the boy with him?"

"No doubt."

"That's good news," exclaimed Harvey. "I congratulate you. But look here, old man: I must go with you, if there's danger afloat. I feel hurt you didn't ask me before."

"I meant to, presently, and should have proposed going to the theatre for an hour," answered Jack.

"That's all right, so long as I am not left out in the cold, when there is a prospect of a row," said Harvey, better satisfied.

Shortly after, Monday handed a parcel to his master, which he hastily put into his pocket.

"Harvey and I are going out to look around," he said. "We shall not be late, but there is no necessity for you to sit up for us."

"Very well," replied Emily.

When they were gone, she turned hastily to Hilda, and taking hold of her hand in a nervous manner, looked her full in the face.

"Hilda, my dear friend!" she exclaimed, "Jack has gone to run some great risk. I know it; I feel it."

"He is after Hunston, I expect," replied Hilda.

"That is what I think. The mysterious telegram dropped by Miles Fenton made the 'Office' in Houston-street a meeting-place. Jack explained to me that the 'Office' was simply a name for a drinking-saloon."

"Yes," said Hilda.

"Do you not think that we might be of use to our husbands, if we put on thick veils and go after them?"

"What an idea!" replied Hilda.

"Are you afraid?" asked Emily, with a tinge of sarcasm in her voice.

"Emily!" said Hilda, reproachfully.

"Forgive me, dearest!" Emily hastened to exclaim. "I would not pain you for the world, and I know your spirit and courage too well. Come with me to this low place. My instinct tells me that we are wanted."

"Why?"

"Can you ask? If Jack and Harvey go to this den, they do so with the hope of encountering Hunston and Miles Fenton, who will fight rather than surrender our child."

"Well?"

"Is not a true woman's place by her husband's side in the hour of danger?" exclaimed Emily, with glowing eyes.

"That is true, dear; but, in the first place, how do you know Hunston is in New York?"

"Let us ask Mr. Mole," replied Emily. "He has been out all day with Jack, and, of course, knows everything."

The professor was placidly sleeping in an arm-chair.

Emily rose, and woke him up by shaking his arm.

"Hullo! What is it? Brigands? Dash my wig!" said the professor, starting up, and looking confusedly around.

"Only a harmless little woman, Mr. Mole, who wants to ask you a question," said Emily, smiling.

The professor presented a grotesque appearance.

In his hurried awaking, he had pushed aside his wig. which hung awry, showing a part of his shorn head, upon which the hair had just begun to sprout.

"What news have you heard of Hunston and Young Jack?" continued Emily.

"Has Harkaway told you nothing?" inquired the professor.

"Only a little. He went out in such a hurry that I had not time to get all the news out of him," said Emily, with a woman's tact.

"You know, of course, that Hunston and the boy were saved from the wreck of the 'Santa Maria'?"

"Oh, yes," replied Emily, eagerly.

"We found that out at Castle Garden, where they were landed."

Emily clasped her hands ecstatically.

"Oh! Heaven above be thanked!" she exclaimed, "my child is safe. He lives—nay, more, he is in this city."

"What! I say, didn't you know it all along?—this isn't fair. You go pumping me, and Harkaway will throw the blame on my back," said Mole.

"Mr. Mole, you have rendered me a service. Do me another," exclaimed Emily.

"Well, that depends. If there isn't any fighting, or not too much lying in it, I'll take the proposal into my serious consideration."

"Come with Hilda and myself to the saloon called the 'Office'"

"What!" replied Mr. Mole. "Go into a den of ravenous wolves? Not if I know it."

"Coward!" said Emily, indignantly.

"I've seen and heard something of New York city to-day," continued Mole, "and I don't want to be brained by a slung-shot, or ripped up by a bowie-knife, or get the bead from a six-shooter. Not much."

"You will not come?"

"With all due respect to you, Mrs. Harkaway, I regret that I must decline your flattering offer."

With a look of scorn, Emily turned to Hilda.

"We must go alone, dear," she said.

"Are you strong enough to venture?" inquired Hilda, tenderly. "Remember your wound. It is scarcely healed."

"Oh, I cannot think of bodily pain and discomfort when my husband is in danger."

"Ah, me!" said Hilda. "We women have big souls, but our bodies are not half strong enough to enable us to carry out our valiant ideas."

"Come, let us go and dress," said Emily, who was fired with impatience. "With a dark dress and a thick veil no one will recognise us."

"I wish we could get some man to accompany us, because we should probably be insulted alone. Women who go to such places as the 'Office' cannot be of high character."

"We must risk anything, everything, in such a cause," answered Emily.

The ladies quickly attired themselves in the oldest and least attractive dresses they could find, hiding their faces behind thick veils.

They would have taken Monday with them, but he would have been recognised at once.

Emily and Hilda both had Italian poniards they had brought with them from Europe.

These were the only weapons they armed themselves with.

On their descent to the sitting-room, Mr. Mole endeavoured to excuse himself for his want of politeness and gallantry.

"You must not think I have no courage," he said; "because I have proved my valour in many a hard-fought struggle, but—"

"It is unnecessary, sir, to say a word," interrupted Emily. "We quite understand your conduct, and appreciate your courage at its real value."

"Oh! if you appreciate my courage, it is all right," said Mole, complacently. "I hate to be misunderstood."

"Now, Hilda," said Emily, "are you ready, dear?"

Hilda was pinning her shawl before the glass, and replied in the affirmative.

Just as they were preparing to start, the door opened, and, to the surprise of the ladies, Felix S. Prye walked in.

"Good evening, ladies," he said. "I saw your arrival at the Gilsey in the evening papers, and guessed I would pay my respects."

"You have come at a most welcome time, Mr. Prye." said Emily.

"How's that?"

"I think my husband told you that our object in coming to America was to look for our lost child."

"That's so. I know all about Young Jack and the one-armed scoundrel, Hunston."

"Mr. Harkaway has gone to the 'Office' to-night with Mr. Harvey. The boy and Hunston are in New York. We want you to take us to this saloon. If nothing happens, we can go back without being discovered; but if our husbands are in danger, we may save their lives."

"I guess many a man has been saved by a woman," answered Felix, "and you two girls are all-fired smart to think of such a thing."

"Will you take us?"

"Will I? Won't I?" replied the young American. "Shall we have Monday with us?"

"He would be recognised."

"He's an awful cunning darkey; I guess we shan't miss him, though. I'm fit to raise Cain to-night, I am so tickled to get back home."

"Good evening," said Mr. Mole.

"Ah! professor, did not see you," replied Felix. "Got your hair again?"

"It is—ahem! a wig, sir."

"Mind you hold it. If you lose that, you'll have to hunt grass. How is it you are not going with the ladies?"

"I'm sick to-night," answered Mole.

"You'll have to keep the knots out of your hair in this country," said Felix.

"Do you doubt my courage, sir?"

"Not much."

"That's all right. If you don't doubt my courage,

I don't mind; let a man once doubt that, and I have done with him for ever," replied Mole.

"Excuse me for hurrying you, sir," said Emily; "but time presses, and you will, I know, readily understand my anxiety."

"Certainly. You may bet your boots I'll place a very large brick on anybody's hat if he interferes with us," answered Felix S. Prye. "If they give me any of their cheek, they'll be worse fooled than they think for."

"I am sure you will protect us, and Mr. Harkaway will never forget your obliging kindness to us."

"My life is always at the service of beauty in distress. How is that for high?" said Felix.

The ladies smiled approvingly, and the three started on their novel and perilous adventure.

We must, however, leave them for a time, to follow Dick and Harkaway, who had about an hour's start of them.

Jack did not ask for the assistance of the police, because he was not sure of meeting Hunston.

He wanted to spy around, and see if he could obtain any information from the proprietor.

"If I grease the boss of the store," he said, to Harvey, "perhaps he will betray Hunston."

"It is clear that Hunston cannot be an old friend of his," replied Harvey, "for he has never been in America before."

"I should think he must have been recommended to go to the 'Office' by some villain who had fled from New York to avoid the officers of justice, and, by force of circumstances, joined the brigands in Italy."

"Most likely."

"I will pay the fellow his price."

"If you bid high enough, you will buy him."

"So I fancy," replied Jack.

By dint of persevering inquiries, they reached Great Jones-street, passed Second and First, coming at the next block to Houston.

Once here, it was not difficult to find the "Office," which was a disreputable-looking drinking-saloon.

Opening the door, they found themselves in a small bar, shut off from the remainder of the room by a screen forming folding-doors, through which those who liked could pass.

Harvey was about to call for something, when Jack exclaimed—

"Hush, Dick! I hear some one speaking!"

"Who?"

"My charitable friend, Sensitive Sheepe, or I'm mistaken."

They listened attentively.

"Look'ee here, Fenton!" exclaimed a voice, which was undoubtedly that of the Mountain Pecker.

"Well?" answered Miles Fenton, the man with the evil eye.

"You think yourself mighty smart, I dare say."

"I'm all there."

"Yet you got chucked into the Atlantic. My! That was well done."

"Dry up about that," said Fenton, sulkily.

"This Harkaway's no fool, I tell you, and if you and Hunston want to ride over him, you'll have to put some more nitro-glycerine into it, I guess."

"We know our game."

"Well, perhaps you do. Yet I've seen a greeney play euchre, and if he holds two bowers and the ace of trumps, it's odd on him for the trick."

"I say that you ought not to be here to-night. Hunston will come down presently, and he should have been met outside. Suppose Harkaway should be on the watch?" said Fenton.

"Haven't I been nursing him all the afternoon?" exclaimed the Pecker. "Didn't he and the professor take quite a fancy to Mr. Sensitive Sheepe, prime

charity organiser of New York city? Ha! ha! ha!"

"That was tall of you. But you wouldn't like the cops to make a raid on you."

"What for?"

"Didn't you boast you had robbed Harkaway of his purse and revolver?"

"Stash that sort of gab!" replied the Pecker. "Do you run this store, or I?"

"You do."

"If a cop comes to me, I can grease him. It's only a question of what you've got with you when you're bounced."

"Don't be offended, Leroy," said Fenton. "I only wanted you to keep out of danger."

"Bet your boots," answered Mr. Sheepe, whose real name appeared to be Leroy, "that I don't mean to have the nippers on me, nor has my time come to dance a jig upon air, though I've killed my man before now, for saying less than you've said to me to-night."

"Well, well."

"If Hunston comes here to-night, I say he is as safe as a church, and Leroy is a man of his word."

This was spoken emphatically, and seemed to put an end to the question.

So engrossed had the talkers been in their conversation, that they had not heard anyone enter.

Jack was pausing, irresolute how to act.

Suddenly the door of the screen opened, just wide enough to allow a man to pass.

To Jack's astonishment he saw Par-a-wau.

The Warning Devil held up his finger as a sign for silence, and, opening the outer door, beckoned them into the street.

They followed.

"My white brother spoke the words of kindness to Par-a-wau," he said.

"Oh! that was nothing," replied Jack.

"They were the first the poor Indian had heard for many long moons. Par-a-wau is grateful. As the parched earth is when the rain of summer falls, so is the heart of Par-a-wau."

"How did you know we were in the 'Office'?"

"Has not the Indian eyes? Has he not ears? Was not his life spent on the prairie and the forest?"

"Why did you beckon us out?"

"The men inside are bad. They talk of Harkaway. That is my white brother's token. My brother's blood must not be shed. I have spoken."

"I'm very much obliged to you, friend Par-a-wau," said Jack; "but it is important I should go back, more especially after the conversation I was so fortunate as to overhear."

The Indian reflected a moment.

"Go," he exclaimed, after a pause. "If my brother is in need, Par-a-wau will not be far off. His knife is sharp, and his hand quick. I have spoken. Wagh!"

Giving a sort of guttural grunt, the Warning Devil leant against the window, on the blind of which was written, in dingy characters, the sign of "The Office."

This was a cant term in use among a certain class of frequenters of this low den.

When they had arranged to take a drink, they would say, "Let us go to the 'Office.'"

Some saloons rejoice in the name of "The Bank." Others are known as the "Counting House," &c.

Pushing open the door, Jack passed boldly in, followed by Harvey, and walked straight into the saloon.

There were five or six men, besides Miles Fenton, lounging about, or standing in front of the bar.

Two were playing euchre at a side-table.

" Pass that," said one.

" I take it up," replied the other player.

Villainous, cut-throat-looking fellows were these customers of Leroy's, *alias* Mr. Sensitive Sheepe.

Miles Fenton and Leroy were greatly astonished at Jack's appearance.

" By thunder," exclaimed the latter, " here he is!"

Fenton replied by a smile, which seemed intended to say—

" Who was right, eh—you or I?"

" Good-evening, Mr. Sheepe," said Jack. " I did not know you kept on Houston-street. How are you, Mr. Fenton?"

" I'm only minding the bar for a sick friend," replied Mr. Sheepe. " Charity covers a multitude of sins, and I am so sensitive, you know."

" Remarkably so," answered Jack.

" You've a good memory, Mr. Harkaway," said Miles Fenton, fixing his terrible eye upon him.

" Yes," Jack replied.

" You do not expect to see Hunston, as he was drowned at sea. Only his ghost can appear."

" Drowned, was he?" replied Jack.

" Of course."

" I know better, old boy," Jack answered. " Hunston is in this city, and will be here to-night."

" Will he?" asked Fenton, with a sarcastic smile.

" You are here to keep your appointment with him."

" To show you that such is not the case, I shall at once take my departure."

" No, you won't."

" Eh?"

" Excuse me. I don't want to be rough on you, but if you stir from this crib I shall bring you back with a bullet."

Mr. Sensitive Sheepe became musical.

" Nix my dolly, cheese it!" he hummed.

Miles Fenton moved towards the door.

" Don't be rash," said Jack.

He drew his revolver, and pointed it at him.

" One step more, and I shoot!" he continued.

Fenton returned, and Jack sat down on the edge of a table, with his back to the wall, so as not to be surprised in the rear.

He could see all that was going on.

His pistol commanded the room.

Harvey was also armed, and he took a place by his friend's side, also displaying a revolver.

The loungers looked inquiringly at Leroy, while their hands sought their pockets.

" If any gentleman draws a pistol, I fire before he can sight the bead. Mind that!" exclaimed Jack.

Leroy gave his friends a warning glance.

" Come, come," he said, " this is foolishness. Since Mr. Harkaway has condescended to visit this poor house of my sick friend, he will, no doubt, further the cause of charity by standing drinks."

" I'll shout," replied Jack; " drinks for the crowd boss."

" Am I to consider myself a prisoner?" asked Miles Fenton, biting his lip.

" For the present," Jack said.

Leroy busied himself in preparing the drinks, and, while he was thus occupied, the Indian came in without taking any notice of Jack.

He sat down at a table, and, letting his head fall on his folded arms, appeared to be asleep again.

" Blarm that Indian," remarked Leroy. " He's always sleeping since he came off the Island."

But the bright, quick eyes of Par-a-wau were not closed.

He was watching all that took place, with the eyes of a hawk in search of prey.

When everyone had been supplied with liquor, and Jack had paid for it, Leroy asked Fenton if he would mind the bar.

" Certainly," was the reply.

" I am very sorry," exclaimed Jack, " but I can't allow anyone to leave this room."

" Why not?"

" Because I don't choose to. That's why."

" You're rather hard on respectable people. I have business to attend to," said Leroy.

" Mr. Sensitive Sheepe, Leroy, or whatever your name is, I know you," said Jack.

Leroy turned pale.

" What do you know about me?" he asked.

" You're Buchu. You're in league with this man Fenton, and Hunston. I have got to get my stolen child back from Hunston, and you shan't stop me."

Suddenly there was a report.

A shot whistled harmlessly over Jack's head.

He turned rapidly.

One of the euchre players was glaring angrily at Par-a-wau, who had seized his arm.

In his hand was a smoking pistol.

" Curse you!" said the man, fiercely. " What do you want to interfere for. I'll be a mark on you for this."

The Indian had been just in time to spring on him as he levelled a revolver at Jack, and knock his arm up, thus disturbing his aim.

He had probably saved our hero's life.

" Thank you, sir," said Jack to the man. " I am indebted to you for a little delicate attention, and shall return the compliment."

" What?" growled the man.

" I owe you a shot."

" Eh?"

" Where will you have it?" asked Jack, blandly.

" I guess you're not going to shoot," said the fellow, becoming ghastly white.

" Indeed I am. Where will you have it?"

There was no answer.

Jack did not wait any longer.

He fired at the would-be assassin, whose arm dropped useless by his side.

The victim uttered a howl of mingled rage and pain.

" You can go," said Jack.

He concluded that the man did not know Hunston, and could not warn him of danger.

Besides that, he would be naturally anxious to have his wound seen to as soon as possible.

With a vindictive glance at Jack, he slunk away, cursing all creation in terrible language as he went.

" If any other gentleman is anxious to be attended to in a similar manner, I shall be happy to oblige him," exclaimed Jack.

The men looked blankly at each other.

They could trace the path of their companion up the room by the great patches of blood which fell on the floor as he walked.

Scarcely had he gone, than two ladies, accompanied by a gentleman, entered.

They sat down near the door.

The gentleman ordered some apple toddy, and talked to the ladies in a low tone.

Miles Fenton lighted a cigar.

" You've got the whip hand, Mr. Harkaway, to-night," he exclaimed; " but it won't be always so, and you're not out of the woods yet."

" I'm not afraid of you," replied Jack. " When I learn what a man is, and what his game is, I can tumble to him. It is only from wolves in Sensitive Sheepe's clothing that I funk."

Since Jack's denunciation of him, Leroy had said nothing.

His face assumed a truly demoniacal expression, and he looked at Harkaway as if he could have knifed him where he sat, with as little compunction as he would have felt in eating his dinner.

Every one was watching Jack with the eye of a lynx.

If he once lost his presence of mind, he would be shot like a dog.

Each of these desperate men were armed.

Five minutes of awful and impressive silence passed.

Then the door of the saloon opened again, and a man entered quickly.

He did not appear to notice Jack and Harvey, who were sitting back.

Advancing to Fenton, he held out his arm.

He had but one.

It was noticeable that one of the ladies, who had come in accompanied by a gentleman, uttered a cry at the appearance of this one-armed man.

Her companion put her hand warningly upon her mouth.

After this, she controlled herself, and was silent.

"How are you, Fenton?" exclaimed the newcomer. "Here I am at last. *I* wasn't born to be drowned, you see. This is our good friend, Leroy, I suppose. Glad to make your acquaintance, sir."

Fenton made no answer.

He pointed in the direction of the two friends, who, revolvers in hand, sat as watchful as Uhlans on sentry duty.

Hunston swerved round on his heel, as if on a pivot.

He was face to face with his old enemy.

"Jack Harkaway, by Heaven!" he exclaimed, and he went the colour of a white-washed wall.

"Yes, my dear fellow," replied Jack. "I am here to meet you on your arrival. Very considerate of me, isn't it?"

"Fenton! Leroy! what does this mean?" demanded Hunston. "If it's a plant—but no, I can't think you'd put up the job for me."

"It means that we're cornered, and can't help ourselves," replied Fenton.

"Is that so?"

"It is," said Leroy; "and, by thunder! it's the first time I was ever circumvented by mortal man."

"Why don't you shoot, and chance it? Here are five of you—six, seven, with the Indian. Go in! Go for them, lads! There is nothing like lead to fetch a man!" cried Hunston.

"I warn you, Hunston," exclaimed Jack, "that I will stand no nonsense. All I want is my child. Restore him, and I will not molest you."

Hunston laughed scornfully.

"You want what you will never have!" he replied.

"How?"

"He is lost to you for ever."

"Do you want money?" said Jack, eagerly. "I will pay—"

"I've got more money than you have," interrupted Hunston. "You don't suppose I was a brigand all that time without making my pile? No, sir."

"What can I offer you?"

"Nothing."

It was noticeable again that one of the ladies trembled so violently that the other had to hold her up by putting her arm round her waist.

"Listen here, Harkaway," continued Hunston. "I hate you, as you know. Your boy is where no one can find him, and, if you were to kill me to-night, you'd be no better off."

"I've always been your friend," said Jack.

"Friend be hanged!"

"So I have. Your life has been in my hands over and over again."

Hunston tapped the stump of his amputated arm.

"Who did this?" he asked.

"You brought it on yourself."

"Bosh! Listen to me, I say," said Hunston, vindictively. "I shall educate that boy of yours to be the most almighty thief in the Union."

Jack shuddered beneath this savage threat.

"He shall learn to curse his father. Oh! you shall have a son to be proud of, you bet," concluded Hunston, with a satanic laugh.

Jack's hand played restlessly with his pistol.

Suddenly Harvey uttered a cry.

He had been seized from behind by a man who had crept up unawares, and thrown him heavily to the ground.

At the same moment, Jack's pistol was knocked from his hand.

He sprang into the middle of the room, defenceless, glaring around with panther-like rage.

In an instant, Miles Fenton rushed at him, and seizing him by the throat, presented a pistol at his head.

"I thought my eye would fix them both," he said, "if they gave the time."

" 'Shoot him! Shoot him!" cried Hunston.

"Say your prayers, Mr. Harkaway!" exclaimed Miles Fenton. "You've got to take the long journey this time."

Leroy had seized him from behind, and he was powerless in the hands of his enemies.

At this juncture, the Indian stood with a drawn knife watching his opportunity.

But as he was going to bound forward to effect a rescue, one of the ladies threw up her veil, uttered a shrill cry, and darted across the room.

Her bonnet fell off, and her long hair flowed in wavy masses over her shoulders.

Throwing herself upon Jack, and standing between his breast and the pistol of Miles Fenton, she looked like a heroine of old.

"Back!" she exclaimed, in a clear, but tremulous voice. "Back! You reach his body but through my heart. If I cannot save my husband, I can, at least, die for him."

It was Emily.

Hunston looked astonished, and then his expression changed to one of pleasure.

"What!" he exclaimed. "My net isn't very big, but I am having a good haul to-night. Eh! my pretty Emily, how beautiful you look when you're excited."

"Coward!" she answered, "I am here to save my husband. Release him. I am only a weak woman, but I can fight for him."

"Fire!" hissed Hunston, between his teeth.

Fenton was about to pull the trigger, which would have sent a bullet crashing through Harkaway's skull.

The pistol, however, was wrenched from his hand.

A blow from the butt-end stretched him senseless on the floor.

"I've got a word to say to this," cried Felix S. Prye.

Harkaway's arms were released, and he clasped them round his wife.

He bestowed a look of gratitude upon Par-a-wau, who had saved him.

"Confusion!" exclaimed Hunston, as Felix struck him on the head with a glass, and caused him to fall back.

Harvey recovered his legs.

"Fire! fire!" cried Leroy. "Let them have it, all of you."

"Heaven protect us!" sobbed Emily.

All at once there was a great noise at the door.

"This way, quick! This way!" exclaimed a voice.

The form of Mr. Mole appeared, followed by Monday and a large body of police.

"Vamoose the ranch!" cried Leroy.

He turned the gas out.

Instantly all was in darkness.

Several pistol-shots rang out with a sharp, cracking noise. The ruffians were firing at random as they endeavoured to escape.

It was some few minutes before the gas could be re-lighted. When it was, Jack surveyed the scene with considerable curiosity.

The saloon was full of police.

Its former occupants were gone, with the exception of Hunston and Par-a-wau.

Hunston was dizzy, and staggering from the effects of the blow dealt him by the Warning Devil.

Hilda was clasping Harvey in her arms.

Mr. Mole was clasping a bottle of bourbon in his.

Leroy and his friends had made their escape by a back door. Miles Fenton had gone with them.

"Is anyone hurt?" asked Mr. Mole. "I think I have done a good thing. My courage was called in question this evening; but, if it had not been for me, you boys would have got into a scrape."

Monday, Felix S. Prye, and three policemen were leaning against the bar for support. They had all been hit by the last discharge of the revolvers.

Jack, Harvey, and their wives were unhurt.

The captain of the ward had come himself, at Mr. Mole's earnest entreaty.

He had long had a wish to make a raid upon Leroy's premises, and this was a good opportunity.

Leroy had played the "Sensitive Sheepe" game on many unsuspecting strangers in New York.

But so skilful had he been, that hitherto he had contrived to escape detection.

Jack had no sooner taken in the situation, than he pounced upon Hunston.

"Lock this man up!" he exclaimed. "I charge him with stealing my child. That offence was not committed in this country; but if that is not enough to take him on, I accuse him of attempting to murder me to-night."

"That's enough," said the captain of the ward.

At a signal from their chief, four men secured Hunston, who was frantic with pain and rage.

Two policemen were so badly hurt by the roughs that they had to be taken home in a coach.

Felix S. Prye was grazed about the ribs, and could not walk.

Monday was shot in the muscles of the neck, and had had a very narrow escape.

Conveyances were sent for the whole party.

The wives were overwhelmed with thanks and congratulations for their brave conduct by their husbands.

As Hunston was sullenly standing in the midst of his captors, Jack approached him.

"Hunston," he said.

The only response he received was a ferocious scowl.

"Tell me where my boy is, and I won't appear against you."

"I'll see you jolly well hanged first, and then I won't," answered Hunston, savagely.

"Take your fate, then," said Jack, firmly.

Mr. Mole went behind the bar and overhauled the bottles on the shelves.

"Very fine old rye!" he exclaimed; "anybody take some old rye? I am the hero of the occasion. Harkaway!"

"Sir," replied Jack.

"Will your wife take a drink?"

"No, thank you, Mr. Mole," answered Emily.

"Well, I guess I will. You see, I am becoming quite Americanised, I guess, and I drink old rye. When you are in Turkey, you must do as the Turkeys do. There is nothing like it. Harkaway!"

"What is it?" petulantly asked Jack, who was talking to his wife.

"Who saved the ship this time—eh?"

"You did."

"Does anyone doubt my courage?"

The professor looked valiantly around him.

No one ventured to find fault with him, or, at all events, they did not express themselves in words.

"That's all right," continued Mr. Mole; "no one doubts my courage. I'll take another drink of old rye."

It was, indeed, lucky, as it turned out, that Mr. Mole had thought of taking Monday down to the Station of the Ward, and asking for a body of police to make a raid upon the "Office."

The result of the desperate situation in which Harkaway and his party were placed might have been very different.

Everyone felt that the professor had acted promptly and sensibly, and he had the thanks of all.

CHAPTER XII.

POOR AND FRIENDLESS.

WHEN Hunston quitted Castle Garden with Young Jack, he proceeded in a coach to the Bowery.

He had obtained the address of a low house where he could be accommodated with a bedroom, and chose the locality of the Bowery in preference to a more aristocratic neighbourhood, thinking there was less chance of being detected.

Leaving Young Jack in the room, he gave him some crackers and a glass of water, daring him to quit it until his return.

His next move was to go to a bank and deposit his diamonds and gold in a false name, keeping only as much currency as he thought he would require to go on with.

Dining at a restaurant on Broadway, he lighted a cigar and strolled on to the "Office," where he expected to meet Miles Fenton and Leroy.

Fenton and he had met before in London and Naples, and he knew him as an accomplished coiner and passer of bad money.

In fact, there was no crime that Fenton would not commit.

He always lived extravagantly, and travelled about from one part of the world to another, robbing in one capital, gaining admittance to good society in another, and gambling with loaded dice and card swindling in another, while he would represent the commercial interest in a third, and forge bills to large amounts.

He had expected to do a large business with Hunston in the States.

The bold stand made by Jack, together with the timely arrival of Mole and Monday with the police, which effected the capture of Hunston, and caused the flight of Mr. Sensitive Sheepe, alias Leroy, put his plans out of gear.

Young Jack hated and feared Hunston.

Since he had been carried off, his captor had cruelly beaten him on the slightest provocation.

The boy was unusually tall and manly for his age.

Though not yet six years old, he had as much intelligence as some boys double his age.

In addition to this, he was strong and wiry.

When Hunston had gone out, he sat by himself until it was nearly dark.

The sky was heavy and overcast.

Thin flakes of snow were falling, covering pavement and roadway with a feathery shroud.

It seemed to the boy a good opportunity to escape.

When hurried on board the "Santa Maria," Hunston told him that his mother and father were dead, that they had been shot by Barboni in the garden at Naples, and he would never see them again.

This cruel statement made the boy cry bitterly; but he was not old enough to detect the lie, and believed it.

He cried bitterly.

Hunston rewarded him for this proof of affection with blows and curses.

No wonder the little fellow wanted to escape from his tyrant.

Opening the door, he crept down-stairs and passed into the street, without his egress being perceived by any one.

Homeless, friendless, without a cent, he stood a wanderer in the streets of New York.

Little did he think that his sorrowing father and mother were in the city, and would, with open arms, have welcomed their darling to all the luxuries and comforts that the palatial hotel they were staying at could afford.

He walked hither and thither, staring at the lager beer and oyster saloons, pushed about by the hungry crowd, until he felt tired and miserable.

Sitting down on a door-step, he began to cry.

A boy with some journals under his arm came by, bawling out, " *Illustrirte Zeitung*   Frank Leslie's *'Lustrated Pepper!"*

No one would buy. The night was cold and cheerless. Snow was falling fast, and those people going by seemed on their way to Fulton Ferry, anxious to get to their homes in Brooklyn.

" Don't I wish I'd sold out!" said the paper boy. " I generally run the *Zeitungs* among the Germans here, but I guess they won't trade to-night. It's too much trouble to put their hands in their pockets. My! ain't it cold!"

He leant against a door-post, and blew on his fingers to warm them.

His tone was rather sad and downcast, but presently he brightened up, and continued talking to himself.

" It don't matter," he said. " My stock's all weeklies; that's better than dailies; dailies are done for when night comes, but weeklies will run straight on. My bank isn't dead broke either, so I shall turn it up for to-night, and go to the theatre."

A child's voice exclaimed, somewhere about the region of his knees—

" Take me with you, please ?"

" Hullo! Who's that ?" said the young merchant in newspapers, astonished.

" Young Jack," was the reply.

The boy, who was about ten years old, with a frank, open countenance, decently dressed, looked down.

" Why don't you go home, little 'un ?" he said, as he perceived Jack.

" I've got no home."

" That's rough. You'll be froze to death, then."

" I can't feel my feet now, and my ears and nose ache ever so," said the boy.

" Have you got any stamps ? Don't you know what I mean ? Any pewter—money ?"

Young Jack shook his head.

" I was stolen from my home," he said, " and brought here in a ship to-day, and I have run away from the man, because he beat and swore at me."

" Poor little cuss!" said the newsboy; " you shall come with me. My name's Kit. I sell papers, and, like you, ain't got any friends."

" Haven't you ?"

" I never knew my father; but I remember my mother before she died, and when I think of her it makes me kinder soft."

Kit rubbed his eyes with the back of his hand.

" I cry when I think of my mamma," said Young Jack.

" It's hard on a boy to get his own living so young," continued Kit; " but we've got to live somehow."

" I'll help you sell your papers," said Young Jack.

" I guess I want a mate. My chum got sent up

for making a swipe, and we should never be fri again, because I will be honest, if I starve for Get up, young 'un; we'll go and have some tea.

Young Jack rose and took his new friend's ha

" Something tells me I shall like you," exclaimed, as they trudged along through the sno

" You couldn't have met a better pal, I guess, replied Kit. " I'm young, but they can't com over me."

" Do you like work ?"

" What do you take me fer ?" said Kit, indignantly. " I can't loaf around."

" Have you always got money ?"

" Pretty much always. I can stay under water a long time, and don't give myself away."

" Where are we going ?" continued Young Jack, whc, child-like, was fond of asking questions.

" To Baxter-street."

" Is it a fine house ?"

" It's not so extensive as it might be if it was in Fifth Avenue," answered Kit, with a smile.

" I don't care what it is, so long as the man who stole me don't find me out."

" Where were you stolen from ?"

" Somewhere in Italy. I don't know where. This is America, isn't it ?" asked Jack.

" That's so."

" I heard the sailors say we were going to New York."

" You'll be fixed right enough with me," said Kit. " I lodge at Hans Dunkerboom's. He's the boss, and keeps a house for boys   He likes me, because I'm smart, and calls me the Right Bower. Here we are.   Follow me."

Young Jack descended some steps leading to a cellar, and followed his new friend into a large kitchen, in which were as many as thirty boys.

Some were sitting on benches, reading by the gas-light; others playing cards; some, again, cooking herrings and other delicacies before the fire, and drinking tea, which they poured from a huge tea-pot.

All were occupied.

A Babel-like din of tongues arose, but it did not seem to disturb the boss, who sat smoking in a rocking-chair near the fire.

He was an elderly Dutchman, stout, rubicund, beer-and-tobacco-loving, easy-going, good-living, and well-liked by his juvenile boarders.

They paid him so much a week. These waifs and strays had good beds, and did pretty much as they liked—all doing something in the day-time for a living, and managing, as a rule, to rub along.

Those who were successful helped those who were not; and, though poor and humble, they were independent, and thought themselves as good as the sons of the richest in the city.

Going up to the Dutchman, Kit exclaimed—

" Pa, I've brought you a new lodger."

Hans Dunkerboom regarded Young Jack with an approving eye.

" You are a goot poy," he replied. " He shall have a ped vat ish emtpy up-shtairs."

" Thank you," said Young Jack, in his politest manner.

" Put he musht pay his ten shents. Oh! yes. You cannot cross de prook unless there ish a priten over de stream."

" I fork out for him to-night," answered Kit, putting down a ten-cent stamp.

" Ah! you ish my Right Bower. Vat a poy that Kit ish!" exclaimed Hans Dunkerboom, with a smile of admiration.

" Now, I guess we'll have an oyster stew," said Kit.

" Young man," said Hans to Young Jack, " Kit

vill pe a prudder to you. You are lucky to meet mit him."

"Dry up!" said Kit. "We're cold and hungry, and want to eat."

"Well, I swow," laughed the Dutchman; "you shpend all your money in eating. You will pe so vat as putter if you do that."

"Not me," said Kit.

"Once I hat a leetle yaller tog," continued Hans. "I give tree dollars cash for him. He say 'pow, wow, wow,' when I first puy him. One day he eat seven quarts sourkrout, and he no more say 'pow, wow, wow,' becos he take sick and tide."

The Dutchman shook his head warningly, and sighed as he thought of the loss of his dog.

Kit led Young Jack to the fire, and told him to sit down while he went out with a saucepan to buy some milk and oysters to make a stew.

The other boys did not pay much attention to Young Jack. They were all busy in their own way, and it was enough for them that he was introduced by Kit.

To be a friend of the Right Bower was a sufficient passport to their society.

Kit presently returned with the milk, which he boiled, then threw in the oysters.

"Set-to," he said, as he poured out the saveury stew before Young Jack, who was hungry.

When he had eaten the oysters, he broke up some crackers in the soup, and eat that, too.

"How do you feel now?" asked Kit. "Your head ain't level if you don't like that."

"It's fine," answered the boy.

"Look at the boss," said Kit. "He's off to sleep. My! Won't I wake him up!"

He walked up to the Dutchman, who had fallen into a sound slumber over his pipe.

Pushing his chair near the stove, Kit placed his feet on the iron, and quite close to the fiercely burning coke inside.

Seeing what he had done, the boys gathered round to enjoy the fun.

Presently Hans Dunkerboom moved uneasily in his chair.

He twitched one leg, and then the other.

He snorted and grunted, and finally jumped up, stamping on the floor like mad.

"Dunder und blitzen!" he cried. "Vat has got my tose?"

Sitting on the floor, he tore at his boots till he succeeded in pulling them off, grumbling and swearing all the time.

"Got in Himmel!" he said; "how my tose burn!"

He rubbed his scorched feet, and made plaintive murmurs, like a dog who has had his foot run over.

"Hello, Dutchy!" exclaimed Kit; "who's set fire to your tenement house?"

"Go to the tufel!" exclaimed Hans, angrily.

"Say, now, did I do it? If you will sit so close to the stove, and go to sleep, I guess that's your fault."

"I dells you how dat vos," said the boss, mollifying a little, "I just tream a tream, and get too near the stove."

"Of course you did."

"I treams that I find a cask of lager beer."

"Is that so?"

"And I shtoops down to trink the beer, when I gets too near de shtove, and dat's what is de matter mit mine tose."

A roar of laughter followed this explanation.

The boys were immensely tickled at the Dutchman's explanation.

"Vere ish Kit? Vere ish my Right Bower?" inquired Hans.

"I'm here, boss," answered Kit.

"Vash anyting done mit me by de poys?"

"I guess not. They're laughing because they saw you hurry off your boots before they could have a hand in the game."

Hans Dunkerboom's suspicions were aroused by the merriment of the boys.

The explanation given him by Kit, however, tended to lull them to sleep.

"Tamm it, my pey, don't you s'pose I know dem fellars?" he said.

"They're right as the mail, pa."

"Dey von't hurt old Hans. Let dem go on mit dare crub, my poy. Dat ish all dey wants."

"There are two or three of them who are always up to mischief, pa," exclaimed Kit, with an eye to mere fun.

"Who dey be?"

"There's Rollins, and Conway, and Young Pete. All the lot who act at the Grand Duke's Theatre."

"Don't pe a tammed vool, Kit," replied the boss. "I dink you ar' scared of dem poys."

"They are always acting at night, boss," said Kit, "and I guess they'll get acting on you."

"I'll pet dey don't. It would not be goot for der 'elth. No, sir. Not much," answered Hans.

"When I'm here, they daren't do it," said Kit, with a wink at his associates.

"Vell, you shtay, Kit. You are my Right Bower, my poy. You shtay."

Kit nodded assent.

"Vell, I guess I shleeps some more," continued Hans. settling himself in his chair.

"Good-night, pa," said Kit.

Soon the Dutchman was snoring again, and the boys were arranging amongst themselves how they should spend the evening.

Young Jack Harkaway began to feel quite at home amongst his new companions.

"Well, little 'un," said Kit, patting him on the back, "how do you foot up now?"

"I feel all right," answered Young Jack.

"Can you strike a balance in favour of the firm, or do you feel as if you could only pay fifty cents on the dollar?"

"I don't understand that."

"Perhaps not; but you'll know what paying fifty cents on the dollar is before you've been long in the news trade," answered Kit, laughing.

"Let me call you my brother, will you?" asked Young Jack.

"If you like. I guess you may."

"My father will make your fortune, when he finds me, if you are kind to me."

"Is your father rich?"

"Yes. Plenty of money, horses, carriages, servants," said Young Jack.

"Do you think he will find you?" asked Kit, thoughtfully.

"He is sure to. My father will never rest," said Young Jack, nodding his head positively, "till he finds me."

"Whether your father finds you or not, Jack, I'll stick to you," said Kit. "I don't want my thanks or money for what I do. My heart's good."

Young Jack took his hand and held it affectionately.

Kit had never felt so proud of himself before as he did this night.

The day had been an unlucky one.

He had speculated in weekly papers, and only sold a few, and his bank was not big.

Yet he had picked up this poor waif, paid for his lodging, given him a stew, and intended to lavish five cents more on him to take him to the Grand Duke's Theatre.

"What can I do for your kindness?" asked the little one.

"You and me will go partners," replied Kit.

"In what?"

"In papers. I shall have a dollar and a half left to-morrow. We'll speculate, and see what we can sell on the cars up-town."

"Will you, really? Oh! you are so good! I shall always like you. I'll fight for you," said Young Jack.

He clenched his little fists, and his eyes burned brightly.

"So you shall, if there is any need," replied Kit. "But, I say, will you come to the theatre?"

"Yes. Is it far?"

"In this street. It's what we call our theatre," said Kit. "They've given it the name of the Grand Duke's, but the actors and audience are all newsboys or boot-blacks, or something of that sort?"

"Are they?"

"You saw Rollins, and Conway, and Young Pete. They act. Put on your cap, and we'll get along," said Kit.

As they were passing Hans Dunkerboom, he continued—

"How do you like the boss?"

"Very much. He talks so funnily," replied Young Jack.

"Oh! my, yes Pa's as right as rain. Wait till Christmas, and if pa likes you, won't Santa Claus fill your stocking!"

"Who's he?"

"Wait and see. Last year I had candies, molasses, cookies, jumping-jacks, peanuts, and sugar-kisses, as well as a drum, a sleigh, and a trumpet; but they did not all come from pa."

"Did the boys give them you?"

"Yes I'm a favourite with the boys."

"Then Santa Claus is—"

"Wait, I tell you, and you'll see before long. When New Year's comes, we'll show you something, too," said Kit.

They had not far to walk before they reached the theatre, which was fixed up in a cellar.

The actors were big boys, the audience little ones, and the performance of the most primitive description.

They had christened the cellar "The Grand Duke's Opera House."

Kit led the way down some damp and mouldy steps, paid ten cents for himself and Jack, nodded to friends right and left, shook hands with the check-taker, and pushing to the foot-lights, watched the performance of the "Mulligan Guards."

This consisted of three boys, fantastically dressed, walking up and down, singing something about "As we march, march, march, we men of the Mulligan Guards."

"Sit down on the stage," said Kit, when the curtain fell.

He placed himself and Young Jack in a corner near the foot-lights, which were four in number, including a big reflector.

The curtain soon rose for the farce of the "Laughing Gas."

A boy with a bag of wind under his arm appeared, and to him entered a youth from the country.

"Do you wish to partake of the gas?" he asked.

"Yes," replied the greeney.

"Then, for Heaven' sake, sit down. Now take the golden mouthpiece between your kissers."

The boy pretended to inhale the gas, and became affected by it.

He pushed and kicked, whereat the gas-man said, "Push and pull. I knew a boy who was good at pushing and pulling. He pulled a pair of pants down Chatham-street, and dragged six months."

"That's not me!" exclaimed the boy.

"You're a Boston boy, I guess," replied the gasman. "Oh, my! lend me ten cents till I see the manager."

The subject of the laughing gas experiment now began to kick violently.

"Hurry up!" exclaimed the showman. "I guess the gas will knock the spots out of yer."

The boy let go the tube, and seemed overcome.

"Go to a bucket-shop, and have a five-cent nip," said the showman, compassionately.

"I'll go and have a seventy-five cent dinner. I must have turkey, or I'll die," answered the victim of the gas.

"I'm afraid you'll die," said the showman, with a laugh.

The victim retired, and another entered.

"Do you wish to partake of the gas?" he was asked.

"I does."

"Then, for Heaven's sake, sit down."

The same business, with variations, was gone through, and the curtain fell.

Then the boys amused themselves by talking, and shouting out—

"Hoist that rag!"

It is needless to describe the remainder of the programme, which varied from a railroad scene with a property engine to a burglary, in which the thieves were more frightened than the people robbed, to the Black Ball Sailors.

Young Jack was glad to get out of the stifling atmosphere of the unventilated cellar, and return to Hans Dunkerboom's.

As Kit put him in his little bed, he said—

"Remember, you're my brother, Kit."

"I'll stand your friend," answered Kit, "and to-morrow we start on business."

"Yes."

"You'll sell lots of papers with your pretty, innocent face."

"Shall I?"

"You bet."

"I'm so glad, for your sake, Kit," replied Young Jack.

"We'll start up-town on the Broadway cars, between Madison and Union."

"Anywhere you like. But—"

"What?"

"I say, Kit!" exclaimed Young Jack, in a terrified whisper.

"Spit it out," said Kit.

"You won't let Hunston have me again, will you?"

"Not much," answered Kit, boldly. "If ever I meet that Hunston, I'll—I'll—"

"What will you do?"

"Smash him!" said Kit, with a sigh of relief, as he got out this tremendous phrase.

Young Jack felt relieved also, and smiled thankfully.

He shook his friend by the hand, turned over, tucked the quilt under his neck, and was soon in the land of dreams.

CHAPTER XIII.

A NIGHT IN A CELL.

THOSE who were wounded in the brawl in the "Office" were taken to the Bellevue Hospital, and had their wounds dressed.

Hunston was conducted to the Tombs Prison, and locked up securely in a cell.

The next morning Miles Fenton applied for permission to see the prisoner, which was granted.

He spoke to his friend through the grating in the door, a warden standing by to see that no "Sharkey" performance was played upon him.

"You've made a nice hash of this," said Hunsten, bitterly.

"How could I help it?" replied Fenton.

"You might have managed things better. Harkaway should never have heard of our place of meeting. It is hard, after all my trials and escapes, to be laid by the heels up here."

"So it is," said Fenton; "but Harkaway has the devil's luck and his own too, or he would have been cold meat now."

"What does Leroy say about it?"

"You'll get a year on the Island."

"Not Sing-Sing?"

"No."

"Is there any chance of getting off the Island?" asked Hunston.

"We'll see to that," answered Fenton. "Leroy says he knows a right screw, and you can swim across the river to Astoria."

"See me through, and I don't care," said Hunston. "And now tell me all about the boy."

"He's bolted."

"What!"

"I've been to the hotel, and he's not there."

"Perdition!" exclaimed Hunston. "How is at?"

"I can't tell; but when I got your note this morning at the Sample-room, I went at once to look after him."

"That's worse than all," said Hunston, with a groan.

"He'll be marching about New York, and I shall drop upon him somewhere," said Fenton.

"If you do, mind you stick to the young whelp tie him up in a room, and leather him well if he howls."

"Never fear."

After some further conversation relative to feeing a counsellor for the defence, Miles Fenton took his leave of the prisoner.

Hunston gnashed his teeth to think that his prey had escaped him.

When his prospects seemed most bright, all his hopes were dashed, and his horizon was clouded.

Harkaway was delighted at having got the better of his old enemy.

Yet he, too, was sad, because he could not find his child.

He offered a large reward for him.

This brought no response.

Jack's only comfort was to think that, at all events, his son, wherever he might be, was, for the time being, removed from the evil influence of Hunston.

Days went by, and Hunston's trial came on.

He was sentenced, for his attempt to murder Harkaway, to twelve months' hard labour in the penitentiary on Blackwell's Island.

This was a great triumph.

Jack did not relax his efforts to discover his boy, but he heard no tidings of him.

Some weeks passed by.

Hunston was duly cropped, according to prison fashion, and clothed in the striped clothes worn by convicts.

He worked with his companions in guilt as well as he was able; but, owing to his only having one arm, he could not do much.

Fenton managed to have another interview with him, in which he assured him that Leroy and he had not relaxed their efforts in his behalf, and hoped soon to enable him to escape.

"If I am to throw myself into the river," said Hunston, "you must have a boat handy. I can't swim far with one arm."

"We won't forget that," replied Fenton.

"Meantime," said Hunston, eagerly, "stick to Harkaway, and try all you know to find the boy. When I come out, I won't forget you. My money is all safe, and I'll give you enough to make you a rich man."

"At first I agreed to serve you for pay," answered

Fenton, "but now I hate Harkaway as much as you do, and will try to ruin him for nothing."

Hunston smiled grimly behind the bars of his cell.

"He shall remember putting my portrait in the rogues' gallery," he said.

"It was lucky they did not gobble both of us up," continued Fenton. "Leroy has a plan to get at Harkaway, and if we don't get you out soon, I have no doubt I shall have some news for you the next time I come up."

"Do your best, and rely upon my gratitude," exclaimed Hunston.

Fenton took his departure, and went back to a small hotel in Jersey City, where he and Leroy were staying.

The "Office" had been given up since the police raid upon it.

Jack and his friends continued to reside at the Gilsey House, and they soon began to make acquaintances in New York society, receiving great kindness and hospitality from the warm-hearted and generous Americans.

Emily grew stronger every day, and lived in constant hope that the large reward offered for her child would bring him to her before long.

A heavy fall of snow was succeeded by a hard frost.

Jack and Harvey started an elegant Albany sleigh, and took the ladies through Central Park, enjoying the sport of skating in the evening, when the lake was alive with magnesium lights, dancing about like fire-flies.

About a month after Hunston's conviction, Jack was surprised to meet Leroy at the door of his hotel.

"Mr. Harkaway, can I speak one word to you?" said Leroy.

"No, sir," answered Jack. "I am surprised at your cool cheek in coming here. If you don't hook it, I shall send for an officer."

"How you misjudge me! I am the best-meaning man in the world."

Jack laughed sarcastically.

"I come here to do you good. Why allow yourself to be prejudiced against me, when I alone can restore your son to you?"

At these words Jack's face flushed.

The man might be lying to him, and, on the other hand, there was a look of earnestness about his face which inclined him to listen.

Drowning men will catch at straws, and, in the hope of recovering his child, Jack would have clutched at the ghost of a beanstalk.

"What do you know about him?" he asked.

"First listen to my vindication. I am not the ruffian you take me to be. I was keeping bar at the 'Office' for the owner, who was sick. Hunston and Fenton were strangers to me. Leroy is a nickname they gave me. My real name is Sensitive Sheepe, as I told you, and I spend my life in works of charity."

The man spoke with such an affectation of seriousness that it seemed as if he really believed the pack of lies he was telling.

Jack shook his head.

"It won't do," he said.

"Your mind is poisoned against me. Some day my character will be cleared. I can give you the highest city references. My father is a Gospel preacher in Maine. Know me once more as Sensitive Sheepe, and let me work with you for the recovery of your child."

"That I have no objection to," answered Jack.

"Ah! that is good of you. I feel like a lost sheep welcomed back to the fold. Your hand, Mr. Harkaway. Let two honest palms meet in a friendly grasp."

This was a very clever bit of acting.

Almost before he was aware of it, and against his better judgment and inclination, Jack found himself shaking hands, while Sensitive Sheepe was murmuring, in a voice husky with emotion and whisky—

"So sensitive, you know."

"The past is forgotten. I am once more your good friend, Mr. Sheepe."

"Call me nothing else," he added, "and I will lay down my life in your service. Come, let us have some dinner together."

"In the hotel?" queried Jack.

"No. I will take you to Delmonico's. There we will have Gumbo soup, bluefish, tenderloin steak, canvas-back duck, and frogs, *a la bordelaise*. I will pay. I am so happy! Forgive me if I gush over some. To be friendly with you again, and have my character cleared, is too much bliss."

In an ecstacy, Mr. Sheepe, as he insisted upon being called, instead of that "horrid nickname," Leroy, once more wrung Jack's hand.

"Ah! Mr. Harkaway," cried Sensitive Sheepe, "a man should be very careful who he associates with."

"That's why I scarcely like being seen with you," answered Jack.

"You wrong me. One is known by one's companions, and my sensitive nature has brought me in contact with a bad lot. I renounce them from this day."

Entering Delmonico's, they dined at this famous restaurant.

During dinner, Mr. Sheepe explained his views.

He had heard that Young Jack, or a boy answering his description, was employed as errand lad at some low place of entertainment, or gambling-house, in the city.

His proposal was to go round to some of the vile haunts, and try to discover if the report was true.

"Well," said Jack, "I will go with you, but mind one thing, Mr. Leroy."

"Sheepe, sir. Forget that horrid nickname. What would my poor father, the Gospel preacher, say if he heard that my charitable instinct had led me amongst bad characters, who altered my name?"

He rubbed his eyes till they assumed the appearance of peeled onions.

"Can't help a falling tear," he whined. "So sensitive, you know."

"I was only about to observe," continued Jack, "that if I find this repentance a sham, and you try on any queer tricks with me, I'll have no mercy upon you."

"If I wronged you in any way, I should be unworthy of the name of man," answered Mr. Sheepe. "Drink up your wine, and come with me."

Quitting the restaurant, at which Mr. Sheepe paid the bill, they walked into Broadway, and turning down a street on the east-side, entered a house in which the strains of music were heard.

"Up-stairs," said Mr. Sheepe. "This is Harry Hill's. We shall see some girls pivoting. Pleasant sight."

Paying at the bar, they ascended the stairs, and found themselves in a music-hall, with a small stage, on which a man was singing a comic song, the refrain of which was, "And all the boys cried out, 'Oh! hang it, shoot that hat!'"

When that was over, several women in tawdry finery came in front of a brilliant lime-light, and began to dance, or pivot, as Mr. Sheepe called it.

Looking carefully round among the motley groups sitting at the tables, Jack could see nothing of any youngster answering the description of his son.

"A blank draw," said Mr. Sensitive Sheepe. "Let us try a keno house."

They retired when the dance was over, and once more found themselves in the street.

Conducting him through several devious turnings, his guide stopped before a house of respectable appearance.

After a peep through an opening, a coloured man seemed satisfied with a mysterious signal given him by Mr. Sheepe, and admitted them.

"This is a first-class club-house or gambling-house," whispered Sheepe.

"Indeed!" said Jack.

"It can't come up to Merrissey's, at Saratoga, or John Chamberlain's, at Long Branch; but it's no small bar."

The "club" was on the second-floor, and consisted of three deep rooms, elegantly furnished.

"Don't be afraid," said Mr. Sheepe, as Jack hung back. "You shall see the elephant without paying."

"It's a fine place," said Jack.

"Oh! my, yes. Some! On that table is a free lunch. Help yourself to turkey or venison, champagne or claret."

"Let's push on to the players," replied Jack.

Business was not brisk that evening. Not more than half-a-dozen men were covering the numbers with the counters or buttons, and seeing who could fill up the row first.

Two were playing old sledge at a side table, and two more were indulging in the pleasant pastime of euchre.

Suddenly one player exclaimed, in a tremulous voice, "Keno!"

His numbers were verified, and the money handed over to him, less the charge made by the proprietor of the table.

"How's that for high?" cried the delighted gambler. "All down but nine. Stick 'em up in the next alley, boss."

"Will you play?" asked Mr. Sheepe. "Only fifty cents a card. Buy four."

"No, thank you," replied Jack. "You know the work we have in hand."

"Certainly."

"The young one does not appear to be here."

"No; but we must try all sorts of cribs, and we may light upon him somewhere."

"I'm ready to go around all night long. It isn't my form to give a thing up," replied Jack.

"That's where you're right," exclaimed Sensitive Sheepe. "We shall get on nobby, I guess, if you show so much pluck."

Jack was about to make some reply, when he felt a peculiar sensation tingling through his veins.

Turning sharply round, he encountered the basilisk eyes of Miles Fenton, which were riveted upon him.

A suspicion crossed his mind that he had been led into a trap.

It was odd that Fenton and Leroy should meet together in such a place as a keno club.

"There's Miles Fenton," said Mr. Sheepe, touching Jack's elbow. "Don't speak. I have shied him ever since I found out his real character."

"Good evening," exclaimed Fenton. "Do you keep your health, Mr. Harkaway?"

"I wish to have nothing to say to you," answered Jack.

"You can be proud if you like," retorted Fenton. "You seem to be having a good time."

"I guess you're pretty well crystallised to talk to my friend," exclaimed Mr. Sheepe, indignantly.

"Your friend? You are not of much account."

"Call me what you like," answered Mr. Sheepe. "I am not going to associate with roughs and gamblers like you."

"Go and drown yourself," said Fenton. "We meet in a public room, and, if Mr. Harkaway wants

THE NEXT INSTANT THE YANKEE WAS SPRAWLING ON HIS BACK.

to be rough on me, I suppose he can take his own part."

"He is here under my protection," continued Mr. Sheepe, "and if you don't sheer off, and mind your own business, I shall have to make you."

Jack listened to this conversation in surprise.

None of the gamblers attempted to interfere, but looked on silently at the brawl, while Mr. Sheepe contented himself with calling out loudly for help.

It is not difficult to see that the result would have been disastrous for Jack, who felt in his pocket for his revolver and found it gone.

Mr. Sheepe had carefully abstracted it while they were at dinner. Kicking the chair on one side, Fenton made a desperate splurge.

His knife was within an inch of Jack's breast, when a loud cry of "The cops!" arose.

Fenton's arm was knocked up by a policeman's baton, and it became apparent that a raid was being made upon the gambling-house.

The gamblers scattered in all directions, but only a few were able to make their escape up a ladder leading to the roof, along which they went to the next house, and so descended to the street.

Among those who got off were Fenton and Leroy, both being well acquainted with the establishment and its resources.

"You are my prisoner," said a policeman, taking Jack rudely by the shoulder.

"What for?" asked Jack.

"Being found in a gambling-house, and a nice

brawl you'd got up. I guess you're a forsaken Britisher, and the hawks meant plucking you."

Jack saw it was useless to resist.

The sergeant in command of the raiding party assigned the prisoners to the different policemen, and a brief walk brought them to the Eighth Precinct Station house.

A large crowd of people, principally from Murderer's Row, followed.

Two other raids had been made on some low houses, and Jack was ranged in front of the desk for examination, amid a throng of thieves, cutthroats, and the scum of the city.

He felt thankful that he had been saved from Fenton's murderous attack, but was not satisfied with the company he was in. More especially as, after giving his name and address, he was thrust into a cell with half-a-dozen noisy, drunken brutes, and told that any complaint must be made to the captain.

He could not get out on bail, nor could he send a letter to his friends, so he resigned himself to his fate, and towards morning he got a few hours' sleep.

A little after six the prisoners were taken to the Jefferson Market Police Court, and put into the prison pen, which was filled with bummers, low women, thieves, and others, but it was nearly ten before the judge took his seat.

Jack explained that he was a stranger in the city, and had gone to the gambling-house out of curiosity, whereupon he was let go at once.

The judge observed that he hoped the gentleman might be more fortunate in the gratification of his curiosity in future.

A coach conveyed him to his hotel, where he was gladly received, his absence having occasioned considerable alarm.

Felix S. Prye, who had become quite a friend of the family, happened to drop in.

He shook his head gravely when he heard of this new attempt upon Jack.

"You've got among a bad crowd, I guess," he said.

"So I think," remarked Harvey.

"If he don't keep his eyes skinned, I wouldn't give a red cent for his life."

"Do you believe it was a put-up affair?" inquired Jack.

"Of course I do," answered Harvey.

"But Mr. Sheepe seemed so sorry for being mixed up with Hunston and Fenton, that I—"

"Oh, my! ain't you soft!" interrupted Felix; "your Sheepe is the black sheep of the flock."

"It may be so. If it is, I am grossly deceived in him."

"You're like the man down in Franklin County, Massachusetts," said Felix.

"What did he do?"

"It's what he didn't do. He'd married, and the first day after the holiday his wife went for him, for some reason or another. When the doctor came, he told him that his face wouldn't be badly scarred, though he might remain permanently bald, and that man still lives with that woman."

"Oh, Mr. Prye!" said Emily, "how hard you are on the ladies!"

"I'm sure," observed Hilda, "he never deserves to get married."

"It's only a tale," observed Felix, "and I told it because Harkaway still believes in Sensitive Sheepe. Why, the name's enough to stamp the man, and I know there is no such person connected with charity in the city."

"Is that so?" asked Harvey.

"Yes, sir; and if the police can't find the boy, it isn't Sheepe's game to do it. You bet!" exclaimed Felix.

Mr. Mole walked in just as Harkaway was observing that all he wanted was to reco child.

The professor's gait was a little unsteady.

In each hand he held a revolver, newly purchased.

"Oh, do take care, please, Mr. Mole!" said Emily. "Are they loaded?"

"No, they are not; but they soon will be," answered Mole. "I have been a month in this country, and I see that a man cannot live without a pistol. Ah, Harkaway, come back!"

"Yes, sir."

"I thought you would. A bad cent is sure to turn up."

"Where have you been, sir?"

"To take an eye-opener. I sleep so much in this confounded climate. It is very trying to the European."

"So you think us rowdy?" said Felix, winking at Jack.

"I do, sir. I have not formed a hasty conclusion. I met a person in the bar who quite agrees with me, and he said that a man would shoot you, if you did not pass the mustard at the dinner table."

"Is that so?" said Felix, his eyes twinkling merrily.

"My informant added," continued Mole, "that you should always carry a pistol, and if you see an American put his hand in his pocket, he means shooting, and you must shoot first. It is a melancholy fact, but so it is."

"I came to-day to invite you and Harkaway to dine with me and a few friends," said Felix.

"It will give me great pleasure to accept," answered Mole.

"Bring your pistols. There is no telling what might happen," continued Felix.

"Sir, they shall be my inseparable companions," replied Mole, looking at them affectionately.

"My opinion of the English is not flattering," said Felix.

"What is it?" asked Jack, with a half smile.

"Every Britisher beats his wife, keeps a bull-dog, and drops his H's."

"That's a gross calumny, sir. Don't abuse my country!" exclaimed Mole.

"You abused mine."

"I spoke the truth," answered Mole.

"Well, I don't know that the professor isn't right," answered Felix. "He'll have an opportunity of judging at my dinner, for I will have some representative Americans."

When Felix rose to go, Jack accompanied him to the door.

"What are you going to do with Mole?" he asked.

"I mean to get some very nice fellows, but I shall tell them to act rowdy, and we'll frighten the professor out of his senses. There will be Lynus Dwyer, from Hokoken, an ex-Congressman; Samson Stockinger, the famous actor at Wallacks; Philip Colwell, a retired merchant from Staten Island, worth thirty millions; Kinny Corksline, a journalist, and editor of the *Light of the Universe*."

"I see!" exclaimed Jack.

"Won't it be bully!" said Felix, rubbing his hands.

"Rather."

"You'll have to see that Mole's pistols are not loaded with ball; only powder."

"I'll take care. When shall it be?"

"The day after to-morrow at the Hoffman House. They know me there," answered Felix.

Jack shook his hand, and Felix S. Prye went away to invite the guests for the dinner which was to show Mr. Mole the Americans as he imagined them to be.

If the joke was a little rough on him, he had only

himself to thank for it, owing to his intolerance and stupidity.

CHAPTER XIV.
MR. MOLE SEES THE AMERICANS AS THEY ARE NOT.

On the morning of the day appointed for the dinner to be given by Felix S. Prye, a letter arrived by mail, marked " Personal," for Mr. Mole.

All the party were at breakfast in their private apartments.

"A letter for me !" exclaimed the professor. " I was not aware that I had any correspondents in this unfortunate country."

" Is it a lady's handwriting ?" asked Harvey.

"No sir," replied Mole, breaking the envelope. "I will read it aloud, to show that there is no foundation for your injurious suspicions."

He began—

" SIR,—I write to remind you of your engagement. You dine with me and some typical citizens of this great republic at six o'clock ; Hoffman House. If you are late I shall cowhide you, and if you don't come at all I guess it will be necessary to order pistols for two, and a coffin for one.

"Yours in equality and fraternity, under th. Star-spangled Banner. (Stars for me and Stripes for you.) "FELIX S. PRYE.

"To that mean Britisher, Professor Mole."

" Well, I never did !" said Mole. " This is a most extraordinary epistle."

" I should go well armed, sir," said Harvey, who had been told of the intended joke.

"It's all blowing," exclaimed Mole. " I've been told that all Yankees are good for their blowing, and to show them that I am not afraid of them, I shall go to this party, and ask them what they think of the ' Virginius.' "

" Sing ' Rule, Britannia,' sir !" said Jack.

" A good idea, Harkaway. But tell me, isn't that letter an insult ? Isn't it enough to make the British lion lash his tail and roar ? Call me a mean Britisher, indeed ! My blood boils. I'm English, Harkaway !"

" Keep cool, sir."

" I can't. Our flag is insulted through me. Talk about the glorious Republic of the United States ! Why, you can't buy birdseye tobacco here. I've bought Lone Jack and Durham, Right Bower and Game Hen, and if I smoke all day I only blister my tongue and get no satisfaction."

" Chew, sir."

" Not I, Harkaway," said the professor, in a tone of deep disgust. " That entails spitting, and I abominate a dirty habit."

When evening came, Mr. Mole and Jack were attired in evening dress.

A coupé came for them, and Harvey presented himself at the door, also dressed.

" What do you want, Dick ?" asked Jack.

" Take me with you. I'm not invited, but I mean to be in this. I know there's some lark on."

" Jump in, and sit on Mole's knee," replied Jack.

The three drove off, and the professor examined his pistol, which Jack had attended to.

It was only loaded with powder and wad, so that, if fired, it could do no harm.

On the arrival at the Hoffman House, they were shown up-stairs into a private room engaged by Mr. Prye, who met them at the door.

" Three Britishers," he said. " Harkaway, Harvey, Mole."

The three Englishmen bowed.

" Dwyer, Stockinger, Colwell, Corksline," continued Felix. " Take your seats, gentlemen."

The party sat down, and the waiters put the first course on the table.

" How do you like the States ?" asked Mr. Dwyer, the ex-Congressman, addressing Mole.

" Not at all, sir," replied the professor. " America isn't a patch on the Old Country."

" It's a pity you didn't stay there," said Mr. Corksline, the editor of the *Light of the Universe.*

" Sir !" exclaimed Mole, with dignity.

"What spoils this country is emigration," continued the journalist.

" Do you call me an emigrant ?" asked Mole. " I, sir, am simply a visitor, a sojourner in this panic-stricken land. I neither buy nor sell."

" Then I calculate you're not of much account here," answered Colwell, the merchant.

" What line are you in ?" asked Mole.

" Dry goods."

" Sell out, sir. Sell out, sir," said Mole. " Realise at once and go to England, where everything is half the price it is here. You have adopted a protection tariff. You have no specie payments. Gold is quoted to-day at 8¼. Follow the example of your estimable Woodwards and Genets and clear out, sir."

At this speech each man rose from the table.

The ex-Congressman took from under his chair a cavalry sabre, and placed it on the table beside him.

The journalist, who was the presiding genius of the *Light of the Universe,* brandished a bowie-knife, and put it in his soup-plate.

The retired merchant from Staten Island displayed a enamelled Derringer, and stood up with it levelled at Mole's head.

The actor from Wallack's exhibited a property battle-axe, while Felix contented himself with the carving-fork, with which he made the most extraordinary flourishes ever seen out of an Indian reservation.

Mole was frightened at this demonstration.

He shrunk into himself and looked small.

But he comforted himself with the reflection that he, too, was armed.

" Ha ! ha !" he gasped ; " I will sell my life dearly. I am not to be fillibustered."

" Minion of an aristocracy-ridden country, do you cave in ?" demanded the journalist

" You'd better apologise, whispered Jack, who sat on Mole's right.

" I—I may have spoken hastily," exclaimed Mole, nervously.

" I guess he caves," said Felix.

The wine was passed round, and every one sat down, though the weapons remained on the table.

" Hail, Columbia !" exclaimed Felix. " I propose the health of the President, Ulysses Grant."

" Ulysses !" said the professor, contemptuously ; " who ever heard of such a name out of the ' Odyssey' ?"

" By Heaven !" said the actor, "he has insulted the President. Let's lynch him."

" I—I didn't mean to," said Mole, trembling. " You snap me up so quickly."

" Give him another chance," said the ex-Congressman. " He's only a tarnation Britisher, and don't know any better."

The ex-Congressman brandished his sabre savagely, and smashed a gas-globe.

After this, he took up a stick of celery and began to eat it.

" That's a salary grab," said Mole, who had imbibed wine enough before he started to make him bold.

" Monarchy-crushed worm !" exclaimed the ex-Congressman, " what do you intend to imply."

" No—nothing," answered Mole.

" Dry up, and eat your fish."

" Your Eagle's had too much ' Fish ' lately, but I don't object," said Mole, plucking up a spirit again.

" Vile spawn of an enslaved and played-out race !" exclaimed the ex-Congressman. " Shall I spill your effete blood at the festive board ?"

Mr. Mole turned to Harkaway with a pitiful look.

"Take me away," he said.

"Where to, sir?"

"Anywhere. I care not whither. They will murder me."

"Pay them back in their own coin, sir," said Jack.

"Promise me one thing, Harkaway?"

"Yes, sir."

"Bury me decently, and put flowers on my grave, if anything should happen to me."

Jack could scarcely speak for laughing.

As for Harvey, he had his napkin stuffed into his mouth, so that his hilarity might not spoil the fun.

"Be brave, sir," said Jack."

"I will, Harkaway."

"The honour of Old England depends on you."

"Give me your hand. I will maintain the honour of my native land against these rowdies," answered Mole.

"Emasculated zoophyte," said the journalist, "retreat!"

"No, sir, I will not," answered Mole, adding, in a whisper, "You will see me through, Harkaway?"

"Yes, sir."

"Right!"

"What are your politics, sir?" asked the journalist.

"Eh?"

"What's your platform?"

"I'm a straight-out Democrat," answered Mole.

"Another insult to the President!" said Felix S. Prye.

Menacing glances were bent upon Mole.

"Grovelling subject of a crowned woman," said the retired merchant, "salute the majesty personified in a free people."

"Never!" replied Mole.

"You won't?"

"No."

"Then I guess it's time to shoot," said the merchant, who began to fire at Mole's head.

"Give it them, sir! Go it!" said Jack.

Mole fired back, and the room was soon enveloped in smoke.

Suddenly he felt himself seized by the neck, and forced on his knees.

The ex-Congressman and Felix S. Prye were standing over him, one with the sabre, the other with the carving-fork.

The journalist waved in one hand the bowie-knife, and in the other the United States flag.

"Kiss it, or die!" he exclaimed, putting the flag before Mole's face.

The professor reluctantly touched the flag with his lips.

At this everybody burst into an uncontrollable roar of laughter.

The ex-Congressman patted Mole on the back.

Felix S. Prye did a war-dance on a chair.

The journalist shook Mole by the hand.

"What does this mean?" asked the bewildered professor.

"It means, my dear sir," answered the merchant in the dry goods line, "that we wanted to teach you a lesson."

"A lesson?"

"Yes. You have been misinformed. You were prejudiced, and we have played a joke upon you. You have seen the Americans as they are not. Now you shall see them as they are."

"Isn't somebody going to cut my throat?" said Mole.

"Not much. You're my guest. Sit down and be jolly," replied Felix; "we mean to have a good time."

"Don't you mean to shoot me?"

"The pistols were not loaded, and the other weapons are 'property' from the theatre. Own up that you are sold."

In a few words, Jack explained the nature of the joke, and why it was played.

He told the professor that he had trifled with his pistols, and that no harm was meant him.

It was simply a bit of fun to cure him of his prejudice against the Americans.

"You were wrong, sir," concluded Jack, "and you must put a good face on it."

Mr. Mole smiled blandly.

"Gentlemen," he exclaimed, "you must pardon my foolishness. I see it now. You have opened my eyes."

"Forgive the joke. We've been rough on you, but it was meant in the spirit of fun," said the journalist, "and before you leave us to-night you will admit that we are not what you have been led to think us."

Mr. Mole shook hands all round.

The dinner proceeded, and under the influence of a tender-loin steak, 'rare,' and plenty of Pommery Sec, he forgot his humiliation, and enjoyed himself immensely.

When the cloth was cleared, he was called upon for a speech.

"A man's nothing in the States unless he can speak," said Felix.

"Well, gentlemen," replied Mole, "I am not much of a speaker. Once I made a speech at an election at Oxford, and it lasted a considerable time. When it was over, I asked a friend what he thought of it.

"'A smart man,' replied my friend, 'would have made that speech in twenty minutes, and a downright smart man wouldn't have made it all.'

"Anyhow, gentlemen, I thank you for your kindness. I shall not forget the 'lesson' you have taught me to-night. To-morrow I will sell my revolver. I find that Americans are perfect gentlemen, and if they like me half as well as I begin to like them, I shan't be in a hurry to put back to the Old Country."

This speech was met with great applause.

"There is one thing I should like to add," said the professor.

"What's that?" asked Felix.

"If you would only try to keep your streets cleaner, I should find New York city more agreeable."

"Oh! oh!" said the guests, laughing in spite of themselves.

"That's a partheon shot," remarked the accomplished editor of the *Light of the Universe*.

It was late when the party broke up.

Mr. Mole's head was inclined to go a little in advance of his feet, and when he got home he went to bed in his boots.

CHAPTER XV.

THE TWO NEWSBOYS.

WHEN Young Jack woke up it was broad daylight, and the sun was glinting over the snow in a hard, unchristian-like manner.

Throwing up crystals and icicles in all their beauty, rough and unadorned as it were, as if it wished to illuminate it, without injuring its virgin purity.

The dormitory was almost empty.

He was the only boy in bed; all the other lodgers of kindly Hans Dunkerboom had gone about their several avocations, though Heaven only knew what they might be during the course of the day.

Looking around, he sighted Kit who was sitting on the foot of the bed.

"You up, Kit?" he said. "Am I late?"

"I guess that depends upon what you call late," answered Kit. "I've been up these six hours, and done a first-class trade, too."

"Why didn't you wake me?" asked Young Jack, rubbing his eyes.

"Because it would have been a burning shame, Tiny. I like to see you sleep. I've sold out my stock of morning papers, and when you've had some grub, we'll go and buy the evening's."

Young Jack shook his head sadly.

"I don't think I shall be of much use to you, Kit," he said.

"Why not?"

"I'm not strong enough."

"Don't you play possum with me," said Kit. "All I want you to do is to run into the cars and sell the papers. If you can't do that, you shall stop at home and enjoy yourself."

"No," replied Young Jack. "I wouldn't let any one pay for me. I'll do all I can, because I love you, Kit."

"Do you?" said Kit, feeling moist about the eyes.

"You've been kind to me. I've had no kindness and no comfort since I was taken away from my home."

"Perhaps your ma will find you yet."

"I hope so, Kit. You'd love her. She's so good.'

"Is she a great lady?"

Young Jack nodded his head.

"Has she got a big house, and lots of money and help?"

Young Jack nodded his head quicker than ever.

"Say, now, Tiny, how much money has she got?"

"Oh! ever so much. It would fill this room, and fill this house, and then it would flow over and fill up the street."

"My!" said Kit, lost in admiration.

"I'm a gentleman," said Young Jack.

"What's that, Tiny?"

"It's—it's—" began the little one—"it's a gentleman's son, Kit."

Kit looked puzzled at this definition.

"We've no gentlemen here," he said. "A poor boy is as good as a rich man's son, if he is honest and works, and does what is right."

"Haven't you got lords and a Queen, and very rich people?"

"We've got rich people. Oh, my! You should see Fifth Avenue, and go over the ferry to Jersey and Brooklyn; but I don't know what a lord is," replied Kit.

"No Queen!" said Young Jack, in surprise.

"Only a President. I might be President of the United States some day. How do you elect your Queen?"

"She's born a Queen or a King," answered Young Jack, getting somewhat confused in his attempt to explain the Constitution of England.

"I guess I'm kinder hunting grass," said Kit. "You must be a queer lot in Europe. Would you call me a gentleman?"

"Well, I don't know. I never met a boy I liked more. I suppose you are."

"Am I good enough for you, Tiny?" asked Kit, with a flash of the eye.

"You're ever so much too good, Kit."

"You aren't ashamed of being with me?"

"No, Kit."

"That's right. If you'd said anything but that, you and I couldn't have been pardners any longer," Kit said, with a sigh of relief.

Young Jack looked at him with an affectionate expression.

"See what you've done for me already," he said. "Why, Kit, if I were the Queen of England, I'd make you a lord."

"I'd rather be an American boy, Tiny, and sell papers."

"And I'll be an American boy, too. Shall I, Kit?"

"You'll be free then, and have no one to trample on you. I wouldn't give a red cent to be a lord, and as for your Queen, I'd make her take in washing at a dollar a dozen, and do something for her living."

This speech seemed to do Kit a considerable amount of good.

He looked himself again, and the young republican cut capers on the floor, snapped his fingers defiantly, and otherwise conducted himself in a manner intended to express his contempt for aristocracy in general, and monarchy in particular.

Checking his democratic antics, he regarded Young Jack with a business-like air.

"Come, Tiny," he continued. "Hoopla! Double up your spine, and be spry. It's time we were at the office, to get the first edition."

Young Jack got out of bed, had a wash in a bucket, put on his clothes, and descended from the dormitory to the large room down-stairs, where, thanks to Kit's forethought, he found a cup of coffee and some crackers ready for him.

Hans Dunkerboom was smoking his eternal pipe, with some lager beer by his side, in a can.

"Ah!" he said. "Dere ish my Right Bower. Vat you going to puy to-day, my poy?"

"Pickled pigs' feet, pa," answered Kit.

"You vash humbug," said the Dutchman, in a tone of disgust. "Vy you vash humbug mit me? I mean vat paper you puy to-day?"

"I shall run the old machine," replied Kit. "I know what sells."

"You try thish," rejoined Hans, holding up a newly-started journal.

"Oh! that's played out," said Kit, looking carelessly at it.

"It's a very goot zeitung."

"I tell you it's gone up since they said they go in a diving-bell and fetch up the sea-serpent from the bottom of the Atlantic," replied Kit.

"Is that so?"

"I'm not going to be stuck," said Kit. "My paper will knock the spots out of yours. I run the *Evening Cable*, and I'm not likely to switch off on anything I can't see."

"Vell, you are a cunning poy, I guess."

"I haven't got the stamps for a bust up rag," concluded Kit.

"You are my Right Bower," said Hans; "you always bay me very goot. How ish our young friend vot you pring mit you last night?"

"As good as new; aren't you, Tiny?"

"Yes, thank you," replied Young Jack, who had just finished his scanty breakfast.

"You have got a goot boss."

"He'll run straight along with me, pa," exclaimed Kit. "We're the Lightning Express News Company, and if we can't live, no other boys can breathe."

"Goot poy—goot poy," said Hans Dunkerboom, rubbing his hands approvingly.

Young Jack being ready by this time, the two started down town, and bought as many papers as the state of Kit's bank would allow.

Then they took their journals up West Broadway and Wooster-street, to Union-square, and up Broadway again to Madison.

It was quite a treat to see how Young Jack learnt to jump on the cars and push in, crowded as they were.

His shrill voice, in imitation of Kit, rang out clearly—

"*Evening Cable*! Buy a paper, please. Latest

news of the masked robbers, and the execution in Jersey City. *Evening Cable*, gents?"

His youth and pretty, innocent face attracted considerable attention, and, the *Cable* being only two cents, he speedily sold out.

Kit had been equally successful, and was beckoning to Young Jack to join him outside the Fifth Avenue Hotel, when an accident happened which was very unfortunate for the partners.

"Take care, Tiny. This way. Mind you don't get run down," he was exclaiming, when a buggy passed swiftly by, and Kit, caught by the wheel, was thrown violently against a lamp-post.

He fell upon the hard-frozen roadway, the blood streaming from a wound in his forehead.

Young Jack ran up, and, kneeling down on the discoloured snow, began to cry loudly.

"Oh, my poor Kit!" he exclaimed; "they have killed you. Poor, dear, Kit! What shall I do if you die? Speak to me, Kit!"

The driver of the buggy had hastened on, without stopping to inquire what was the result of the reckless pace at which his roadster went.

What did it matter to him if there was one poor and friendless boy the less in New York?

The passers-by took no notice of the two boys, and Young Jack sat on the edge of the pavement, holding his friend's head on his knees, crying bitterly, and moaning for help.

Poor Kit looked very white.

His pale face presented a strange contrast to the blood-stained snow on Broadway, stained by the warm red current which flowed freely from his wounded forehead.

Suddenly a boy who was going by stopped, and peered curiously at Young Jack.

"What's this?" he exclaimed. "Is it a dodge? What lay are you on?"

"It's Kit," answered Young Jack. "My only friend. He was knocked down, and won't speak to me. Oh! what shall I do?"

"What, Kit? Move a bit, and let the gas-light fall on him."

The boy took a steady look at the wounded one.

"Why, hang me, if it aren't the Right Bower!" he exclaimed. "He used to work with me before I took to gunning."

"Did what?" asked Young Jack, raising his tear-stained eyes.

"Turned thief. I'm a 'bug-hunter' now, and peaf about the 'lush drums' for drunken men, and 'run through' them if I get the chance."

"Do you?" said Young Jack, to whom this explanation was not particularly clear.

"You ask any one at the Dutchman's if they don't know the Shyser. I do a bit of 'hall-sneaking sometimes with a blank back and a Betty—that's a latch-key, you know."

"You're a bad boy, I'm afraid," said Young Jack.

The Shyser laughed scornfully.

"A chap must have the price of a meal, and a night's lodging," he answered, "and it's got to be had somehow. But see here. It won't do to leave the Right Bower like this. Shall we take him to Bellevue?"

"Oh, do something! I will pay you. Look! I have money," said Young Jack, drawing forth a large handful of cents.

"No; bless me if I take anything from you," answered the Shyser. "But I guess I'm stuck to know what to do. Is he badly hurt?"

At this moment Kit opened his eyes, and stared wildly round him.

"Where am I?" he asked.

"You've been run over."

"Is that you, Tiny? My head feels so bad.

It's all dizzy, and I can't see straight. Have I been took sick?"

"Yes, it's me," replied Young Jack. "What shall I do, Kit?"

"Who's that? He's like the Shyser. Say, Shise, is that you?" continued Kit.

"You're right. Get up, Kit, and lean on our arms. We'll see you through, and take you back to the Dutchman's."

With difficulty Kit rose to his feet, and by the help of his friends, staggered along, until, after many stoppages, and an hour's painful exertion, he reached the boys' tenement-house.

"Mine Got!" cried the Dutchman, as the boys entered, bearing Kit's aching form. "The tufel! vat's the matter with mine Kit—the Right Bower the boy of mine heart?"

"He has had a very sad accident," Young Jack said. "It is a wonder that he is alive."

"Mine Got!" Hans Dunkerboom exclaimed, extending his hands, and opening his eyes very wide, "thish is very drefful, very drefful accident. Tell me, my goot poy," patting Kit tenderly on the head, "how this happen?"

Kit's explanation was very brief, but he exalted the conduct of Young Jack, and thanked the Shyser.

"Bat poy, Shysher," said the Dutchman. "You will come to no goot, my poy. Petter sell papers and get ride over, than turn thief."

"Oh! that's your opinion, is it?" the Shyser returned. "All right, you stale cheese, I know which is the best. Listen here."

And the young American pickpocket rattled a quantity of money he had in his pocket.

"Vell, vell," the Dutchman said, "I vill not lecture. I very sorry my poor poy is hurt. He must go to ped at once, and he shall pe looked after as if he vas the son of Hans Dunkerboem."

"I don't think I am very much hurt," Kit said, endeavouring to stand alone; "the cold has made me weak."

"Mine Got! it ish cold," Hans said, rubbing his hands. "My poy, you shall have your head dressed, and have some supper, and then go to ped; but, my poy, vere are your papers? Vot you puy vith your monish?"

An expression of alarm came over Young Jack's face, as he said—

"I am afraid that in our hurry we left them behind. Shall I run back, and see if I can find them?"

"Ha! ha! ha!" roared the Shyser, "that's not bad. Oh, no; not by any means. Will somebody hold me while I have my laugh out? I say, youngster, you're greener than corn in June. Ha! ha! ha!"

"What's the matter?" Jack said, rather angry at being laughed at in this manner. "What do you mean?"

"Are you really so green as to suppose you would find the papers if you did go back for them?" cried the Shyser.

"Yes? why not," Young Jack replied. "I should let them be if I saw them."

"You!" cried the Shyser, in a tone of contempt; "you! Why, you sucking baby, what do you know of the world? Wait till you have been here a month or two, and then you'll know better."

"Hold your tongue, Shysher," the Dutchman said, shaking his finger warningly at the young thief. "Vat you want to laff for? Master Jack is von goot poy. He is very fond of Hans Dunkerboom."

"I like you all very well," Young Jack said; "but I should like to get back to my own friends."

"Hoopla! Pigs and perriwinkles!" cried the Shyser. "A young haristocrat in disguise—eh?

Lost his way a-getting out of the way of the cops. Which ?"

He asked these questions of the Dutchman, who was by this time attending to Kit, and made no answer.

"Do I hurt you, my goot poy ?" he asked the suffering Kit, as he applied the bandages as tenderly as possible. "Mine Got! vot a plow. You have got von hole in your head as if it had been made vith a pullet. Do you feel petter, my poy ?"

"Much better, thank you," Kit replied; "I shall be all right soon."

"But de papers," moaned Hans. "Vat vill you do? I very poor, and can't advance you any monish. Dunder and blitzen! I net like dis," continued Dunkerboom, as he shook his head gravely, looking first at Kit and then at the Shyser. "But I might know vell no goot would come if he was mit Shise."

"Dry up, you old tub!" exclaimed the Shyser. "I found him, and I've brought him back, haven't I? Bind his nut up and put him to bed."

"You sling out," said Hans Dunkerboom, growing red in the face. "You have not bay me when you leave here. I tell you, Shise, you ish de piggest gun der ish on dis ward."

"That's no news," answered Shise, with a grin. "Good-night, boys. See to Kit. I drew a stake last night. There's a dollar bill. It's for Kit. See to him, boys."

With this, Shise put his hands in his pockets, and carelessly left the room.

Degraded and lost as he was, the lad's heart was not yet thoroughly hardened.

So true it is, there is some good in the worst of us.

Kit was taken upstairs and put to bed. He had lost a great deal of blood, and soon became insensible again.

It was very cold up in the dormitory, where there was no hot-hair and no stove.

But Young Jack would not leave his friend, and sat by his side all the long night through, keeping the weary vigil of love.

The tears flowed from his eyes at times, and his little hands turned blue with the cold; but still he watched, though he shivered till his frail body shook, and his feet were chill and numbed.

Young as he was, the little boy was a hero, without knowing it.

Hans Dunkerboom had left some water, with lemon-juice squeezed into it, for the invalid to moisten his feverish lips with when he woke, and Young Jack handed it to him at intervals during the night, with all the tender solicitude natural to a girl.

Towards morning Kit became delirious.

He did not know any one.

He would call out for Tiny, and when the boy grasped his hand, he would push him away roughly.

"You're not my Tiny!" he exclaimed, angrily. "Don't try it on with me, Shise. I know you. The dodge is too thin for me, I guess."

"It is me, Kit," answered Young Jack, crying afresh.

"Cheese it, Shise, or I'll lick you till you ask for your mother."

He grated his teeth together in hysteric agony.

"Dear Kit, try and know me," sobbed Young Jack.

"You've done this, Shise," continued the sufferer. "You've killed my Tiny because you saw I began to love him, and you've tried to kill me, but you can't do it, Shise. I'm tough, and don't mean having my six feet of earth yet."

He took the patient watcher for the Shyser, who was a boy he had a strong dislike for, owing to his bad habits and thievish way of living, for, with all his faults, Kit was honest to the back-bone.

His fits of anger soon wore him out, and he sank back on the dirty pillow, breathing heavily.

In the morning Young Jack fell asleep from sheer exhaustion.

When he woke up, Kit was no better, and the Dutchman was obliged to call in a doctor.

Kit's illness lasted a long time.

Soon—very soon—all the money the boys had was gone, and the Dutchman took Young Jack on one side.

"You are a goot poy," he said. "You vatch mit your friend. That ish all right, but I must have my money, and as Kit cannot do de work, you must go out into de vorld and see vat you can pring home."

Young Jack saw the force of this reasoning.

He went out, but having no money wherewith to buy papers, he was obliged to beg, and look out for horses to hold or parcels to carry.

This was poor work, and Hans Dunkerboom shook his grave old head as Young Jack put a few cents into his hand some nights, and at others none at all.

How the boy lived was a wonder.

He would scarcely buy a bit of bread, so that Hans might not turn Kit out and refuse him the broths and medicine he required, because he thought if he could give him all he could earn, if it was ever so little, it would induce the boss to be merciful.

The other boys gave him part of their food, for they saw what he was doing for his friend.

Twice they made a subscription amongst themselves for him.

The first realised eighty cents, and the second a hundred, all but one.

This was a lift up for him and Kit, and he bought a pound of grapes for Kit, for twenty-five cents, and was never so pleased in his life as when Kit ate them all.

"You're getting on fine, Tiny," said Kit, who was recovering himself by degrees. "But I'll help you when I'm strong."

Young Jack did not tell him how he struggled, and what his privations were.

"How long does the doctor say I shall be in bed?" continued Kit.

"Several weeks yet."

"It's very hard on you, Tiny."

"It is worse for you, Kit. I brought you bad luck," answered Young Jack.

"Oh! I can stand hardships and knocking about, but you're not used to it," said Kit.

The days dragged along wearily, and Young Jack continued his exertions on behalf of his friend, sometimes making a little money, and oftener bringing home nothing.

Kit's illness took an unfavourable turn.

The hope of his speedy recovery was dashed to the ground, for, getting up too soon, he caught a severe cold, which settled on his lungs, and he wasted away gradually.

Young Jack had only a vague idea of death, but he grew frightened as he noticed the change in his friend.

From being a fine, healthy boy, Kit wasted away to a shadow.

His face was pale and thin, his hands transparent, and his skin of an unearthly whiteness.

Sometimes in Spring the sun will burst forth with splendid brilliancy, gladdening all hearts, when suddenly the dark clouds will hide the glowing orb of day, and everything will look sombre and wintry.

So it was with Young Jack.

He had hoped that Kit would soon be running about with him again, helping to fight the hard battle of life.

But this expectation died away, as he saw him

grow thinner and paler, weakening every day, and drawing nearer the grave.

"Tiny," said Kit, one day, when they were alone in the dormitory

"What is it, Kit?"

"Listen here."

"Do you want anything, Kit?"

"No; my wants will soon be over. I shan't run the machine much longer," said Kit, solemnly. "The doctor thought I didn't hear him, but I did. Do you know what he said, Tiny?"

"No, Kit."

"He said—'That boy will die.'"

"P'raps he didn't mean you, Kit," exclaimed Young Jack.

"That boy was me, Tiny. Say, now, Tiny, did they ever teach you much about Heaven?"

"I can say, 'Our Father,'" answered Young Jack, "and I used to know 'I believe,' and the evening hymns; but I don't recollect them very well."

"A man who runs a Gospel store," said Kit, "once wanted me to come to his school. I didn't. Wish I had, now. Don't the good boys go to Heaven, Tiny?"

"My mamma used to tell me so."

"Where is Heaven, Tiny?"

Young Jack pointed to the ceiling.

"Up there, somewhere, Kit; ever so high up in the clouds," he answered.

"And where's the other place, where they say there's fire to burn the bad boys, Tiny?"

"That's down under our feet, Kit," answered Young Jack, with a shudder.

"I wonder where I shall go when I die?" said Kit, with a dreamy expression about his large, lustrous eyes.

And Young Jack wondered, and sat by the bed-side, wondering, until Kit, who was also speculating on the mysteries of futurity, looked up, and saw the tears running down his cheeks so fast that they chased one another, and when they met, they formed up into big tear-pools, and dropped with a sullen splash on the floor.

"What are you crying for, Tiny?" he asked.

"It seems so hard to lose you, Kit. It seems as if I was never to be happy and have a friend. If God is good, what does He want to take you for, and leave me? Why can't He take us both?"

"Hush! Tiny," exclaimed Kit, reprovingly. "You mustn't talk like that. I'm not very good; but I know it's wrong, and when you're sick like me, it makes you think deep, I guess."

Young Jack was silent under this rebuke.

Nothing was heard but the heavy breathing of Kit, and Jack's tears falling mournfully on the boards.

"Heaven's a steep road to travel, I guess, Tiny," said Kit, suddenly.

"They've got angels up there, Kit, and they fly with wings," replied Young Jack.

"Fly with wings!" repeated Kit. "Do tell! I never heard that. Is that in the Bible?"

"Yes. My mamma's read that to me."

"My! The Bible must be a fine book, Tiny. Wonder how I shall look in wings, flying with the angels? But—"

He paused, and an intensely miserable expression came over his face.

"I'm not good enough to go there and fly with angels, Tiny," he added. "I wish I'd gone to that Gospel store now, and listened to the boss that runs it. Say, now, Tiny, couldn't you go to that boss and bring him here to me? It isn't too late, is it?"

"Not as long as you live, I guess, Kit."

"My!" continued Kit, "I'm mighty tickled to think it isn't too late. When you die, Tiny, it's like putting the candle out when you go to bed.

But the candle ain't out yet. It's got a bit more to run, ain't it, Tiny?"

Young Jack said he thought so.

"Do I look bad Tiny?" continued Kit.

"Awful bad," replied Young Jack, with childish candour.

"Ah!" said Kit, with a melancholy shake of the head, "it makes you look bad when you've been sick long, Tiny."

"I've never been real sick," answered Young Jack.

"Tiny," continued Kit, very earnestly, "go and get that boss of the Gospel store. It don't do to waste time when the grave's kinder dug for you."

"Where is he, Kit?"

"Way down Chatham-street. He hangs out his rag at a brick house, and there's 'Little Bethel' wrote up over the door, just like the title of a paper, Tiny,"

"Will Dutchy let him come in?"

"If Dutchy asks you anything, just tell him any lie as comes up first," replied Kit; but his face clouded as he added, "My! ain't I a wicked boy, telling you to tell lies! I shall never fly amongst those angels you told me about, Tiny."

He sighed deeply.

"Just own up the truth," he continued; "there can't be much harm, Tiny, in having in the Gospel boss to talk about the Bible things and square you up a bit before you die. Eh! Tiny?"

"It can't be quite right, or Dutchy would have had him in to talk to us boys before," answered Young Jack. "But I'll do it, Kit. I'll chance a hiding for your sake."

"Thank you, Tiny. You're true grit," said Kit.

Young Jack went away, looking very grave, as if he felt he had accepted a great responsibility, and was going to do something altogether contrary to the rules of Hans Dunkerboom's establishment.

The cold pale rays of a wintry sun streamed in a half-hearted way into the dormitories, showing up the white-washed walls, the little beds, and the carpetless floor in all their poverty-stricken nakedness.

And the dying boy shut his eyes to think more deeply about the new and strange matters which occupied his uncultivated mind.

Nearly an hour passed before Young Jack returned with the minister of the Gospel, a Mr. Saveall, who preached in a Baptist chapel to a small congregation gathered from the slums of the Five Points.

He had gladly consented to come when he heard that a dying boy wanted to see him.

"Say, Tiny, is that the boss?" inquired Kit, as the footsteps approached his bed.

"Yes, Kit."

"What's the bank, Tiny."

"Fifteen cents," answered Young Jack, feeling in his pockets.

"I want a fifteen-cent talk with the boss. Cash up, Tiny."

"My dear boy, I make no charge," said Mr. Saveall. "It is my vocation to attend death-beds, and bring glad tidings."

"Say, now, pa, you're fooling me," replied Kit. "I thought you Gospel chaps were all-fired smart in picking up the stamps. Don't you charge nothing at all?"

"No."

"My! Ain't this bully! It's better nor a free lunch. Give us some chin-music, pa," continued Kit, delightedly.

"Will you listen to me attentively, my poor child?" said the good clergyman.

"You bet."

"Have you anything on your mind?"

"I feel kinder mad," replied Kit, "to think I've

been such a wicked boy, though I never was a gun. Now, pa, I've been starving, and I wouldn't sneak a peanut."

"Have you had no religious instruction? But I needn't ask. I can see how it is. There are hundreds like you growing up in our midst without God," said the clergyman.

"Tiny says, pa, that the good boys fly up with angels," continued Kit. "Now, I'm dead sure I'm not good enough for that, pa, and that's what's the matter."

"Did you ever hear of Christ?" asked the reverend gentleman.

"You bet!" answered Kit. "But that's swearing. The boys only say 'Christ' when they want to swear."

The clergyman held up his hands in horror at this dense ignorance.

Taking Kit's hand in his, he gently and plainly began to talk to him about the sublime truth of revelation, and soon the dying newsboy began to see through a glare darkly.

Then came a clearer consciousness, and he recognised the glorious fact that a Saviour had died for sinners on the cross, and that there was hope for those that repent, even on a death-bed.

The dark shadows of falling night—sad precursors of coming death—began to wrap the room in their black embrace before the good man's earnest voice ceased.

Kit had taken in all he said.

Grasping the pastor's hand, he pressed it warmly, and his eyes sparkled with gratitude and joy.

"Pa!" he cried. "Pa! I guess I'll fly. I guess I'll fly yet."

A smile of triumph and satisfaction hovered for a moment round the corners of Mr. Saveall's lips.

His usually meek and subdued face was lit up with an inward fire.

He felt that he had snatched a brand from the burning.

Young Jack had listened to his unadorned eloquence with wrapt attention.

He, too, saw a new world opening up before him.

The reverend gentleman was a constant visitor to that bedside after this.

But Kit grew weaker and more shadow-like day by day, so that it was easy to perceive the end was drawing nigh.

CHAPTER XVI.

AT THE CONVENT.

It was the last Sunday in the old year. The weather was gloriously fine, though bitterly cold.

Jack and his wife, with Hilda and Harvey, went to church on Fifth Avenue, and as they were walking back to their hotel, they met Felix S. Prye, with his father, mother, and two sisters.

An introduction took place, and Felix promised to come to lunch.

When he entered the apartments at the Gilsey House, which were the handsomest that money could procure, he exclaimed—

"You've had a chance to-day of seeing our ladies. What do you think of them?"

"I am astonished," replied Emily. "Never did I see such expensive dresses."

"The American ladies," said Hilda, "seem to lavish money on their attire. I saw one lady with lace on her dress that must have cost a thousand dollars; and then the furs! Sealskin and astrakhan, sable and grebe! Considering that everything is twice as dear here as in England, it must cost a fortune to dress a woman."

"I guess that's so," replied Felix. "Last year my married sister paid two thousand dollars for flowers on New Year's."

"Really, your ladies are very elegant," said Emily.

"And the men are not far behind," said Jack. "A London swell could not find fault with them. Neither Hyde Park nor the Bois de Boulogne could beat them."

"I thought," said Harvey, "that Americans were careless about dressing, and that we left luxury and taste behind when we quitted the Old World."

"Well, you've found out your mistake—own up."

"I do," answered Harvey, laughing.

"It wasn't a bad crowd on Fifth Avenue?"

"Not at all. The wealth of London and the taste of Paris is combined in New York."

"Shall we go to Central Park this afternoon?" asked Emily.

"I guess not," answered Felix. "You won't see our good people there. The Park's not nobby on Sunday."

"Harvey and I arranged to sleigh up to the Convent, and smoke a cigar before dinner," said Jack.

"Perhaps I'll meet you there," replied Felix. "I shall take father's Portland; the girls are going out in the Albany."

Mr. Mole appeared in the doorway.

"If you have a seat to spare, Mr. Prye," he said, "take compassion on a humble individual of the name of Mole."

"With pleasure, sir. Where have you been?"

"Over to Brooklyn, to hear Beecher."

"What's your opinion of him as a preacher?"

"He is excellent. Far ahead of most of our divines in common sense, earnest gospel eloquence. I am told his pew-rents come to over fifty thousand dollars a year."

"Yes, sir," said Felix; "religion pays here just as well as in Europe, if you know how it's got to be run. I thought a little going around in New York would knock the spots out of you Britishers. Don't take me as a sample of the straight-out tip-top White House American. I am a little rough, and perhaps can trade better than I can talk."

"Now, you're fishing for compliments, Mr. Prye," answered Hilda.

"Is that so, Mrs. Harvey? Say something nice; I like to be tickled."

Hilda laughed, but had no time to reply, as Monday announced lunch. When it was over, Felix said to Mole—

"Will three suit you? It will. Very well, I'll be in time."

Jack and Harvey had started earlier, and as Jack had made good use of his time since he had been in New York, he could run a sleigh as well as any one.

He knew that the rule of the road is the reverse to what it is in England, where the maxim is, "Go to the left, you'll be right; go to the right, you'll be wrong."

The snow was beaten down into a hard mass on the roads, no effort being made by the authorities to clear it away.

Turning into Fifth Avenue, at Madison-square, Jack sped along towards the Park.

The sleigh-bells on all sides made merry music, and visions of fair women wrapped up in furs were frequent.

"Isn't this jolly?" said Harvey.

"Rather," answered Jack. "I like New York life immensely. Aren't the people gay! Sleighing in the day-time, theatres and parties in the evening, and hospitality always."

"Shall we pull up at the Convent, and have a smoke and a warm?" asked Harvey.

"Certainly. That was what I came for. I hate going out without an object."

They were close to the picturesque building, once a convent and now a restaurant, which attracts the fashionable world to its comfortable precincts.

Jack pulled up, and having procured some one to

mind the horse, he walked into the sitting-room, and did his furs, and ordered a bottle of wine in a private cabinet.

While smoking a cigar, he heard a man passing along the passage utter his name.

"Harkaway."

The sound was readily transmitted, because, in these cabinets, there were no doors, the opening being hidden only by a curtain.

"Do you know that voice, Dick?" he asked.

"I fancy I do," replied Harvey.

"Whose would you say it was?"

"Miles Fenton's, for a dollar."

"So I think," answered Jack. "Now, if that fellow is here, talking about me, he means mischief. Can't we smoke him? I smell a rat, and should like to get to the bottom of this thing."

"All's fair in love and war," said Harvey.

"It would be fair to listen, if we could."

"Rather; but the difficulty is, how to do it. Let me try. If I go out by myself, and play 'possum with them, they will not be so likely to notice it as if we both went."

"Dick," said Jack, "you're worth a Jew's eye. Slip along, and I'll wait here. But—"

"What?"

"If they twig you, sing out, and I'll be there like a flash."

Harvey nodded his head, as if he perfectly understood that Jack was always there when he was wanted.

He quitted the cabinet, and began to explore the Convent, to find where Miles Fenton had gone.

For some time he could not discover any trace of him.

There were many people at the Convent, ladies and gentlemen, who were talking and laughing together.

He peered carefully into the different groups, walked hither and thither, and at last opened a door leading to a wooden balcony.

Here were two men smoking.

Their backs were turned to him, and there was something about one of them which led him to more carefully examine them.

"Yes," he muttered, after awhile, "that's Fenton; I know his build."

Passing carefully by, he hid himself in an angle of the wall, which was the more easily done as it was growing dark.

The white snow was stretched out all around in all its spotless purity.

Miles Fenton and his companion seemed deeply interested in their conversation.

Their flushed countenances and thick voices betokened that they had been drinking.

From his position of 'vantage, Harvey could hear the larger part of their conversation.

This he drank in with a greedy ear.

"It was a fine idea, Leroy!" exclaimed Fenton. "By thunder! it was a splendid idea, anyway."

"Hush!" said the other, nervously. "Don't call me Leroy. Call me Sheepe. That name's not so well-known, except to Mr. Harkaway."

"Ha! ha!" laughed Fenton. "You practised on him like an old hand."

"That's so; but he was a stranger, and wanted to find his boy, which he never will. If I can't find the whelp, how can he?" said Fenton, savagely.

"You've got the advantage of my talents, and can't drop across him. It's a wonder to me where he can have got to."

"Dead, perhaps. Eh, Leroy?"

"Don't!" exclaimed Leroy, anxiously. "Superintendent Matsell's got spies about everywhere."

"What good are they?"

"Well, well, don't talk so much. Call me Sensitive Sheepe. That's my name."

"You're a nice sheep to fleece," said Fenton, who had been drinking until he lost his accustomed caution.

"Dog don't eat dog, I guess," replied Leroy, "and you needn't try the game on with me. But do be careful. You London men don't seem to mind what you risk when you get on the drunk."

"Why should we?" answered Fenton. "See how easily we got Hunston out of the Penitentiary."

"Not out of it."

"Well, off the Island, anyhow."

Harvey held his breath.

This was news to him.

"It will be in the papers to-morrow," said Leroy.

"Dash the papers," replied Fenton; "Hunston's away from Astoria by this time, and on his way up to Albany or Troy. He'll meet us up West, as soon as we've burnt out our wasps' nest."

"My!" said Leroy, with a fiendish chuckle, "won't it be a Fourth of July!"

"Hope it won't be a fizzle!"

"Fizzle? Not much. Didn't I make it myself?" exclaimed Leroy, indignantly. "You've heard of Fieschi?"

"Yes."

"Well, he made an infernal machine to blow up a King of France, and I've improved on his model."

"Is it sure to work?"

"Is it?" replied Leroy, contemptuously. "I have made a handsome mahogany box—looks like a writing-desk. Inside is a bag of powder and cartridges. When the lid is opened, it is connected with a spring, which draws some matches along sand-paper, and as the matches strike, they light a train of touch-paper, which, in a few seconds, communicates with the magazine, and I'll bet there's nothing much but arms and legs about that room directly afterwards."

"Did you direct it properly?"

"I did."

"How?"

"'Jack Harkaway, Esquire, Gilsey House; from Felix S. Prye, Esquire, with compliments of the sender.' You told me Prye was a friend of theirs."

"Yes. They met on board ship. Harkaway has a pleasant manner, and a knack of making friends," replied Fenton.

"And enemies, too," replied Leroy, with a laugh, "if I may judge by what I see."

"Oh!" said Fenton, "every man who is worthy the name of a man has enemies. A fellow can't be everlastingly polite to every one he meets. I never could make myself agreeable to a man I didn't like."

"Nor I," said Leroy; "my idea, when I don't like a fellow, is—"

"To send him an infernal machine," interrupted Fenton.

"Don't talk so loud," said Leroy; "you might ruin us by an incautious word."

"Bosh!" exclaimed Fenton; "you're as timid as a hare. They are all dead by this time."

"It isn't my fault if they're not."

"What time did you arrange the box to get to the hotel?"

"Just after lunch, when they were likely to be all in a family group."

"Good!" said Miles Fenton. "Let us have another bottle of wine, and then we'll go down-town, and gather up the news."

"We must be at the Central Depot by seven," answered Leroy, "or we shan't join Hunston, by the Hudson River Railroad, as we promised."

"I'll see that is all right. Come and drink."

"Where?"

"In number three," said Fenton. "There's some bully boys we know in there; Black Dick, the President, and Little Howard, and the Indian."

"Which one?"

"The one you call the Warning Devil. I think he is square enough now, though I had my doubts about him at first."

"Oh! Par-a-wau's right as the mail," said Leroy, sharply.

They threw their cigars away, and prepared to leave the balcony.

Harvey was in a state of the utmost excitement. What had he heard?

First of all, that Hunston had escaped from the Penitentiary, probably swimming across the river to Astoria, by the help of some friends in a boat.

Secondly, that the devilish ingenuity of Fenton, Hunston, and the Pecker, had prompted them to send Harkaway an infernal machine.

Apparently, a handsome present.

But, in reality, a messenger of death.

A fearful thing, filled with powder and ball, which would be discharged in all directions on simply opening the lid.

There was no time to be lost.

He followed them into the passage, and saw them enter number three room, in which four men were playing euchre.

"The jack of clubs," said the dealer.

"I pass all bowers," said the second.

"That's me." remarked the third.

"I'm by," observed the fourth.

"I turn it down," said the dealer.

"Next. That's what I make it," said the second. "Spades are trumps, boys; play to the ace."

Harvey waited a moment, and saw Fenton and Leroy greeted by their friends.

Nothing more was said.

The players were intent upon their game.

Hurrying back to Jack, he came in, looking very white and scared.

"Come along, quick!" he said.

"Why?" asked Jack.

"It's life and death! Come!"

"How?"

"I'll tell you as we go along," said Harvey, impatiently.

"I haven't paid for the wine."

"Square up some other time."

"Hang it, Dick," said Jack, "we've been through a good deal together, and I never saw you look or act like this."

"Hunston's escaped from the Island!" exclaimed Harvey.

"The deuce he has! That's smart."

"Fenton and Leroy—"

"Who?"

"The man you call Sensitive Sheepe, but whose name is Leroy, have sent you a present."

"Very kind of them, I'm sure. What is there to be annoyed about over that?"

"A lot," answered Harvey. "It is, in reality, an infernal machine."

"What's that?"

"Why, a thing to explode when it's opened, and blow everybody in the room to little bits!"

"My!" exclaimed Jack. "Is that so?"

"I've overheard enough of their conversation, Jack, to know that they think we are all dead by this time. They are gloating over it, and intend to go down-town to get the news of our death and our wives', and then they are going by the Hudson River Railroad to join Hunston at Troy."

"Forgive me, Dick, for not taking all this 'in' at once," said Jack.

"Come along," replied Harvey.

"Wait a moment."

"I can't. I love my wife, Jack, and we may be in time to save all our party."

"You mean they may not open the present till we arrive home?"

"Exactly."

"Look here, Dick," said Jack, whose face was unusually grave.

"Well?"

"Listen to me. If Emily or Hilda felt inclined to open this 'present,' they'd have done it before now. An hour or two won't make any difference."

"But I want to get home," said Harvey.

"So do I, but I want to do something else now."

"What's that?"

"Go for these men."

"Go for them?"

"Yes. Smash them up. Play Small Peter with them, if they're in this building."

"Don't be foolish," said Harvey.

"Knowing what I do, I won't quit till I'm level with them."

"Think of our wives."

"I've discounted that, Dick, and I mean to go for these villains," answered Jack.

"Do you know how many you're going to fight?"

"No."

"Only six."

"Six?"

"Yes. If you like to go for six in a country where such men always carry revolvers, do it. I shan't."

"This is the first time, Dick, I ever saw you cave in against odds," said Jack.

"What's the good?"

"Very well. You take the sleigh and go home. I'm on for a fight. What's happened at home in our absence can't be helped, but I've got these beauties under my thumb, and I mean to squeeze them."

"Jack!"

"They may break my heart, and rob me of wife and child, but, by the Heaven above, I'll be even with them!" said Jack.

"All right," replied Harvey. "When you screw your lips down like that, Jack, I know you mean business, and I won't leave you. Let's go for them."

Jack wrung his hand cordially.

"Don't you see, Dick," he said, "I should be a fool to let them go, now I have them in the next room?"

"Perhaps you're right," replied Harvey, "though I'd give the world to be back at the hotel."

"Come with me. We'll make it hot for them?" said Jack.

The two friends quitted their cabinet, and went to the one in which Harvey had seen Miles Fenton and Leroy join their associates.

To their astonishment, it was empty.

The birds had flown.

Perhaps Jack had spoken too loudly, and so warned the villains, who had taken their departure in a hurry.

At all events, Jack was baulked of his revenge for that time.

He went outside, followed by Harvey.

Some one touched him on the shoulder.

"Par-a-wau!" exclaimed Jack, in surprise.

The lithe and sinewy form of the Indian was drawn up to its full height.

"My brother is in much danger," he said. "Bad men sent him death in a box. My brother will beware."

"I have just heard of this," answered Jack, "and we are going home at once. God grant no harm has happened in our absence to those who are dearer to us than our lives."

"The Great Father will watch," replied the Warning Devil.

"Par-a-wau!"

"My brother can speak. The ears of Par-a-wau are open."

"Watch these bad men. Come to my hotel, and tell me where they go to."

The Indian nodded, and glided away, serpent-like, in the darkness, his tall form stealing away like a shadow over the gleaming snow.

Jack and Harvey got into the sleigh, and drove rapidly back to town.

The park regulations, forbidding any horse to go at a greater speed than seven miles an hour, was disregarded.

"Drive like mad!" said Harvey.

There was no reason to say this, as Jack was urging his horse at his best pace, and the sleigh flew over the snow.

Suddenly they came on some obstruction.

The sleigh was upset, and its occupants sent flying in various directions.

Harvey found himself on a bank, not much the worse for his fall, and from his elevated position he looked round for his companion.

"Jack! where are you?" he said.

"Up a tree," was the reply.

The voice seemed to come from the clouds, and, looking up in the direction from whence it proceeded, Harvey saw his friend astride a bough.

"Drop down, soh! softly, don't!" he said, scarcely able to refrain from laughing.

Beyond a severe shaking, and a few cuts and bruises, they were unhurt.

The sleigh was set up again, and was found to have sustained no important damage.

Getting in, they continued their journey, though Jack drove more carefully, not caring about another aëriel flight.

It was, indeed, a race for life.

Who could tell whether the curiosity of the women had triumphed over their prudence?

What was more natural than that Emily and Hilda should open the box containing the infernal machine?

If they had done so, Heaven help them!

The gates of the park were reached, and away sped the sleigh like lightning down Fifth Avenue.

Would its occupants be in time?

Jack scarcely dared to ask himself the question.

In a few short minutes he would receive the answer.

CHAPTER XVII.

THE INFERNAL MACHINE.

EMILY and Hilda were seated together in their drawing-room at the hotel.

"How warm the Americans keep their rooms!" remarked Emily.

"It is the hot air, dear," answered Hilda. "I have got used to it already, and really it is so very cold that warmth is a necessity."

There was a knock at the door.

"Come in!" said Emily.

Monday entered, bearing a good-sized box carefully wrapped up in paper.

"What have you there?" asked Hilda.

"Um present for Mast' Jack, mum," replied Monday.

"Set it down on the table. Christmas presents already!"

"Thursday is Christmas Day," remarked Hilda.

"I wonder what it is, and who it is from?" said Emily; "cut the string, and let us look at it."

Monday did so, carefully removed the paper, and revealed a handsome box, made of polished mahogany.

In a piece of paper was wrapped the key, and underneath was written, "With Felix S. Prye's compliments."

"How kind of Mr. Prye!" said Hilda. "I suppose that is what he would call one of his father's notions. Shall we open it, dear?"

"I think we ought to wait until the men return," replied Hilda.

"Very well," said Emily; "you can go now, Monday."

The black retired, and the ladies gazed curiously at the present.

Surely some good angel was at that moment whispering to Hilda, and warning her of danger.

Its guardian voice must have restrained her from being hasty.

"Perhaps there is some jewellery inside for us," remarked Emily.

"We shall see presently, dear," answered Hilda, looking at the clock. "They cannot be long now; it only wants an hour to dinner-time."

"I should so like to open it," said Emily; "we could lock it up again, and no one would know that we had taken just one little peep at its contents."

"Remember the fate of Bluebeard's wife!" laughed Hilda.

"Curiosity is a failing of our sex."

"Yes, but how often has it been punished! Think of Lot's wife."

"My dear child," replied Emily, "I feel as if I could risk being turned into a pillar of salt just to have one look."

"What a baby you are!" said Hilda. "Do wait. It will be much more fun to examine it when we are all together."

"Very well," answered Emily, with a reluctant sigh. "You are as bad as a severe governess we had, when I was at school, who would never let us open a letter from home till lessons were over."

"Quite right, too. The mind cannot be fixed on two things at once."

"Oh! you hard-hearted tease!" said Emily, with a half smile.

The door opened, and Mr. Mole appeared with Felix.

"I am so glad you've come, Mr. Prye," said Hilda. "Did you see anything of our husbands?"

"No," answered Felix; "we did not get as far as the Convent. Mr. Mole complained of the cold, so we stopped at a restaurant, and had hot Tom and Jerry, which our friend Mole found so much to his taste that I could not get him away from Thomas and Jeremiah until it was too late to go further."

"I am ashamed of you, Mr. Mole," said Emily.

"Fine thing, Tom and Jerry," replied Mole, thickly. "'Sure you that Tom and Terry—I mean Sherry and Tom—bother these Yankee names. Anyhow, Tom and Sherry's a tall thing in drinks. Eh, Felix?"

"Certainly, sir."

"Now I'll tell you why I'm glad you've come, Prye!" exclaimed Hilda. "But of course you can guess!"

"Indeed, I can't."

"Really, to use one of Mr. Prye's favourite expressions," said Emily, "he's playing possum with us."

Felix looked puzzled.

"Well," continued Hilda, "if you will be bashful, we must thank you very much for your handsome present."

"Present!"

"HE IS HERE UNDER MY PROTECTION," MR. SHEEPE SAID; "SO YOU HAD BETTER SHEER OFF."

"Precisely," said Hilda.

"I have not sent you anything," he said.

"Oh! Mr. Prye, how can you say so, when it is on the table, with your compliments written on the paper the key was wrapped up in?"

"You're trying to bluff me," said Felix.

"Go and look for yourself," said Emily and Hilda in a breath.

He approached the table. They all crowded round him, while he examined the outside of the box, and read the writing on the paper.

His face assumed a grave expression.

"That's not my writing, nor did I send you the box!" he said.

"No!"

"Somebody's been playing a joke, I guess."

"Well, this is the strangest thing I ever heard of," said Emily.

"There is more in it than appears on the surface," observed Hilda.

"It can't have come wrong, for I see it is directed to Mr. Harkaway," continued Felix. "But why should my name be used? I don't like it. The thing looks ugly. It's not fixed up square."

"P'raps it's got Tom and Sherry inside; let's look," said Mole, with a side-lurch against the table.

"There can be no harm in opening it," said Emily.

"Hold on there, sonny!" cried Felix, as Mr. Mole took up the key.

"What for?"

5

"I wouldn't touch that box. Jack's got enemies, and—"

He broke off abruptly.

The ladies looked inquiringly at him.

"I scarcely like to say what I have in my mind. It seems too terrible," he continued.

"Say it! say it!" cried Emily and Hilda.

"There may be something to destroy life inside."

"Oh, what nonsense!" laughed Emily. "What danger could that pretty box contain?"

"You bet," said Felix, "that some one's been trying to skunk us."

"Rubbish!" said Mr. Mole. "Who's afraid?"

"Stand back!" said Felix, "till I tell you a story. Once I was on a Mississippi steamer. We were racing. There was a nigger sitting on the safety-valve, and he kept bobbing up and down like a cork on a wave. 'Fire up, boys; put on the reserve,' said the captain, 'and those gentlemen who haven't paid their passage will please go to the ladies' cabin.' I went, because I knew what it meant."

"What?"

"The ladies' cabin was at the end of the boat, and pretty safe, if she burst up, so that there was a chance of getting the dollars for the passage. Now, it's my opinion that we ought all of us to go to the ladies' cabin."

"I tell you," said Mole, "that I'm going to open that box."

"Oh, do!" cried Emily.

"Well," replied Mole, "as you seem so anxious, Mrs. Harkaway, I'll let you do it."

Emily took the key.

"How far is it from the window to the street?" asked Felix, retreating with an anxious expression.

"Now for it," said Emily. "Oh! I do love a mystery. What do you say is inside, Hilda? Let us have a bet—diamonds?"

"I'll say pearls, for half a dozen pairs of gloves," said Hilda.

Emily fitted the key in the lock.

There was a moment of breathless suspense.

The key clicked in the lock, and it was turned.

It only remained now to lift the lid.

This Emily was about to do, when the door was thrown violently open. Jack bounded in, struck his wife rudely on the arm, and threw her across to the sofa.

"Saved! saved! thank God!" he cried, half-laughing, half-crying with excitement.

Harvey had followed him closely.

Taking him in his arms, Jack danced round the room like one insane.

Emily was very angry.

"Are you mad, Jack?" she asked.

"Getting on that way," replied Jack, adding, "Didn't the old horse go, Dick? Wasn't I right to tan him? We weren't a moment too soon."

"What on earth is all this fuss about?" said Emily. "You have hurt my arm, Jack; you never did such a thing before; I am surprised at you."

"Turn it up, Dick; let's be sensible once more. It's all over now, but it was almost more than I could bear at first. To think that we should have nicked it by half a second! Hurrah!"

"Hurrah-rah-rah!" cried Harvey, tossing his sealskin cap up to the table, and catching it like a schoolboy.

"Sold again, ain't they, Dick?" said Jack.

"Rather! My! how is that for high?" answered Harvey.

Then Jack caught his wife in his arms, and kissed her, Harvey doing the same to Hilda.

After that, they shook hands wildly with Felix and Professor Mole, finally sitting down and trying to be calm.

"First of all," said Jack, "that thing on the table is an infernal machine."

The ladies screamed.

"What did I say?" remarked Felix.

"Secondly, Hunston has escaped from the Island, and got safe off to Astoria, from whence he is going to Westchester County, and up to Troy."

"Never!"

"Fact," said Jack. "And now listen; you shall have the full details of the story."

He proceeded to relate how they had overheard the plans of the conspirators, and what fear they were in that they would not reach the hotel in time to stop the explosion.

"Hunston has lost no time in letting us know he is free," observed Mr. Mole.

"Hang him, no; he don't let the grass grow under his feet," replied Jack.

Emily and Hilda burst into tears.

They could now realise how near they had been to a sudden and awful death.

Mr. Mole was very indignant.

He turned up his sleeves and extended his right arm, clenching his fist savagely.

"I wish I had that fellow Hunston here," he said, "I'd hammer him. See my fist Mr. Prye; how does that look?"

"It isn't very clean, sir, and I should say it looked as if you had gone short on your soap," answered Felix.

"Nonsense! This is no time for joking. I hurl my malediction upon Hunston."

"Gentlemen will please copy," said Felix, laughing.

It was with a very poor appetite that the party sat down to dinner, and as soon as it was over, Jack had the box taken into a cellar.

He fastened a cord in such a manner to the lid that when it was pulled from without it was raised up.

A terrible explosion followed, and the walls were found to be indented with slugs, nails, and bullets, showing conclusively the villainous nature of the infernal machine.

"This is something like the wooden horse the Greeks gave the Trojans," remarked Professor Mole. "Virgil says, 'I fear the Greeks when they bring gifts,' and we may apply the line to Hunston and his friends."

"It is the most rascally thing the scoundrel has yet done," said Jack.

"Miles Fenton has had a hand in this," said Harvey. "It is just the fiendish trick he would delight in."

"I guess that's so," answered Felix.

Jack informed the police of what had occurred, and when Par-a-wau came, later in the evening, to inform him that Fenton and Sheepe had gone somewhere by train from the Harlem Depot, he at once forwarded the news to the detectives.

But either the luck of the conspirators was in, or their purse was long, for no arrest was made.

Hunston and his friends were at large.

More villainy might be expected from such a significant fact.

CHAPTER XVIII.

PAVONIA PANTS, THE CLOWN.

As surely as the leaves fade and wither and drop from the trees in the fall, did the sick newsboy draw near his end.

Towards the end, his mind seemed to be brighter and more vigorous.

There was a preternatural clearness in his understanding, which enabled him, in a remarkable degree for a boy of his years, to comprehend all that was said to him by the kind clergyman.

"I'm going soon, Tiny," he said, "and I'm not afraid to die. Say good-bye."

"Good-bye, Kit," replied Young Jack, choking back a sob.

"Tiny!"

"Yes, Kit."

Young Jack was obliged to place his head close to his friend's lips, because his voice was so faint and feeble.

"You'll see where they bury me. I'm only a poor boy, and I don't suppose they'll muss about much to mark the grave. Now, I should like you to carve a wooden cross."

"I can do it with your old jack-knife," said Young Jack.

"That's so. I shall leave you my jack-knife and my clothes, Tiny. That's all I've got to leave. The clothes aren't worth figuring about, but the boots are good, though they ain't quite your fit."

"Never mind that, Kit."

"Well, you'll carve a cross, and stick it up over the grave, and write 'Kit' on it, 'aged eleven years,' won't you, Tiny?"

"Yes, Kit," replied Young Jack, making his invariable answer when appealed to.

"Do you think you could put, in small letters, 'He died in the Lord?' Small letters, mind. I don't want to sweat you about too much, because you've got your living to get. But of evenings, this winter, you might do it—bit at a time."

"I'll do it, Kit. No fear."

"The boys might like to come over and have a look at the grave, Tiny, and if there was no head-piece they wouldn't know where I was laid, would they?"

"No, they wouldn't."

"'Kit' will be enough; and, Tiny, if flowers aren't dear, you might plant a few roots. It will make it look kinder homely. I always did love flowers."

"Snow-drops and crocuses?" suggested Young Jack.

"Yes; and heart's-ease in summer, with a rose and mignonette; that stuff that smells so sweet."

"And a sun-flower?"

"No," said Kit, shaking his head, "I don't think I should like a sun-flower. It's too big like, for a little boy like me, and wouldn't match. Don't put no sun-flower, Tiny."

"All right, Kit."

The important question of the flower-planting over the grave being settled, Kit was silent for a time, the oppressive stillness being broken only by his occasional coughing and heavy breathing.

"I'd like you to learn and read that Bible the boss gave me, Tiny," he continued; "and you know Plummer—him as runs the peanut-store, corner of Chamber-street?"

"The one that sells peanuts on a basket?"

"That's him. Well, he's been kind, while I've been ill, giving me peanuts. I couldn't eat them; but he meant it well, and I'll leave him my toy sleigh—that is, if you don't want it, Tiny?"

"No, Kit."

"Plummer's mighty good at going a belly-gutter on a sleigh. There ain't a boy that can beat him on belly-gutter. You'll see he has my sleigh, Tiny?"

"Yes, Kit."

"I think I'll go to sleep now, Tiny. Give me your hand. God bless you, Tiny. I can say God bless now, and know what it means. My! ain't I happy! When I get up to Heaven, Tiny, and fly with the angels, I'll keep a place for you, and you must be a good boy, and never lie or steal like Shyse; think of that, Tiny, will you? Good-night! It's got dark sooner than usual, and I feel very tired. God bless Tiny!"

These were the last words the poor boy uttered.

It was not dark, for the sun was shining over the house-tops, and on the crisp, white snow, flooding the room with its radiance, but it was not a messenger of glad tidings to him.

The shadow of death had come, and cast its black funereal wings over him.

He went off to sleep—his last long sleep, from which he was never to awake in this world, and he held Young Jack's hand in his beneath the bed-clothes.

"God bless Tiny!"

These last words rang in Young Jack's ears, as the last words of the dying will ring in the ears of those who are with them in their death-bed moments.

Gradually the hand that Young Jack held in his grew colder and colder, until it was like ice.

Getting frightened, he took his arm away, and ran down-stairs to the Dutchman, who, as usual, was smoking, and warming his lower extremities by the stove.

"Vell, my poy," said Hans Dunkerboom, "ish he ted?"

Young Jack said he feared so, as he was so cold and still.

"It must have come shome time, I gues. Kit, he vash my Right Bower; he vash your he vash own me a long pill. You vash own me money, too. It ish twenty tollars. If you do not pay me my pill by Saturday, you musht not shleep no more mit te poys at Hans's."

This was a lengthy speech for the Dutchman to make, and it took him some time to deliver it.

Feeling sick at heart, when he comprehended that he was alone in the world, and would soon be homeless and an outcast again, Young Jack went out into the street.

Where could he obtain the large sum of twenty dollars?

It was impossible.

He had not gone far before he met the Shyser, who recognised him in a moment.

"Hoopla! you young Britisher! come here. Where are you off to, marching like a Mulligan Guard?" he asked.

Young Jack thought of Kit's last dying words, and tried to get past him, but this he was unable to do.

"Come here, or I'll fetch you with a brick!" cried the Shyser.

The boy obeyed, tremblingly, and with evident reluctance.

"You look scared. What's up?"

"Kit's dead," said the boy, beginning to cry. "Let me go, please, I'm so wretched, and I want to get along to see if I can make a cent or two up Broadway."

"Kit's dead, is he?" repeated the Shyser. "Bust up, has he? My! who'd ha' thought it? The glass is empty; fill it up, boss, and put some nutmeg on top."

With this rather vague remark, he cut a caper on the snow, and then gave vent to a prolonged whistle.

"What are you running on now, young 'un?" he asked.

"Nothing."

"That's filling at the price It don't take much figuring, I guess. You'd better join me."

"What in?" inquired Young Jack.

"Oh, the young possum!" cried the Shyser, "he pretends he don't know how I pick up the stamps. Now, say, what am I?"

"I don't like to—"

"Say, or I'll lick you."

The Shyser extended his muscular arm threateningly.

"Don't hit me, please, Shise. I didn't want to say it—you made me."

"You haven't said it yet. What am I?"

"A thief! Oh, please, Shise, don't! Oh!" cried Young Jack, as the Shyser playfully knocked him over with a blow on one side of the head, and with equal cheerfulness helped him to recover his balance by a blow on the other.

Reeling from the effects of the blow, panting with rage, smarting with pain, Young Jack's spirit was aroused.

He was a very little boy, compared with the Shyser.

But, doubling his fists, and squaring up to him, he exclaimed—

"You big coward! What do you mean by hitting me like that? I'll give it to you, if you kill me for it!"

He rushed in, and, more by good luck than skill, succeeded in striking his enemy on the nose.

The Shyser's language immediately became more forcible than elegant, and he consigned the various parts of his body, together with his eyes, to eternal perdition, if he didn't smash Young Jack.

"I'm not going to be a thief!" cried the young one, his father's spirit showing itself in him at this moment.

"Who asked you?" replied the Shyser.

"You did; but I won't do it! I'd starve first! Mind your shins!"

Young Jack dodged under the big boy's arms, and kicked his shins violently, darting away again without being hurt.

"You all-fired young skunk!" cried Shyse, rubbing his shins. "I didn't think you'd got it in you!"

"Let me alone, and I'll be quiet," replied Young Jack, trembling at his unlooked-for success, and expecting it would bring a terrible punishment presently.

"Oh, yes, I'll let you alone! Just come a little nearer to me, will you?" answered Shyse. "Hoopla! I'll make you look as if you'd murdered your uncle, and wanted to hide the body! Oh, you're a bully boy, and don't know nuffin at all, you don't!"

Young Jack picked up half a brick which was laying in the road, ready to his hand.

He knew it was cowardly to throw half bricks.

But self-preservation is the first law of Nature. Shyse was double his size, and he knew that he might expect a terrible licking when the unequal combat came to a close, and he was caught.

Consequently, he did not hesitate.

Like another David attacking an over-grown and boastful Goliah, he hurled the half brick at Shyse.

It struck him in the pit of the stomach, and doubled him up for a moment.

Young Jack took to his heels and ran, not waiting to see the result of the shot.

"Oh!" said Shyse, with a gasp; "my belly's bust entirely. Who'd have thought of his chucking 'arf bricks like that? I'll thank him for that, I guess."

Recovering himself, he rushed off in the gathering darkness, and managed to overtake the little fellow, after about a hundred yards' run.

Young Jack struggled, and kicked, and bit, and scratched, to get away, but all to no use.

His captor held him in a firm grasp.

He did not beat him immediately.

He held him like a cat does a mouse, and played with him, torturing him with a few playful pinches, twists of the ear, and pulling of the tender hair at the nape of the neck and under the temples.

"Say, now," he said, "don't you deserve what you're going to get? I'll hammer you out till you'll stretch from one side of the road to the other. Tap me on the smeller, will you? Bark my shins

like a hickory log, and heave 'arf bricks at me, will you? Oh, you're a nice boy for a Boston tea-party, you are. I'll give it to you, red-hot!"

This was said with sarcastic emphasis, and interspersed with the small attempt at torture we have mentioned, Shyse appearing to enjoy the sport as much as a Red Indian does tormenting a victim at the stake, before the consuming fire is kindled.

Fortunately, Young Jack saw a man passing by.

"Help, sir, help! He's going to kill me!" he cried.

The passer-by stopped.

"What are you doing to that boy?" he asked, sternly.

"Nuffin," answered the Shyser, readily. "He's my little brother. Been out in the streets all day. Mother says it ain't O K. I've got to bring him home. Oh! oh! A reg'lar young rip, and won't go to school, nor do nuffin at all, but play with the bad boys, who teach him to steal."

"It isn't true, sir. I'm—" began Young Jack, when a sharp twist of the ear made him break into a prolonged howl.

The passer-by was a middle-aged man, with a round, benevolent, German sort of face, having a merry twinkle in his eye, and a sort of constitutional or professional smile hovering round the corners of his lips.

"Let him go!" he exclaimed. "I'm going to see this thing through."

"I guess you may take him altogether. Take him home and kiss him, as you seem so fond of him," replied Shyse, impudently.

He pushed Young Jack away from him, and strode off, but before he was aware of his intention, the stranger had made a wonderful bound after him, and with two blows, right and left, rolled him over in the gutter.

"That's for your cheek," said the stranger. "I see what you are, and I calculate you feel mean."

Like all bullies, the Shyser was a coward, and he lay in the gutter, on the hummocky snow, squealing for mercy.

He could beat little boys, but he daren't tackle a grown-up man.

"Oh, how you did jump, sir!" exclaimed Young Jack, admiringly.

"It's my profession," replied the stranger. "I'm Pavonia Pants, the clown. I belong to the troupe playing at the Rink."

"That's where the circus is, sir, isn't it?"

"Yes; Barnum's got the rink; but we'll talk about that afterwards. Come along with me. You shall have a cup of coffee to warm you, and tell me all about yourself."

He took the lad by the hand, and Young Jack trudged along merrily, for the sadness occasioned by the death of Kit, and his forlorn condition, seemed to be lifted from his heart.

There is an instinct in children which tells them when they have met a friend.

A child will not make friends with some people, because his feelings tell him, or rather warn him or her, that such people are hard and wicked, and do not like children.

Young Jack felt instinctively that in Pavonia Pants he had found a friend.

After walking as far as Bowery, Mr. Pants turned into a store, and, changing his mind about coffee, ordered a stew for the little waif he had so providentially met with.

While eating, the boy poured out his little life's history, which the clown listened to attentively.

"We must see what can be done for you," said he, thoughtfully. "Don't you remember the name of the city you were stolen from?"

"No, sir. It was very hot, and it had the sea near it; that's all I recollect."

"Would you like to join the circus, and be a boy-clown? I want a juvenile funnist—eh, my lad?"

"If you would teach me, sir, I'd be so glad!" replied Jack, the tears of gratitude starting to his eyes.

"That's settled. You shall board with me and my wife and child. My little boy is about your age, and he's learning to be a boy-clown. You shall appear together as the Brothers Momus, the most laughable, strike-you-comical, juvenile funnists and bully-boy clowns ever presented to the public."

Young Jack laughed for joy, and clapped his hands with delight at this speech.

"That's the idea, and I guess you'll do well," continued the clown, "and now let's trot. We'll take the Third Avenue cars as far as Forty-seventh-street, where I locate."

"Won't you have something, sir? I've got a few cents," said Young Jack.

"That's not me," answered Pantalia Pants. "Mr. Barnum says he's got a few curiosities, but I'm the most strikingly original of all, and he's going to get me a glass case."

"Why, sir?"

"Because I live in the States, and neither drink, smoke, nor chew. Come along, Jack," said the clown.

They quitted the store together, and once more the poor, lost boy found a resting-place and a friend.

Lately, he had been taught that there is One above who watches over little children.

He believed it now

———

CHAPTER XIX.

MR. MOLE SEES A LITTLE MORE OF THE HUMOROUS SIDE OF THE AMERICAN CHARACTER.

THE frost continuing, the snow became hard, and excellent sleighing gladdened the hearts of the New Yorkers.

Fast-going cutters and family sleighs jostled one another in the Park, and critical judges stood on St. Nicholas Avenue to pass judgment on the respective teams of the Commodore and Bonner.

Felix Prye drove up to the Gilsey House on a bright sunny morning, in an Albany sleigh, and getting out, ascended in the elevator to Jack's rooms.

He knocked at the door.

"Come in!" exclaimed Jack.

All the members of the little party were at home, the ladies being engaged in performing various little feminine tasks.

The men reading the *Times* and *Herald*, and talking politics, in which connection the withdrawal of Cushing and the appointment of Conkling to the Chief Justiceship, together with the riot in Tomkins-square, took prominence.

"Ah! Felix, my boy!" exclaimed Jack; "glad to see you!"

"Where have you been, Mr. Prye?" said Emily; "we haven't seen you since New Years'.'

"Been down to Baltimore on business," replied Felix. "Did you have a good time, Mrs. Harkaway?"

"Oh, yes!" answered Emily. "We gave out downstairs that we would receive, and Hilda and I sat in state, with lunch and wine on the table, and we got about fifteen calls, which, as we haven't been here long and don't know many people, was not bad."

"Not at all," said Felix. "Jack and Harvey went round with me and father, and I guess he's told you we made about sixty calls. What did Mole do?"

"Oh, I must tell you about Mr. Mole!" cried Emily.

"I beg you will do nothing of the sort!" exclaimed the professor.

"I must! I must!" exclaimed Emily, laughing. "It was dinner-time, and Mr. Mole did not come down, so I ran up to the room and knocked.

"'Come in,' said he.

"'What are you doing?' I asked, as I opened the door.

"He was sitting on the floor with a new hat between his knees, and in his hat was about two quarts of water, and in this he was stirring up with the end of his umbrella half-a-dozen dried herrings.

"'Mr. Mole!' I exclaimed, 'what on earth are you doing?'

"'I,' he replied, with a hiccough, and look of surprise. 'Why, Mrs. Harkaway, I'm shtarting an (hic) aquarium for you, Chrithmas (hic).'"

"Mr. Professor," said Felix, "this won't do. I shall have to send you to Yale, and let the Sophomores talk to you as they do to the Freshmen."

"Really, Mr. Pyre," replied Mole, "there is a slight amount of exaggeration in Mrs. Harkaway's manner of telling this story. I will explain it all to you privately. Suffice it to say for the present that I was merely trying an experiment in fish culture."

"Let it be," said Felix. "I have come to ask you to go out for a sleigh-ride."

"You are kind," said Emily.

"Not to you, Mrs. Harkaway. This is a stag party."

"A what?"

"Gentlemen's party. Just got room for Jack, Harvey, and the professor."

"Oh! you disagreeable thing," replied Emily. "Isn't he, Hilda?"

"Yes. I don't like him at all," said Hilda.

"We will have our revenge," said Emily. "We'll order the coupé, and go out shopping."

"Capital!" cried Hilda. "Let us go to A. T. Stewart's, on Broadway, Arnold and Constable's, and Tiffany's."

"Won't it be lovely!" replied Emily. "Tiffany's is charming, and I am so fond of spending money."

"I never knew a woman who wasn't," growled Harvey.

"Oh, you bear!" said his wife.

Felix laughed, and the men speedily got themselves ready.

Putting on furs and caps with ear-laps, and thick gloves to keep out the cold.

"How you lords of the creation tyrannise over us poor women!" remarked Hilda.

"We must go in for women's rights," said Emily, "to redress women's wrongs."

"A woman's mission in this world, my dear," exclaimed Harvey, "is to nurse the baby, cook the dinner, sew buttons on, and read the evening paper to her husband, as, after dinner, he elegantly lounges on the sofa, lazily smoking his twenty-five cent cigar."

"And a man's mission?" asked Hilda.

"Is to love his wife when she is obedient, and to enjoy himself after his own fashion, as seems good to him."

"Oh, you wretch!" said Hilda. "I've a good mind to punch you."

"Hurry up," said Felix.

The men promised to be home in time for dinner, and started on their sleigh-ride.

When they reached the Park, they saw an animated scene.

The "boys in gray" who watch over Central Park stood at different points.

Past the Croton went the sleigh, down the hill beyond Mount St. Vincent, where they obtained a magnificent view of the upper portion of Manhattan Island, and at last emerged on the Boulevard.

They pulled up at Point View House, to have a hot drink at friend Sturges's and see his cunning dog, who can go for a base-ball as well as any player in the States.

Then mounting again, they drove over an un-sheet of snow to Breakneck Hill, afterwards going up to Harlem Bridge, and coming back to Captain Tillson's, when they once more stopped and joined the motley crowd, to refresh the inner man.

Their last call was at Claremont, and here Felix had a long conversation of a private nature with Jack.

"I'm on," exclaimed Jack, smiling.

"You quite understand?" asked Felix.

"Perfectly."

"First," continued Felix. "we take Mole to our house, and my sisters will make him join the B. Y. F. Club."

"Yes."

"Second, he comes to the S. D., or sham dinner."

"Right."

"Third, we make him a Knight of Malta."

"Very good," replied Jack; "I'll help you all I can, old boy."

Felix shook hands with Jack, and they rejoined Harvey and the professor, the latter being quite unconscious of the new plot against his peace of mind.

He had to see a little more of the humorous side of the American character.

"Where's Mole?" asked Jack, as Harvey came up.

"Buying a horse and sleigh," replied Harvey. "He says he's going to start on his own hook."

"Wants to be boss of his own team?" asked Felix.

"So he says; but the horse looks more like a mule than anything else. Come and see it."

Mr. Mole was outside, talking to a sharp, horsey-looking man, who exclaimed, as Jack came up—

"Well, are we to trade on this animal?"

"If you want to commit suicide, professor, you'll trade," said Felix.

"Suicide, my dear Felix," replied Mr. Mole, "is a mistake. Ours is a short life, and must end in a few years, and why kill yourself and then enter upon one which lasts for ever, of the evils of which you know nothing?"

"What have you got to say to this deal?" inquired the owner of the horse, savagely.

"Not much. I only say he's half horse, half alli-gator. He's goose-rumped, cat-hammed, dish-faced, ewe-necked, and got as much slink in his eye as a New York bummer."

"Did you ever see a horse before?" inquired the seller, sarcastically.

"I have; but if that isn't the toughest piece of mule meat that ever looked through a horse-collar, I'm no church-member," replied Felix.

"Look here, captain," said the dealer, "that horse would a heap liefer work than eat. I know I'll be sorry for trading with you. Look at his coat—slicker than a mole's. See him blaze the road."

"You have alluded to a Mole's coat, sir!" exclaimed the professor. "This is an insult! I shall not buy your mule! Take him away; we cannot trade!"

"That's bully," said Felix; "you can fool a coon, but you can't get over a mole."

Mr. Mole walked away, wrapping his fir coat round him, and paying no attention to the would-be horse-dealer, whose mission at that particular moment was decidedly to "cuss."

Felix ran after him and said—

"This way, sir; we're off again. You needn't talk like a Kickapoo Indian."

Mr. Mole only caught the last two words.

"Kick a poor Indian!" he exclaimed. "Who wants to?"

"You'll be the death of me," cried Felix, "if you make me laugh so much."

"I wanted to buy that horse and sleigh," said Mole; "but the man was too familiar. What there is to laugh at in that, or to make you talk about kicking a poor Indian, I can't imagine."

Felix went on laughing, and the party embarked once more in their snow cutter to return to town.

The horse-dealer pushed his way up, and, handing out a pasteboard, said—

"There's my card, sir, if you like to call about the cattle. You're a brick."

"Sir!" exclaimed Mr. Mole, "you have made yourself personal once; I forbid you to do it again!"

"What's to pay now?" inquired the man "Here's my card; my name's on it; Urick Raymond Andy Brick. That's U. R. A. Brick, isn't it?"

"I beg your pardon," replied Mr. Mole; "you have such strange names over here. Excuse me. Come and see me at the Gilsey House, and bring your roadster with you. Good-night."

This little difficulty being settled, the party returned down Eighth Avenue to town.

During the drive, Felix said to Mr. Mole—

"Will you dine with me to-day?"

"With pleasure. Are Harkaway and Harvey coming?" answered Mole.

"Yes. We sent a messenger to ask the ladies to join us."

"That is right. I have enjoyed my stag parties very much, Mr. Prye. I was in doubt whether or not to hit that horse man, but he seemed very civil. You never saw me fight. Some day you shall. I will put on the gloves with you. It is a pretty sight—the prettiest in the world—to see an English gentleman box. We guard with the right, and hit with the left, but you fight with the pistol and the knife here."

"Don't you run away with such a mistaken idea, Mr. Mole," answered Felix.

"Why?"

"You ought to know better by this time. I tell you, I have lived in New York City all my life, and never carried a revolver yet."

"Is that so?"

"If a man wants a row with you, ask him to take a drink, and you're brothers directly. The Americans are no more rowdies than the English."

"I can bear witness to that," replied Jack; "for I have found as much good breeding in New York as I have in London or Paris, and a great deal more warmth and genuine good-feeling."

"Quite agree with you," said Harvey. "There is a hollowness about London society, and the only real hospitality to be found in England is in a country-house."

"If we don't treat you well to-night, I'll give you leave to strike a bee-line for home, right off," remarked Felix. "This is a banquet in honour of the professor, and we mean to do the thing real elegant."

Mr. Mole bowed in acknowledgment of this compliment, and the party returned to the hotel to dress, finding Hilda and Emily nearly ready, they having received a message some time before.

Felix had a short conversation with them, and they nodded their heads and smiled, as if they quite understood that they were to express no surprise at anything they saw.

"We shall make his soul sore, and give him double extract of delirium-tremens before we've done with him," said Felix.

When they were all at Mr. Prye's house, they were introduced to Felix's three sisters, Miss

Statistical Prye, Miss Metaphysical Prye, and Miss Astronomical Prye.

"Dear me! what strange names!" said Mr. Mole to Felix. "Do you christen all your girls like this in America?"

"We wait till they grow up before we name them," answered Felix, "and then we give them suitable names. If a girl shows a liking for the study of history, we should call her Historical. If her mind runs to cats or dogs, we'd name her Catorial or Dogogriphal, so that a man would know the sort of woman he was going to marry by just hearing her name on introduction."

"A strange plan, but a good one," said Mr. Mole "Yours is indeed a singular country."

A coloured help announced dinner, and the professor led in Miss Astronomical Prye.

"You are from Europe?" said Miss A. Prye.

"Yes," answered the professor, for about the six-hundredth time since he had been in New York.

"And how do you like America?"

"I have scarcely had an opportunity of judging," said Mr. Mole, for about the six-hundredth and fifty-first time since his arrival in the country.

"I am told that your skies are not so clear as ours. You have fogs?"

"We have fogs," said Mole, with the air of a man who is admitting an evident truism.

"That would not do for me. I could not view the stars. Stars are my study."

"Indeed!"

"I love stars," continued Miss Astronomical Prye. "I have a telescope. I should have discovered a new planet by this time, had not my mamma forbidden me to sit on the window-sill, nights, for fear of catching a cold in my head."

"Speaking roundly," observed Miss Statistical Prye, "there are seven millions of stars visible to the naked eye, and about 99,900,000 myriad billions of millions invisible to the peeled optic."

"Impossible!" said Mole, aghast at this display of information.

"Oh! it's a fact. Statis makes statistics her study," said Miss Astronomical Prye.

"The heavens, sir," observed Miss Metaphysical Prye, "conceal more mysteries than can be penetrated by human ken. You ascend a mountain and reach the limit of earth; what do you see beyond?"

"I once saw an eagle," replied Mole; "an eagle in the air."

Miss Metaphysical Prye bent a withering look of scorn upon him.

"That eagle, sir," she answered, "should have compelled your thoughts to fly upward, and consider that the soul is merely a fragmentary sparkle of the great pearl of eternity, and will ultimately return to that vast spiritual essence which leavens this dough-like world."

Mr. Mole gasped for breath.

"Metty makes metaphysics her study," observed Miss Astronomical Prye. "What a wife she would make for a studious and thoughtful man!"

"Wonderful!" replied Mole, who did not see it in the same light.

"Are not our girls in advance of yours?"

"Advance is no word for it," replied Mole. "They are tip-top singers, and I should think would drive an average Englishman out of his mind in about six weeks."

"Ah! it is easy to see, sir," answered Miss Astronomical Prye, severely, "that Venus was not in conjunction with Minerva when you were born, and I pity your ignorance, deplore your prejudice, but forgive you, because you are only a benighted Britisher."

Some soup was placed before the professor.

It looked like hot water with a stick of firewood in it.

He tasted it, and did not approve of it.

"May I inquire what this is?" he asked.

"Hard-hickory-hammer-handle soup—a great American delicacy," answered Miss A. Prye.

"Ah! thank you," replied the professor, who tried another spoonful, and, putting his hand on his waistcoat, added, "I think I will wait for the next course."

Everybody else appeared to be relishing the delicacy, for spoons were being raised to mouths, and the company went through the form of eating, if they did nothing else.

When the fish came, a thing that looked like a bit of boiled rope was placed before the professor.

With difficulty he cut it, and tried to eat it, but in vain.

"Is this fish peculiar to the country, may I venture to inquire?" he said, with a ghastly smile.

"This is our famous sensation sea-snapper," answered Miss A. Prye.

"Really, I find it difficult of mastication and will —a—with your permission, wait for the meat."

When the meat was placed on the table, it had the appearance of papier-maché or pulped paper.

The professor was helped to a slice, which he cut, and tried to chew, but his teeth were not equal to the occasion.

"Another American delicacy, I presume?" he said, faintly.

"Oh, yes! this is bear meat."

"Bear!"

"The brown bear of Arkansas."

"Dear me! Fancy eating bear! I will for-bear," answered Mr. Mole. "This is a bare-faced imposition, and more than I can bear. Madame, you must bear with me if I appear rude, but I bare my mind to you, and say frankly I cannot bear this bear."

"Hullo, professor!" said Mr. Prye, senior, "are you through?"

"I am sir," replied Mole, "and if you will permit me, I will withdraw to the nearest restaurant, and have my dinner. I am growing weaker every moment. Up to the present time I have had nothing to eat, and what with hard-hickory-hammer-handle soup, sensation sea-snapper, and Arkansas brown bear meat, I have had enough of American delicacies."

"Come, come," said Mr. Prye. "Wait for the famous feathered fowl of the pathless prairie."

"No, sir; not if I know it."

"Try chicken on the shell."

"Ah! that sounds better. Give me chicken on the shell," replied Mole, brightening up a little. "It sounds odd; but I dare say it eats good."

The coloured servant handed him an egg which had a yellowish appearance.

He broke it open, and a most disagreeable stench came out, while sundry dark-looking fragments swam about in a blackish sort of liquor.

"Ugh! this is an addled egg! The chicken is only half hatched," cried the professor, in disgust. "Ugh! Bah! how it smells! Ugh!"

"That's just the idea. Chicken in the shell," said Mr. Prye.

Everybody burst into a roar of laughter.

"Carry me out. It's gone right down to the bottom of my stomach," continued Mr. Mole. "Oh! that I should have lived to see such a day as this!"

"If it's gone down, you've had something at last," said Miss A. Prye.

"Yes, madame, but a man can't live upon smell," answered Mole, furiously.

Getting up, he rushed from the room, but the whole party came bounding after him, laughing heartily.

Mr. Prye, senior, seized him by the arm, and dragged him into another room, where the table was laid for dinner, just as it had been in the other room.

He forced him into a seat, poured out a glass of champagne, and exclaimed—

"Sit down, my dear sir. It was only a joke. You have had a sham dinner; now you shall have a real one. Serve up! Look spry, there!"

"A sham dinner!" repeated Mole, feebly.

"Yes, sir. Felix was dead sure you would enjoy a little joke, as you are rather down on us Americans, so we treated you to a sham dinner."

"Harkaway," said Mole, "did you know of this?"

"Yes, sir," replied Jack, laughing. "I had a hand in it."

"Just like you," said Mole, trying to smile under the influence of Pomery Sec. "Perhaps Miss Statistical Prye will kindly inform me how many hard-hickory-hammer-handles it takes to make one pint of soup?"

"Don't call me Statistical," replied the young lady, tossing her curls. "My name's Polly; that's my sister Annie; and there is my youngest sister Laura."

"Bless me, ain't you statistical?"

"I know as much about statistics as a lamp-post."

"Ain't you metaphysical, and you astronomical?"

"Not in the least, Mr. Mole. It was only our fun," was the reply from the laughing girls.

The professor looked in a bewildered manner from one to the other.

They crowded round him, smiling like three rosy-faced darlings as they were, and begged his forgiveness.

"My dear young ladies," he said, "I am only glad that Three Graces like yourselves have been clever enough to get some amusement out of an old man like myself."

"Will you try and think better of American people and American institutions?" said Polly.

"I will."

"And never abuse us again?" said Annie.

"Never."

"Now he's good," said Laura, "and we'll make him a member of our B. Y. F. Club, after dinner."

"What's that?" asked Mole.

"You will see. It's a ladies' club, and gentlemen consider it a great honour to belong to it."

"Thank you; I shall be charmed to be admitted to such a society as the B. Y. F.," replied Mole.

An excellent dinner was now served, and every delicacy of the season put before the guests.

The professor forgot his vexation, and warmed into geniality under the influence of the wine.

He forgave soup made of hot water and matches, he pardoned rope stewed with onions, and he forgot brown paper mashed into a pulp and called bear meat.

CHAPTER XXI.

TWO SECRET SOCIETIES.

AFTER dinner, Mr. Mole was left by himself in the dining-room to smoke a cigar, while preparations were made for his initiation into the B. Y. F. Club.

In half an hour's time, Miss Polly Prye came for him.

"We have a small gathering to-night," she said; "only eight. My two sisters and myself and mamma, four; and the others are widow ladies of our acquaintance, who keep their veils down as required by our rules."

"I am ready," replied Mole, "and I consider it quite a distinguished honour to belong to your society."

Miss Polly led him into the drawing-room.

The gas was lowered. The four widow ladies were tall and ungainly. They sat as stiff as pokers on the sofa. Annie and Laura sat at a table.

Polly took her place at the head, and Mole was requested to stand before her.

"Mr. Mole," began Polly, "the society has no authentic history, but the association yearly gathers on its records all the noblest names of the land.

"There is no blackballing, for we never refuse a new member. We have no treasurer, as we receive no fees. I am the president, and my sister Annie is the secretary.

"The grip is given after my remarks are ended, and the password, which is 'Oh,' always follows after the grip.

"Our motto is 'hold fast.'

"The object of our society is to enlighten the ignorance of our fellow-creatures, and to teach them to bear pain with fortitude.

"We may be called the anæsthetics of society.

"When receiving the grip you must not sing, or dance, or otherwise express your joy, or you will cease to be a member of the B. Y. F. Club.

"With this brief exposition of our society, I will proceed to give you the grip, and begin the business of the evening.

"Sister secretary, blindfold the neophyte."

The fair secretary tied a handkerchief over the professor's eyes, and seated him on a chair.

Sounds of badly-suppressed mirth seemed to come from the sofa, where the four tall, veiled widows were sitting.

"Are you ready?" asked Miss Polly Prye.

"Yes," answered Mole.

"You speak in a nervous tone. There is yet time to retreat, should you feel so disposed."

"No. I will go through with it," answered Mole. "I am not so mean as to be frightened by a parcel of girls."

"That shows a right spirit, Mr. Mole. Extend your left hand."

The professor did so.

The president of the B. Y. F. Club seized it in her mouth, and her teeth met it a firm grip.

Mr. Mole sprang to his feet, and uttered the most dismal cries.

"Oh! oh! oh!" he exclaimed. "Let go; you'll bite my finger off! Oh! oh!"

He tore the bandage from his eyes with his right hand, and Polly fell back laughing.

"You are now a member of the Bite Your Finger Club," she said, "and the password 'Oh,' followed the grip as I told you it would."

"Another joke," replied Mole, in a reproachful tone, as he rubbed his finger. "Well, I can say one thing for the American ladies—if they are all like you, they have good teeth."

"Did I hurt?" asked Polly, with a pretty simper.

"Some; but I will forgive you, if you'll not tell Harkaway or Harvey."

"Oh, I promise that."

"And your sisters?"

"Yes," replied Annie and Laura, in chorus.

"That fellow Harkaway is so fond of chaffing, and Harvey is as bad," said Mole. "I daren't tell them anything—they are just like two children."

The four tall widows had burst into a loud guffaw.

Their veils were lifted, and, to his horror, Mr. Mole perceived that he had been watched by Jack, Harvey, Felix and his father, disguised in feminine attire.

"My!" said Felix. "Look at our Johnny! Who will care for mother now?"

"This is another outrage," said Mr. Mole; "but as ladies are concerned in it, I shall say nothing."

"You declared, Mr. Mole, that it was a distinguished honour to belong to the Bite Your Finger Club," said Polly, with an arch look.

"Never mind, sir; I'll make up for it, I guess," continued Felix. "It is the meeting evening of the Knights of Malta. We'll introduce him to the knights, father, shall we?"

"Certainly," replied Mr. Prye, senior. "All distinguished visitors to New York city join the Knights of Malta."

"No more jokes," said the professor.

"Is it likely?" replied Mr. Prye. "We will take off these clothes, and conduct you to the hall in Fourteenth-street, where we shall find the Knights in council."

"I suppose I have to go the whole animal," said Mr. Mole, with a sigh. "A man can't see too much of the manners and customs of a strange country."

"I guess that's so," replied Felix. "Hurry up, father; we must be in time, or the initiations will be over."

Jack and Harvey elected to stay with the ladies and have a musical evening.

Mr. Prye, senior, and Felix took Mr. Mole in charge, and promised to bring him back as soon as possible.

"Have a drop of fusil oil to keep your courage up?" asked Felix.

"What's that?" inquired Mole

"Whisky. There is some Jersey City lightning in that bottle. Try it, before you start."

Mr. Mole did not want to be asked twice.

He took his "lightning" "straight," and quitted the house with his friends, to go to the hall of the Knights of Malta.

A couple of hours later he wished he had stayed at home.

Scarcely had they gone, than Jack heard a disturbance down-stairs.

"That sounds like Monday's voice," he said. "I thought I told him to stay at home."

The noise came nearer, and an altercation on the stair-case between Monday and Washington, the coloured servant of Mr. Prye, was audible.

"Tell you, sar," said Monday, "that I come see Mist Harkaway; know nothink 'bout niggers like you."

"I guess you're no better than a nigger yourself, sar," replied Washington.

"How dare you call me a nigger, sar?" cried Monday. "I prince in my own country."

"You're mean trash, anyhow, and I'd like to set you to hoeing corn on a plantation."

"Want um head punched? Me do it berry soon, sar."

"Go way, you mulatter trash. If I was Mr. Harkaway I'd not keep such a nigger as you. Go 'long, you poor darkey. Heu! heu! heu!" laughed Washington.

"You berry cheeky nigger, me comb um wool," said Monday, angrily.

He rushed upon Mr. Washington, and soon a heavy body was heard falling down-stairs, and going bump, bump, bump, till it rolled on the bottom mat with a dull thud.

"That teach um not to give Monday too much of um cheek," muttered Matabella.

The thickness of a negro's skull is proverbial, and Washington got up none the worse for his fall, vowing vengence upon the "mean counterfeit who had wipped him."

Monday entered the drawing-room, looking the picture of innocence.

"What's that noise?" asked Jack.

"What um noise, sar?" replied Monday. "Oh, a black man, him slip down um stairs, sar."

"Well," said Jack, repressing a smile, "what brings you here?"

"A sort of um nigger come to hotel, sar. He say his name Par-a-wau."

"The Warning Devil!" cried Jack.

"Him very much want see you, sar. Um business not wait, so I bring him on to you."

"Is he here?"

"Yes, sar, um down below."

"Will you allow me, Mrs. Prye, to have him up here? Par-a-wau is an Apache chief, and has already rendered me important services. He mixes with my enemies, and plays the spy on them," said Jack.

"By all means, Mr. Harkaway. Make my house your own," answered Mrs. Prye.

"Show Par-a-wau up," continued Jack; "and look here, let me hear no more quarreling."

"How it my fault, sar, if cheeky niggers fall down um stairs?"

"Don't answer me. Be off."

Monday departed grumbling, and sent up Par-a-wau, and, as Washington carefully kept out of his late antagonist's way, there was no repetition of hostilities.

The Indian entered the room with perfect self-possession, and did not seem astonished at the evidences of wealth and luxury around him.

To his untutored mind, diamonds were little better than glass-beads, and the fact that the lace on some of the ladies' dresses had cost over a thousand dollars did not strike him any more forcibly than a guady mocassin on a squaw's foot would have done.

"Par-a-wau," he said, in his rich, deep, sonorous tone, "has come to warn his white brother."

"About what?" asked Jack.

"Hunston, Fenton, and Leroy were together in Canal-street this day. Par-a-wau make believe to sleep, and overheard their talk."

"Well?"

"They are going to put my white brother in what they call a lunatic asylum, and Hunston will carry off Miss Emily to the Far West. He will pay Leroy and Fenton much big sum of money, and they go to California to mine for gold."

Everybody looked astonished at this revelation of the new plot.

"They can't do it!" said Emily, indignantly. "Put you in a lunatic asylum, indeed! They must be mad to dream of such a thing!"

"Hold on a bit, Emmy," exclaimed Jack. "Let me ask a few questions. Tell me where these men are living, Par-a-wau."

"I do not know. They cross the North River, and live somewhere in Jersey City or Hoboken," was the reply.

"Is that all you have to tell me?"

"That is all."

"I am much obliged to you, Par-a-wau," said Jack, "and I will show you my gratitude by making you a present. Take these bills; you will find one hundred dollars there. Go back to your native plains and your people, and think that one white man stood your friend."

"Par-a-wau never forgets. There is no Winter in his mind; his thoughts are ever green," replied the Indian.

He took the notes with a grateful smile.

Polly Prye took her emerald and diamond drops out of her ears, and handed them to him.

"See," she exclaimed; "here is something for your wife, if you are married."

"Par-a-wau has a squaw, whose heart is beating for him, and his papooses strain their eyes to see him coming. The poor Indian will think of his white sister."

"And here is a Bible," exclaimed Laura Prye. "Read that, Par-a-wau, and become a Christian."

"Par-a-wau cannot read," answered the Indian. "He will not take the book."

"Good-bye," said Jack; "start early to-morrow, and get West. If we should meet again, it will be far from here, but I shall always think of you as a good sort of fellow."

Par-a-wau advanced a step, and seizing Jack's hand, raised it to his lips.

Then he stalked from the room, looking grand and majestic, in spite of the ill-fitting rags that clothed him.

Civilisation could not hide the dignity natural to the Apache chief, nor could the degradation he had suffered among the whites subdue his native pride, or stamp out his wild spirit.

"That's an extraordinary creature," remarked Harvey.

"Poor fellow," said Jack; "he is lost in a city, and I shall be glad to think I have enabled him to return. Rum is the curse of such as he, and he has found it out, to his cost."

He proceeded to tell Par-a-wau's history as it had been related to him, and the ladies expressed a good deal of sympathy for him.

Laura was indignant that he should have refused her Bible, and predicted that he would come to a bad end.

The conversation, however, soon turned upon the singular communication made by the Warning Devil.

It was something to know what the enemy was about.

Hunston, Fenton, and Leroy were hiding, preparatory to striking a final blow at Jack, before they separated.

It had always been Hunston's purpose to get rid of Jack, and then possess himself of Emily, whom he had loved with a savage passion since he was a mere boy.

"I don't understand the law over here," observed Emily; "but it seems to me impossible to put a man into a lunatic asylum when he is sane."

"The certificate of two doctors will do it, and if the proprietors of a private asylum row in with the doctors, it is difficult to get a man out," answered Mrs. Prye.

"Indeed?"

"About seven years ago there was a fearful exposure of the system. A lady was illegally confined in a private asylum. She escaped, and the matter came before the courts."

"We will soon have you out, Jack," said Harvey.

"My dear fellow," answered Jack, "I have the strongest possible objection to go."

"You must be careful, now you know what the villains are about."

"You bet I shall be."

"Have you had any news of your child?" inquired Mrs. Prye.

"Not a word," replied Jack. "Par-a-wau said, some time ago, there was no child with Hunston. I cannot make it out."

"Perhaps he ran away when Hunston was in prison."

"It may be so."

"I would rather believe he was a wanderer in the streets of New York than think him in the power of that dreadful man," said Emily.

"Time will show," replied Jack.

A dead silence fell over the group, and Mrs. Prye saw, when it was too late, that she had started a disagreeable subject of conversation.

Soon the ladies rose to go.

Tears stood in Emily's eyes, for she could not refrain from weeping when she thought of her child.

"It's late," said Hilda, "and I do not think we will wait for Mr. Mole. Will you kindly say good-night to Mr. Prye and Felix?"

"Certainly," answered Mrs. Prye. "We shall be glad to have you come again soon."

The carriages were ordered round, and the party returned to the hotel, where they found Felix in the hall.

"Where is Mole?" inquired Jack.

"Oh! he's mad!" answered Felix. "I thought I would wait and tell you. I followed him here, but he won't speak to me."

"He'll be all right in the morning. Won't you come up?"

"I guess I'll get back. I want to have you go skating with me on the lake. The flag's up on the cars, and the ice bears," answered Felix.

They shook hands, and Jack followed the ladies and Harvey upstairs.

Mr. Mole was pacing the room in an agitated manner, and talking to himself.

"What have they being doing with you, sir?" asked Jack.

"Another sell, Harkaway," replied the professor. "That Knights of Malta Society is as big an imposition as the sham dinner, or the B. Y. F. Club."

"How's that?"

"You shall hear. I was taken into a large hall, where there were nearly fifty men, wearing black cloaks and masks. Some were clad in armour, and had drawn swords."

"It was imposing."

"Yes. In more senses than one. The president ordered me forward, and said I must answer his questions truthfully, and pass the ordeals before I could become a Knight."

"Did you?"

"He asked me if I wore my own hair, and, not liking to say no, I replied that I did, whereupon a man behind me whipped off my wig, and every one roared. Then he asked me if I drank, and I replied 'Nothing but water,' when the same man pulled my private flask of whisky out of my pocket and handed it round."

"You didn't pass for telling the truth," remarked Harvey.

"That's what the president said, and he ordered me to go through the ordeals. They took me up in a gallery and bandaged my eyes. Then they sent me sliding down a plank, and, when I reached the bottom, I fell into a blanket and was tossed up and down for ten minutes.

"After that, I was told to sit down and rest myself, but I soon jumped up, as the seat was studded with needles. Oh! my! I boil with rage when I think of it.

"Telling me I was hot, they put me under what they called the cooler, and, pulling a string, about a ton of water came down on me. I fell on my face, and couldn't get up. If they hadn't stopped it, I should have been drowned.

"What more they would have done to me I don't know, but I got mad, rushed at the president, knocked him down, seized his sword, cut my way through the crowd, hit old Prye on the head, and bolted."

"It's a great shame!" said Emily.

"I thought I was going to join an ancient and honourable society, instead of which I was made a fool of, and I don't like it," replied Mole.

"It was very silly to do what Nature had done already," remarked Harvey.

"If I catch you, Harvey, you'll regret joking at my expense," cried the professor.

"It is your own fault," said Jack. "You run down the people and their institutions, and they have their revenge upon you."

"Please God I once get back to England, I'll stay there," answered Mole, with a groan.

Emily mixed him a glass of hot grog, and persuaded him to go to bed, w   bling bad language to himself, and consigning his tormentors to a place which shall be nameless.

CHAPTER XXII.

THE CHAMPION JUVENILE FUNNISTS AND BULLY-BOY CLOWNS OF AMERICA.

"I LIKE you, Jack," exclaimed little Jeff Pants, a month after his father, the clown, had found and brought the lost boy to his home.

"So do I you, Jeff," answered Young Jack. "I never saw a boy I liked so much, except Kit."

"Ah!" said Jeff, with a grave shake of the head, "you've told me about Kit. That was sad, some. Did you plant the flowers on his grave, he spoke about?"

"Yes, I did that when I had a holiday last Sunday."

"Poor Kit!" said Jeff, tossing up three balls and catching them, which was a part of his performance.

"When do we appear?" asked Young Jack. "Are we underlined yet?"

He was becoming quite proficient in professional slang.

"Haven't you seen the bills?" replied Jeff; "we're out as large as life in all the posters. We're the Brothers Momus."

"Are we?"

"And the Champion Juvenile Funnists, and Bully-Boy Clowns of America."

"My!" said Young Jack, "that sounds well."

"To-morrow night we come on at the Rink. Do you think you can go through?"

"I can tumble, and have got my patter by heart, and know how to gag."

"Ah! but you can't tumble like me," said Jeff.

"The riding on the ponies is the most difficult," said Young Jack. "You've got to jump well, to go through the hoops, and 'light on the pony's back."

"Oh! that's nothing. Father says you've learnt very quick. We shall make a sensation"

"I hope so, for his sake. He's been so good to me."

"Father's real kind," said Jeff. "Every one likes him. Stand steady, Jack; I'm going to run up you."

Young Jack steadied himself, and Jeff sprang up his back, landing on his shoulders, on which he stood, kissing his hands to an imaginary audience, while Jack held his feet and walked round.

Sitting down, he tumbled over and over, made himself into a ball, unrolled himself, let Jack make a wheelbarrow of him, then take him by the leg and throw him away, he always alighting on his feet, and making a bow to the said imaginary audience, and saying, "La! la!"

Then Young Jack said "La! la!" and allowed himself, in his turn, to be rolled about and twisted. At last he lay down flat, and Jeff ran over him, to show that he was flat, and stepped on him, and otherwise mangled him, only in the end to lift him up horizontal and rigid, whereupon they both made wonderful head-and-heels somersaults, crying "La! la!" louder than ever to the imaginary audience, finally kissing hands and making bows, in acknowledgment of loud applause from phantom spectators.

"That ought to fetch them," said Jack, rather short of breath.

"It will. Now let's do the Heathen Chinee. You be the Chinee. Get a euchre pack of cards, and put the jacks up your sleeves. So, when I go for you, dodge me all around, and trip me up until I say 'La!' when you must let me get a hold of your pigtail. That comes off and you exit."

This was one of their set bits of acting, Young Jack being dressed as a Chinaman, and Jeff as a California miner. It was very comical, and entitled "The Heathen Chinee; or, a Harte-full Game," being a delicate allusion to Mr. Bret Harte, and a cunning violation of grammar in the use of the word "artful."

When the eventful night came for the Brothers Momus to make their first appearance before a New York, or any other audience, they felt a little nervous.

The gas dazzled them, and the sea of faces swam before their eyes; but the applause which greeted their first contortions encouraged them.

"Get on, Jeff," whispered Young Jack; "they can't eat us."

"They'd find us tough, I guess, if they did, for we'd tumble about inside," answered Jeff, in the same tone.

The boy-clowns made up very well in their quaint dresses and powdered, painted faces.

Young Jack's "Here we are again!" and Jeff's "Give me a slice of puddin', or I'll have to burgle a candy-store!" was received with roars of laughter.

When they came to their tricks, and did their tumbles, and performed the Heathen Chinee, there was no mistaking the hearty appreciation of the audience.

"They're a hit! they'll run!" said Pavonia Pants, delightedly.

Sundry policemen, and people with baskets of meat and fish, came on, as in a pantomime, and were cruelly robbed and shamefully ill-treated by the Brothers Momus, as is the custom in such entertainments.

At length the ponies were brought in, and the Juvenile Funnists showed how they could ride the bare-backed steed, and jump through paper hoops.

But when the Bully-Boy Clowns pretended to be afraid, and sat with their backs towards the horses' heads, and held on to the horses' tails, the laughter and applause culminated, until the Rink fairly shook with the enthusiasm.

Then the Brothers Momus, *alias* Juvenile Funnists, *alias* Bully-Boy Clowns of America, sprang into the saw-dust and contortioned and went on anyhow, doubling up their spines, and trying to make believe they had no bones, and cried, wildly, "La! hoopla! la! la!" and eventually made pretty bows and kissed their hands, as has been the custom of boys in a circus from time immemorial.

Then they ran wildly behind, only to come on again in answer to the prolonged applause, and make more bows and do more kissing of hands, until the audience screamed itself hoarse, and thought fit to subside.

"That's bully," said Pavonia Pants, as he patted the heads of the infant clowns.

The members of the company were unanimous in endorsing this opinion.

Even the manager smiled, but a snake lurked in his grass, for he had only made a three months' engagement, at a low price, and knew he would have to give a rise of fifty cents on the dollar to renew.

The boys were not old enough to excite envy in the heart of any one, and they were congratulated on all hands.

"At their age," said Pavonia Pants, "I could not have done it better myself. In fact, I could not have done it at all. It's bully, I tell you."

Changing their property-dresses for their own clothes, the Brothers Momus returned home with Pavonia Pants, who stood treat on the way, and gave them each a box-stew, and bought them some candy to put under their pillows, and suck at if they woke in the night.

Whereat the Brothers Momus were highly delighted.

They now knew what fame was, and eagerly looked forward to a sight of the morning papers.

They had worked hard, Young Jack especially, and at an early age he had solved the problem of life.

Hard work meant success, and success brought fame, and fame brought its own reward in the shape of oysters and subsequent candy.

What more could little boys under ten years of age desire?

We pause for a reply.

CHAPTER XXIII.

YOUNG JACK'S BLOOD SEEMED TO FREEZE IN HIS VEINS. A DIZZINESS CAME OVER HIM, AND HE FELL HEAVILY TO THE GROUND.

ALL the sight-seeing portion of New York flocked to the Rink, to witness the performance of the Juvenile Funnists.

The Boy-Clowns were pronounced something novel, and worthy of a visit.

About ten days after Young Jack's first appearance, the Rink was crowded to overflowing.

A gentleman in the front seats seemed to take a great interest in the performance.

By his side sat another, who spoke hurriedly to him as the boys came on.

"I'm off," he said. "It won't do for me to be seen in it."

"Are you sure?" said the other.

"Quite."

"He is the lad?"

"I'm dead sure he is, or I shouldn't say so."

"Right. Leave me to work it."

The man rose and took his departure, and it was remarkable that one sleeve of his coat hung down by his side, as if he had only one arm.

In the eye of the man who remained was a fascinating gaze, which was fixed upon Young Jack.

The boy did not feel it until the pony trick came on, and he had to go round the Rink.

When this happened, he was close to the man with the fascinating eye, and he trembled all over.

A second time he passed him.

Young Jack's blood seemed to freeze in his veins. A dizziness came over him, and he fell heavily to the ground.

Instantly there was a great commotion among the spectators.

The pony cantered on, and the attendants hastily bore the boy into the rear.

"Shame! Shame!" cried the women. "He was too young for this sort of thing, and I guess any one might have told how it would end."

"Perhaps he's dead," said the men.

The man with the evil eye slipped away in the confusion, and went behind the scenes.

At this moment the manager stepped forward.

"Ladies and gentlemen," he said, "I regret to inform you that one of the talented Brothers Momus is slightly injured by a fall from his pony. He will appear before you again in a few days. The performances will this evening proceed with the wonderful equestrian feats of Miss Victoria Vincent."

The man with the evil eye was Miles Fenton.

He heard the disapprobation of the audience at this speech, and smiled with satisfaction.

It was his infernal gaze which had upset Young Jack's equilibrium and caused him to fall.

The poor boy was lying on some sawdust near to where the elephants were fastened.

Round him stood a sympathising group, prominent among whom was Pavonia Pants.

A dog known as the elephant's dog, on account of the fondness displayed towards him by those animals, licked his hand.

On his knees, by Young Jack's side, was Jeff, who was deeply grieved at the accident which had occurred to his friend.

"I'd have given a thousand dollars rather than this should have happened," said Pavonia Pants.

"Are you in pain much, Jack?" asked Jeff.

"It's very bad about the right leg, Jeff," said the boy.

"What a time that doctor is coming!" said Pavonia Pants, in an impatient tone.

Miles Fenton, sure of his prey, pushed his way through the crowd.

"Stand back there!" he said. "I know this boy!"

"Are you a doctor?" asked Pavonia Pants.

Fenton stooped down and examined Young Jack carefully.

"I know enough of surgery to tell you," he replied, "that the lad's leg is broken. But, what is more to the purpose, I am his uncle. He has been stolen from his home, and I shall at once restore him to his family, by whom he will be well taken care of."

"What!" exclaimed Pavonia Pants. "Take my Boy-Clown? Take my Juvenile Funnist? After I've trained him? No, you don't!"

"If you will have the goodness to tell me what right you have to detain him, as a means of earning your bread, I shall be obliged," answered Fenton.

This question rather staggered Pavonia Pants.

He knew he had no legal claim to the boy.

"Ask him," he answered. "Ask him whether he'd rather go with you, or stay with me."

"I shall do nothing so utterly absurd," said Fenton. "The boy is my nephew, and I shall remove him from an influence which has already resulted in a broken limb."

"How can you prove that you are his uncle?" asked the old clown.

"If I am asked by the proper authorities, I can give chapter and verse, but I shall merely give you my card."

The clown took a card, on which was written in ink, "Mr. Browenbark, 499, West Fifty-ninth-street."

"How do I know this is not a fake name and a fake address?" said Pavonia Pants.

"Don't talk to me," replied Fenton. "The boy requires surgical assistance, and I must take him away in a coach at once."

"But—"

"There is no but about it. You found the boy in the street, and you could not substantiate any claim to him in any court in the States."

"Is that so?" asked the clown, scratching his head.

Fenton cut short the discussion by taking Young Jack in his arms, and bearing him, groaning, along the corridor.

Lions, tigers, hyenas, monkeys, and other caged creatures looked curiously at him as he passed by them.

Pavonia Pants followed, not knowing what to do.

When Miles Fenton looked into his eyes, he was, as it were, petrified, and lost his energy.

The terrible glance of the evil eye unnerved him.

Jeff was half tearful, half angry.

"Say, pa," he exclaimed, "you ain't going to let that man run off with our Jack?"

"He's a relation, Jeff," replied the clown.

"But our Jack isn't well enough to go. He's hurt badly."

"That's so. Still, I can't help it."

"Well, I call that real mean," said Jeff. "Can't you go for him and fetch him back? Oh, don't I wish I was bigger! He shouldn't tote off our Jack like that. Where'll I be without my Brother Momus? Why, I'll be only half a boy-clown."

THE DOOR WAS THROWN VIOLENTLY OPEN, AND JACK BOUNDED IN AND SEIZED HER BY THE ARM.

At any other time Pavonia Pants would have laughed at this speech.

But just then he did not feel like laughing at all. It was a very serious matter to him.

They had reached the entrance by this time, and Fenton was about to emerge on the street.

"Where are you going to take him to?" cried the old clown.

"You've got the address. What more do you want? Stand out of my way!" answered Fenton, angrily.

Young Jack had fainted, owing to the pain he was suffering.

But just then he came to himself, opened his eyes, and saw that he was being borne away from his friends and protectors.

"Save me! save me!" he exclaimed. "If you send me away, I shall die! Jeff, don't let them take me!"

His piteous and dispairing accents rang through the air, touching a chord in the hearts of father and son.

"I'll bite his legs, and hamper him, dad," said Jeff, "while you hammer on to his face."

Pavonia Pants approached Fenton threateningly, but the gleaming barrel of a pistol was presented at him, and he hesitated.

"Advance another step, and, by Heaven! I fire!" cried Fenton.

The clown did not dare risk his life, or run the chance of being wounded, for his living depended upon his being "sound in wind and limb," as they say of horses when they want to sell them.

"It's no sort of use, Jeff," he exclaimed; "we must be by this."

Lower down the street was a coach, and out of the window of it a man was frantically waving his arm.

"Come on!" he exclaimed, fiercely. "Why the deuce don't you make haste? One would think you'd turned fool!"

Miles Fenton expedited his pace, and opening the door of the coach, pitched his burden on the front seat, regardless of the suffering caused by his brutal conduct.

"Drive on across town," he said to the hackman, "and get to the Christopher-street Ferry. We're going over to Hoboken."

Presently the coach was rattling down Third Avenue, and then cutting across through Fifty-second-street.

The man in the coach was Hunston, and a savage gleam of triumph, such as a fiend might have indulged in. sat on his hard face, the lines of which were drawn tightly down.

"Sit up, you young whelp!" he exclaimed. "I want to have a look at you. My eyes haven't had such a feast for a long time."

"He can't," said Fenton.

"Why not?"

"His leg's broken. I gave him one of my magnetic mesmeric looks, and he went off his pony in the circus."

"Curse him, he shall sit up, I say!" cried Hunston. "What do I care if he has a broken leg? I've only one arm through his father's firing at me. It would be a good revenge to make the son a dot and go one."

Without showing the slightest pity for the poor boy, Hunston forced him to sit up on the seat, which he did, his eyes full of tears, and moaning with the pain.

"You're a precious young skunk to run away, aren't you?" continued Hunston. "I'll teach you to give me your leg another time. You cannot run now."

With a refinement of cruelty, he struck the child heavily on the head and over the arms, twisted his ears, and pulled his hair, and thumped him on the back of the neck, as if he had been a rabbit he wanted to kill.

"Curse you! how I hate you for your father's sake!" he said. "I hate you worse than poison!"

"Don. ... .. now, please," implored Young Jack. "I'm not strong enough to bear it, and you may say what you like about my father, but he wouldn't be such a coward as to hit a little boy with a broken leg."

"Call me a coward, will you?" thundered Hunston. "Curse him! I think I shall kill him, Fenton!"

He rained a shower of blows upon the defenceless head of the little fellow.

"Not good enough, Hunston," said Fenton. "Turn it up. Hang it all, we are-men!"

Young Jack saved Hunston any further trouble in making up his mind whether or not he would continue his inhuman treatment.

His eyes closed once more, he drew his breath shortly. His head fell back, and he fainted for the second time.

"The little viper. I believe he's shamming," said Hunston.

He drew his scarf-pin from his shirt-front, and ran it into the boy's flesh.

Not a sound of consciousness was elicited.

"He's off right enough; let him be," said Fenton.

"Very well," Hunston replied; adding, "My! isn't this a lucky night? Who'd have thought when you and I started for a bit of a spree up-town, that we should make such a glorious haul as this?"

"Our luck's on," answered Fenton.

"Now, we've only got to let Harkaway gnaw his heart out in a lunatic asylum, run away with Emily, and get right away out West," said Hunston.

"Remember," said Fenton, "that you have promised me fifty thousand dollars for what I've done for you."

"You shall have the money."

"I think I've earned it."

"Just wait until you've finished your work," said Hunston, "and I'll pay up. Leroy shall have ten thousand, and you fifty. I've got plenty of dollars. You don't suppose I was with the brigands for over a year without making my pile?"

"That's all right. I thought I'd remind you of our bargain."

"You're entitled to your pay as agreed upon, and, as things appear to go smoothly now, I'll cash up shortly. We must get this young cub's leg set to-night."

"Shall you take him West with you?"

"No. I shall apprentice him to a burglar, and give him his right name, 'Jack Harkaway,'" replied Hunston.

"Why?"

"Because I want to hear that Jack Harkaway is a villain, a thief, and a fiend, who gets hung for murder."

"Who will teach him his business?" asked Fenton.

"Leroy. Isn't our Sensitive Sheepe, as he calls himself, the prince of villains and hypocrites?"

"I guess that's so."

"Well, I shall pay Leroy to take this young Jack Harkaway, and make him a bigger scoundrel than any in New York, and that's going high."

"It is."

"That boy," said Hunston, emphatically, pointing to the insensible child, "shall spend half of his young life in prison, and end it on the gallows."

Miles Fenton regarded Hunston with admiration.

"You're a genius," he said.

"I tell you," replied Hunston, "that revenge on Harkaway is the business of my life."

"What's he done to you, that you should hate him so bitterly?"

"I always did hate him. We were enemies at school, and when we went to sea. He always did things better than me, and got on better I always got the dirty end of the stick, and, after all he shot my arm off. Curse him! I hate him!"

The bad, vindictive man ground his teeth and clenched his fists savagely.

"By Jove!" he went on, when the paroxysm was over, "isn't mine a splendid revenge? Isn't it, eh?"

"It's mighty fine," answered Fenton.

"I put the father in a lunatic asylum. That's better than killing him, because a mad-house is a living death to a man like Jack Harkaway."

"Yes."

"I apprentice the son to Leroy, who will make him the king of thieves and villains."

"Yes," said Fenton again.

"And I run away with the wife and mother. I make her my paramour, and finally cast her off to go and earn her bread as best she may in the wilds of the Far West."

"By Jove!" exclaimed Fenton, "you're the tallest hater I ever met with, and. as I admire original geniuses, I feel proud of your acquaintance, and esteem it an honour to shake you by the hand."

The hands of the two men met in a cordial grasp, and the coach drew up at the Christopher-street

Ferry. The boat was just in, they drove on board, crossed the North River, and were taken to the house they lived in at Hoboken.

Young Jack was lifted out of the coach, and put on a bed, while a doctor was sent for.

His hurt was found to be an oblique fracture of the femur, which was reduced and set in splints.

Young Jack was in the power of his enemies.

His horizon was clouded over once more, and the hand of Fate had dealt roughly with him.

What would his future be ?

Time alone would show.

CHAPTER XXIV.

" CALL ME MAD, DO YOU ?" CRIED JACK. " I'LL LET YOU KNOW WHETHER I'M MAD OR NOT !"

" HULLO! I've overslept myself," said Jack, jumping out of bed. He looked at his watch, and found it was twelve o'clock.

Hastily getting into his bath, he dressed himself and rang for Monday.

He had been to the Heavy Weights, or Fat Men's Ball the night before, and after that, he had gone to the French Ball.

This accounted for his feeling rather heavy in the morning

Monday answered the ring.

" Where are the ladies ?" inquired Jack.

" Missy Emily and Missy Hilda gone out in um soupé, sar," replied Monday.

" To make calls ?"

" No, sar. Gone to um drygood's store, and to um Tiffany's."

" Where's Mr. Harvey ?"

" Him gone with um, sar."

" And Mole ?"

" Mr. Mole gone out to get um first swiggle, sar," replied Monday, with a grin.

" Order me some fried oysters and a canvas-back in my private room. I shall be down directly," said Jack.

He completed his toilet, and ate his breakfast, running over the columns of the *Times* and *Herald*.

Just as he had got through, Monday appeared.

" Two gentlemen to see you, sar," he said.

" Their names ?" demanded Jack.

" Doctor Crore and Doctor Sankin."

" What, in thunder," said Jack, " do two doctors want to see me for ? By Jove! this may be Hunston's dodge. Par-a-wau warned me. Two doctors! that means mischief. Send them up, Monday, and stay in the room."

" Yes, sar."

" Have you got your knife ?"

" Me always carry um knife, sar," said Monday, displaying the keen-edged weapon which had done so much good service among the brigands.

" Look here, Monday," said Jack; " you and I are old friends, aren't we? You like me as much as I like you ?"

" Monday try to show that he would die for Mast' Jack, if that any good."

" I know you have, lots of times," replied Jack.

" What wrong now ?" asked Monday.

" Hunston is at work, and wants to shut me up in a lunatic asylum. Once there, I should be helpless, and the proprietor could do what he liked with me. Unarmed, I should be unable to fight against the keepers."

" You not mad, Mast' Jack," said Monday, with a scornful smile.

" Of course I'm not; but it's Hunston's game to have me locked up; and these doctors who want to see me are probably sent by him."

" What they do, sar ?"

" Sign a certificate, and seize me when and how they can," replied Jack, shuddering at the prospect.

It took a great deal to frighten Jack, but he did tremble at the idea of being confined in a madhouse, the proprietor of which would be in the pay of Hunston, and not at all scrupulous as to the means he employed to turn a sane man mad, if he was well enough remunerated for it.

Monday brandished his knife.

" Me go and stick um, sar ?" he asked.

" Don't do anything, unless I tell you. Show them up, and don't leave the room."

Monday was not gone long, and when he returned he had with him two gentlemen of middle age, both of whom wore spectacles and had long noses. They were dressed in black, and carried their hats and gloves in their hands.

" Mr. Harkaway, I presume ?" said one.

" That is my name," replied Jack, stiffly.

" Ah! don't be excited, my dear sir. I am Doctor Sankin. This is my esteemed friend, Doctor Crore. Ahem! Doctor Crore, Mr. Harkaway; Mr. Harkaway, Doctor Crore."

" What do you want with me ?" inquired Jack.

" We have called in a friendly way to ask you a few questions," said Doctor Sankin.

" Indeed !"

" A few simple questions. That is the way to put it, Crore—eh ?"

" Certainly," replied Doctor Crore. " We have come to interview you, sir."

" Ahem! glad I meet with your approbation. Now, tell me, is it not a fact, Mr. Harkaway, that you labour under the delusion of having peritonitis in the diaphragm, and that your alimentary canal is crowded with rats ?"

" Which is the reason he will not eat Indian corn on Sundays," put in Doctor Crore."

" Exactly."

" Look here," said Jack; " I can see what your game is, and if you don't clear out, I shall have to make you."

He made a threatening movement, and the doctors retreated precipitately towards the door.

" Do *not* be excited, my dear sir," said Doctor Sankin, persuasively.

" A symptom of the disease," remarked Doctor Crore.

" One question more," said Doctor Sankin. " Are you not subject to a vertebrate spasm, which leads to an enlargement of the cerebellum, and makes you imagine that you have an elastic or india-rubber mind, which expands with heat and contracts with cold ?"

" You couple of miserable quacks !" said Jack. " Get out !"

" Clear case—eh, Sankin ?" said Crore.

" Never was a clearer; the man is mad !" replied Sankin.

" Mad !" cried Jack; " am I mad? I'll let you know whether I'm mad or not. Call me mad, do you ?"

He went for Sankin, who had neared the door, and was closely followed by Crore.

" My dear sir, do not be excited," said Sankin.

" Yes, pray be calm," said Crore.

Jack seized Sankin, and administered such a severe thumping to him that he yelled with pain.

Crore tried to escape, but Monday intercepted him as he had his hand on the door-handle, and, imitating his master's example, beat him within an inch of his life.

" Out you go !" exclaimed Jack, as he kicked the wretched Sankin into the passage.

" You go and join um friend," cried Monday, casting the equally miserable Crore after him.

The doctors picked each other up, and with bloody noses, torn clothes, and aching limbs, descended the stairs, feeling sorry they had not staid at home that morning.

Jack threw himself into a chair and laughed heartily.

"The vagabonds won't come here again," he said.

"Me got um knife ready!" exclaimed Monday, adding, "Who do this, sar?"

"Hunston."

"Oh!" said the black, reflectively, "that Hunston bad man. If had him in my own country, Limbi, kill, eat him."

"I wish he'd break his neck," answered Jack. "There is no peace for me while he lives."

He got up and put on his hat.

"Um going out, sar?" asked Monday.

"Yes. If I am asked for, say I have taken the cars to the Park to have a good walk. I feel rather cobwebby about the head, and want a spin," answered Jack.

He took an umbrella, in case it should rain, as the wind had changed, bringing about a rapid thaw, and the sky was heavy and lowering.

It was about as disagreeable a day as could well be imagined for walking; but Jack had his gum-shoes on, and a thick coat, so he cared little for the weather.

His mind was not at rest.

He had been some weeks in America now, and had made little or no progress in the work he had crossed the Atlantic to accomplish.

All his efforts to discover Young Jack were made in vain.

Hunston, Miles Fenton, and Leroy were conspiring together.

There was danger ahead.

But he was the last man in the world to cave in and give up because he was threatened with peril.

As he walked along, plunged in deep thought, with his eyes cast on the ground, he did not remark two men who were closely following him.

When he hailed the cars on Broadway, they did so too.

Instead of getting inside, they jumped on the board with the driver, and stood there smoking.

When the Park was reached, and Jack got out and walked over the fast-melting snow, they kept him well in view.

Behind them came a coach at a walking pace, and once one of the men spoke a few words in a low tone to the driver.

The man then proceeded at a trot, and got in advance of Jack.

He was thus between two fires.

All unsuspicious of being dogged, he threaded the Park, his spirits rising as he went along, for he began to feel that exhilaration which always comes of vigorous exercises in the open air.

Though not much in the humour to raphsodise, he could not help admiring the way in which Art had aided Nature in this beautiful and picturesque Park.

Clad as it was in wintry garments, there was something to be charmed with at every step.

The graceful pines, firs, and other trees were yet laden with their snowy burden, and the rugged, undulating masses of rock were white with the same virgin covering.

Grand and spacious as Hyde Park, in London, pretty and well laid out as is the Beulogne Wood of Paris, these gems of Europe are eclipsed by the Central Park of New York.

There were very few people in the Park, the heavy weather keeping the pleasure-seekers at home.

Jack had come to a lonely and sequestered spot, and paused to light a cigar.

The men who had been so diligently following him crept up noiselessly, their footsteps being deadened by the melting snow.

One raised a heavy club and dealt him a blow from behind.

He staggered and fell on his knees.

A mist came over his eyes, and all was dark.

He had lost consciousness, and as he extended himself on the ground he was seized and rapidly conveyed to the coach.

The men placed him inside, took their places by him, and as his head sunk on the shoulder of one of them, the other, in a hoarse voice, exclaimed—

"Drive on!"

"That's well done," said the other. "Eh, Leroy?"

"Yes," growled Miles Fenton, "I thought we should have had some trouble with him—he is so cursedly strong."

The coach rolled rapidly away in the direction of Washington Heights, and Jack lay like a log of wood between his captors.

CHAPTER XXV.
A PUNCH FROM A TRIP-TICKET.

WHEN night came, and Jack did not appear, his friends became alarmed.

Monday threw all the light he could upon the matter, and spoke of the visit of the men who called themselves doctors, and asked the ridiculous questions which had put Jack in a rage.

Emily became violently hysterical, and it was as much as Hilda could do to keep her from fainting away.

Unfortunately, she was deprived of the services of her maid, Ada, who was unwell, and Monday was constantly in attendance on his wife.

Mr. Mole and Harvey sent for Felix Prye, in whose judgment they had great confidence.

They fancied that his experience and knowledge of the country would be of service to them in this emergency.

Besides this, they knew that Felix really liked Jack, and was just the sort of whole-souled young American who would leave no stone unturned to serve a friend.

When Felix came in, he was at once placed in possession of the facts, as far as they were known, and his opinion was asked.

"There isn't a doubt in my mind," he replied.

"As to what?"

"He's been carried off to some asylum by Hunston and Co."

"Jack's been in many a tight fix before this," said Harvey, "but he's never been in a mad-house. I wonder what he'll do?"

"Do?" repeated Felix. "Why he's got a right smart chance to make them squirm."

"Poor Jack!" said Emily, checking her grief. "Perhaps they will drive him mad altogether."

"Drive Jack mad!" cried Harvey. "That's a good joke. When they do that, the sky will fall, and we shall catch larks."

"He's a great deal more likely to send them mad," remarked Mr. Mole. "He has very often placed me on the verge of insanity with his tricks."

"It's my opinion you've staid there," said Harvey.

"Where?"

"On the verge."

"Now you're going back on Mole," said Felix. "Just hush right up, and let us talk this matter out."

"No," said Mr. Mole. "You may talk amongst yourselves. I have a private room, and I am going to it. If Harvey thinks he can insult me with impunity, he is mistaken, as I shall resent it in my own fashion. I could have assisted your deliberations —but no matter."

Mr. Mole walked away in high dudgeon to his own room.

"You've sent him a-humpin'," said Felix. "I guess Mole's an awful wise chap, and can't stand sass; best let him alone, and he'll simmer down."

"Never mind him," said Harvey. "Will you give us the benefit of your advice in this crisis?"

"Why, certainly."

"What's to be done about Jack?"

"We must find out in what asylum he has been placed, and get him out. We'll advertise and put on some private detectives. That's all that can be done at present," replied Felix.

"Do you think we shall find him again, Mr. Prye?" asked Emily.

"Do you expect to see the sun again, to-morrow, Mrs. Harkaway?"

"Of course."

"Then you may calculate upon your husband's appearance on the festive scene in a short time. Bear up, and congratulate yourself it's no worse."

"I'm glad you've come," said Emily, more cheerfully. "It always does me good to see you, Mr. Prye. You're so cheerful and hopeful."

"It's my sanguine temperament, ma'am We Americans have got a spring of hope continually bubbling up inside. What did we do when we burnt down Cargo? Didn't we set to work and build another city?"

"Now I come to think of it," replied Emily, "I am not so very much afraid about Jack."

"We'll get him out."

"It's not nice to be called mad, when you're not mad, and placed among lunatics; but Jack isn't easily frightened."

"They'll be like the boy that caught the skunk," said Felix.

"What did he do?"

"He wished he hadn't touched that animal, for he couldn't come within a mile of himself with any comfort, for a month afterwards."

"I say, Felix," said Harvey, "it's too late to do anything for Jack to-night, so let's go and bait Mole."

"Why, certainly; we'll catch him on the fly. He'll be doing his bourbon and a cigar all alone," replied Felix.

Drawing Hilda and Emily together, they walked along the passage until they came to Mr. Mole's room, and Harvey opened the door unceremoniously, discovering the professor in an arm-chair, a pipe in one hand, and a glass of grog in the other.

"Harvey, this may be a specimen of American manners; but I should have thought you would have known better than to have come into a gentleman's room without knocking," said Mole.

"It was Felix's fault, sir," replied Harvey.

"Mr. Prye!" said Mole, eyeing him sternly.

"Colonel!" answered Felix, gaily.

Mr. Mole presented a pistol at the intruders on his privacy.

"You get—" he said.

"You bet," replied Felix, retreating to the door.

"I say, sir!" cried Harvey, "this isn't your usual form; we came to have a quiet and cosy half-hour with you. If we have offended, we are very sorry."

Mole put down the pistol.

"That will do," he said. "I only want you to understand that I'm not to be trifled with. I may be what Shakespeare calls a 'foolish, fond old man,' but I will not submit to ridicule at the hands of beardless boys. Sit down!"

"'Beardless boys' is good," said Felix.

"Mr Prye, you are a cultured American," continued Mole.

"Thank you, sir; do you want me to loan you a quarter, or shall I treat?"

"No, no. I was about to remark that Harvey is an unfavourable specimen of his country. Is he not?"

"Queer sort of purp," answered Felix.

"What?"

"No more manners than a dog, colonel," said Felix.

"What?" said Harvey. "Is my Felix going back on his own particular pal, his pet Britisher. I conclude, guess, reckon, and calculate, that I shall have to punch his head."

"Harvey, be silent!" exclaimed Mole. "I am talking to Mr. Prye, who is what you'll never be—a sensible man, for his age."

"I'm glad you qualified it, sir," replied Harvey.

"I have been dipping into your literature, Mr. Prye," continued Mole, "and it seems to me that an American cannot write a book without speaking of the Fourth of July, Benighted Britishers, the Great American Nation, and Horace Greeley."

"Well, sir, those are patriotic fixings," answered Felix.

"I never know when you're laughing at me or not, Mr. Prye."

"I'm not laughing, sir. If you think so, switch off on that subject. What's the price of pigeon's milk in the undiscovered islands?"

"Really, Mr. Prye, you are laughing at me."

"Think so, sir? Let's take a drink, and call it square."

Mr. Mole passed the bottle, and at that moment Monday burst unceremoniously into the room.

"It am all right, sar!" said Monday, grinning from ear to ear.

"Have you found Jack?" asked Harvey.

"No such luck, sar. Um talk about umself, sar. It all right."

"What's all right, Sambo?" asked Felix.

"Got um boy, sar. The doc' he come and tell me."

"Oh! I know what he means," said Harvey. "Monday, you know, has been expecting to be a happy father for some days past, and the event's come off."

"Is that all?" answered Felix, adding, "Simmer down, my coloured friend. This sort of thing has occurred before and since the birth of Cain and Abel, the novelty's worn off."

"You should call the child Tuesday," said Mr. Mole.

"How dat, sar?"

"Doesn't Tuesday come after Monday? Ha! ha! Take a drink. Here's to the health of the little stranger."

Monday drank a little whisky, and ran off. He was a proud and happy man at moment, and too excited to sit still.

Several days passed by, and the private detectives brought no news of Jack.

Wherever he was, his captors had carefully hidden him.

Monday could not rest; he went out early in the morning, and came home late at night, searching in every direction for his lost master.

He explored Manhatten Island, Brooklyn, Jersey, Staten, and Long Island, without success.

But Jack's friends did not give up hope.

They persevered manfully, expecting to be triumphant in the end, but in the meanwhile Jack's whereabouts remained a mystery.

Deprived of her husband and child, Emily began to droop again, and hang her head like a fading lily over its stem.

Mr. Mole also went around, but did no more good than the others.

One day he got into the cars near Madison-square, to go down-town, and at the corner of Eighteenth-street a young and pretty-looking lady entered, and sat by his side.

She wore what the American ladies seem very much to affect, a black silk dress and a seal-skin jacket.

Now that Mr. Mole's wife was dead, his friends remarked that he was a gay widower, and paid the fair sex a large share of attention.

Harvey had decided that Mole wanted to marry again.

But Jack thought not.

"Once bit, twice shy," is an old motto, and Mole had been so badly bitten, that it was not very likely he would be anxious to tie with his teeth the fatal knot one cannot undo with one's hands.

At all events, he looked admiringly on this occasion at the lady, and catching her eye, he smiled.

She smiled, too.

"Sweet creature!" murmured Mr. Mole.

The car-conductor approached and demanded the unknown's fare.

"Oh, dear me!" she exclaimed, feeling in her pockets, "I have left my purse at home."

"Five cents, ma'am, please," said the conductor.

"I haven't any money to pay for a punch from a trip-ticket," she continued.

"What on earth is that?" asked Mole.

"Why, sir," she replied, entering readily into conversation, "the conductor has a slip of paper, which is called a trip-ticket, and when he is paid by a passenger he must punch a hole, with that steel thing he has in his hand, in the paper."

"Oh, I see!" answered Mole, much relieved by this explanation. "Allow me, madame, to have the honour of paying for a punch from a trip-ticket for you."

"Oh, sir! you are too good."

"Not at all. Don't mention it."

He paid the money, the lady was freed from her embarrassment, and smiled sweetly.

"I get out at the corner of Twelfth and University," she said.

"Indeed! So do I," replied Mole, who, until then, had had no idea of doing anything of the sort. "May I be allowed to escort you on your way?"

"Why, certainly," said the lady. "You have been so kind to me that I should not like to refuse you."

"Are you married, may I ask?" inquired Mole, boldly.

"I have been," she replied, casting down her eyes, while her lovely face was suffused with blushes.

"Ah! a widow, I presume? Interesting, and dear creature."

The professor squeezed the lady's hand, and she returned the amorous pressure.

"Twelfth-street," said the conductor.

Mole got out, and handing the lady out, put himself by her side.

"I am going to see an old friend near Washington-square," said the lady. "You must not come quite to the house with me, sir, but you can walk part of the way."

"Divine being, accept my heart-felt thanks," answered Mole.

"Are you from Europe, sir?"

"I am."

"Long resident in the States?"

"But a few weeks."

The lady stopped, as if by accident, in front of a store, and looked in at the window.

A placard in large letters informed the curious that Elijah Jones ran a wheel of fortune. All prizes, no blanks. Prizes from ten cents up to a hundred and fifty dollars.

"How tiresome I left my purse!" said the lady. "I am so lucky at games of chance, and I should so like to try the wheel of fortune!"

"Would you?" replied Mole. "I have money. Let me take you in, and I will stand you chances all day long for one smile from those ruby lips."

"Ah, sir! you are too good," she sighed.

"My dear Mrs—"

"Jones."

"The boss of this store is named Elijah Jones," said Mole. "Singular coincidence."

"It is such a common name. I want to change it," she replied.

"My name is Mole. How would Mole do?"

"Oh! you naughty man!" she replied, with an arch smile. "We have not known one another half an hour."

"I feel as if I had known you for years. What do you think of Mole?"

"Mole is charming," she replied. "I always liked moles, they have such soft, sleek coats. Oh! I think moles are divine little creatures."

"I—I am not so little," said Mole, drawing up his tall, gaunt figure.

"Ah! I was not alluding to you, sir. But will you indeed humour me so far as to take me into this store?"

"A Mole is always a man of his word. Come; command me to the extent of my last dollar."

The professor opened the door, and they passed in.

If he had been on the look-out, he would have noticed that a sharp glance passed between the lady and the proprietor of the store.

But the professor was in love at first sight, and saw nothing but the lovely creature for whom he had purchased a punch from a trip-ticket, and whom he was going to treat to unlimited chances in the wheel of fortune.

He happened to have about a hundred dollars with him, which Harvey had given him to pay a private detective down-town for looking after Jack.

The wicked and amorous professor was actually infatuated enough to spend what ought to have been a sacred trust, and to squander money not his own, upon a fair creature whom he did not know from Adam.

The proprietor of the store was a tall, thin, active, man, dark-haired, and wearing a thick moustache; the rest of his face being shaven in American fashion.

"Wheel of fortune, ma'am," he said; "fifty cents a chance. All prizes and no blanks. Here are gold and silver watches, a silver cream jug, a gold champagne vase, and other valuable prizes too numerous to mention. Try your luck, ma'am?"

Mr. Mole put down a five-dollar bill.

"Give the lady ten chances," he said.

Mrs. Jones saw the wheel revolve, and put in her daintily-gloved hand.

Fortune did not seem to favour her until the ninth chance, for she drew numbers entitling her to such trifles as thimbles, scissors, pin-cushions, &c.; but the ninth chance was a silver jug.

"You have won this, ma'am," said the proprietor.

"Oh, how charming!" answered the lady.

"I don't think the number of the gold watch is in the urn," said Mr. Mole. "Take this number, fourteen. I will put it in the urn, and let it represent the watch."

"Very well," answered the proprietor; "number fourteen is the watch. Now, see I put it in the wheel there, and I'll tell you what I'll do with you, colonel."

"What?"

"You shall give me five-and-twenty dollars for the chance, and if the lady draws the number, she shall have the watch. The wheel shall stand as it is. I won't touch it. There's the number—see."

Mr. Mole hastily counted out the money.

"If you would prefer cash, I'll hand you over one hundred and fifty dollars instead of the repeater."

"Done!" exclaimed Mole, adding, in a whisper to the lady, "That is the number on the left."

"This one?" she asked, pointing to the wheel.

"No, the next one. I saw him fold and put it in." The lady put in her hand and drew out a number.

"Fifteen," said the proprietor.

"Confound it! She's drawn the wrong one," said Mole, angrily.

"Try again, my gallant sportsman. Your bank's good. It's all square. Don't let the luck break you. Put down fifty dollars this time, and I'm on again."

The professor paid the money.

"Don't make a mistake this time," he said; "that's the number."

"I see," replied the lady.

She drew again and handed out a number.

"Thirteen," said the proprietor.

"Oh, how stupid I must be!" cried the lady. "I am making you lose all your money!"

"Come out of this," said Mole, getting mad.

He had lost eighty dollars in ten minutes.

"Thank you, sir," answered the lady; "I am not going any further."

"What?"

"I stay here."

"How's that?" asked Mole, in perplexity.

"The lady's my wife," said the proprietor, with a mocking glance at Mole.

"Your wife!"

The professor turned pale, and leaned against the counter for support.

"I'm much obliged to you for your kindness to my wife," continued the proprietor of the store; "but when you next pick up with a lady in New York, wouldn't it be best to find out if she is married?"

Mr. Mole shook his fist at the man.

"This is a swindle," he said.

"Of course it is. What else did you take it for?"

"As sure as my name's Professor Mole, and I'm staying at the Gilsey House, I'll have the law of you. You're a swindler, sir, and your artful wife is your accomplice. She wouldn't see the right number. I'll expose you. It's a public duty. I owe it to society."

"Try a new gag, colonel," replied the man. "Who's put your eye out?"

"You're on the edge of the burning gulf," said Mole, furiously.

"Let her burn. You're rather heavy on the preach, colonel, but you can't fool this child. Clear out."

"Give me back my money!"

"Go and wean the baby, you old woman, or go out as a wet-nurse. It's all you're fit for."

"Police! police!" cried Mole.

The lady vanished through a side-door, after bestowing a most provokingly bewitching glance at the professor.

"Dry up, colonel," said the proprietor. "I'd be sorry to have to make you squirm, but I'll have to, if you don't sit on the safety-valve, and that's shoe-maker's talk up to the handle."

Mr. Mole saw he was done.

He strode towards the door, but stopped on the threshold to say—

"If I don't have you held to bail for this, call me a story-teller."

"Make haste over it, colonel. My wife and I are off South this evening. Your dollars will just come in handy. Can I send you anything from Florida?"

"Alligator!" ejaculated Mole, hitting upon this word as a term of abuse.

"Send you an alligator? So I will. You shall have it at the Gilsey House as soon as possible. Good-bye, professor. I've caught most things in my life, but I'm kinder tickled to think I've turned mole-catcher at last."

The professor bounced out of the door, and strode angrily down the street.

He was wild, he was mad, for he had lost his money, and his charming widow, too.

Altogether, he was eighty dollars five cents out of pocket.

This he did not so much care for, as he did for being sold.

To paraphrase Brett Harte, Mole might have said, "For ways that are dark, and tricks that are vain, the ladies of New York are peculiar, and the same I am free to maintain."

Mrs. Jones had just got into a car to look for a victim; she had seen Mole, and selected him as the fly to walk into Mr. Jones's little parlour, where he was very neatly fleeced.

He walked on till he came to a lager beer saloon.

"Beer will cool me," he said. "I will walk in."

Pushing the door open, he saw a group of young men assembled, in the midst of whom was Felix Prye

"I have forgotten most all my conjuring tricks," said Felix, as Mr. Mole entered; "but I remember one."

"What is it? what is it?" asked his companions.

"If any gentleman will give me his hat, I will cut a round piece out of the crown, and bet a twenty-five cent drink that I can replace it without the cut being seen."

"Ah! Felix," said Mr. Mole, "that would be clever, but you can't do it."

"Here's the professor, gentlemen; Professor Mole," said Felix. "Mr. Mole, allow me to introduce to you the future Presidents of the United States—Mr. Buggins, Mr. Muggins, Mr. Huggins, Fuggins, Tuggins, and Luggins."

Mr. Mole bowed, and handed in his hat.

"This is a new eight-dollar hat," he said. "I will bet you twenty-five cents—"

"Drinks for the crowd!" cried Mr. Prye's strangely-named friends.

"Well, the loser shouts all round," said Felix.

He took Mr. Mole's hat, and added—

"I've got to cut a round piece out of the crown, and put it back again without leaving any mark on the fur."

"Yes, yes."

He produced a penknife, and carefully cut a bit out of the crown of Mole's new hat.

It was a large piece—nearly all the crown, in fact.

Holding it up, he endeavoured to replace it, but at length put the hat down on the table with a sigh.

"Take your hat," he said. "I've lost."

"What!" exclaimed Mole.

He looked aghast at the big hole in his new hat.

"I've forgotten the trick," said Felix. "Take your drink."

A roar of laughter greeted the professor.

"But you've spoilt my hat."

"Is that so?" asked Felix, innocently.

"Look at it, sir! Look at it! Here's a good hat ruined!"

A fresh burst of laughter greeted Mr. Mole, who, putting on his hat, rushed madly from the place.

"This is an unlucky day," he said. "Confound those Dutch saloons! Confound Felix Prye! Confound Mrs. Jones! Bother everything and everybody!"

Mr. Mole was seeing a little more of the playful side of the American character.

CHAPTER XXVI.
THE CAVE IN THE PALISADES.

OWING to the pressure put on the police authorities of New York by Jack's three friends, a fierce hunt was kept up after Hunston and his companions.

They were obliged to shift from Jersey City, and, knowing the lines of railroad were watched, they dared not go up the country.

The tact of the Pecker was now of use to them, and he conducted them through Weehawken to the Palisades.

In this mass of rocks, Leroy had discovered a cave, and here the gang found refuge.

They established a press for the manufacture of counterfeit money, and lay hidden from the police.

In the evening they would sally forth, disguised, to pass their counterfeit two and five-dollar bills, leaving Young Jack in the cave.

The boy was slowly recovering from the effects of his broken leg, and stumped about on crutches.

There was an entrance to the cave from the top, being caused by a natural fissure in the rocks, but the principal entrance was from the water, it being easy to row over from Spuyten Duyvil Creek in a small boat, or to cross at Bull's Ferry.

In crossing from New York city, Hunston and his friends usually took the Forty Second-street Ferry to Weehawken, and walked up, though they sometimes, when down town, took the Elevated Railroad as far as it went, and then travelled by the Hudson River Road to Washington Heights, and crossed in their boat to the cave.

It was a rough and uncomfortable sort of dwelling. They had only the rudest articles of furniture, and nothing but rugs to cover them at night.

But in their work of counterfeiting, or making bad money, they required the strictest secrecy.

Had not Hunston been influenced to some extent by Leroy, he would not have embarked in the counterfeiting buisness.

Fenton and Hunston intended to go to California together.

Leroy's purpose was to remain in New York, and the others were assisting him until the winter was over, and their plans were settled.

There was another reason why Hunston lingered. Young Jack was not well enough to travel.

His broken leg was getting better gradually, but some weeks had to elapse before he would be able to walk.

It was a bitter cold night, and the icy blast howled over the surface of the Palisades, darting in and out of holes and crannies, and screaming in its wild career, as it swept away into the darkness.

Hunston and Fenton entered the cave together, and found Young Jack crouching over a stove in which a fire was burning.

"Get up, you young cub!" said Hunston, raising his arm threateningly; "or I'll let you know the reason why."

The boy retreated into a corner.

"Unpack that bag of yours," continued Hunston, "and let's have some whisky."

Fenton produced several parcels from his bag, and from amongst them he drew out a bottle of whisky, with which the men refreshed themselves.

"Jack," said Fenton.

"Yes," replied the boy, surlily.

"Where's Leroy?"

"He told me to say he was going into the city, and would be back early."

"When did he go?"

"About two hours after you and Hunston."

"How's your leg to-night?" inquired Hunston.

"Bad. It hurts."

"You'll have to get well quick, as we're going to leave here. Pass that bottle, Fenton, and if you can find a bit of loose coal, chuck it at the cub; he's sulky, and wants it knocked out of him."

Fenton was not slow to do as he was directed.

A lump of coal struck Young Jack on the forehead, causing him to fall back bleeding on the rough floor of the cave.

He was creeping away into the darkest recesses of the singularly-shaped cavern, when a few more favours of the same sort quickened his movements.

"I hate that cub like poison," remarked Hunston.

"Can't say I have any more affection for him than I have for his father," replied Fenton.

"I shall take him up to Chicago, and send him to rob somebody, so that he may be sent to gaol, and have the taint of the thief on him."

"Good," said Fenton. "If he gets twelve months, you'll know where he his, and have him safe, though he'll be off your hands. I wonder where Leroy is?"

"Shoving the paper about; I can see from the press he's been at it this morning. Any news of Harkaway?"

"No," said Fenton. "I haven't been up to the asylum lately. From last accounts, he was quieter."

"I see the advertisements are still in the papers, offering a reward for Jack's present whereabouts. Don't they wish they may get it? The doctor's true as steel, and we pay him too well for him to split upon us."

"No fear of that. Harkaway's caged for the remainder of his natural life," replied Fenton.

"I don't suppose he will live long," observed Hunston, "among all the horrors with which he is surrounded. I know I shouldn't."

"For my part," said Fenton, "I'd ever so much rather be in prison than in a mad-house."

"So would I."

"Harkaway will go mad himself, and die raving, I expect," continued Fenton.

"Have you told the keepers to be strict with him?" asked Hunston, with a savage gleam in his twinkling eyes.

"They had fifty dollars apiece to knock him down, strait-waistcoat him, whip him, shower-bath him, and use all the rest of their tortures on the slightest provocation."

"That's right. When shall we flit?"

"As soon as possible, I vote. You've settled Harkaway and got the boy. What's the use of stopping?" said Fenton.

"We've been safe from the hue-and-cry of police here, and the youngster is not quite well. Besides, we've been making money, and, though we are tolerably well off, money is one of those things we can't have too much of," replied Hunston.

A noise was heard at the river entrance to the cave.

"Leroy!" ejaculated Fenton.

The form of the Mountain Pecker appeared in the narrow passage, and Hunston dropped the pistol he had seized on the first alarm of footsteps.

He was not alone.

Behind him walked a man, who was dressed in the ordinary clothes of a respectable citizen.

"A friend of mine, by name Banks," said Leroy. "He has been helping me to put the paper about in small parcels, and he now wants a larger quantity."

"Sit down, sir," said Hunston.

Banks looked uneasily around him, and evidently tried to appear at his ease, but the effort was a failure.

Hunston and Fenton glared angrily at Leroy, as if

they were annoyed at his rashness in bringing a stranger into the cave.

But the Pecker telegraphed back a glance which was intended to reassure them.

"I can trust Banks," he said. "We have known one another for a whole week, and that's long enough to tell what a man is."

"Rather," remarked Banks.

"He was bumming around Canal-street, and I spotted him at once as a sure card."

"How much does he want?" asked Hunston.

"I'll take five thousand dollars worth," said Banks.

"You shall have it. Hand over the stiff."

The exchange of good money for bad was made, Banks paying only half price for the counterfeit bills.

"Take a drink?" said Hunston.

"Why, certainly," answered Banks, accepting a glass of whisky straight, and adding, "My respects."

"Will you play a little poker?" inquired Fenton.

"Not to-night," replied Banks. "I want to get back. Got to meet something very nice by ten. I'm sure you'll excuse me, and, in fact, I'm so used to boxing the cards that I shouldn't like to play along with you gentlemen. Dog doesn't eat dog."

"Well, that's so. Good-night. We'd like to see you again soon, Mr. Banks," said Hunston. "You'll remember our den?"

"I think so, though I didn't take particular notice."

He rose to go.

Leroy had put himself at the entrance to the passage, and his hand was hidden behind his back.

"Do you mean going?" he asked.

"Yes, it's time," answered Banks.

"I'm very sorry to disappoint you," continued Leroy, "but you'll never go out of this cave again alive."

The man turned deadly pale.

"You're joking," he said.

"Not much."

"What do you mean?"

"You must have taken me for an everlasting fool. Do you think I didn't know you all along! I'm called the King of the Standards, and there isn't a police officer in New York I don't tumble to, disguised or not."

Banks's hand also sought his pocket.

He uttered a cry of dismay.

"You've robbed me of my pistol!" he said.

"That's for certain," laughed the Pecker. "I did that coming along, and I thought you'd have tumbled to it before now. How clever you thought yourself, didn't you? Fancied you'd spot the cave, and come down on us in the night. Oh! my! isn't this a sell!"

"Let me pass," said Banks. "You are mistaken."

"What!" cried Leroy, with a demon-like chuckle. "Think I don't know Larkin, the cleverest detective of the Sixth Ward. Come, Larkin, old man, I'm sorry for you, but you'll be found a floating corpse before morning, stiff and stark, in the North River."

"I'll buy my life," said the officer, who saw that he was discovered, and that further concealment was useless.

"Have you got a gold mine in your pocket?"

"No."

"Then we can't trade. You darned fool! couldn't you see I was playing with you all along? Is it likely an old hand would bring any one, if he was ever so good a pal, to the very place where the stamps are cut?"

"I must have been mad," answered the officer. "But, for God's sake, let me go. I'll not round on you. Think of my young wife and child. Give me

my life, Leroy, and by Heaven! you've got a friend for ever in Tom Larkin!"

"What use is there praying? Did you ever show mercy to any of us? How many have you sen' up the Island? How many poor fellows are there groaning their lives out at Sing Sing? No, Larkin, you've got to die."

"Finish him right away, or let me," said Hunston. "I want my supper."

Detective Sergeant Larkin saw that there was no hope.

He could see that these desperate men did not know what mercy was to one of his class and profession.

In this terrible moment he lost his presence of mind; brave as he had always shown himself to be, he turned craven, and fell on his knees before Leroy, who spurned him.

Fear had robbed him of his power of speech.

Unable to utter a word, he cowered before the intending assassin, and clasped his hands, while he made a piteous moaning noise like an idiot.

"Shoot! hang you, shoot!" exclaimed Hunston.

"I like it," answered Leroy. "Look how he squirms! Thunder, ain't it fine? He used to be a good chinner, and now he can't speak a word."

Impatiently Hunston produced a pistol, and fired it at the poor quivering wretch, breaking his leg.

A long, loud, fearful cry resounded through the cave, making weird echoes, which terrified Young Jack, who was an involuntary spectator of the awful scene.

Larkin dragged himself up to Hunston like a wounded snake, leaving a long trail of hot, steaming blood behind him on the floor.

"Mercy! mercy!" he pleaded.

It was pitiable to witness the agony of this young man, cut off from the world at a moment's notice.

"Dry up, colonel!" said Leroy. "It's my shot, I guess, now. I'll make you squirm!"

He walked up to the detective, pistol in hand.

Young Jack's blood had been boiling over, and he could bear no more. Rushing forward, he placed himself in front of Larkin, and, throwing his arms round him, exclaimed—

"You shall not kill him!"

"Hullo, you young spawn!" said Leroy. "What do you want to put your finger in the pie for?"

"Let him go!" cried the boy. "Oh, I wish I was armed! I'd shoot you!"

The brutal ruffian swung out his left hand, and knocked the lad in an insensible heap on the ground, cursing him the while through his clenched teeth.

"That will teach you," he said.

The next moment a ball went crashing through the brain of the unfortunate policeman, who fell, with a groan, to the blood-stained rock.

Thus was acted the tragedy of the Palisades.

Leroy dragged the body out of the cave, and tumbled it into the river, as if it had been so much lumber.

Returning to the cave, he shook the fast-falling rain-drops from his coat.

"It's an awful night," he said. "Just the sort of night for a bit of work like this."

"You're no fool, Pecker," remarked Hunston.

"Not much. There's where Larkin was wrong. You thought I'd made a slip when I brought him here, but I had my knife into Larkin, and wanted to stick him quietly."

"Why?"

"You didn't know the Dutchman? Dutch John we used to call him?"

"No."

"Larkin got him twenty years in the State Prison. Poor Bob! he and I were like brothers. We'd worked together for years, and never wanted for sugar while we were pardners."

"What did he do?"

"Nothing, much. He only strangled a woman in Water-street, in one of the dance-houses, one night, when he was kinder playful. She'd offended him by talking to a sailor."

"Is the kid dead?" asked Fenton, looking curiously at Young Jack.

The boy was lying motionless.

"Not he," answered Leroy.

"I hope not," said Hunston. "It isn't my game for him to die yet."

"Get up, you whelp!" said Leroy, kicking the boy.

Young Jack moved uneasily, and opened his eyes.

"Oh, my head!" he murmured.

"Rouse up. Dy'e hear? Hurry up, or I'll warm you!" shouted the Pecker.

The boy staggered to his feet, and looked round him in a dazed sort of manner.

"No shamming, curse you! Go and lie down in your corner, and mind you get my coffee by daylight, or I'll break every bone in your darned young carcase."

Young Jack slunk off, bestowing a look of deadly hatred at the Pecker.

His evil passions were beginning to work within him.

He was in a good school for going to the bad, and the effect of the training he was subjected to was commencing to show itself.

CHAPTER XXVII.

A SURPRISE PARTY.

"WHAT's the matter with my Felix?" said Harvey, as Mr. Prye entered his room at the hotel.

"I want to do something to get a laugh out of," answered Felix. "The fact is, trade is very bad, and the governor has been blowing me up because I haven't made a dollar this week."

"Infelix puer!"

"I'm all that, though I don't know what it means."

"It's Latin, and means unhappy youth."

"It may be Persian, but it's true," said Felix.

"'Penicos ode,' as Horace says. That's the Persian. Now, tell me, Felix, what we can do to dissipate this gloom. I'm down, too, because we can't find Old Jack or Young Jack, and our expedition seems to be stumped."

"We scored over the enemy at first, but we're out on the second base," replied Felix, adding, "can't we have a lark with Mole?"

"What should we do?"

"Give him a surprise party."

"What is that? Remember, I'm an ignorant Britisher. I know I ought to drop my H's, but I don't. Condescend to enlighten me, my Felix, as to the scope and purpose of a surprise party."

"Why, certainly," answered Felix. "The joke consists in sending out invitations to a lot of people in Mr. Mole's name. Of course he knows nothing about it, and is surprised to see a party of pleasure-seekers, who take possession of him and his apartments, intending to make a night of it, whether he will or not."

"And he hasn't asked a soul?"

"Not one."

"We'll do it," said Harvey, rubbing his hands. "Who shall we ask?"

"Well, you see, you haven't many friends as yet in New York, so I'll invite a few of mine."

"Can't we send in a piano, and have some music, if we ask some girls?"

"I guess that's part of the idea," replied Felix.

They sat down, and between them wrote a couple of dozen letters in this strain—

"Professor Mole, of Oxford University, England, has the honour to invite —— to his rooms at the Gilsey House, on Thursday evening next, to hear his initial lecture (private rehearsal before making a tour of the States) on—"

"On what shall we say?" asked Felix. "Look it up."

"On Cheek," suggested Harvey

"No. That's more in my line," replied Felix. "So it is. Suppose we say 'Woman's Rights'?"

"That notion's gone up. I guess. Let us say on the 'Suppression of the Liquor Traffic.'"

"Good enough, my Felix," said Harvey, laughing loudly.

"N.B.—Professor Mole may add that he is one of the foremost champions of the temperance cause in the world," said Felix, "and has drank nothing but water for fourteen years."

"And a half," said Harvey.

"Will that do?"

"Couldn't word it better. Fix the time at seven."

"We'll mail those to-night," said Felix. "To-day's Monday. On Thursday look out for a lark."

The letters were posted, and Mole was altogether unconscious of the joke.

On the eventful day he dined very heartily, and retired to his room to indulge in an after-dinner nap.

Felix and Harvey repaired to his apartment, and found him asleep in a chair.

The piano had come in, and was placed near a window, not having attracted the professor's attention.

Holding up his hand, Felix said—

"Hush!"

He took a champagne cork, and cut a cleft in the lower end, sticking the top, or bulky end, full of lucifer matches.

The cork he gently fitted on Mole's nose.

Then he lighted a piece of paper, and set fire to the matches, which caught with a fizz.

The flame woke the professor, who started from his chair, wondering what on earth was the matter

He saw fire plainly before his eyes, but where it came from was more than he could guess.

"Fire! Fire!" roared Felix.

And "Fire! Fire!" screamed Harvey, wildly.

The professor darted about the room, dashing his hands right and left.

His eyebrows got singed, and his wig caught fire, blazing up like flax.

"Put him out," said Harvey.

"Where's the water?" asked Felix.

This delicate act of attention on their part was rendered unnecessary, owing to the fact that Mr. Mole, in his frantic struggles, pulled down his wig over his eyes.

It fell on the cork and dislodged it.

Wigless and panting, he stood confronting his tormentors.

"Is he ugly when he's mad?" inquired Felix.

"Don't be afraid," replied Harvey.

"How dare you put a fiery cork machine on my nose?" said Mole, furiously. "I will not bear it!"

"It wasn't me, sir," said Harvey.

"Then it was that American. I hate Yankee tricks."

"Not me, sir," said Felix. "Wouldn't do such a thing."

"You can't make a fool of me," answered Mole.

"Confess that you did it between you, and promise not to do it again."

"Well, sir, I did do it," said Felix.

"Ah! I've found you out, Mr. Prye," cried Mole, triumphantly. "That's a new wig up your sleeve. I shall have to make reclamations. How my nose burns! Is it red?"

"Kinder purple colour, sir; like a sunset in a fit."

"Fortunately, I have another wig. Don't do it again. I owe you one for this. Really, you are old enough to know better," said Mole, calming down a little.

He adjusted himself before the glass, and ended by inviting them to spend an hour with him.

"Take a drink, boys," he said; "and when you want to play another practical joke, select a fresh victim. Never put all your eggs in one basket."

He placed several bottles on the table, which were labelled, respectively, rum, whisky, brandy, gin, Catawba, and California wine.

Quite a formidable array for a temperance lecturer.

Presently a waiter came up with a card.

Mr., and Mrs., and the six Misses Martinique, sir, to see you," he said.

"Bless my soul! I don't know them. Some mistake," cried Mole.

"Here they are, sir!" replied the waiter.

The party entered the room.

Mr. and Mrs. Martinique were tall and lean. So were their daughters. They all lived together.

"Mr. Mole, Professor of Temperance Principles, from Oxford, England, I presume?" said Mr. Martinique.

"I am Mr. Mole, sir."

"Come to hear your lecture. Sit down, girls," said Mr. Martinique, eyeing the bottles curiously.

Felix was acquainted with the Martiniques, and at once began talking to them.

Mole would have demanded an explanation, had not a dozen more people been ushered up.

He was almost beside himself with surprise and vexation.

What did it all mean?

One fussy little man seized him by the hand.

"Glad to see you, sir," he exclaimed; "my name is Drinkwater. I have devoted a life to the glorious cause, sir, and am proud to know you. Temperance must triumph, sir, and I am pleased to see Old England lend us a helping hand, and send us her gallant sons to aid us in the fight against drink and the devil."

The Misses Martinique groaned and looked leaner than ever, while their mother surreptitiously took a pinch of snuff, and indulged in a pious snuffle.

"I am sure," said Mole, "that I abhor drunkenness as much as anyone."

"Hear! hear!" from Harvey, in a corner.

"But," continued Mole, "why you should call me a gallows—I mean a gallant son, I don't know."

"You are modest, sir," said Mr. Drinkwater.

"What have I done to deserve this?" cried Mole, in despair.

"Your fame has penetrated all lands. Who has not heard of Mole, of Oxford?—glorious old Mole!"

"Bless him! May he be a fruitful vine!" sighed an old maiden lady.

More people appeared, and the room was full.

"Order! silence!" exclaimed Mr. Drinkwater. "Let us open the proceedings of this glorious night with prayer. I can see Deacon Teaurn. The deacon will ask a blessing."

"For Heaven's sake, hear me, good people!" exclaimed Mole.

There was an instant hush again.

"There is some mistake here," continued Mo'
"I did not advertise——"

Twenty letters were drawn with a rustling noise from as many pockets.

"I am not a temperance lecturer, nor am I temperance, though a temperate man."

A great uproar arose.

"For Heaven's sake sit down, and hear me out!" continued Mole. "This is a trick—a practical joke, and I think I see the author of it."

"Name! Name!" cried several.

"Mr. Felix Prye. Look at the writing of the letters. But, as you are all here, I should be sorry to disappoint you, and I will give you a lecture on the 'Rise and Fall of the Roman Empire.' First of all, though, let me not forget the duties of hospitality —will you take a drink?"

He pointed to the bottles on the table.

His voice was drowned in groans and indignant exclamations.

Had New York and Brooklyn sent their shining lights to be hidden under this bushel?

"Look here!" exclaimed Mole, "I will make Mr. Prye confess, and then you will be satisfied."

He seized Felix by the arm, and held him firmly, while several indignant supporters of the temperance cause surrounded him threateningly.

"Rascal!" said Mole, "what do you mean by it? Confess."

"Yes, yes,—own up, own up!" chorused the indignants.

"I do own up," answered Felix. "Let go, and stop your chin-music, or—"

"What?" furiously demanded an old lady, brandishing her articles in his face.

"I'll publish this hoax in the Herald, and put in the names of all those present."

There was considerable hesitation in that crowd.

Felix had got the laugh of them, and they began to see how very neatly they had all been sold.

Mr. Mole went about from one to another, explaining, as well as he could, that he was not reponsible for their disappointment, and that he was a classical, not a temperance professor.

"But," said Mr. Drinkwater, "you will join us?"

"I will," replied Mole.

He was in a mood at that moment to promise anything.

"You will help us to exorcise this demon of drink, that is sapping the energy and preying upon the vitals of the community?"

"I will! Oh, I'll do anything, if you'll go!" replied Mole.

The servant appeared again at the door.

Behind him were four others, carrying a large and very long deal box, with holes perforated all along the top.

"Packing-case for you, sir," he said.

"For me? Where from? Is this another joke?" asked Mole, with a faint and weary smile.

"Comes from Florida, sir."

"Open it. Put it down near the fire-place. Open it; I am equal to anything to-night. I am equal to new-born babies, and even to corpses sent by rail in deal boxes."

The visitors crowded round the box with eager expectation.

Not the least curious of the throng were Felix and Harvey, who, knowing they had no hand in this last arrival, were as anxious as any one else to know all about it.

Hammers and chisels were produced, and wielded by steady hands.

"Remember," said Felix, "this is a surprise party."

"I am reckless; proceed," answered Mole.

"Ain't we to have no singing?" asked one old lady or 'nother.

"; don't you hear it's a surprise of that young

"Drat him! I'd like give him a bit of my mind. That's me."

The box was slowly opened.

The long lid was lifted, and out stepped——

There was a general stampede to the door, and loud cries arose from the ladies, who mounted on chairs, and screamed, and otherwise conducted themselves in an incomprehensible manner.

Mr. Mole sprang upon the table, and wrapped the ample folds of his Cashmere dressing-gown around him.

Felix and Harvey were not behindhand in seeking a place of safety, and found it on the top of the piano.

The intruder was a formidable creature.

At last the mystery of the box was solved, for out stepped AN ALLIGATOR!

On his head was a bit of paper, written on which was——

"For Mr. Mole, with Mr. Elijah Jones and Mrs. Jones's compliments."

The boss who ran the wheel of fortune had kept his word, and sent the unlucky professor an alligator, real and alive, from Florida.

Its arrival was very opportune, for it completed the surprise party, and did what all Felix's threats, and Mole's entreaties and explanations might have failed in effecting.

It cleared the room.

Soon, only Felix and Harvey were left on the piano, Mole on the table, and a few grinning servants outside the door.

The temperance surprise party had vanished like snow in summer.

As for the alligator, he looked round in a hungry manner.

A plate of biscuits had fallen on the floor; he condescended to eat one, but a cat, that had strayed under the table, caught his glassy eye, and, with one snap of his ponderous jaws, puss was cut in half and eaten.

"Harvey," said Mr. Mole, "oblige me by turning out this unwelcome intruder."

"Thank you, sir," replied Harvey; "I'd rather be excused."

"What's to be done with him?"

"I don't know."

The professor regarded his unwelcome visitor with an air of perplexity.

"This wasn't my doing, sir," remarked Felix.

"That I am aware of," replied Mole. "I know perfectly well to whom I am indebted for this act of delicate attention. Ugh! get out, you beast!"

This observation was addressed to the alligator, who stared up at Mole, as if he would have liked to stand on his hind legs, if the accomplishment of such a feat was possible, and help himself to a bit of Oxford professor.

Mole retreated to the centre of the table, and took up a bottle of spirits, from which he drank.

"Give him some fusil, sir," cried Felix; "I guess it kills Christians, and why shouldn't it settle the heathen? Make him squirm, sir."

"A good idea," replied Mole.

He advanced to the edge of the table, and looked down into the distended jaws of the cayman.

Turning the bottle upside down, he sent a flood of whisky into its mouth, making the creature retreat rapidly, and go for the door.

At this moment the table, being a two-leaf one, gave way in the middle beneath Mole's weight, and collapsed, the professor falling to the floor amid a wreck of bottles and glasses.

"Lord help me!" gasped Mole. "I'm gone up! I deserved a better fate than a grave in the stomach of an alligator! The Lord be good to me!"

Fortunately, the officials connected with the hotel arrived on the scene with ropes, knives, and

pistols, and after a deal of trouble the alligator was despatched on the landing.

Never had there been such excitement in the hotel before.

When he saw that the creature was on its back, and at its last gasp, Mole strode up to it.

"Harmless creature," he said giving it a kick. "It is never dangerous, if properly handled. Never be afraid of such things, boys; I have killed scores of them in my time."

The alligator gave a final and expiring snap with its fearful jaws.

Mole jumped about six feet.

"Ha! ha!" laughed Harvey. "Never be afraid of such things, boys."

"Who's afraid?" replied Mole, angrily.

"What made you jump, sir?"

"I jumped for joy, that the huge beast was dead. I feel as if I had put a hook through the nose of that great Leviathan," answered Mole, who added, "Take him away, boys. I will pay for any little trouble and expense you may be put to. Come inside, Felix. Harvey, step in."

The door was closed, and the room partially restored to order.

Whisky toddy was mixed, and Mole recovered his serenity.

The wind howled and whistled without, making the shutters bang and the windows rattle.

"This is what I like," said Mole, settling himself down in his chair. "Let the wintry wind howl. We are under shelter, and feel not its angry blast. This is peace."

"Well, sir, we'll leave you to enjoy it," said Felix.

"Good-night, Mr. Prye," replied Mole, with a smile. "I thank you for past favours, but by no means require a continuance of the same, and recollect I owe you one, and you, too, Harvey."

"All right, sir," laughed the young men.

They departed, and Mr. Mole drank his grog with a sigh of relief.

"I have had temperance people, and I have had alligators. I wonder if they will let me rest now?" he muttered. "Imps of mischief! But it doesn't pay to be cross with them. They'd only make it red-hot for me."

CHAPTER XXVIII.

THE FIGHT IN THE COUNTERFEITERS' DEN.

FOR a little while the birth of his first child kept Monday in a flutter of excitement.

"Now young Mast' Jack," he said, "when um find him, have some one to play with."

He did not like the idea of calling him Tuesday, but thought of having him christened Washington, out of compliment to the nation among which he was staying.

Monday's Malay name was Matabella.

Would not Washington Matabella sound well? But he would not decide until both young and old Jack were found and brought back.

Days glided by, and were merged into weeks, and yet no sign was seen of either.

Ada was anxious to have her child christened, and both Emily and Hilda were of opinion the ceremony should not be delayed.

"It's an awful thing for a young baby to die without being christened," said Emily.

"But mine is not going to die, ma'am. He's strong and hearty," replied Ada.

"I hope he will remain so," said Hilda.

"Wait till Mast' Jack and young Mast' Jack come back," said Monday. "Um never do anything without Mast' Jack. Say, now, Missy Emily, shall um go out on the war-path, and not come home till um find 'em?"

MONDAY, SEIZING MILES FENTON BY THE SHOULDER, PLUNGED THE KNIFE INTO HIS BODY.

"Oh, yes, Monday! Please do go and have a thorough hunt all round," Emily hastened to answer.

"Yeu've done it before successfully, and you may be fortunate enough to do it again."

"That's settled," said Monday.

Disdaining the use of a pistol, he armed himself only with his knife, and started on the chase.

Willingly would he have dispensed with his clothes and gone in his native buff, but in New York State this was out of the question, and he wore a loose-fitting coat, a pair of whity-brown pants, and a seal-skin cap, discarding the ear-flaps, as they prevented him from hearing as well as he could wish.

Thinking it of little use to go down-town, he wandered up the Island of Manhatten, very much as the musician Blondel wandered after his master

Richard the Lion Heart, when he was held in captivity by the Emperor of Austria.

All at once he heard a man walking behind him, and quickened his pace, thinking he might be "shadowed" by some spy of Hunston's.

A hand was laid on his shoulder, and a deep, guttural voice said—

"My brother has forgotten the lost chief of the Apaches."

It was Par-a-wau.

"How am do?" said Monday. "Can't stop for um palaver, now. Um on the war-path. Apache ever go on war-path?"

Par-a-wau smiled scornfully.

"In the wigwam of Par-a-wau," he said, "there hang many scalps When a brave falls by the

Indian's hand, he takes his scalp, and they are plentiful as leaves in autumn with the chief of the Apaches. He is a great chief, and his young men mourn him for dead."

"Scalp um enemy!" said Monday. "Dat queer custom. In Limbi we eat um."

"Is my brother a chief beyond the sea?"

"Um a King," replied Monday.

"Ugh! the Indian eats not his enemy. It is not well," said the Warning Devil, in a tone of disgust.

"What black man like you know about war customs?" asked Monday. "You drink too much rum. Mast' Jack gives you money to go home. Why um not go back and take more scalps?"

"I got drunk," replied the Indian, hanging down his head, as if ashamed of himself. "Par-a-wau is very sorry. Now he has no money, and is obliged to stay."

"What are you doing up here? This is Tenth Avenue. What um Indian up to?"

"Par-a-wau saw Hunston yesterday here, and followed him. Then he lost sight of him. To-day come to try and find him."

"I'm not going back until I have found Mist' Harkaway or Young Jack. Par-a-wau come with um on the war-path?" asked Monday.

"Harkaway is a great chief. He was kind to the poor Apache. Par-a-wau will give his life for the great white chief."

"Now um speak like a man," said Monday. "Give um hand. So. Monday and the Indian make friends."

"Par-a-wau will be like a brother to the young brave."

They shook hands and held a long consultation, the result of which was that they agreed to cross the river to Weehawken, thinking it likely that some trace of Hunston and his confederates would be found in the wild country about the Palisades.

Nor, as the reader knows, were they wrong in their conjecture.

Once Par-a-wau stopped, and asked Monday to buy him rum, which the latter refused to do.

This showed how strong a hold intoxicating liquors take upon a red-man when he comes amongst us; he being led by his natural instincts to imitate our vices, while he is blind to our virtues.

It has been said that we approach the savages with a sword in one hand, a Bible in the other, and small-pox and rum hidden up our sleeves; and yet we wonder that the Indians are decreasing in numbers, and are unsatisfactory subjects to deal with.

After walking some distance, Monday led the way up the rocks, feeling a savage pleasure in surmounting the difficulties of the rocky scenery.

Par-a-wau followed.

A change seemed to have come over both of them.

They were no longer the quiet, languid creatures of civilisation, but as they reached the open country, sniffed the invigorating air, and beheld the wild tracks around, they hunted about like dogs looking for tracks, and seemed to be all ears, nose, and eyes.

"Some one been here," said Par-a-wau.

"How um tell?" asked Monday.

Par-a-wau pointed to some signs which would have passed unnoticed by a less keen eye.

"Yes," said Monday; "um quite right. Stay here while I hunt round."

He scrambled up the rocks, and Par-a-wau continued to make further examinations.

Suddenly he heard a cry, and looked up.

"Ugh!" he ejaculated; "where is my brother?" Monday had disappeared.

He was nowhere to be seen, and the Warning Devil in vain stretched his eyes in every direction.

Instantly he fell flat on his belly, so as to escape observation, and crawled over the rocks in search for some trace of Monday, who had vanished in so mysterious a manner.

Where could he have gone?

If he had been shot by some unseen enemy, there would have been the report of the gun.

If he had been stabbed, there would have been the sound of a scuffle.

But the quick ear of the Indian had detected no noise, save that smothered cry, which came up, as it were, from the bowels of the earth.

All at once Par-a-wau stopped.

Not a sound escaped him, nor did he in the slightest degree relax the rigidity of the muscles of his face.

He, however, imitated, with remarkable accuracy, the croaking of a frog.

This was a signal agreed upon between him and Monday.

He had not long to wait for an answer.

The shrill screech of a parrot came up from a fissure in the rocks.

Without hesitation, Par-a-wau lowered himself through this hole, and disappeared as suddenly and mysteriously as had Monday.

He found himself inside a cave of large dimensions.

When his eyes became accustomed to the semi-darkness, he distinguished Monday.

The black was hugging and kissing a little boy, who was equally delighted, and returned his caresses.

"Par-a-wau, that you?" said Monday.

"Ugh! my brother goes quick. I want time to find him. He went like the spirit of the wind. Lo! it is here, and then it is gone; but the eye of the Indian is not easily deceived. I am here. Wagh."

"Here um lark," cried Monday; "not find Mast' Jack; but, by golly, find Young Jack."

And he fell to kissing and hugging the boy, and dancing about like mad.

"I am so glad you've come, Monday," said Young Jack, who recognised his father's faithful retainer at once.

"Who keep um here?"

"Hunston, Fenton, and Leroy."

"Where um now?"

"Gone out. Mind my leg. It is not quite well. I ran away and sold papers, then I was a boy-clown and did real tumbling—think of that, Monday—but one night I fell and broke my leg, and Fenton took me away, and at last they all came here, where they make bad money."

"Dat so?"

"The other night they killed a man, and they threw him in the river, and they beat me shamefully. Next week they were going to take me a long way off."

"They say anything of your papa?"

"Yes. I hear them say he's settled in a mad-house. But we'll have him—won't we, Monday?"

"We have um, sure 'nuff, sar," replied Monday.

"How's my mamma, and Hilda and uncle Dick (this he called Harvey), and Mr. Mole?"

"All quite well, sar. Feel better when they see you."

"You take me away, Monday?"

"Right straight off, sar."

"Ain't this bully, you finding me, Monday? How did you do it?"

"Kinder instinct, sar," replied Monday, proudly.

"Won't Hunston be mad when he finds I'm gone, and won't my mamma be pleased?"

"She'll be tickled to death, sar," replied Monday. "Here, you nigger, Par-a-wau, get up those rocks, and I'll hand um Young Jack up. We clear out dis mighty quick."

The Warning Devil held up his hand.

"Now come," he said.

Monday listened intently, and distinctly heard the sound of voices and footsteps outside the cave.

"Mast' Jack," he whispered.

"Yes."

"You strong 'nuff to climb up um rocks? Par-a-wau and I stop and fight."

"I'll try. My leg's much better," answered the boy.

He went to the foot of the aperture, and was soon busily engaged in clambering up the fissure, through which his friends had descended a short time before.

But with his lame leg it was not an easy task, and his progress was necessarily slow.

"Got um pistol?" queried Monday.

Par-a-wau grunted.

Monday drew his knife, and waited with a vindictive gleam in his eyes, but his heart did not beat any faster. Accustomed to danger from his infancy, this child of the East was as much of a stoic as his companion of the West.

"Come on, boys!" said Fenton.

A dark figure hurled itself against him. A knife penetrated his flesh, and he sunk heavily to the ground.

"Oh, God! I'm stabbed!" he said, in a faint tone.

Hunston was at his heels, and he turned to fly, overthrowing Leroy in his headlong speed.

A ball from Par-a-wau's pistol flattened itself against the rock over his head.

"Where are you coming to?" asked Leroy,

"The cave's surprised!"

"What is it?"

"The cops, I think; hook it, you fool!"

Hunston disappeared, but Leroy was not so nimble, and another ball grazed his arm.

He, however, followed Hunston, but Monday was upon him before he could make his escape.

A terrible fight ensued.

Knives were freely used, and blood flowed in streams.

At length Leroy struck the right arm of his enemy, and Monday fell back.

That moment would have been his last, had not Par-a-wau come to the rescue.

Seeing the odds were against him, and not knowing how many men might be in the cave, he, too, fled and joined Hunston, just as the latter was shoving off the boat to cross the Hudson.

"Where's Fenton?" asked Leroy.

"Dead, I guess," answered Hunston. "All is lost; we must be off to-night, somewhere. Curse the luck!"

"That's what I say," growled Leroy.

"Take an oar."

"How can I, when I'm bleeding like a pig? It was that black servant of Harkaway I struck, but he's slashed me all over, as if he'd been carving a pig."

"Was it Monday? Then they've got the boy. It's as well to know that, because we shall have a better chance of getting him back. Sit down; I'll pull. Perdition seize the whole lot!"

"Ditto," said Leroy, looking ruefully at his bleeding wounds.

The boat was propelled swiftly across the river.

Par-a-wau did not attempt to pursue them; he turned his attention to Monday, whose right arm was hanging uselessly by his side.

"Much hurt?" asked the Warning Devil, in his laconic style.

"Tear bit of um shirt, and bind it up. Stop blood, and um get all right," answered Monday, faintly.

Par-a-wau bandaged the wound with as much surgical skill as he possessed.

There was no doubt that Fenton was stone-dead. The knife had penetrated to his heart, which had ceased to beat.

"Leave um here; um dead as mutton," said Monday, spurning the body of Miles Fenton with his foot.

"Why not my brother eat him?" replied Par-a-wau, with a smile.

"You want um scalp?" answered Monday.

The hint was sufficient, and the savage nature of Par-a-wau asserted itself.

Once a savage, always a savage.

Casting aside the artificial scruples of civilisation, half-hearted and imperfect, he whipped out his knife, knelt down, and soon hid away in his breast the still warm and reeking scalp, the fairly-earned trophy of a hard-fought battle.

The body of the versatile Miles Fenton, citizen of the world, as he loved to call himself, remained in the cave to rot, until, when Summer came, some children strayed into the cavern, and ran shrieking away at the sight of the blanched bones of the ghastly skeleton—sad relic of mortality.

Unwept, unmourned, abandoned in death by his late companions, he was cut off without any warning.

Those that live by the sword shall perish by the sword, and it was a fit ending for a bandit like himself—a blot on life, an ulcer on society, an enemy of mankind.

The mournful ripple of the flowing river was his only requiem, except when the wind soughed and sighed without, and sang his dirge.

"You go and see to Young Jack," said Monday. "I get out this way; not able to climb now."

Par-a-wau nodded, and disappeared up the fissure, while Monday threaded the winding passage giving entrance to the cave from the river.

He walked along the edge of the rocks until he gained the level ground.

Here he was joined by Par-a-wau.

Young Jack had got down safely, and was limping along in a fine style, with a stick, which did duty for a crutch.

"Come on, Monday," he exclaimed; "I want to get back and see my mamma."

"So you shall, sar."

"I've seen the world since I was stolen, and I'm quite a little man. You feel more of a man since you've seen the world, Monday?"

"Ever so much, sar."

"And our red-skin friend, here?"

"Par-a-wau seen a little too much," answered the Indian; "white men bad; drink, swear, cheat—want to get back."

"Do you know my father?" asked Young Jack.

"My brother Harkaway is a man," replied Par-a-wau.

"That's all right," said the boy. "I love my father, and I'd have gone for you with my crutch if you'd abused him. All white men are not bad. Don't Indians lie, steal, and take hair?"

"White man teach them."

"Not to raise hair. That's their own invention," said Young Jack, who added, "Monday!"

"Yes, sar."

It was amusing to see how the boy ordered Monday about, and spoke to him in a commanding tone, while the black, instead of resenting it, seemed rather proud of it.

"What was that firing? Have you killed th whole gang?"

"Fenton's gone up, sar. Hunston and t'other one, they escaped."

"I'm glad Fenton's settled," said Young Jack. "But you should have killed Hunston."

"He run too fast."

"My! Wouldn't father have given you something! You've missed a good chance, you black stupid."

"No black men here, sar," said Monday, with a grin "All gentlemen of colour, sar."

"You dry up, and carry me the rest of the way. My leg hurts."

Monday pointed to his bandaged arm.

"What!" said the boy. "Are you hurt! Poor fellow! I wouldn't have chaffed you if I'd known. Who did that?"

"Mr. Sheepe, sar."

"That Leroy fellow! He's a beauty," said Young Jack. "Didn't you mark him?"

"Yes, sar," replied Monday, with a smile of admiration. "Tell you what, sar, you quite young man of the world."

"Pretty well for my age. Living with such men, and going through what I have, sharpens you up a bit. You want to be a newsboy, Monday, to get sharp. Couldn't I sell them and blow on the news! *Tallygram, Grarphic!* They used to go like steam."

"Um quite a wonder," said Monday, raising his hands in admiration.

"Here, you lazy skunk, you Par-a-wau," said the boy. "You've done none of the fighting, and you haven't got a scratch. Carry me to the ferry."

Par-a-wau took him up like a baby, and, holding him in his two arms, carried him to Weehawken, where they crossed the Hudson, and took the cars to the hotel.

Monday conducted them to the elevator, and they got in, being taken to the second-floor.

"Come to Mast' Mole's room first, sar," said Monday. "Perhaps be too much for Missy Emily, if she see um on a sudden."

"Bosh!" answered the boy. "I'm going straight to my mamma. What's her number?"

"What um know 'bout numbers?"

"I was in a small hotel with Hunston, and we had a number."

"Oh, my!" said Monday. "Isn't um a beauty? Bet he'll beat all um creation."

"What's her number?" persisted the boy.

"Twenty-six, sar."

Young Jack started off up the corridor, looking at the numbers.

"Um go first," said Monday. "You got game leg, Mast' Jack. Race um for a dollar."

"Done with you," replied Young Jack.

As Monday passed him, he put out his crutch, and sent him rolling on his nose, and, before the black could recover himself, he had gained twenty-six, and, throwing open the door, cried—

"Who's last, eh?—old bag of soot!"

Emily and Hilda were sitting together, moping. Emily wouldn't talk. She did nothing but cry, and Hilda got tired of trying to comfort her.

When she saw Young Jack, she uttered a loud scream, and stared wildly at the boy.

But when Monday appeared with his bandaged arm, and said—"It all right, Missy Emily. Um got him back, sure 'nuff," she then opened her arms, and Young Jack rushed into them, while they clasped round him, and he was covered with kisses.

"Don't cry, mamma," said the boy. "Monday has found me, and we've killed Fenton."

Emily couldn't speak. She could only sob, and press him to her bosom.

Monday danced and cried, too, and, the example being catching, Hilda followed suit.

In the midst of the excitement, Mr. Mole and Harvey entered.

Young Jack caught up a paper lying on the table, and went up to the professor, saying—

"Buy a paper? *Tallygram.* All the news, sir."

"Get out, you young scamp!" said Mr. Mole. "Monday, what does this mean? Why is a newsboy allowed up here? Get out, lad!"

"Don't you know me?" asked the boy.

"No, and don't want to. I've read the *Advertiser* and the *Post.* Get out, I say, or I'll make you, you limping young vagabond!"

He raised his hand as if to box his ears.

"Smack me on the nose, will you?" said Young Jack. "No, you won't."

With considerable dexterity, he thrust his stick into Mr. Mole's stomach, and doubled that gentleman up.

"Oh, my!" said the professor, "what are we coming to? I will visit this insolence with condign punishment."

He ran after the boy, who took refuge at that safest of all places for a child—his mother's knee.

"My angel!" said Emily.

"Are you mad, Mrs. Harkaway?" said Mole, pausing. "Do you intend to adopt this ragged and dirty urchin?"

"He is my son."

"What?"

"I'm not too clean, and shouldn't be any worse for a new rig-out," replied Young Jack. "But my name's Harkaway, and Monday's found me. Ain't moles blind, that's all?"

"Bless us and save us!" cried Mr. Mole, holding up his hands. "Can this be possible? I might have known he was a Harkaway by his playful disposition, to which my internal organisation will testify at this moment."

Harvey shook the boy's hand.

Emily was warmly congratulated, and Monday heartily thanked.

Then all came round Young Jack, and listened to his adventures with intense interest.

After this, Monday was heard, and Par-a-wau, who had been standing at the door, asked in.

"This is wonderful," said Mr. Mole.

"He's taller and thinner," remarked Harvey.

"Poor, dear child, who can wonder at his being thin? Think of what he has gone through!" said Emily.

"Fancy his being a newsboy and a clown!" said Hilda.

"Suppose you put on some grub, mamma," said the boy, "by way of fattening me up a bit?"

"Why, certainly. Monday, order the best in the hotel."

"I haven't had a good square feed since I broke my leg in the circus. Oh, isn't Hunston a nice boss to serve under! It's kicks and blows all day long."

"If your father was only here, wouldn't he be pleased!" said Emily.

"One thing's clear," remarked Harvey. "Roughing it as sharpened him up. He's not the innocent he was a year ago."

"I fear I shall have some trouble with him," replied Mole, "though we will begin lessons to-morrow, and I will try to put that polish on his mind which always distinguishes my pupils."

"That's what you say," said Young Jack. "Put a polish on your boots—they want it."

"This is a case," muttered the professor, "in which the child will be spoilt if the rod is spared. Evil communications corrupt good manners *Noscitur a sociis.* He has had evil companions, and it is difficult to eradicate a noxious weed."

"I heard you say 'case' and 'weeds,' sir," said Harvey, offering Mr. Mole a cigar.

"Thank you, Harvey. I was imperfectly understood; but no matter, let us be merry. *Nunc est bibendum.*"

"What's that, old boy?" said Young Jack.

Mr. Mole raised up his hands in horrified astonishment.

"I never thought," he said, "that I should live to be accosted in such terms by a pupil of mine."

"You must make allowance for him," remarked Emily.

"I do, ma'am. I discount his backslidings, but there is a heavy *per contra*. John Harkaway—"

"Call me Jack," interrupted the boy. "Jack's good enough for the governor, and I'm not going back on him."

"Jack is familiar, but since you wish it, Jack let it be. The words that excited your curiosity are Latin. We had just commenced to study that language when you left Naples, stolen by the scoundrel Hunston, whom I may justly designate the arch-villain of the world."

"Bully for you, sir. That's good," put in Harvey.

"Now, Jack, let us see what you remember. What is *Musa?*"

"A song, sir."

"Right. Give me the genitive case."

"Bother genitives! You're all vocative," replied the boy.

At this apt reply, Harvey laughed loudly, and even Mr. Mole himself was obliged to smile.

"A sharp boy," he said. "I am compelled to admit that he resembles the edge of a razor, and to me is sharper than a serpent's tooth, for he is a thankless child. However, I will proceed. My quotation was from Horace. *Nunc est bibendum* means, ' Now is the time for drinking,' "

"That's a frequent complaint of yours, sir, isn't it?" said Young Jack, with a mischievous wink at Harvey.

"I drink when I am dry, lad—only when I'm dry," replied the professor, severely.

"You've altered since I saw you, then."

"Silence!" cried Mr. Mole, with a gesture of the hand, as if he were in class. "Let me proceed with my exposition of Horace. The lines go on. *Nunc pede libero pulsanda telus.* Translate that, Harvey."

"Literally," replied Harvey, "it is, ' Now is the earth to be struck with a quick foot.' In other words, it is a metaphor for dancing, and the passage, if I remember rightly, occurs in the first book of Odes.' "

"Right. You are a good boy. Take the head of the class. I shall give you a good mark—bless me, I thought I was in school!" exclaimed Mr. Mole, scratching his wig.

"Once a schoolmaster, always a schoolmaster. Eh, sir?" said Harvey.

"Well, well," replied Mr. Mole. "What have you to say against schoolmasters, Harvey?"

"Nothing, sir. They are all very well when you are young, but you don't want to go to school all your life."

"The world is a school, Harvey."

"How do you make that out, sir?"

"We are ever learning, and the wisest men admit they have always something to learn."

"Caught on the fly, Harvey," said Young Jack.

"You precious young brat," replied Harvey, "I shall have to attend to your education."

"I'm a man of the world," said the little fellow

"Come," exclaimed the professor, "let us be merry. Let us follow the advice of Horace. Let us drink. Can't we have a carpet dance?"

"How can I dance with a game leg?" said Young Jack.

"Young shrimp," replied Mr. Mole, "who was talking of you?"

"Wait till my leg gets well, and I'll show you a trick or two."

"What can you do?"

"Go through you any day. I'll bet my bottom down, against your top shutter, that I can run up your back and stand on your head before you can say hoopla."

"Go through me! Bottom down! Top shutter! Run up my back! Stand on my head! What language is this?" repeated Mr. Mole, in blank dismay.

"That's circus slang, up to the handle, boss."

"Oh, dear me! this is dreadful!"

"Carry me out, and bury me decently," said Young Jack, laughing.

"Well, I must say, my darling," said Emily, "that you are strangely altered since you have been away."

"That's nothing, mamma," said the boy. "Wait till we find pop; he'll understand me."

"I hope he may."

"I'm like my poor friend Kit," said the boy. "Young America, straight out. That's my platform, and I vote the whole ticket."

"But you are English."

"Was. I'm American now, and mean to take out my papers."

Harvey laughed till the tears ran down his cheeks.

"That boy will be the death of me, if he goes on like that." he said.

"They've taught him something," remarked Mr. Mole.

"I can do what you can't," said Young Jack.

"What's that?"

"Talk Schneider."

"Do what?"

"Sprechen sie Deutch? Nein. Gaseuntheit—dat ish, I will trink your 'elths like a goot poy, in the goot Rhien wein. Gaben mir a bretzel und a glass of lagar. Das est goot. Trink halle. I am a Dutchman, sir, and I give a barty to-night to my kind friend Mr. Mole. Prosit."

"Isn't he a beauty?" said Harvey, rubbing his hands delightedly.

"You shut up, and grin through a horse-collar! I haven't been a boy-clown for nothing. No, sir," answered Young Jack.

"That boy will give me some trouble," thought Mole, as he eyed him anxiously.

Monday had brought in some wine, but as his arm was stiff and painful, he had to get Par-a-wau to do his duty.

"Pop um cork," he said.

"No," said the Indian. "The Apache chief waits on no one. Ask your squaws."

He turned haughtily on his heel, and left the apartment.

"Nice sort of um chap for um quiet party," said Monday to himself.

Harvey saw what was the matter, and opened the bottle himself, pouring out the wine, which every one drank, Young Jack just sipping out of his mother's glass.

"Ladies and gentlemen," said Mr. Mole, "I can't refrain from saying a few words on this auspicious occasion." ("Hear, hear," from Harvey.) "We have found the lost sheep." ("Hear, hear," from Hilda, and "Thank God!" from Emily.) "Our best thanks are due to Monday." ("So they are.") "We must not relax our efforts." ("No, no.") "The enemy is discomfited. He has been smitten hip and thigh. We will smite him again. There shall be no truce till we find Jack Harkaway. Here's his jolly good health. God bless him, and long life to him!"

"Bully for you," said Young Jack.

Mr. Mole sat down amidst great applause.

The evening passed, and Monday went to have his arm dressed by a doctor, see his wife and kiss his child.

Emily soon retired with Hilda, and took Young Jack with her.

When she put him in his little bed, she clasped his hands together, and said—

"My darling, say the prayers I taught you long ago, and thank the Almighty for his goodness."

"God bless mamma and papa," said Young Jack, reverently. "I am very thankful for all his mercies. I feel very glad to come back to my dear mamma, and have such a good home again, and I hope God will always make me good to my kind mamma. That's all I can say. I don't remember what you taught me, only little bit's of 'Our Father' and 'I believe.' Will that do, mamma?"

Emily kissed him tenderly.

"What comes from the heart, my child, is better than what is merely said by rote by the lips. Good night," she replied

She left the room, and he sank off to sleep; but she stole in several times during the night to have a peep at him.

Each time she found Monday lying on the door-mat.

"You here, Monday?" she said.

"Yes, Missy Emily. They not steal um again, if Monday know it."

Bestowing a look of gratitude upon the faithful fellow, she retired, feeling confident that her darling was safe.

CHAPTER XXIX.
YOUNG JACK ASKS A FAVOUR.

CARE and rest soon made Young Jack's leg quite well, and he astonished everybody by his acrobatic performance and tricks—standing on his head, doing handsprings and somersaults, sliding up and down bannisters, and appearing in apparently impossible positions at unexpected times.

His mother and Mr. Mole found him a little rough, and tried to tone him down, with some success.

The search for Harkaway continued, but he was completely buried from the world, and could not be unearthed.

Neither could the police find any trace of Hunston or Leroy, though it was supposed they were hiding in the outskirts of the city, waiting for another chance of capturing the boy.

The latter was never allowed to go out alone.

Monday was his constant attendant, and carried arms to defend him against any attack.

"Mamma," said Young Jack, one fine morning, "I want you to do me a favour."

"Certainly. What is it?" asked Emily.

"Give me ten dollars."

"What for?"

"To buy flowers. You have heard me talk of Kit? My poor Kit, who saved me from starving in the snow?"

"Yes, dear."

"He asked me to plant flowers on his grave, and I promised him to see it done. The Spring has come. There is no snow and ice now, and flowers will grow. I cannot be happy until I plant the flowers on Kit's grave."

"That shows you have a good heart, my darling," said Emily. "You shall go with Monday and buy the flowers, and then we will go to the cemetery and ornament the grave."

Young Jack was delighted.

He kissed his mother, and thanked her very much.

All the time he had been in the cave with the counterfeiters he had been thinking of Kit and his dying request.

It would have been a great blow to him if he could not have kept his word.

Monday took him to the florist's at the corner of Forty-second-street and Fifth Avenue, where he bought all he wanted, and had the roots and shrubs packed in a hamper.

This Monday carried, his arm being quite well

again, and, a coach being procured, they started for Greenwood.

The grave was a very simple one, and Young Jack easily recognised it. Permission was obtained to plant the flowers, and they approached the little mound, under which lay the remains of the poor newsboy.

At the head was a marble cross, on which was carved, "Kit. He is not dead, but sleepeth."

"Why, mamma!" exclaimed the boy, "some one's done this!"

"I had it done, my dear," replied Emily, "when you first spoke to me of your friend. I thought it would please you."

"Oh! that is very kind of you. How can I thank you?" said Young Jack, in delight. "I am going to say a little prayer, mamma, for Kit, and then we will plant the flowers."

He knelt down at the foot of the grave and prayed, while his mother and Monday looked on with their heads bowed.

When he had concluded, he said—

"Kit is with the angels now."

"I hope so, dear," replied his mother, in whose eyes the tears had started.

There was something so simple and unaffected about the boy's proceedings that she was touched.

Children are always genuine, and in the absence of art, they appeal very forcibly to grown-up people.

"Can Kit look down from the clouds and see us?" continued the boy.

"Yes, dear."

"Do you think he is pleased with me?"

"I cannot tell whether spirits are pleased or not, but if they can be pleased, he must feel a delight in what you are doing."

"It seems to me, mamma, that he is talking to me, and saying, 'Put these roses at the head, and the lilies at the foot,'" said Young Jack. "Now, Monday, just level the ground, and we'll plant the flowers. That geranium will go in the middle, and the ivy must twine round the cross."

"We fix um up all right, sar," answered Monday, setting to work.

Emily watched the two performing this labour of love, and her tears fell fast.

She was more proud of her boy at that moment than she had ever been before.

He had a good heart, his nature was fond, affectionate, and generous, and there was a strongly-rooted sentiment of piety and religion in his young mind, which a mother is always glad to see in her offspring.

Rough though his adventures might have made him, they had neither corrupted nor hardened him.

In about an hour Young Jack got up from his knees, and surveyed his handiwork.

The grave was very neatly covered with flowers and shrubs, and all round ran a bordering of white, innocent-looking flowers, and not a weed was allowed to remain to sully the purity of the same.

"What do you think of it, mamma?" asked the boy.

"It is very nice, and very pretty, my dear, and does you great credit. I hope your heart will always be so good, and incline you to such sacred and holy thoughts."

"Kit must be happy," said Young Jack. "I'll bet my—"

Emily interrupted him—softly, but solemnly.

"You must not talk about betting, my dear," she said, "at such a time. Take my hand, and let us go home."

The boy was abashed, and allowed himself to be silently led away from the cemetery.

Suddenly Monday pointed to a grave-stone.

"See there, Missy Emily!"

"What?"

"Hunston behind that grave. I see um look up, and his eyes like um tiger's!"

"Nonsense. Hunston cannot be watching us," replied Emily, holding her child tightly.

Monday went up to the grave, but could see no one. If his eyes had not deceived him, Hunston must have glided away like a spirit.

"It dam odd," he muttered. "Um fit to swear I see um one-arm thief."

"You were mistaken, you see, Monday," exclaimed Emily, drawing a deep sigh of relief.

"Um get home fast in um coach, Missy," replied Monday. "The blackguard's 'bout somewhere, that for certain."

He held his pistol in his hand, to be prepared for any emergency ; but nothing more was seen of the intruder.

CHAPTER XXX.

HOW JACK GOT ON IN THE LUNATIC ASYLUM.

THE injury inflicted upon Jack, when attacked by Leroy and Fenton, was very severe. It produced concussion of the brain, and he was insensible for some days.

They took him in the coach to a private lunatic asylum at the upper end of Manhattan Island, where he was put to bed, and placed under surgical superintendance, and it was fully two weeks before he began to look about him, and wonder where he was.

It was a fine Spring day, and the sun shone in through the window of the narrow room in which he was confined. But few articles of furniture were to be found, and the bed on which he was lying belonged to the commonest trestle sort. The walls were kalsomined, and devoid of pictures. The windows were grated with iron bars, and as he gazed fully upon the surroundings, events came back dimly to him.

"Hullo, there!" he exclaimed. "Is anybody around?"

The door opened, and a young man, about five-and twenty, entered. He was tall and thin, having rather a comical cast of countenance, dressed in a slovenly manner, but looking jolly under the circumstances.

"Did you call?" he asked.

"Yes," replied Jack ; "I'm getting better, and I want to talk to some one. Have I been sick long?"

"About a fortnight," answered the young man. "You had an ugly crack on the head, when you were brought here, and have been raving awful. I happened to be passing by when you called, and have come in to cheer you up a bit."

"Who are you?" inquired Jack.

"My name is Pleasant Hook, but they call me the Deputy Governor," he replied, "because I can do most what I like here."

"Where am I?"

"In a private lunatic asylum. Didn't you know that?"

"Well, I guessed it. Where is it situated?"

"In New York City. It's called Paradise Lost by me, but the governor, in his circulars, terms it the Sanatorum."

"There is a chance of my friends finding me?" said Jack,

"If they do, they are cunning, and if they get you out, they are cunninger. That's not grammar, but it's expressive," replied Pleasant Hook.

"I have been knocked down and carried off," exclaimed Jack, "and it's a scandalous outrage."

"I have heard a good many say that, but they are still here."

"What am I to do?"

"Keep quiet." said Pleasant Hook. "The boss of this show is named Mr. Persuasive Power—and a good name it is, too. He goes in for the persuasion dodge first, and if that don't answer, he comes down upon his patient powerfully hard."

"Are you mad?" exclaimed Jack, leaning on his elbow, and eyeing his new acquaintance curiously.

"I!" exclaimed Mr. Pleasant Hook, bursting into a roar of laughter. "Of course I'm not. That's the joke. They say I'm mad ; but I'm no slouch, if I do have fits, you bet."

"Then you're not mad?"

"Not much. I'm an epileptic subject, and have been here six months now. My friends are rich, and pay heavily for me. The fact is, when I'm out, I can't keep away from the lush drums. Late hours, and drink and dissipation, brought on my fits, and my father put me in here. I don't blame him. When I'm right again, I shall get out."

Jack thought this was sensible, and was pleased to meet with some one who could speak rationally.

"What's your craze?" asked Pleasant Hook.

"Mine?" repeated Jack, in astonishment.

"Yes."

"I'm not mad," said Jack.

"Come, now, that won't do," exclaimed Pleasant Hook, with an incredulous smile. "You might just as well own up, and have done with it. Are you the President of the United States ?—or Queen Victoria ?—or the Prince Imperial ?—or any other bloated swell ?"

"Upon my honour, I'm not mad," replied Jack ; "I'm only the victim of a base conspiracy."

"Don't, for goodness sake," cried Pleasant Hook, holding his sides to check his laughter. "You'll make me bad, if you go on like that."

"Why?"

"I've heard so many of them talk like that. It was only last week that a bloke came in, as mild as milk, and the next day he tried to murder a keeper, swearing he was the only original Bengal tiger, and must have blood for supper."

"Well," said Jack, gloomily, "I won't contradict you. Listen here. I'm Jack Harkaway."

"What! The hero of all those bully stories?"

"Yes."

Mr. Pleasant Hook smiled with an air of compassion.

"You must be mad!" he said, "if you fancy you are Jack Harkaway. I suppose you have been reading too much. Poor fellow! I'm sorry for you. But look here, Jack—I shall call you Jack—I've taken a liking to you, and will try to make you comfortable,"

"Thank you," replied Jack, who, in spite of his weakness, began to be amused.

"Just so long as you're quiet, and do what you're told, you will have the run of the place, and you must promise old Persuasive Power that you won't try to escape."

"That I never will do," replied Jack, " for I mean to get out of this as soon as I can."

"That's what I said when I first came here, but it's easier said than done. Take my tip, and don't try it on. You'll find it a mistake, you bet."

"But I want to get back to my wife," said Jack.

"You may in time," replied Mr. Pleasant Hook, thoughtfully. "For the present, be quiet, be docile, as they call it. If you're violent, it will be bad for you. Don't throw yourself away."

"Can I have a drink of lemonade?" asked Jack.

"You can have a Croton cocktail."

"That isn't up to much."

"Will a Boston float do?"

"What's that?"

"A glass of water with a cork in it."

"No, thank you," replied Jack.

"Then I'm afraid, my blooming shrub," replied Pleasant Hook, "that I can't do anything for you. The doctor will be round soon. Ask him. Good sort of fellow is the doc. I kinder cotton to him. Good-bye for the present. Keep up your pluck, and remember that the deputy-governor is your friend."

"Very many thanks," answered Jack, who felt that it was something gained to have a friend of any sort in such a dreadful place as a lunatic asylum.

"By-the-way," said Pleasant Hook, "did I say anything to you about my diamond?"

"No."

"I've got the biggest diamond that ever was found. It's buried at the foot of a tree in Limpia Canyon, near Camp Stockton, in Texas. I was all over there three years ago, and when I speak of my diamond, they all laugh at me. But wait a bit. I'll have it when I get rid of my fits and am free again. Then we shall see who'll laugh."

Jack regarded him with pity. "After all," he thought, "he his mad, and his insanity consists in his thinking himself the owner of a buried diamond in the wilds of the Far West."

At that moment Jack did not dream of ever being in those regions, but not many months were to pass over his head before his feet would be treading the pathless solitudes of Western America, battling with Indians, and meeting with adventures which would throw into the shade all he gone through hitherto.

"Well," said Pleasant Hook, "I must go my rounds. I dine with the governor, and he is sure to ask me at dinner if all's well. I shall try for you to dine with us at private table when you are strong enough to get up."

"That will be bully," said Jack.

"Recollect all I have told you. Don't get riled with the keepers. Keep your wool straight. If you try to sick them, you'll get euchred, and I shan't be able to help you."

"I'll remember," said Jack.

"That is right, my blooming shrub. Don't throw yourself away. Ta-ta, till we meet again."

Mr. Pleasant Hook kissed his hand to Jack, and left him alone. Turning round at the door, however, with a short laugh, to say—

"Fancy your delusion being that you're Jack Harkaway! That is good. Ha! ha! ha!"

After this, Jack began to recover himself rapidly, and the doctor pronounced him well enough to leave his room.

Mr. Persuasive Power paid him a visit for the first time, and Jack recollected all that Pleasant Hook had said to him.

The governor of the asylum was a little man, with long, dark hair, and a quick, active manner. He took in everything at a glance, and through being constantly with lunatics, his glance had acquired an almost supernatural acuteness.

He could see in an instant if an inmate was about to be ugly, and altogether was a right smart man for the situation he held.

"Well, sir," he said to Jack, as he entered his room. "The doctor reports you to be convalescent."

Jack was sitting up, reading a book which had been lent him by one of the nurses, and replied that he was getting quite well, though he still felt a little weak.

"Your stay here," continued Mr. Power, "will be either agreeable or not, just as you like to make it."

"I do not wish to stay," answered Jack, and not being mad, I trust you will recognise the liberty of the subject, and let me go."

"According to my patients," said the governor, "I am the only lunatic here. They are all sane.

Dismiss that idea from your mind. Here you are on the certificate of two doctors, and here you will stay."

"I thought this was a free country. Is that a delusion?"

"As far as you are concerned, it is. Now make up your mind that you are a fixture, and that there is no moving, even on the first of May. If you do, I will accord you all the liberty I can, but first of all you must promise not to attempt to escape."

Jack hesitated.

"Tell me who has put me in here?" he said, "and what is the meaning of it all?"

"All I know is, that I charge a thousand dollars a year for a patient, and that I have received two years' pay in advance for you."

"I will get you twice as much to let me go."

"Can't be done. It would not pay me to accept ten thousand, for if I broke faith with those outside who patronise me, I should lose my connection. We wish to treat patients well. It saves trouble, but if they are ugly, so can we be."

"Do not Commissioners of Lunacy come round to inquire into cases?"

"Certainly; but we get over that difficulty. A patient can be driven temporarily mad, by having his feet tickled with feathers. We can shave a man's head, and shower-bath him till he's silly, or put him in one of our underground dungeons. Believe me, you are helpless, and your best chance is to listen to me."

"If I promise all you require, what then?"

"Then you will have the privilege of the reading-room, the garden, and, as I have a vacancy at my private table, you may dine with me. I wish to act squarely with all."

Jack thought of his friends without, of Harvey, Mr. Mole, his wife, Monday, and Felix.

Surely they would not let him languish long where he was, and their efforts to find him must be crowned with success, sooner or later.

It was best to fall in with the governor's views, and he determined to do so, but, with a smile, he said—

"Can a lunatic keep a promise? Does not your request go to prove that you think me sane?"

"We will not discuss that question now. Am I to place you amongst the tractables, or the intractables?" replied Persuasive Power, biting his lips.

"I consent to all you require," said Jack. "Let me be a tractable."

"Sensibly spoken," said the governor. "Come with me, Mr. Harkaway. I will introduce you to the head-keeper, and I do hope we shall run along smoothly."

Jack followed Persuasive Power along a passage, into a large reading-room, in which a few patients were languidly looking at prints, or turning over the leaves of books in a listless manner.

A tall, robust man was standing by.

"Goliah," said Mr. Power, "this gentleman is admitted to all the privileges of the asylum. If he does anything to forfeit this indulgence, let me know at once."

The keeper bowed, and Mr. Power opened a door leading to the garden, which was a pleasantly wooded tract, inclosed with high walls.

It was a lovely Spring day, and Jack's heart felt quite glad at the chance of roaming about the pretty garden.

"Now, walk about. Do what you like," said Mr. Power. "But when you hear the gong beat, come in to dinner."

Jack thanked him, and strolled along, coming to the conclusion that it was better to knuckle down and knock under, than to be violent and subjected to ill-treatment.

The keepers would all be against him; he was weak and unarmed. What could he do against alarming odds?

He concluded to keep quiet, and wait for what turned up, believing that his lucky star would soon be in the ascendant again, and his friends would find him out.

Before he had gone far, the voice of Pleasant Hook reached his ears, and he turned round.

"Ah! my blooming shrub!" said Hook, "how you feel to-morrow, Schneider? They told me you were out, and I have come to post you up in all the peculiarities of the place."

Jack shook the hand of the "deputy governor" warmly, and they walked along the garden-paths together, looking at the flowers, and the chirping birds, and the shadows dancing under the leafy branches of the verdant trees.

"Fancy being landed in a place like this, at such an early age," said Hook, in a moralising tone. "It all comes of being a forward boy. I used to run down old women on my three-wheeled velocipede, throw rocks at old gentlemen with spectacles, go for people on the side-walk with my gumboshooter, walk on stilts, and draw devils in chalk on the fences."

"Is that so?" asked Jack, amused at his young friend's deception.

"Ah! if I had only been a young Bostonian, and my idea had been taught to shoot in another manner, I should have been walking along the street with eye-glasses at three years old, serenely perusing my multiplication card, or learning the seraphic fact in verse, that 'dogs delight to bark and bite, for 'tis their nature to."

"How do you amuse yourself?" Jack inquired. "Isn't it dull?"

"Not a bit of it. I like observing human nature, and I am a general favourite. I told you they all call me the deputy-governor. I go for things lively, that's me. I'm like the boy who would not read his geography, and said, 'I ain't an angel. Give me a lively dime-novel, with lots of Injuns scalpin' a soldier.'"

Jack sat down on a seat under a tree, and began to laugh.

"It seems awfully funny, my being here," he said. "I'll be hanged if I can help laughing. You see, I've been in so many tight fixes in my life, that this is nothing wonderful. It is only a detail."

"Well," replied Pleasant Hook, "we've got to hang up our hats in some shanty, and all that worries me is that I can't go and look after my big diamond."

"Perhaps you'll be able some day."

"You bet. I am not fixed for life. As you say, being here is only a detail. What we want is our liberty."

"We never know how blessed liberty is till we lose it," answered Jack.

"Tell you," said Pleasant Hook, "I'd rather accept a chore in a junk-shop, and work from six to eight, than be shut up here, and doing nothing. Eh?—my blooming shrub!"

"Quite of your opinion," replied Jack.

"What do you think of the circus, as far as you've seen? It ain't exactly as bully as it might be, but with a chew of bacca and a book, it isn't so bad on a fine day out here. See there!"

Jack looked in the direction pointed out, and saw a melancholy individual moving along with his hands behind his back, and his eyes cast down.

"That is our historian," continued Pleasant Hook. "He's writing a history of England, which is a played-out country, I guess, which has made all the history she can, and that don't amount to much."

"You dry up," said Jack, good-humouredly. "I

don't allow any one to run down the U.... Jack. If you and I fall out, you will have to be swept up when I'm through with you."

"And when I am through with you, there will be only a grease-spot left," answered Pleasant Hook; adding, "Aren't we two lively and highly intelligent lunatics?"

The historian approached slowly.

"Hi! my blooming shrub!" continued Hook. "what are you splashing around for?"

"Good morning, gents," replied the historian. "I am engaged in collecting materials for Chapter V. of Book II. of my History of England, complete and unabridged, with a portrait of the author."

"Give us part of Chapter V.," said Hook.

"With pleasure. We are now under the head of Raleigh. This distinguished man was passing through a forest with his cousin, William the Conqueror, when Walter Tyrrel, called Rufus, on account of his red hair, shot an arrow at him, and Raleigh fell dead. He was buried in Westchester Kerfederal."

"Thank you," said Jack "May I inquire, sir, who Washington was?"

"Washington was the inventor of postage-stamps. He tried to impose a stamp tax on Great Britain, and sent an army there, but he was badly whipped by Queen Elizabeth, and ever since then the British Isles have been free, with the exception of Ireland."

"What were the principal battles of the civil war?" inquired Pleasant Hook.

"There was the battle of the Crimea, and the war of Bull Run, in which the Red Roses whipped the Confederates, and after that Beauregard took Charleston, and Baltimore surrendered to General Jackson, while Abraham Lincoln received the swords of Wellington and Nelson, for the First Napoleon on the field of Waterloo, which classic plain is somewhere about the centre of the Northern Pacific Railroad, between California and Cape Sable."

"Quite correct. I'll mark your ticket O. K. You can run and play," said Pleasant Hook.

The historian inclined his head, and walked on in the same melancholy manner, mumbling to himself, and jumbling his historical facts together for his own especial edification.

"The old fool!" said Hook. "It would be an act of charity to fix him for a tombstone in Greenwood."

Turning round, the old man said to Jack—

"Pardon me, sir; but are you Julius Cæsar?"

"I have not that honour," replied Jack.

"He's his first cousin thirty times removed," said Hook.

"Ah! I thought there was a family likeness," answered the historian, "and I feel proud to make the acquaintance of a relation of so distinguished a man. Come and see me."

He shuffled off again, and another lunatic walked up rapidly, saying to Jack—

"Fine day for the race, sir."

"What race?" asked Jack.

"The human race, sir. Sold again. Good-morning," replied the lunatic, walking away, rubbing his hands with glee.

"You've got a lively lot here," remarked Jack.

"Oh! that's nothing. I can introduce you to the inventor of the flying machine, and the discoverer of perpetual motion—that is not a woman's tongue. No, sir, though that comes near it, and the owner of the patent elixir of life, which keeps people from dying, and the man who can make diamonds out of charcoal; but, I say, they can't touch my big diamond stone in Limpia Canyon—eh? Not much, you bet, my blooming shrub."

Jack repressed a smile, and they strolled on, coming to one of the side-walls.

"That does not look difficult to climb," said Jack.

"Try it," replied Pleasant Hook. "It might be done by the help of a tree."

"No," answered Jack. "I have given Persuasive Power my word of honour that I will not attempt to escape, and I always keep my word."

"Perhaps you're right," said Hook, "though I wasn't brought up to regard the truth, unless it paid to be truthful."

"It always pays; a liar is a contemptible worm," answered Jack, "and when a man once begins lying, he never knows when to stop. It is as much a disease as drinking."

"I'm afraid I've had both diseases badly."

"That accounts for your being here."

"You're going back on me, my blooming shrub," said Pleasant Hook, angrily.

"Excuse me," replied Jack. "I didn't mean anything, and certainly don't want to quarrel with my only friend in this place."

"Well, shake hands and call it square. There's the gong for dinner. Come along. Won't I give the grub Jessie! Hurry up, my shrub," exclaimed Hook, smiling again.

They went in to dinner, and Jack found his life in the asylum more agreeable than he had expected it would be.

But in his heart there was a burning desire for freedom.

He wanted to get out to push his search for his child, whom he did not know was restored to his mother's arms. He wanted to persecute Hunston, and be amongst his friends once more.

Freedom was what he longed for, and many a poor wretch has echoed from his dungeon the silent prayer that Jack put forth for liberty.

CHAPTER XXXI.
MR. MOLE STRIKES OUT.

YOUNG JACK soon became himself once more, and forgot all his trouble and misery in the happiness with which he was surrounded.

He wished to return the kindness that Pavonia Pants and his son had shown him; but, on making inquiries at the Rink, he found that the clown had gone to Chicago, to fulfil an engagement out West.

Everybody admitted that the boy had wonderfully improved. His roughing it had made quite a little man of him, and his mother felt proud of her son.

His leg got well, and he could run about and climb like a monkey. He astonished his friends by his clownish tricks, and his tumbling. Despising the elevator as a thing only fit for girls, he slid down the bannisters, coming down-stairs in a way that frightened Emily into fits.

Mr. Mole thought a little schooling would do him no harm, and gaining his mother's consent, he told the boy after breakfast that he must begin work again.

"I am your private tutor, specially engaged by your father, who was once my pupil, as you are now," exclaimed the professor.

"Yes, sir," replied Young Jack.

"I have spoken to your mother, and she has agreed that we ought to resume our studies, which were so abruptly broken off when you were stolen by Hunston after the fight in the garden."

"I can read and write a little," said Young Jack. "But not much, and I can say A was an archer, who shot at a frog, and B was a butcher, who had a big dog. C was a cat, who eat a small mouse, and D was a Dutchman, as big as a house."

"We shall soon get on," said Mr. Mole. "Come into my room every day from ten till twelve, and from two till four, and let us make a start at once."

"It won't hurt my leg, sir, will it?" asked Young Jack.

"What nonsense! Who ever heard of such a thing?"

"The doctor said I was to be left quiet."

"This looks like trying to shirk your work, my boy, and that won't do. You will find that I am a strict disciplinarian, however mild I may be out of school. Come, we will resume our studies of the English language, and I hope you will turn out as good a scholar as your father."

"You bet," replied Young Jack.

"When addressing me, be more respectful," said Mr. Mole, with a reproving glance.

He quitted the room, followed by the boy, and together they entered the professor's private apartment, the latter going to a box to get out a spelling-primer and a book of fables.

When he looked round, Young Jack was nowhere to be seen. Mr. Mole gazed around, astonished, and exclaimed—

"Can the young rascal have given me the slip?"

A low laugh over his head made him look up.

The boy was hanging by his twisted feet to the gaselier, and making more grimaces in a minute than a monkey could in an hour.

"Come down, sir. How dare you!" cried Mole.

"All right, colonel," replied Young Jack. "Stand still, and I'll 'light on your back."

The next moment, a heavy substance fell on Mole, who tumbled forward, knocking his nose against a chair, and the boy was standing before him, bowing and kissing his hands to an imaginary audience.

"I say," said the professor, getting up and rubbing his nose, "this won't do, you know. I can't have this."

"A was an acrobat on a long pole. B was a bummer who drank from a bowl," replied Young Jack. "Go ahead, sir. I'm ready. Who's afraid?"

"My dear child," answered Mole, solemnly, "I am afraid that it will take a long time to civilise you. The adventures you have gone through have made you a wild Indian."

"Who's he when he's at home, sir?"

The professor groaned.

"Sit down, and sit still, if you can. I must really buy a cane if this is to go on," he said.

"My mamma won't have me beaten, so you'll have to try a new start," answered the boy.

"What am I to do?" said the professor, in despair.

"Turn it up for to-day, and let's go and look for pop."

"Well, now, that's a good idea," said Mr. Mole. "Suppose we do take an excursion, and see if we can find any private lunatic asylums. We can talk and learn as we go on. But this must not be an example. You will promise to be a good boy in future?"

"I can't be too good," replied Young Jack. "It isn't natural for a boy to be too good."

"You will have to go to school," said Mole, "if you do not obey me."

"What! over here in America?"

"Yes. Why not?"

"Won't that be bully!" said Young Jack. "I'll lick all the Yankee boys if they chaff me about Bunker Hill. See if I don't."

Mr. Mole smiled, and patted the boy's head.

"You're like a young bear," he said. "All your troubles have to come, though I must admit you've seen something of life at an early age. Put that primer in your pocket. I will ask you questions as we go along. Youth is the time for learning. When you grow up, the cares and pleasures of life will take up all your time."

"Shan't we go back to England when we've found my father?" asked Young Jack.

"Perhaps. I cannot say."

"I should like to stay here," said Young Jack. "England isn't big enough for me. I want to go out, when I'm bigger, and shoot bears, and kill Indians."

"That's your father's spirit," replied Mole, smiling again.

Monday knocked at the door as the professor was taking his hat down from the peg, and being told to come in, entered.

"Hullo! Sambo Gumbo," said Young Jack, "what fox has got into your hen-roost?"

"Mast' Young Jack," replied Monday, "if you ain't the cheekiest young varmint in the States, I'll not eat any more pie, as long's I live, sar."

"Never mind him," said Mr. Mole. "Do you want me, Monday?"

"Yes, sar. Letters have come by the mail from England, and Missy Harkaway want to 'sult you 'bout it, sar."

"Oh! indeed. Say I'll be with Mrs. Harkaway in a moment. Jack, go and get your cap; we will take our walk later on," answered Mole.

The boy ran to Monday, and climbed up his back, holding on to his black hair, and biting one of his ears, till he kicked and bellowed like a vicious mule.

"You drop it, sar," said Monday. "You get down quick, or I jam um up against the wall. So."

Monday backed up against the wall as hard as he could, but Young Jack was too quick for him, and threw a somersault over his head, alighting on his feet just in time to see the black go bang against a picture, the glass of which he broke in a hundred pieces.

"You run 'way and laff," said Monday, rubbing his shoulders. "All right, young fellow; me give it you hot, sar."

"Dat so, Sambo," replied Young Jack, half way up the passage.

He put his thumb to his elbow, and extended his fingers in the derisive manner known as "cocking a snooke, or taking a sight," and added—

"Take it out of that, old ebony."

"Well, I nebber see such a rip in all my life. No, sar," said Monday, laughing in spite of himself. "But he good boy after all, and I guess he like old Monday."

Mr. Mole at once repaired to the drawing-room, where he found Emily, Hilda, and Harvey.

"Sorry to disturb you, Mr. Mole," said Emily; "but we have received some important letters from England."

"Is that so?" replied Mole.

"Jack's father is dead."

"How?"

"He was out hunting, and fell from his horse receiving injuries which resulted in his death. Jack's mother writes to tell us this, and to say that they have lately lost a great deal of money in an American mine. But you had best read the letter, which, in Jack's absence, I have taken the liberty of opening."

Mr. Mole did so, and read—

"MY EVER DEAR BOY,—It is with the deepest grief I write to inform you of the sudden death of your father in the hunting-field. His last words were of you."

Full particulars of the disaster followed, and then the letter resumed—"Your father has been very unfortunate lately in speculations. I find that, after paying all debts and liabilities, I shall have only a small income of three hundred pounds a year, with which I mean to retire to a sea-side

place and reside till you return, which I hope will be soon."

"Poor thing!" interrupted Emily, "she does not know what trouble we are in about Jack."

"It will be necessary," continued Mole, reading aloud, "for you to do something to maintain yourself while you prosecute your search after your lost child. I scarcely know how to help you, but will try to send you a small sum as soon as my affairs are settled, hoping that your education and experience in a country like America will enable you to do something for yourself."

"You need never want for money, Emily, dear, while I have any," said Hilda.

Emily's eyes were streaming with tears, and she pressed her friend's hand warmly.

"Our great loss," continued Mr. Mole, reading from the letter, "has been the robbery of our bankers, Messrs. Froom Brothers, of Cornhill. Your father had advanced very large sums for the Missouri United Lead Mining Company, receiving bonds and mortgages on the company. These were at Froom's, and were stolen."

"That is bad," said Harvey.

"Very," answered his wife. "If we had the bonds and mortgages, Jack is just the man to go and work the mine successfully."

"Let me go on," said Mole. "I am interested in the letter."

"Certainly, sir."

"Oddly enough," continued Mole, "the clerk who is suspected of robbing the bank is a brother of your old enemy, Hunston. His name is Alfred, or Alf Hunston, and the brothers are said to be very much alike."

"Two scamps in the same family," remarked Harvey.

"This is very strange," said Hilda.

"The most remarkable thing that I ever heard of," said Mole. "But hold on, please, till I get through."

Every one was silent again.

"It is not known where Alfred Hunston has gone to," pursued the professor. "The detectives are on the look-out, but he will, perhaps, disguise himself. It may be as well for you, my dear son, to look out for him in New York, though the general opinion is, that he has gone to Spain with his booty, as there is no Extradition Treaty between that country and England, in cases of felony."

"I'll bet he is coming here to join his precious brother," said Harvey.

"I should not wonder at all if it were so," observed Hilda.

Mr. Mole continued reading the letter to himself, and at length looking up, said—

"There is not much more of any importance."

"One thing is clear," said Harvey. "Jack's allowance is stopped."

"But we have plenty of money, my dear," said Hilda, "and I am sure that both Emily and Jack are welcome to use our purse."

"Of course," replied Harvey, "yet I know Jack so well, that I am sure he would not live upon us."

"Not he," said Emily, who was proud of her husband's independence. "If ever we get Jack back again—"

"If!" interrupted Mole; "we won't have any 'if's' about it. Why, Young Jack and I are going out to-day on an exploring expedition."

"Really!"

"Yes, and as our friend Felix would say, we mean to strike oil."

"I hope you may."

"Tell you what," said Harvey, "I believe that Alfred Hunston is in communication with his brother, and will come over here right away with the plunder of the bank."

"We must look out for him," said Mole.

"By all means. Don't you see, that if we could recover these mortgages on the mine, Jack could go out and work it as his own, and by personal super-intendence make a fortune out of it?"

"Why not?" replied Emily.

"The first thing to be done is to get Jack back again, and I'll start right off. I feel like a morning star to-day," said Mole, "and I'm sure something will come of my expedition."

"Are you going to take my boy with you, Mr. Mole?" asked Emily.

"It was the proposal that we should go."

"You must be very careful, please. I am miser-able when the boy is out of my sight. Hunston and Leroy are on the look-out for him, I have no doubt."

"I shall take my pistol," replied the professor, "and if I can't come back with the boy, I won't come at all. My life for his, Mrs. Harkaway. Will that do?"

Emily smiled faintly.

The professor went to the door and called for Young Jack, who came into the room, looking annoyed.

"What's the matter, my pet?" asked his mother.

"This won't do, mamma," answered Young Jack. "I've just put on my new pants the tailor sent home last night, and there's no pistol pocket in them. I can't stand that, anyway."

Everybody laughed, and Harvey said—

"Won't a pea-shooter do as well?"

"I tell you what, Dick Harvey," replied the boy, "if you cheek me, I'll tell your wife where you go of evenings."

"Where does he go, dear?" asked Hilda.

"I ain't going to split on him, unless he drives me to it; but he'd best not rile me up to the hilt, or I'll spring a torpedo on him."

"I shall have to pull your young ear," said Harvey.

"That's more than you dare do, Dick," replied Young Jack.

"Don't be rude," said Emily. "Go with Mr. Mole and learn to behave yourself."

"All right, ma. Now, pro-fess-or, are you ready? If so, make your bow, and fire away. I can't wait all day for you," answered the boy.

The professor nodded, and, followed by Young Jack, left the drawing-room.

"I never saw such a boy," exclaimed Hilda.

"Nor I," remarked Harvey. "He's a perfect young demon."

"You must make some allowance for him," exclaimed Emily. "Look how he's been knocked about lately, and I don't think there's any harm in him."

"Not a bit," Hilda hastened to reply. "I didn't mean to say there was."

"Recollect how he went to his friend Kit's grave. Poor little fellow, he has a good heart."

"He wouldn't be his father's own son if he hadn't," said Harvey. "I wish we had one like him. I'll buy him, if you want to sell."

"I wouldn't part with him for all the world," answered Emily.

Hilda said nothing. She, too, would have liked to have such a boy, and had he been hers, she would have forgiven him all his impudence, which, after all, was only the result of animal spirits, and a sort of native wit, which had been developed unusually early by the adventures he had gone through.

The professor took the boy's hand, and they walked up Broadway. When they had got as far as Thirty-fifth-street, they met a well-dressed boy walking quickly along.

He stopped and looked sharply at Young Jack, who returned his gaze with equal astonishment.

"My!" said the boy "Euchred, if it ain't Kit's Tiny."

"Is that you, Shise?" said Young Jack.

"If it ain't me, it is my ghost. What have you been a-doing of. You're in luck, ain't you?—and so am I."

Mr. Mole frowned angrily.

"Come along, Jack," he said. "I can't have you stopping in the street to speak to boys."

"Say, colonel," cried Shise, "who's been tread-ing on your corns? Tiny and me is ole pals. Ain't we, Ti?"

"Not pals. I knew you, and that is all," replied Young Jack.

"I'm not gunning now," said Shise.

"Aren't you?"

"Not much. I've got a place. Regular up-to-the-knocker crib. We are finanshal and minin' agents. I'm door-boy. We keep on Broadway, and ain't our offices a picture!"

"Is it square?" asked Young Jack.

"I would not be in it, if it was," replied Shise, with a solemn shake of his head, which was quite comical. "If I ain't on the gun, my bosses are sure to be. The firm consists of three. One is late from England, the second is a one-armed cove, brother of the first, and the third is the cleverest man in the States, bar none. His name is Leroy, or the Sensitive Sheepe."

Mr. Mole pricked up his ears.

"What is that you say, boy?" he demanded, eagerly.

Recollecting the news that had come from England that morning, the revelations of the Shyser were of great importance.

"Who spoke to you, old run-to-seed?" replied Shise. "You're a parson, aren't you? What is your text?"

"He is my tutor," said Young Jack. "Good-bye, Shise. Be honest, and you'll get on."

He was about to walk along, feeling rather ashamed of the Shyser's company, when Mr. Mole pulled his hand and stopped him.

"If you have been a friend of this boy's," he said, "I shall be glad to assist you, my little man."

"Perhaps you'll wait till you are asked," replied Shise, impudently.

"There is a quarter for you," said Mole, present-ing him with a twenty-five cent stamp.

"Chip in. I'll go you a dollar better. Bluff away, colonel," answered Shise.

"Won't you take it?"

"I never say 'No' to a good thing, but what is it for? Am I to do anything for it?"

"Where are you employed?" asked Mole.

"Do you see any green in my eye?" replied the Shyser, adding, "What is your graft? Cheese it, sonny. I was not born yesterday."

With this speech the Shyser nodded his head to the professor, and quickly disappeared in the distance.

Mr. Mole pondered what he had said in his mind, and was very grave and unusually silent.

The Shyser had said just enough to set him thinking.

Was it not likely that Alfred Hunston had come over to New York, communicated with his brother, and set up a financial agency with Leroy to help them?

The name Leroy, the one-armed man, two brothers, all combined to fix this belief in Mole's mind.

"Wasn't it funny that Shise should be with Leroy?" said Young Jack.

"Very," replied Mole. "Who is Shyser?"

"A bad boy. Kit didn't like him, and Shyser was going to lick me the last time we met."

JAN RAN UP AND STOOD OVER HIM WITH HIS FISTS CLENCHED, WAITING FOR HIM TO RISE.

"Indeed!"

"Couldn't you do something to Leroy? I hate him. He was very cruel to me," said Young Jack.

"If we could find him."

"Of course you can. Didn't Shise say he and some others had an office, and Shise is office-boy, so that wherever Shyser is you will find Leroy."

"Very good reasoning," replied Mole, admiring the boy's intelligence.

"Shyser said they kept on Broadway. Let's go and look for Shyser, and then we shall spot them."

"Not now. We have something else to do. This is a lucky day, and so I want to make the most of it. I feel like a man on the eve of a great discovery," said Mole.

"All right, I'm your man. March, march, march, march, and march away, from Baxter-street, 'way down to Avenue A," replied Young Jack.

They walked on in silence, for Mr. Mole was deep in thought. If it was as he imagined, a great discovery had been accidentally made.

Jack Harkaway's father was dead. His mother had only enough to live upon, and it would be necessary in future for him to work, as he could expect no more money to be sent over from England.

The only property which Jack's father had not lost in speculation was the shares of the mine in Missouri, and these had been stolen by Hunston's brother, who, oddly enough, happened to be a clerk in the bank in which they were deposited.

It seemed fated that the Hunston family should always be a thorn in Jack's side.

If Mr. Mole's reasoning was correct, the situation stood thus—

Alfred Hunston, the defaulting clerk, had come over to New York and found his brother.

Defying the police, and perhaps escaping detection by his very boldness, Hunston had joined his brother in a financial agency on Broadway, assisted by Mr. Leroy, who had retained the Shyser as office-boy.

Who would think of looking for them in a handsomely-furnished sitting-room on Broadway, connected with elegantly-furnished offices, into which the unwary might been trapped to their ruin?

Suddenly Mr. Mole's chain of meditation was abruptly broken.

"I don't know," said Young Jack, in a tone of disgust, "if you are going to tramp about these streets all day, but I'm getting jolly tired, and this doesn't look like finding pop."

The professor stopped and looked round.

"Where are we?" he said. "Ah! Corner of Forty-second and Eighth Avenue. I have been lost in thought. Let us get into that car. Hi!"

He beckoned to a car which was going to McComb's Dam, and they rode up as far as a Hundred and Fifty-fifth-street, where they got out.

The intimation that lager beer was sold in a saloon hard by attracted the professor's attention.

"I will slake my thirst," he said. "Lager beer is good. Come inside, Jack."

They entered the saloon, and Mole drank some foaming lager.

"Nice day," he exclaimed. "How's real-estate about here?"

"Looking up," answered the saloon-keeper. "All we want is rapid transit."

"Any lunatic asylums near by?"

"There's one. The Sanatorium kept by Persuasive Power. Turn to your left, and then keep straight on. Then take the sixth turning to the right, and go to the left again, and after that, turn down the hill, and you'll come to it after a bit."

"Thank you," said the professor. "You're as good as a guide-book."

"Do you want to leave yourself in the asylum?" inquired the saloon-keeper.

"When I do, I'll come and tell you."

"I thought you looked a little like it."

"Take your five cents for the beer," replied Mole, "and if I come in here again, tell me of it. I'm not to be insulted by the bar-tender of a Dutch saloon."

"You can do the other thing," replied the man. "The loss of your custom won't break me."

The professor seized Young Jack's hand, and hurried away, vowing that he would never drink lager again. Which vow he kept until he was thirsty again.

More by chance than by following the rather vague and confusing directions given him by the bar-tender, he reached the asylum, which frowned down like a fortress in the middle of its high walls.

"This must be it!" he exclaimed. "A very formidable Bastile-like looking place."

"Do you think papa is in there?" asked Young Jack.

"I can't tell, my dear boy," replied the professor. "We don't know where he his; all we can do is to examine all the asylums we can find, because we have every reason to believe that he is confined by Hunston in one."

"What makes Hunston hate us so?"

"Because he is a bad man. He and your father were at school together, and even then Hunston disliked him."

"That's a long time ago."

"It is. In after-life they were continually at variance, and Hunston lost his arm through a shot fired at him by your father."

"I've heard that," replied Young Jack, "and I should like to shoot off his other arm."

"You mustn't say that," said Mr. Mole. "Youthful minds should not harbour revenge."

"Isn't it natural to hate an enemy."

"Perhaps but it is divine to forgive. We are told if an enemy smites us on one cheek to turn the other to him and let him smite that."

"Well," said Young Jack, with a wise air, "it may be all right, but I guess if a boy came smiting me, I should smite back precious quick. You bet."

"I am a Christian, I hope," replied Mr. Mole, "and Hunston in my varied experience has smitten me more than once, but I think I should hit back, and hit hard, if we met; he's a wily scoundrel."

"Wouldn't it be bully to hire an Indian to scalp him?" remarked Young Jack.

"Scalping is too good for him. I would have him tomahawked out of hand. See here; some one has been loping a tree. Suppose I take this ladder, put it against the wall, and have a peep over on the other side."

"Go on, sir; I'll back you up," answered Young Jack.

Mr. Mole looked at the ladder, and measured the wall with his eye.

It would just about enable him to reach the top.

Without any further hesitation, he grasped the ladder in his long, bony arms, and placed it against the wall, ascending carefully, while the boy placed his little foot on the bottom rung to steady it.

"Stand fast," said Mr. Mole.

"Aye, aye, sir!" replied Young Jack.

When the professor reached the summit, he got astride the wall, and looked down into the garden.

Sitting on a rustic chair was a young man indulging in a pipe of tobacco, which had been privately obtained for him by a keeper.

It was Jack's friend, Mr. Pleasant Hook.

"Hallo! down there," said Mole.

"Say, my blooming shrub, where are you coming to?" inquired Pleasant Hook, looking up in surprise.

"Is this a lunatic asylum?"

"If you adorned its ancient walls it might be; but as you are on the right side, we'll call it Sanity Hall."

"Poor fellow!" replied Mole; "it's easy to see you've got a slate loose."

"Who's your hatter, my blooming shrub?" inquired Pleasant Hook. "It's easy to see you've got a tile off."

"Tell me, if you can, whether there is a gentleman here of the name of Harkaway?"

"We've got a bloke inside who calls himself Harkaway, but that's his delusion."

"What's he like?"

"Tallish, stoutish, good-looking, and a darned Britisher. That's the bloke's description, my blooming shrub."

Mr. Mole with difficulty suppressed a cry of joy.

"I've struck oil!" he exclaimed, "and hang me if I can help it! I must say hurrah, if I die for it! Hurrah!"

A childish voice at the foot of the ladder echoed the cry, saying—

"Hurrah!—rah!—rah!"

"Tiger!" said Pleasant Hook. "Go it, and pile up the agony, my shrub. It pleases you, and don't hurt me."

"Where is Harkaway now? Is he well? How do they treat him?"

"He's splashing around. He's bully—they treat him well."

"Go and fetch him here," said the professor.

"Where have you been nigger-driving, my blooming shrub?" replied Pleasant Hook. "I'm not everybody's dog to fetch and carry. You don't boss er me; I'm not to be bossed over by any one. No, sir."

"I beg your pardon," replied Mole. "Forgive my excitement. I am Professor Mole. Harkaway's friend, and I am so pleased to think I've found him, that I could dance on the top of this wall."

"Well, my shrub," said Hook, "if dancing will suit your complaint, you can have a real good time of it as far as I'm concerned. I shan't chuck half-bricks at you."

"Tell Harkaway we'll soon have him out," continued Mole.

At this moment, Goliah, the keeper, happened to stride up, and seeing the professor on the wall, became angry.

"What are you doing up there?" he cried.

"Are you a lunatic, or an officer of this establishment?" asked Mole.

"I'm a keeper, and you've no business there. Slope, or I'll make you."

Goliah took up a handful of stones and began to pitch them at Mr. Mole, picking him off twice without hurting him much, but shaking his balance.

"Say, my blooming shrub, how's that for high!" cried Pleasant Hook.

"Hold your jaw, will you?" said the keeper, striking him with his fist, and brutally knocking him down.

Pleasant Hook got up, and shook his head, as if he wasn't quite sure if it was fixed on all right.

"Cheese it, my shrub!" he muttered, "or you'll rouse the eagle. If I go for you, I'll sick you, you bet!"

"Quit," said Goliah, threateningly.

"All right, my shrub," replied Pleasant Hook, keeping out of the way. "You'll bust if you hallo so loud. I'm off. I've seen enough of the elephant, and it's quite time to quit the circus."

"You dastardly coward!" said Mr. Mole. "I'll report your conduct. It's a shame to see a poor lunatic hit like that for nothing at all. How dare you do it, you ruffian!"

"Who are you, when you're at home. I don't think much of you when you're out, you old scarecrow!" replied Goliah.

"I'm your superior, anyhow," said Mole, "for I'm not a cowardly brute."

"Get off that wall!"

"I shall when it suits me."

Goliah aimed a big stone at the professor, and so accurately was it thrown that it struck him in the pit of the stomach, doubled him up, and sent him rolling over the other side.

A loud burst of laughter came from Pleasant Hook, who, at a distance, witnessed this achievement.

"Good-night, my blooming shrub," he said. "Why did you throw yourself away?"

Mr. Mole lay for a moment half-stunned.

Young Jack bent over him with tender solicitude.

"Are you much hurt, sir?" he asked.

"Not much," replied Mole, rising.

"Did you see my father?"

"No, but he is in there. We must make haste back to the city, and organise a rescue party. This is a great day. We're in luck, Jack, and shall bring glad tidings to your mother."

"Shall we get father out, and be even with Hunston?"

"Yes, that indeed we shall," replied Mole.

"That's what I like. I don't care so long as we get pop back, and euchre old Hunston," said Young Jack, in high glee. "Step out, sir; put your best leg forward."

Together they walked hurriedly along, the professor taking huge strides, and the boy trudging manfully at a trot by his side.

They had discovered Jack's whereabouts, and

that was an immense gain, for Mr. Mole did not doubt the possibility of releasing him from the den in which the lying malignity of his enemies had confined him.

But this was a difficult task.

More difficult than that the professor had any idea of, for Persuasive Power was a man who did not like to part with a healthy paying patient.

It was money out of his pocket, and an inmate of the asylum, when he rejoined the world, spread tales which did not do Mr. Power any particular credit.

So he always concluded to keep his patients as long as he could, and stuck to them with leech-like tenacity.

CHAPTER XXXII.
A STRANGE PROMISE.

GOLIAH, the keeper, was in a bad temper, and it seemed to him outrageous that an inmate of the asylum should hold converse with an outsider.

This outsider, too, was coolly seated on the wall, and had used language which was not calculated to soothe the keeper's feelings.

It was true that the audacious professor had been very neatly bowled over, and had fallen down on the other side with more quickness than dignity.

True it was, also, that the inmate who talked to the intruder was a priviledged person, for the "deputy governor" was generally allowed to do as he liked.

But the devil rose in Goliah's breast that morning, and he went up to Pleasant Hook with a threatening look in his grey eyes.

"What do you mean by breaking the rules?" he asked. "We don't want any strangers prying into our affairs."

"I didn't ask the man to come, and when he spoke, I only chaffed him," replied Hook.

"Don't give me any of your cheek," said Goliah. "I'll have to take you down a peg. Take that!—and that!"

He began to beat the slenderly-made young fellow in a shameful manner, this operation not being difficult, as he was twice as big, and three times as strong.

Pleasant Hook in vain put up his hands to protect his head and face from the shower of blows that fell upon him.

At last, dizzy and confused, he sank upon the ground, and the brutal keeper began to kick him in the side with his heavy iron-tipped boots.

"I'll warrant you'll not do it again," he said. "This will teach you to respect me, I guess."

At length Hook's cries became fainter and fainter, subsiding into low moans, and then ceasing altogether.

Attracted by the noise, Jack ran to the spot. He had been reading a book under a tree, and was afraid that something dreadful had taken place.

When he saw Pleasant Hook lying on the ground, and Goliah kicking him, the blood rushed to his head, and he felt mad to think that a harmless fellow like Hook should receive such severe punishment at the hands of the giant keeper.

"What's this for?" he asked.

"Find out," replied Goliah. "Do you want to be tarred with the same brush?"

"You'd better not try," answered Jack, taking the man's measure with his keen flashing eye. "I'm well and strong now, and I warn you that if you try to touch me, I shall pound you."

"Oh!" laughed Goliah, sarcastically, "you're boss of this show, are you? While I've got my hand in, I will tackle you."

"I didn't seek the row," said Jack; "but I'm ready for you."

Goliah advanced, and aimed a blow at Jack,

which the latter parried, and watching his opportunity, he made a flint at the keeper's head ; lowering his first, and striking him a desperate blow in the stomach.

This doubled the man up, and Jack, raising his knee with all his might, caught him just under the chin, loosening his teeth, and sending him heavily to the grass, feeling as if he had gone to pieces.

Jack ran up and stood over him, with his fists clenched, waiting for him to rise.

The brute hadn't had half enough yet, and Jack knew he would be as vindictive for half thrashing as for a whole one.

"Get up!" he said.

It was fully half a minute before the keeper made a move, and when he did, he staggered uncomfortably.

Jack let out at him, right and left, with the skill and force of a Heenan or a Morrisey ; and, with his face all cut open and bleeding, the bully rolled over a second time.

Seeing that he was getting the worst of it, the giant was artful enough to lay perfectly still, and Jack thought he had stunned him.

Not knowing exactly how to act, Jack looked from him to Pleasant Hook, and then up at the windows of the asylum, as if he wished some one would come to his assistance.

Luckily, Mr. Persuasive Power had seen that something unusual was going on, and he hastily ran down the garden.

"What's all this?" he asked, angrily.

"This brute," said Jack, pointing to Goliah, "has half-killed my little friend Hook, and when he attacked me, I showed him that he couldn't boss over every one."

"You have beaten Goliah," said Persuasive Power, "whipped my giant! You could not have done it fairly."

Goliah got up, looking like a fiend, and trembling with rage.

"I'll show him, sir, if you'll let me go at him again," he said.

"Not now," replied the governor. "We'll see to him afterwards. How did all this occur?"

"Hook was talking to a stranger on the wall, and I tapped him about a bit, to make him mend the rules."

"Go in and get your face seen to. Mr. Harkaway, assist me in carrying Mr. Hook into the house," said Mr. Power.

Goliah slunk off, shaking his fist at Jack, and muttering more oaths in a minute than he could repent of in a week.

Pleasant Hook was carried into his room and placed upon the bed. He was very pale, and so still that he might have been dead, had not a faint motion of the heart shown that he still lived.

"I shall send the doctor here in a moment, Harkaway," said Persuasive Power, "and I shall trust to your discretion to say nothing about this."

Jack made no answer, and taking his silence for consent, Mr. Power went away.

Shortly afterwards, the surgeon arrived, and made an examination of the poor victim of the keeper's brutality.

"This is a bad case," said the doctor. "There are three ribs broken, and one has perforated the lungs, producing internal bleeding. I fear he will not live. It was a sad accident."

"Accident!" repeated Jack.

"Yes. Mr. Power tells me he fell down from the wall when attempting to escape, and tumbling upon some stakes, inflicted the wounds he is suffering from."

"It's a gross falsehood," exclaimed Jack. "and I won't keep silent if they will kill me for it."

"A falsehood!"

"Yes, sir. The poor fellow was kicked and beaten like this by the tall keeper they call Goliah."

"Indeed ! If that is so, and he dies, as I fear he will, I shall have to notify the coroner," replied the doctor. "Though Mr. Power may be right. You are a lunatic, of course, or you would not be here, and lunatics have always strange delusions about the brutality of the keepers, which, when they take the shape of accusations, and are examined into, nearly always turn out untrue."

"I am as sane as you you are," said Jack, "and I am only telling the truth."

"Well, well, don't get excited over it, my good fellow. Hold your friend's head up, while I give him this draught."

Jack did so, and Hook swallowed the medicine, which quickened the action of the heart and revived him.

The doctor then dressed the wounds on his head, and departed, leaving Jack in the position of nurse.

"How do you find yourself now ?" asked Jack, kindly.

"A heap better," replied Pleasant Hook, faintly, "though I've got my ticket. My throat and mouth are full of blood, and I've got a dreadful pain in my side."

"I licked that brute, Goliah," said Jack, "and gave him a bouncing he won't forget in a hurry."

"Bully for you, my shrub," answered Hook, trying to smile, but making a ghastly grimace instead.

"I hope you will be better presently," said Jack.

Pleasant Hook shook his head.

"I've been kicked too badly to get well," he replied, "and I think I am going home. In part, I feel it. Now look here, you take me for a crazy fool, don't you?"

"No," said Jack.

"Yes, you do. I could see it in your eye when I was talking about my big diamond ; but it's all true. I killed a man, Jack, to get that diamond."

"What !"

"I did. There is blood upon my hand. It's been like a curse to me. It drives me to drink, and brought on my fits. I might have done well out West. I've been all over Texas colonies, Missouri, California, and Nevada. Young as I am, I've seen the world."

A fit of coughing interrupted his utterance, and a thin stream of blood rolled up over the pillow.

"That's one of the last nails in my casket," he said. "But I'll tell you all about it. The bloke who had the big diamond had come from the Brazils, where he had been a convict, working in the Government mines. He found this diamond, and escaped with it. One night, over a camp-fire, he showed it to me, and I fell upon him and beat his brains in with a hatchet."

Jack shuddered.

"You shrink from me, and well you may," continued Pleasant Hook. "I know I'm a wretch, and when I had the diamond I was afraid to carry it about, and so I buried it in Limpia Canyon, near Camp Stockton, that's in the lower and wildest part of Texas."

Another fit of coughing intervened, leaving him weaker than before.

"If ever you're that way, you'll know the Canyon by its wonderful rocky scenery. The walls are a thousand feet feet high," continued the young man, his eyes flashing with a fluting glare. "It seems as if the rocks were cut into great pagan idols with worshippers kneeling at their feet. Beside these stands a gigantic sentinel, eyeing an enormous rock, and near this is a rock which resembles a sharp-nosed wolf. Do your hear ? I want you to mark this."

"I do," replied Jack.

"That diamond shall be yours, my friend."

"Mine!"

"I give it you. What matter that it cost a

man's life. It is my dying bequest to you," said Pleasant Hook.

"It isn't likely I shall ever find myself in the wilds of Texas," said Jack.

"You can't tell. Two years ago, I didn't think I should die in a lunatic asylum."

"And if I were in your Canyon, how should I discover the diamond?" said Jack, still having great doubts as to the location of the famous stone.

"I'll make sure of that," said Pleasant Hook, a wild inspiration breaking from his face.

"How?"

"I'll make sure of it, I tell you. Listen here, won't you? Put your head nearer mine. I'm growing fainter."

Jack bent down till his ear almost touched the lips of the sufferer.

Lips upon which a purple froth was gathering, and which quivered as if the death-rattle was already gathering in the throat.

"I'm going to die," said Hook, in a hollow, sepulchral tone.

"Not you."

"I am. 'Tis the sunset of life gives in mystical love, and coming events cast their shadows before," as the poet Campbell says.

"It's awful to think you should be cut off like this."

"One greater than we are arranges that, and what seems good to Him, must be right. I will pray presently to be forgiven. But I want you to listen to me."

"Go on," said Jack.

"If ever you're in that Canyon, my ghost shall rise as the clock strikes twelve at night, and stand right over the spot where I buried the diamond."

"Your ghost! What nonsense! There are no such things as ghosts," said Jack.

Pleasant Hook's head fell back, another rush of blood came to his mouth, and he breathed heavily for several minutes.

"Are you easier?" asked Jack.

"What have I been talking about?" inquired Hook, whose mind was beginning to wander a little.

"Oh! nothing much," replied Jack.

"I shall soon be gone, my blooming shrub," said he, with an affectation of his old cheerfulness. "I think I promised you something. I can't recollect, my memory's so bad, but whatever it was, I'll keep my word. You bet."

Jack regarded this strange promise as the raving of a disordered mind, but a time was to come, when this singular death-bed scene was brought to his remembrance in a vivid and startling manner.

There was a noise of many feet outside the door, and Mr. Persuasive Power, followed by Goliah and another keeper, rushed into the room.

"There's the villain who is trying to ruin me!" said the governor, pointing to Jack.

"Hush!" said Jack, "respect the dying."

"I guess you'll be that way soon," replied Mr. Power. "Seize him, boys; knock him down!"

Goliah and the other keeper required no further bidding.

They rushed upon Jack with a will, and soon overpowered him. Goliah, getting his hand twisted in his neckerchief, pressed his knuckles against his throat so that he could scarcely breathe.

Then he forced him down on his back, and knelt on his chest.

"D—don't s—strangle me!" gasped Jack.

"I'll teach you to tell a pack of lies to the doctor about me," said Mr. Power. "Take him to a cell on the basement, and shut him up close."

The keepers dragged Jack away, treating him as brutally as if he were dead sheep, and did not amount to more than mutton for the next day's market.

He was hauled off and placed in a dark, narrow cell, the size of which was about seven feet by three, a dim light was admitted through a narrow iron grating at the top. It was entirely destitute of furniture, and only some mouldy straw was to be seen in a corner.

Jack heard the door bang behind him, and began to breathe again, thanking his lucky stars that he had escaped with his life.

Two hours later, Pleasant Hook breathed his last.

Goliah swore that his injuries were the result of an accident, and the surgeon believed this statement, being all the more willing to do so as he was handsomely paid by Mr. Persuasive Power for being accommodating in the matter of giving certificates in cases of sudden deaths, which were not unfrequent in the asylum.

It was about tea time when Mr. Power was apprised that three visitors wanted to see him.

He at once received them in his office.

The visitors were Mr. Mole, Harvey, and Felix Prye.

"In what way can I serve you, gentlemen?" asked the governor, with his most pleasant smile.

"We have every reason to believe that you have a patient here named Harkaway," replied Mole, "who is perfectly sane."

. "I do not know the name," replied Mr. Power, his face clouding over.

Pleasant Hook had forgotten to tell Harkaway of Mr. Mole's visit, and the message he sent him.

Had he done so, it would have been a ray of sunshine for him in his miserable captivity in the wretched dungeon into which he had been cast.

"Do you refuse to give him up?" asked Harvey

"I cannot give up a man I have not got," was the reply of the governor.

"Perhaps he is here under some other name. Can we look round?" inquired Felix.

"By all means, gentlemen. I will myself show you every ward and every cell. Come. I do not like to be thought harshly of by the outside public, and am always willing to give the friends of my patients every facility they can wish for."

This rather staggered the three friends.

Mr. Mole had returned to the hotel full of his important discovery, and at once Harvey sent a messenger for Felix, who came up without delay.

A coach was ordered, and the party started immediately for the asylum, fondly hoping to return with Harkaway.

Persuasive Power blandly took them all over his establishment, allowing them to peep into every hole and corner, except the particular cell which contained the person they were searching for.

This, from its peculiar position on the basement, escaped observation, and the party returned to the office without making any discovery.

"Are you satisfied, gentlemen?" asked Persuasive Power.

"No," replied Mr. Mole. "I am not."

"Nor I," said Felix.

"Same here," said Harvey.

"Well, really, gentlemen, you are very difficult to please. I cannot see how I can render you any further assistance," said Mr. Power, while a peculiar smile played around the corners of his mouth.

"We're not going without him. Eh, boys?" said Felix.

"Not much," replied Harvey.

"For my part," said Mr. Mole, "I mean to see this thing through, and will stand by you two, even unto the death."

The professor took a little flask from his pocket, and sipped at its contents, as if to fortify himself for a coming struggle.

Mr. Persuasive Power looked from ene to the other in bewilderment.

He did not quite understand what the action of the three friends might be.

Their attitude was dreadfully hostile, but what could they do?

He had not long to wait before they enlightened the darkness of his understanding, showing him that Jack Harkaway had friends who were not to be thrown off the scent by a paltry lie, but were prepared for just such a block as had occurred.

CHAPTER XXXIII.

THE RESCUE PARTY.

THE governor of the asylum was, as befitted one in his position, a man of action.

"Gentlemen," he said, promptly, "if you don't quit, I shall have to make you."

Harvey drew a pistol, and replied, with equal promptitude—

"If you don't sit down on that chair, and do as you are told, I shall break your leg with a bullet."

Mr. Power sank back in his chair, looking slightly uncomfortable.

"This is an outrage," he said, "and if I had been aware of your intentions, I would have met you on your own ground."

"Unhappily," remarked Felix, "one cannot always be prepared. A man out West once met a bear. He quitted the locality as soon as possible, remarking, 'If I had known you were coming along, I'd have brought my shot gun.'"

"Mr. Mole," said Harvey, "stand sentinel over this man, if you please. You have a revolver?"

"Yes, here it is," replied the professor, drawing something out of his pocket.

It was his flask, and, in some confusion, he put it back, saying—

"That's the wrong one. I have another one somewhere. Ah! this it. Let the Philistine dare to move, and he is done for!"

Leaving the professor standing guard over Persuasive Power, Harvey and Felix went once more into the wards of the asylum.

They had not gone far before they met Goliah, who eyed them curiously.

"Say, you boy," said Felix, "come here."

The keeper approached.

In one hand Felix presented a pistol, in the other, a bundle of bills, amounting to about one hundred dollars.

"Which would you rather have?" he asked.

Goliah grinned.

"The currency," he replied, "for choice, by a long sight."

"Very well. It is yours, if you conduct us to an inmate of this place named Harkaway."

"I'd rather you'd have asked for any one else," he said. "He and I are bad friends. He painted my face this morning, and we've got him in chokers."

"Is that so?" cried Harvey. "Bully for Jack."

"He's wonderfully strong and cunning at fighting," said Goliah. "I haven't got a firm tooth in my head. He kicked me like a horse, but if he's got to quit, I may as well have the rocks as any one else. Hand over."

Felix gave him the money, and the keeper led the way to the cell in which Jack was confined. He shot back the bolt, and disclosed the captive, who was comfortably lying down on the straw, with one arm under his head as a pillow.

"Rouse up!" said Goliah. "Here's some friends of yours."

"Can't you let a fellow sleep in peace?" said Jack. "I thought I warned you sufficiently this morning to make you civil; but if you want any

more, and will fight fair, I'm game for another tussle."

"Jack," said Harvey, "don't you know me?"

Jack sprang up.

"My dear Dick," he said, delightedly. "I didn't expect this any more than the man in the moon. How did you do it?"

In an instant they were shaking hands cordially.

"And my Felix, too!" exclaimed Jack.

"It's all owing to Mole and your plucky young son."

"My son! Have you got him? Don't trifle with me," said Jack, eagerly, as he shook the straw out of his hair, and rubbed his eyes with the back of his hand to see more clearly.

"Yes. Monday found him, and Mole found you," replied Harvey.

"And I thought I had no friends left. Wasn't I a beast to indulge such a thought, Dick?" said Jack.

"Not at all. A place like this would make a fellow think anything. Come along. Let's get out."

"Certainly. It's a lovely crib, isnt it? But I'm not sufficiently taken with it to wish to stay any longer. Say, ugly!"

This was addressed to Goliah.

"Just walk into that straw, will you, and squat yourself down," continued Jack. "I should like you to have a turn."

"I'd rather be excused, sir, if it's all the same to you," replied Goliah.

"No, you wouldn't—that's your modesty. He's the most modest cuss out, Dick."

"Is that so?"

"Why, certainly. He killed a man this morning, and I'll bet if you asked him, he'd deny it. Oh! he wouldn't put himself forward for the world. Now, my friend, step inside, as the spider said to the fly, or do you want me to help you?"

Very reluctantly Goliah took up a position on the mouldy straw.

"Squat," continued Jack. "This lot's a free gift, and you may pre-empt without so much as rising a shanty on it. Dick, lend me your fire-iron."

Harvey handed him his pistol, wondering what he was going to do.

"A friend of mine," pursued Jack, "was once shot in the foot, and he was lame for life, an awkward place is the foot to get shot in. How would you feel, friend Goliah, if you were condemned to wear crutches for the rest of your natural life?"

A cold sweat broke out all over the wretched man.

"Oh, sir," he said, "You're only joking. I can see you like your fun."

"I do, you bet," replied Jack, severely. "Just stretch out that right leg of yours, will you?"

Goliah did as he was requested, without believing that Jack was in earnest, but he soon found out his mistake.

In an instant the trigger fell, and the ball went crashing into the bones of the man's foot, and lodged there near the ankle.

A terrible cry broke from Goliah, who rolled on the straw with agony.

"That's for what you did to Pleasant Hook, and I hope you will bear it in mind when your ill-temper next inclines you whack into a patient," said Jack.

"Oh, Lord!" groaned Goliah, "it's more than I can bear! Kill me at once! Oh, I'm done for, and ruined for life! Oh! oh! oh!"

Jack led the way out of the cell, followed by his friends, and shut the door on the bellowing giant, who continued to roar like a bull—at one time shrieking with pain, the next, bewailing his misfortune, and then cursing Jack like a Bowery boy, or a prairie scout whose trail had been struck by Indians.

When they were outside, Jack shook hands again with his friends

"God bless you!" he exclaimed. "I never felt so pleased in my life to get out of a tight fix as I do out of this, and the news about Young Jack is all I wanted to make me as good as new."

In spite of the sundry bruises which he had received in the morning, Jack bounded along like a three-year-old, and seon reached the vestibule.

A noise proceeded from the private office of the governor, and Mole's voice was heard in a tone of authority.

"You base worm," he said, "I've a good mind to shoot you where you sit! How dare you keep in confinement a friend of mine? Do you know who I am, sir?"

"Don't blew, colonel," replied the governor.

"I don't know what you mean by blowing, but you will be good enough to understand that I am an intimate friend of all the crowned heads in Europe, and if I take out my papers, I don't know that I shan't run for governor of New York State."

"Dry up!" said Mr. Persuasive Power, curtly.

"If this pistol should go off accidentally, it won't be my fault," replied the professor.

Suddenly there was a report.

He had been trifling with the trigger too long, and the revolver went off. Fortunately, it did no harm, as it was pointed at the ceiling, in which the ball imbedded itself.

Jack and his friends entered the apartment at this juncture, and seeing Mr. Power unhurt, burst into a fit of loud laughter.

"Dear me," said Mr. Mole, "the confounded thing went off of its own accord. It's like everything else in this country. It's got a will of its own. Who would have thought it would have gone off at half-cock?"

Mr. Power looked gratified at the appearance of Harkaway and his companions.

"Will you take this lunatic away," he said, pointing to Mr. Mole; "or, if net, will you give me time to go and get my life insured?"

Jack took the pistol out of Mole's hand.

"I have no reason to care for your life," he replied. "But I am not the man to bear malice, and just now I could forgive my bitterest enemy. You have a certain amount of dirty work to do, and I suppose the dirty work of this world must be done by some one. I call you a social scavenger."

"That's rough on me," said the governor.

"I like that," said Mr. Mole. "Give it him, Harkaway! Social scavenger is good. Sick him, as Young Jack would say. This fellow called me a lunatic, but social scavenger is a dab in the eye for him; and excuse my hilarity, but the fact of seeing you again, alive and well, makes me young again."

"Mr. Harkaway," said Persuasive Power.

"Well, sir?" replied Jack.

"Are you going to raise Cain over this?"

"No, I'm not," answered Jack. "I've done with you, and the worst wish I have is that poor Hook's ghost may haunt you till the day of your death, which I hope won't be far distant."

The governor did not seem much concerned at this outburst.

"Remember," he said, "that you were brought here on the certificate of two doctors. What I have done was legal."

"Was it legal to have a man kicked to death by one of your keepers? I suppose poor Hook is dead now. He could not have lasted long. What sympathy did you show for him? Get out! I've no patience with such humbugs as you, and I'd rather get my living as a plantation hand than in your way."

"Bravo, Jack!" said Felix; "I guess you've touched him on the raw. He shows alarming symptoms of stings of conscience, and I can see the worm

that never dies on his classic brow, and the fire that is never quenched on his rubicund nose."

"Well, gentlemen," said Persuasive Power, "it's your go in. I'm out on the first base, and when you've done your innings, you can tell me, as I shall feel kinder tickled when you're through."

"You are a contemptible hound!" exclaimed Harvey.

"Thank you," answered Mr. Power, with a polite bow. "Anybody else want to chuck dirt?"

"You're worse nor a bed-bug, and I could stamp you out of creation!" exclaimed Felix.

"Go it, gentlemen! I like things lively. Keep the ball rolling!" replied Mr. Power.

"Sir, you're a rank humbug and an impostor!" said Mr. Mole.

"That's mild. Can't you give it me hotter than that?" inquired Mr. Power, with a half smile. "I've been accustomed to more severe Webster, and when you come to humbugs and impostors, I feel elevated in the social scale."

"Sir," continued the professor, "I will tell you what are you. I have ransacked my vocabulary in vain, and I will hurl an expressive Americanism at you!"

"Hurl," replied Persuasive Power, calmly.

"You are a scalawag, sir, and a bad one at that!"

"I subside. I cave," said the governor, with a crestfallen air. "When a Britisher calls a free and enlightened citizen of the United States a scalawag, it is time for him to send for his Consul, and if it isn't a case of war between two nations, he'd best make his will and die right away."

"Harkaway," said Mr. Mole, "is this man really penitent, or is he chaffing me?"

"I'm afraid, sir, he is chaffing," replied Jack, who could not help laughing.

"You're a bad lot," said Mole, furiously, as he shook his fist at the governor, "and I'm afraid you'll come to the gallows some day."

"Oh! we only hang foreign scum now," replied Mr. Power.

"If you provoke me too far, I'll—"

"Talk United States to me, and don't be a fool," interrupted the governor, impatiently; adding, "Good-day, gentlemen. You've gained your point, and I'm euchred."

Jack beckoned to Harvey, and said—

"Let us get out. If you'd been here as long as I, you wouldn't care about stopping. Besides that, I am dying to see Emily and the kid. Come on, or that old fool, Mole, will jaw to everlasting."

"I'm ready, my dear fellow," said Harvey.

They walked out, and were followed by Felix, who had almost to drag the professor from the office, so enraged was he with Persuasive Power.

"Say, Mr. Harkaway," cried the governor, bawling after them, "can't you leave the old one with me? I'll take him cheap. I'll have him for nothing, just to amuse me. I guess I want a clown."

"Let me go!" exclaimed Mr. Mole. "I'll shoot him!"

"Come along," said Felix; "you're excited, sir."

"I had a sunstroke once, and it affects me at times," replied the professor.

"Had a sunstroke!" repeated Mr. Power, who had heard this answer. "Oh! that's what's the matter with Hannah. I bar sunstrokes. Take him along, gentlemen. I won't rob you of your British curiosity. Barnum might trade with you. I'm not on for this deal."

His loud laughter rang in their ears, until they quitted the establishment, and shut the heavy doors of the wretched place behind them.

They all got into the coach which was in waiting, and were driven quickly back to the hotel.

Imagine Jack's delight at seeing his wife again, and his child! He was wild with joy, and when

Emily told him that there were letters from England which he ought to see, he replied—

"Shunt them. I shall switch on to something lighter than business."

"That's right, Jack," said Harvey; "one doesn't kill a pig every day."

"Right you are, Dick," replied Jack. "I mean to be jolly. Felix, be a gay and festive cuss for once, and join us in a spree."

"You're not going out, pop, are you?" asked the boy, looking up into his face.

"Not if I know it," answered Jack. "I mean to enjoy myself in the bosom of my family."

He sat down on the lounge with his boy on one side, and his wife on the other.

"If this isn't happiness, I don't know what is," he continued.

"Tell me all about your confinement in the asylum, Jack dear," said Emily.

"Not now, darling. I will to-morrow. I want to hear those I love talk. Jaw away, young one. I could listen to you by the hour. Bless your old heart."

He hugged him tight, and then embraced Emily, and laughed, and talked, and otherwise made a fool of himself, which was excusable under the circumstances.

"I say, pop," exclaimed Young Jack, "there is old Mole at the whisky."

Mr. Mole was standing at the side table, and he certainly had a bottle in one hand and a glass in the other.

Everybody laughed.

The professor, finding attention turned towards himself, said—

"It's a poor heart that never rejoices, Harkaway. Here's to your health; but if that boy of yours was a little less forward, it would—ahem!—redound more to your credit."

"I'll see to him, sir, when I've got time," said Jack.

Jack's return was celebrated in quite a pleasant manner.

Felix went home for his sisters, and a dance was arranged on the carpet.

It was late when the party broke up, and those who composed it retired to rest.

In the morning, Jack asked Harvey to accompany him to Mr. Mole's room.

When they entered it, they found the professor ooking over some school-books which he had purhased for Young Jack.

"Good morning, Harkaway," he said. "This eems like old times. I welcome your return as the commencement of a happier state of things."

"That depends upon circumstances, sir," replied Jack.

"How is that? You have your boy, and I do not see that anything can interfere with your happiness. Our happiness, I may say—as anything that vexes you worries me equally."

"I know your attachment to me and mine, sir; and I thank you heartily for it," answered Jack.

"The question I had on the tip of my tongue to ask you was, When shall we return to Europe?"

"Certainly not for some time."

"Indeed!"

"My home, Mr. Mole, must be in this country for some years," answered Jack. "Perhaps for ever."

"Well," said Mr. Mole, philosophically, "it is a great country. I am cosmopolitan in my tastes, and I am getting used to America; but tell me why you think of remaining here?"

"With pleasure. You know that my mother has written to say that her husband is dead, and has only left her sufficient to live upon."

"Yes."

"She cannot afford to send me any more money as an allowance."

"That is clear."

"All she can give me is the right to work the lead-mine in Missouri, in which her husband had invested so much money without getting any return."

"Exactly," remarked Harvey; "and that is a poor look-out, because, from your mother's letter, it appears that the mine has never paid a dividend."

"No matter," replied Jack, "it may be made to do so. The mine was mortgaged to us for the money advanced upon it, and we had the title deeds."

"Which Alfred Hunston has stolen," said Harvey.

"All the better. We have reason to believe that Alfred Hunston is in this city, in partnership with his brother. We will soon find them out, get the deeds from them, and I will go and superintend the working of the mine."

"All alone?"

"Yes. I shall take no one with me. It may be that I shall have to encounter many dangers, and I feel, Dick, that I have dragged you all into trouble enough."

"I have never complained," said Mr. Mole.

"Nor I," replied Harvey.

"I know that," replied Jack. "You are both of you too thoroughbred and too good-hearted to do anything of the sort, yet I have my private feelings about the matter."

"Well," said Mr. Mole, folding his hands, "let us understand what it is you propose to do?"

"I mean to find the Hunston's, get the title deeds, and go West to work this mine."

"Better give up the idea," said Harvey. "I've got plenty of money. You know how rich my wife is."

"Dick," said Jack, "I thought you knew me better."

"Why?"

"Did you ever see me sponge on any one?"

"No."

"I'm not going to begin now. All I will ask you to do is to stay here for a time, and look after my wife and child and Mr. Mole. I make them a charge upon you, and will pay you all you expend when—"

"Don't talk about payment," interrupted Harvey.

"I must. It isn't my principle to owe anybody anything. Not even my best friend. Don't be offended, Dick."

"Why can't I join you?"

"Because I'm determined not to give you any more anxiety on my account."

There was a pause.

"Where's this confounded lead mine?" said Harvey, abruptly.

"In the south-western part of Missouri," replied Jack, "as well as I can make out from mother's letter."

"That's near Arkansas, and the Indian Territory, isn't it?"

"Somewhere down that way."

"Oh! wouldn't I like to go with you!" said Harvey.

"Your scalp's safer where you are, Dick."

"Bother scalps! Wigs are cheap."

"They couldn't scalp me much," observed Mr. Mole. "I wear a wig, and have only got a little stubbly hair under it, thanks to your joke on board the 'City of Athens.'"

"Go to Europe, if you like, Dick," said Jack. "All I want is to work out my fortune my own way."

"No. I shall stay in New York. You may want me, Jack, and recollect that a telegram will always fetch me."

"Thanks, old boy. I know that my great regret at going away is leaving you."

"But you're not gone yet. Where are the title deeds of this confounded mine?'

"I'm after them. A detective is now looking out for the firm of Hunston Brothers, or whatever they call themselves."

"Is that so?"

"Yes. I was up this morning at five o'clock, arranging matters, and I expect the detective here every moment with his report."

"Won't you take me with you, Jack?" asked Harvey.

"If you were not a married man I would."

"But Hilda won't mind."

"Yes, she will, lad. I never knew a woman yet, who loved her husband, that liked him to run into danger."

Monday knocked at the door.

"Um gen'leman to see you, sar," he exclaime."

"Tell him to wait down-stairs in the hall, and I will come to him," replied Jack.

After addressing a few more remarks to Mr. Mole and Harvey, Jack descended by the elevator, and met the detective in the hall.

He was a man named Davis, who was well acquainted with New York, and whose cleverness had resulted in the capture of many notorious evil-doers.

"Well, Davis," said Jack, "have you found out anything?"

"Yes," replied the detective. "I think I have spotted our gentlemen."

"So quickly?"

"It was not a very difficult thing to do. First of all, you gave me the locality, Broadway. I had only to inquire in the business-quarter of that thoroughfare for all offices recently let."

"Exactly."

"When I came to an office with new tenants, I asked if one had lost an arm. At length I received an answer in the affirmative. You see, there are not many movings going on till the first of May, and my task was not a long one."

"Your reasoning is excellent," said Jack.

"Three men," said Davis, "answering the description you gave, are located in Broadway, between Walker and Spring Streets. They trade under the style of Delavanti & Co., and are financial agents."

"Capital!"

"If you have breakfasted, I will take you down there. What do you propose to do?"

"Simply this," answered Jack. "I will leave you outside, and enter myself. If I do not show in ten minutes, you will come in search of me."

"Very well. I will secure the service of the policeman on the beat, and you need not fear anything."

"Come along at once, then," said Jack. "I am anxious to see this thing through."

They quitted the hotel and walked down Broadway, which was thronged with pedestrians.

"Get into a stage," said the detective.

"You're the leader," answered Jack.

They stopped a stage, got in, and were driven to the locality at which they expected to find the Brothers Hunston.

When they got out, the detective said—

"I did not ask you why you were so anxious to find these men."

"It's a private matter," answered Jack.

"All well and good," replied the detective. "I don't want to pry into your private affairs, but you must keep your eyes peeled."

"I know that."

"There's a man of the name of Sheepe, or Leroy, Mr. Harkaway, mixed up with them."

"Oh, you've found that out, have you?"

"Yes, sir. He's managed to keep out of our clutches for a long time, but he's wanted, and is bound to end his days at Sing Sing."

"I don't care if he does," replied Jack, who added, "Now, look here. Get hold of a policeman, and if I don't appear in ten minutes, or you hear pistol-shooting, come straight up."

Davis nodded his head.

"I understand fully," he replied.

Jack looked at the door-post, and saw written up, "Delavanti Brothers."

He went up to the second-floor, and knocked at the door, which was opened by Shise.

"Is your master in?" he asked.

"Who do you want?" inquired Shise.

"Either of the Mr. Delavantis."

"Mr. Alfred's in, but his brother started on a journey this morning."

"Alfred Delavanti will do," replied Jack.

"What name shall I give?" said Shise.

Jack pushed past him, and walked towards the private room, without making any answer.

Shise, however, ran forward, and put his back against the door.

"You can't go in without your name!" he exclaimed.

Jack took him by the arm, and swung him round.

Then he opened the door.

He saw two men in the room. One was seated at a desk, which was covered with papers; the other occupied a chair, and was smoking a cigar.

The latter jumped up directly he saw Jack, and said—

"Harkaway, by jingo!"

"Yes, Mr. Sheepe, alias Leroy," said Jack. "I have the extreme satisfaction of finding you out in your lair."

The man at the desk was tall and thin, with dark hair, and a cadaverous face, which was closely shaven.

He did not move when he saw Jack, but his face became as white as a sheet when he heard Leroy address him as Harkaway.

Jack was perfectly self-possessed, and unconcerned.

"I presume," he said, with a bow which was a mockery of politeness, "that I am addressing Mr. Alfred Hunston?"

"On the contrary," replied Alfred, "I am—"

"Save yourself the trouble of telling falsehoods," interrupted Jack. "I have got precise information respecting you, and I know you to be the person I have named."

Alfred Hunston looked at Leroy, as if he wished to ask his advice.

Leroy took the hint, and said—

"Mr. Harkaway and I are old friends. We thoroughly understand one another."

"If you mean that I know you to be a scoundrel, you are right," answered Jack.

"Take a seat. You are here on business, or you would not have come," replied Leroy.

"Yes, take a seat, by all means," said Alfred Hunston, eagerly.

A rapid glance passed between him and Leroy.

Jack saw it, but was at a loss to understand its meaning.

A chair was placed for him in the centre of the room, and he sat down, always keeping his eye fixed on the door, and his right hand upon a pistol which he carried in his pocket.

"Now, sir," said Alfred Hunston, "I am at your service"

"You admit that you are the brother of my old enemy, Hunston?" began Jack.

"I admit nothing," was the reply. "You are pleased to confuse me with that individual."

"Own up," said Leroy, impatiently. "It will facilitate matters greatly."

"Well," said the young man, sulkily, "I am Alfred Hunston."

"So far, so good," said Jack "Where is your brother?"

"He has gone on a journey."

"In what direction?"

Alfred Hunston hesitated, and looked again at Leroy.

"Tell him," said the latter.

"He has gone to Missouri."

"As I suspected," said Jack. "You stole the title deeds of the Hail Columbia Lead Mine from the bankers in England, brought them over here, and have given them to your brother, I suppose, who has gone to see what he can make out of them; and when you have collected some plunder in this city, you will go to join him."

Leroy laughed.

"You have a wonderful mind, Mr. Harkaway," he said; "and have guessed everything correctly."

"Don't you think you are a nice set of villains?" said Jack.

"I rather pride myself upon being a big thing in villains," answered Leroy, impudently. "But Alfred, here, is young, though I hope he will improve under my tuition."

"You will be separated for a time, anyhow," said Jack.

"How is that?"

"I shall have the painful duty of arresting you both. You, Leroy, will be tried here for your various crimes, and Mr. Alfred Hunston will be sent back to England, under the Extradition Treaty, to answer an indictment for robbery."

"There is one thing you have not taken into your calculations; and that is, we are not caught yet," laughed Leroy.

"The house is watched, and I have assistance at hand."

At this moment Shise entered the room in a hurry.

"What's the row?" inquired Leroy

"Cheese it!" said Shise. "There's Davis, the detective, and a cop below."

"That will do. You can go, sir," replied Leroy, whose calmness equalled Jack's, if it did not exceed it.

He approached the wall, in which was a brass knob, and touching it suddenly with his finger, kept his eye fixed upon the door.

To his great surprise, Jack felt a peculiar motion. The chair on which he was sitting seemed to be sinking through the floor with a rapidity that was alarming.

Before he could realise his situation, his head had passed the level of the carpet.

Leroy had set in motion some ingeniously-contrived machinery.

This had the effect of lowering rapidly a certain square piece cut out of the floor.

Down went Jack, till the basement was reached, and he in vain clutched at the walls to stop his unexpected descent.

All at once the downward motion was arrested, the chair tipped forward of its own accord, and threw Jack on his hands and knees.

So quickly was this accomplished that, when he rose to his feet, the trap was already far on its upward way, leaving him a prisoner in a damp and mouldy vault, some yards below the level of the roadway.

All was dark as pitch.

Sitting down on the cold, hard floor, Jack could not help admitting that the thieves up-stairs had been too clever for him.

"That's the cutest trick I ever heard of," he said to himself, "and how I'm going to get out of such a tight fix, I'm blessed if I know."

While Jack was deliberating in his new prison, events of importance were taking place up-stairs.

Davis had become impatient at Harkaway's non-appearance.

He fancied some foul play was in operation, though he was far from thinking that the diabolical ingenuity of Leroy and the Hunstons had consigned Jack to a dark and dismal dungeon, in which it was their intention he should spend the short remainder of the life they hoped to cut short.

They had had this trap specially constructed for just such an emergency as the present.

The workmen who made it were told that it was to insure easier and rapid access to a vault for storing deeds and papers.

To the masons, it was simply a clever invention or a modern improvement. They did not connect it with a death-trap.

The detective beckoned to a policeman who was on duty, and to whom he had confided his intentions.

Together they ran quickly into the office, headed by Shise, who, as usual, was on the watch.

Davis's first act was to seize Shise, and slip a pair of handcuffs on him.

"What's this for?" indignantly demanded the Shiser.

"You'll see, if you live long enough," replied Davis.

He and the policeman were armed with clubs and pistols.

But Davis's orders were—"Don't fire unless I give the order."

Leroy looked angrily at the detective, and exclaimed—

"Explain the meaning of this outrage upon a boy in the service of our firm. Delavanti Brothers are not to be trifled with."

"Delavanti humbugs!" replied Davis. "I have a warrant for your arrest, Leroy, and also for that of Alfred Hunston and his brother."

"On what charge?"

"You and the elder Hunston are wanted for making bad money. Alfred is required on the other side for robbery. You know all about it, as well as I. Hold out your hands for the bracelets."

Leroy's reply was to fire point-blank at the detective's head.

Davis had been expecting this, and he dodged on one side.

The bullet firmly imbeded itself in the wall.

"Club them!" exclaimed Davis, preserving his coolness of action and demeanour.

The policeman fell upon Alfred Hunston, as did Davis on Leroy.

So sudden and unexpected was the attack, that the latter was unable to fire again.

The pistol fell from his hand, which was broken at the wrist by a blow from the club.

It is a terrible sight to see a man clubbed by an angry policeman.

The long, heavy staff, weighted with lead, flew about like a flail on a threshing-floor.

Leroy put up his arms to guard his head and protect his face, but in vain.

He roared for mercy, but received none.

Soon he was on his knees, the blood streaming down over his eyes, and blinding him.

Then he sank on the floor, his head a gory mass, and Hunston, junior, was not in a much better plight.

"That settles it," exclaimed Davis, leaving off.

He looked round the room.

Shise was horrified, and had not attempted to move, lest he, too, should be clubbed.

"Where the dickens is Mr. Harkaway?" exclaimed Davis; then, turning to Shise, he added, "Boy, did you not see a gentleman in here?"

Shise hesitated.

"Do you want a touch of the persuader?" asked Davis, touching his club suggestively.

This question, in police parlance, "fetched" the Shyser.

"No, sir; please sir. Not for me, sir," he answered.

"Answer my question, then, truly. Did you or did you not see a gentleman here a few minutes ago?"

"Yes, sir."

"Where is he now?"

"I don't know," replied Shise.

This was the truth, for the secret of the trap had been kept carefully a secret from the inquisitive eyes of the boy, who might have chattered inconveniently about such a stratagem.

Davis was a good judge of character, and could, as a rule, tell, by looking in a person's face, whether he was speaking the truth or not.

This time he evidently believed the Shyser.

"Go to the precinct," he said to the policeman, "and bring stretchers to remove these men on."

He did not place the handcuffs on them, because they were both so dreadfully beaten by the clubs, that there was no possibility of their moving.

His only fear just at that moment was that he had killed Leroy.

Still, it was done in self-defence, and Leroy was known to be a desperate ruffian.

Soon the wounded men were conveyed through a gaping crowd to the station, where their wounds were dressed by the surgeon, who pronounced them severe, but not mortal.

Shise was locked up.

He said, in a pathetic tone, to the sergeant who had him in charge—

"What will be done to me, sir?"

"Do you want to know?" replied the sergeant.

"If I didn't, I shouldn't ask," said Shise, with a show of his usual impudence.

"You'll be taken off the streets."

"I'm not on them."

"You'll be sent up to the Refuge on Randall's Island with the other bad boys, and kept there till you're twenty-one, and made to learn some trade to get an honest living by."

"Is that so?"

"You may bet your boots on it," replied the sergeant.

"And they call this a free country!" said Shise, with a groan.

This was actually the Shyser's fate; and as it was a species of imprisonment with hard labour, it may be readily imagined that he did not like it at all.

To a boy who has been accustomed to get his living by his wits in the streets, confinement is a great punishment.

But the Shyser was known as a clever thief, and it was deemed advisable to keep him shut up for a few years.

Lately he had been doing no harm as an office-boy, but his previous bad character told against him.

"This all comes of being honest," remarked the Shyser, in the solitude of his cell.

When well enough, Leroy, *alias* the Sensitive Sheepe, was put upon trial and sentenced to twenty years' imprisonment in Sing-Sing.

Alfred Hunston was sent back to England, where he was dealt with by a jury of his own countrymen, who appreciated his enterprise so highly that they found him guilty, and the judge ordered him into penal servitude for fourteen years.

And now having disposed of those dangerous ruffians, who so richly deserved their fate, and had reaped the fruit of their crimes, we must return to Harkaway.

Having seen the prisoners safely cared for at the precinct, Davis returned to the office of the pretended Delavanti Brothers.

It was certain that Jack had been in the room, and the fact had been admitted by Shise.

Where, then, could he have gone to in such a mysterious manner?

Solid flesh cannot melt or vanish like a flash of lightning.

Davis argued that either he or his dead body must be somewhere about.

He began to examine closets, and sound the walls with his club.

At length the knob in the wall which concealed the spring attracted his attention.

A detective is a man whose mind never neglects a trifle.

He touched this, pulled at it, and eventually pressed it.

A slight creaking behind him fell upon his ear, and turning half round, he saw a yawning chasm in the floor.

Jack had been impatiently watching for some sign from above.

Directly he saw the light come down the sides of the shaft, which grew wider towards the base, he got on one side, and when the trap touched the ground he jumped upon it.

Just then, Davis let go his hold of the knob, and ran to the middle of the room to look at the gulf.

To his astonishment, the trap rose up with considerable velocity, and on it was Jack, who appeared very much like Jack-in-the-box.

"Mr. Harkaway!" he said, in surprise.

Jack grasped his hand eagerly, and shook it warmly.

"Davis," he said, "you have acted like a man, and saved my life. How did you do it?"

The detective told him what had happened as briefly as he could.

"You have made a clean sweep of them. I shall never forget you," said Jack.

"Who would have thought of their getting up such a dodge as that?" remarked Davis, pointing to the floor.

"It's just like Hunston," said Jack. "He's a wonderful fellow, and, as a rule, I can't touch one side of him; but I hope to run him to earth soon."

"I'll wait here," remarked Davis, "and catch him as he comes in."

"Wait, will you? How long do you reckon to wait?"

"An hour or two."

"A month or two, you mean," said Jack.

"How?"

"Hunston has gone to Missouri with the title deeds of the lead mine my father has left me."

"Is that so?" replied the detective.

"Yes, sir," said Jack; "and I'm after him at the double."

"Well, Mr. Harkaway, I wish you luck; but you'll be getting out in the wilds before you know it, and sometimes a stranger falls into a bad crowd."

Jack thanked Davis for his kind wishes, and having rewarded him handsomely for the service he had done him, returned quickly to the hotel.

He was profoundly thankful for his narrow escape.

If Davis had not thought of coming back to look for him, he might have pined to death in the narrow vault to which the ingenuity of the Hunstons had consigned him.

CHAPTER XXXIV.
JACK MAKES A START.

A PECULIARITY of Harkaway's character, which our readers will have already noticed, was an aptitude for striking the iron while it was hot.

He never allowed the grass to grow under his feet.

If a thing was to be done, he did it at once, and if he could do it himself, he never employed any one else to do it for him.

Returning to the hotel, he went upstairs, and found his friends assembled at luncheon.

Monday was in attendance, as usual.

"Pack my valise," he said, as he entered.

"Yes, sar," replied Monday.

"And order me a coach to go to the Central Depôt at Forty-second Street, at four o'clock," continued Jack.

Everyone regarded him with astonishment.

"Jack, dear," said Emily, "are you going a journey?"

"Yes, my pet," he replied.

"Far?"

"A little over two thousand miles," said Jack, carelessly.

"Good gracious! What do you mean?" exclaimed Emily, nervously.

"I have business to attend to."

"Of what nature?"

"That I will explain to you. Horace Greeley's advice to young men was 'Go West.' I am a young man, and I am going West."

Emily turned pale.

"Jack, old fellow," said Harvey, "are you really in earnest about what you said this morning?"

"I am," replied Jack.

"Harkaway is a man of determination," remarked Mr. Mole, helping himself to the wing of a fowl, and adding, "The poultry in this country is exceptionally fine."

Emily sprang up, and clasped her husband's arm.

"Are we not to return to England?" she said.

"No, my pet."

"But you've got me back, pop," said Young Jack.

"Yes, you young rascal," replied his father, putting him on his knee; "and you'll have to go to school."

"I guess I've forgotten as much as Mr. Mole knows," said the boy.

"Silence," said Jack. "I will not allow you to make an impertinent remark in my presence. Do you hear, sir?"

The boy hung his head, for though not afraid of his father, he didn't dare to answer or disobey him.

"Just let me pitch into this corned beef," resumed Jack, "and I will tell you all that has happened. Fire away, Dick; I know you haven't half done. Mr. Mole, don't stop at your second chicken. Mrs. Harvey, Emmy, dear, don't let me spoil your appetites."

In spite of his cheerfulness, everyone's appetite, except Mr. Mole's, was spoilt.

Seeing this, he went on eating and talking.

He told them what had occurred during the day, and what his intentions were.

"Oh, my!" said Young Jack, clapping his hands, "I'm jolly glad that fellow, Sheepe, has got into choky."

"What, my dear?" asked his mother.

"I'm glad he's copped."

Emily looked disgusted, and Jack said—

"Mole, you must see to the young one's mode of expression, won't you?"

"I will do my utmost in that direction," answered Mr. Mole; "though if the soil be barren, you cannot expect the seed to yield a good crop."

"Oh! the soil's good enough," said Jack, "if you plough it up properly."

"Are you really going to Missouri after Hunston?" asked Emily, whose face betrayed the annoyance she experienced.

"Yes, my dear, I am going after Hunston, and yet not so much after him as after my property."

"Can't you let him alone?"

"Not by any manner of means. See here, Emily," said Jack, "my father is dead. My mother has only enough to live upon. All my father had to leave me was the title to this lead mine in Missouri, and Hunston has stolen this."

"Well," replied Emily, "can't you get something to do in New York?"

"I dare say I could," said Jack. "It doesn't matter to me what I do, so long as I get an honest living. I'd accept a chore in a junk-shop if I couldn't get anything else, for I hate poor gentility, which consists in starving in your own pride, or living at the expense of others."

"Bravo, Jack!" said Harvey. "I admire your spirit."

"You're all right, Dick, so you may dry up."

"You are welcome to what I've got."

"And I'll not touch a cent of it. All I want you to do, Dick, is to look after my wife and child while I'm gone," said Jack.

"That I will do with pleasure."

Emily burst into tears.

"I've enough money left," said Jack, "for what I want, and I start to-night for the West."

"You will not leave me, dearest," said Emily, throwing her arms round his neck.

"I do it for your good," said Jack

"Won't you take me with you, papa?" said Young Jack.

"No, my boy, you will stay here; or, if you all want a change, you can go on by the Pacific Railroad to San Francisco, and wait there till I join you."

"Perhaps you never will. You'll be scalped or tomahawked by the Indians," said Hilda.

"Oh!" said Emily, "the very thought of Indians makes my blood run cold."

"Why?"

"I remember what we suffered in the Malay Islands."

"The poor beggars won't hurt me, if I don't hurt them," replied Jack.

"Won't they? Don't make too sure of that?"

"Perhaps I shan't see any."

"I'll have your hair," said Young Jack, jumping up on the back of his father's chair, and making a grab at it.

"Let my scalp-lock alone, young 'un," said his father, smiling.

"Well," said Harvey, "I'll look after everything at home while Jack's gone, though I'm sorry he won't have me with him."

"I'll write to you, Dick, from Missouri," said Jack, "and you can come on if all's serene."

"Harkaway is right," said Mr. Mole. "It is best for him to go alone. We should only encumber him with useless lumber."

"If I can't tackle Hunston singly, I must be a duffer," answered Jack. "Leroy and Alfred Hunston are beaten, and when I have settled the elder brother, my task is accomplished."

"Quite so," replied Mr. Mole. "You can work your lead mine, I can educate the boy, and all will run smoothly."

"If I find there is a living to be got out of the mine, I shall settle there," continued Jack; adding, as he saw Felix Prye enter, "Ah! friend Felix, how are you?"

"Cheerful, thanks; how do you find yourself? Ladies, glad to see you. Harvey, hope you keep your health. Mr. Mole, what's the best news?" replied Felix.

"Jack's going away," said Emily, tearfully.

"Never! where is the great man going to travel?"

"West," said Harvey.

"That's rather vague. When you talk of going West, it isn't like saying you're going from England to Scotland. Your little island isn't so big as one of our large States. When I was over there, I was afraid to go for a long walk, in case I might come to the end and fall off the cliffs into the sea. But, seriously, tell me all about this."

"ROUSE UP!" SAID GOLIAH. "HERE'S SOME FRIENDS OF YOURS."

"With pleasure," said Jack, who related all that had happened.

"It's the best thing he can do, Mrs. Harkaway," said Felix.

"Every one seems to think so," replied Emily; "and I suppose I must not grumble any more."

"That's the way to look at it, my pet," said Jack. "Nothing will happen to me."

A boy came up to say that a man wanted to see Mr. Harkaway.

"What's his name?" inquired Jack.

"Says his name is Hank Smith, and he's come from Mr. Davis's. He's a roughish sort of a man. Shall I show him up?"

"Why, certainly."

In a few minutes, a tall, well-proportioned man entered the room, keeping his otter-skin cap on his head; his face was frank and open, his eyes bright, his manners genial, though blunt, and his appearance generally was that of a weather-beaten prairie-hunter, or a backwoodsman."

"Happy to see you," said Jack.

"Are you Jack Harkaway?" asked the man.

"Yes. These ladies and gentlemen are my friends. Mr. and Mrs. Harvey, my wife and son, Mr. Prye, Mr. Mole."

Hank Smith gave a series of nods as an acknowledgment of the introduction as each name was mentioned.

"I knew a man of the name of Mole," he observed. "He was a great coon-hunter."

"Very likely a relative of mine," said Mr. Mole. "We are a sporting family."

"Mayhap you don't have coon around in England? Maybe you've never killed a coon?"

"No," replied Mole. "I realise that I've never shot a coon."

"Ah!" said Hank, with a grave shake of the head, "that's bad. I'll allow you've killed a coon in your day, Mr. Harkaway. No? Well, you'll do it before you leave this Continent. I guess I'll sit. Suppose I take the big chair? I spread some when I sit."

"There's the lounge," said Emily "Would you prefer that, Mr. Smith?"

"This will do. There's worse chairs than this, and then, again, there's better," replied Hank, seating himself, and looking round, as if to take in the bearings, and adding, "You seem to have a pleasant camp spot here."

"Yes, we're well fixed," replied Jack; "and now, Mr. Smith, may I venture to inquire to what fortunate circumstance I am indebted for the honour of your visit?"

"I'm coming to it. Never you hurry a man up, Mr. Harkaway. We've all got our ways of coming to a thing, and mine is slow and sure."

"Take your time."

"You bet. I happened across Davis; he and me is old friends, Mr. Harkaway."

"I'm glad to hear it," replied Jack, who said this because Hank paused, and looked at him, as if he wished him to acknowledge his remark.

"I was born in New York city, and I've been back to bury mother. Leastways, I didn't bury her, but I put a stone up over her. You see, Mr. Harkaway, mother died last April twelve months, but I didn't hear of it till quite recent. I was out on the plains, when a man I met give me the news, and I quitted at oncet to come up to York."

"What are you by trade or profession, may I venture to ask?" said Jack.

"I'm a hunter, that's what I am. I've been stock-keeper, miner, all sorts. I've got to go back to the prairies. It's no use talking—I can't live in cities. Mother's left me a bit of money in the bank. Let it stop there. I don't reckon to touch it."

"Oh!" observed Jack, who began to see his way. "Davis sent you to me as a likely man to travel with to Missouri."

"That's it; we go the same road," replied Hank. "Now, I'm tickled 'most to deff to think you should have hit it off in a few words, when I've been all this time trying to tell it. Does that come of book larnin'?"

"Education is a great part, my dear sir," said Mr. Mole.

"Can't say. I never had none of it," replied Hank.

"Is it possible? Can't you read and write?"

"Nary word."

"Poor benighted creature! What a disgrace to the boasted civilisation of the United States!" said Mr. Mole.

"Hold on, stranger; don't you say nothin' agin the Union. I fought through the war to preserve it, and I won't have no goin' back on the Union."

"I didn't mean anything disrespectful," replied Mole, apologetically, as he saw Hank's manner was rather threatening.

"Many a better man than you's had the lead give him for less than that," continued Hank. "If I'm no scholard, I'll tell you what I can do. I'm a hunter since I was fifteen, and now I'm forty-two. I can track bar and buffalo. I've killed a heap of Injuns in my time, and I could live any day where such as you would starve. The school marm wern't about as she is now when I was raised."

"I shall be very pleased, Mr. Smith," said Jack, "to accept you as my fellow-traveller, and I hope you will honour us with your company at dinner to-night."

"Dinner! What do you mean?" exclaimed the hunter. "I had my food at twelve."

"We dine late."

"Then you may dine for me; and, see here, call me Hank. I don't want no 'misters' stuck on to my name. If you like to play a little whisky poker, I'm agreeable."

Jack excused himself, on the ground of having a great deal to do, and the hunter got up and took his leave, saying he'd come back about six, and see about making tracks for the cars.

Everyone agreed that the hunter would be a very valuable companion for Jack.

In fact, he could not have had a better one.

Hank Smith was known by most people beyond the Mississippi as a mighty hunter, the Indians dreaded him, and he was one of the kings of the prairies.

Presently, Mr. Mole, Harvey, and Felix went out; Hilda retired, the boy sought Monday, and Emily was left alone with her husband.

"I am sure, darling," he said, "that you will feel I am doing everything for the best."

"Yet it is so hard to be left alone," she answered.

"You haven't got half the pluck you had when you were a girl, Emmy," said Jack.

"Then, dear, I had only myself to care for and think of. Now, you are all the world to me. If I were to lose you, I should be miserable indeed."

"I wouldn't go away," said Jack, "if it wasn't necessary; but we haven't much money left, and I must go and see what I can make out of this mine."

"Perhaps it is worthless."

"I can't help it, if it is. I'm bound to strike oil somewhere."

"Well, dear, I shall say no more," replied Emily. "You have my best wishes, and take my fondest love with you. Write to us often, and send for us as soon as you can, if you conclude to stay."

Harkaway promised to do so, and went to look after his baggage.

Young Jack had heard that his father intended to go away, and that his journey would not be unattended with danger.

He also learnt that he was going at once.

The boy's heart burned with a fierce desire to accompany him.

He knew it would be useless to ask his permission, so he sought Monday, who was always his friend in need.

They sat down on a bench together in the hall of the hotel.

"Monday," said Young Jack, "I want to talk to you seriously."

"Well, sar, what am up?" replied the black.

"You've heard papa is on the move."

"Um take a journey, sar, and come back soon. That all."

"I'm not sure about that. Hunston generally leads him pretty long chases."

"Wish he'd take me along, sar. Why he leab us all here?" said Monday.

"He wants to be on his own hook, I guess. I did hope he'd have taken me with him. It's the most old sell I ever saw. I don't blame him for leaving mamma, because women are always a bother when you're travelling."

"What um able to do?" asked Monday.

"He'd be safer if he had us around," said Young Jack, with a look of self-importance.

"That's for sartain."

"Can't we work it somehow?"

"I like to know in what way," replied Monday, scratching his head.

"You've got to meet him at the Depôt, haven't you?"

"Yes. Take um baggage."

"Very well. Take me with you. Don't you see?"

Monday shook his head.

"When the train starts, you and I can jump in the last carriage, and when we've gone too far to be sent back, we'll tell him what we've done."

"That um splendideferous scheme, sar."

"Will you do it?"

"Just give me time to think it over. The boss will be in dam tearing rage. That sartain as um sun shines to-morrow."

"He can't kill us, and it's nothing very wrong," replied Young Jack. "We only did it for his sake."

"It'll cost a heap of money, and I've put um wages in um bank," said Monday.

"How much have you got?"

"Fifteen, twenty dollars."

"That's lots to start with," replied Young Jack, with the recklessness of consequences peculiar to rash and impulsive childhood.

"P'raps get along somehow," said Monday

"Will you risk it?"

Monday's answer was interrupted by the arrival of Harkaway on the scene.

"What are you two sitting there for?" he said. "You look like a couple of conspirators."

"We're only talking about your journey, pop," said Young Jack.

This was an evasion without being an untruth.

"Run up-stairs to your mother. I don't like your hanging around here; and you, Monday, hurry up with my valise. I have laid out what I want to take with me."

They both scattered in double quick time.

One of the men attached to the hotel came up and said—

"A horse has come for you."

"A horse? I haven't ordered one."

"It's outside. Will you look at it?"

"Certainly."

Harkaway went to the door, and found a small crowd collected at the entrance in Twenty-ninth-street, round a magnificent animal.

It was thorough-bred, and as white as snow.

The groom who held it said—

"Are you Mr. Harkaway?"

"Yes, I am," replied Jack.

"This horse is for you, sir."

"There must be some mistake."

"None at all. It comes with Mr. Harvey's compliments for Mr. Harkaway. We call the horse Lightning, because of its speed. What stable shall I take it to?"

Jack's face flushed with pleasure.

He was proud to be the owner and master of such a splendid creature as the one that was pawing the ground impatiently before him.

It was the admiration of all the beholders.

"This is kind of Dick," he said to himself.

While he was deliberating what he should do with it, a second man arrived, leading a big dog.

I was of enormous size, and of the Siberian blood-hound breed, and seemed possessed of great strength and ferocity.

"Who's dog is that?" he asked.

"A present for Mr. Harkaway, from Mr. Felix Prye," answered the man.

"A dog for me!" exclaimed Jack, still more surprised.

"What will I do with it?" inquired the man. "If it's for you, I suppose you'll send it somewhere out

of the way of children. It's death on babies, this dog is."

"Wait awhile, and I'll see."

The dog now divided the attention of the curious, who were loud in its praise, as they had been in that of the horse.

Just then, up came a third man, carrying a rifle of the very best workmanship, ornamented wherever it was possible with silver and gold.

"Anyone know Mr. Harkaway?" said the man.

"I am he," replied Jack.

"Rifle for you, sir; presented with the compliments of Mr. Mole."

"Bless me!" said Jack. "It's raining presents. Take it inside."

"This gun, Mr. Harkaway, has a name," said the man. "It shoots so true that we've called it Grim-Death."

"Thank you," answered Jack. "By-the-way, what is the dog's name?"

"The dog," replied the man who led him, "is called Republican, or Rep, for short."

"Oh! There's the dog Republican, the horse Lightning, and the rifle Grim-Death. I shan't forget."

After reflecting awhile, he determined to take the presents with him on his travels, and had them forwarded to the Depôt, to be in readiness for the steam-cars.

He thanked his friends for their kindness, and took an affectionate leave of all of them.

Harvey accompanied him to the Depôt, and asked him if he was sure he had all the money he wanted.

"Quite," replied Jack. "I found I had over two thousand dollars at the bank, half I gave to my wife, and all I want you to do, Dick, is to look after her."

"That you may rely on," said Harvey. "I wish you every success, old man, and hope to see you again soon."

They shook hands. Harkaway got into the drawing-room car, where he engaged a seat for himself and Hank Smith.

"Good-bye, once more," said Harvey; "I wish you luck, old boy."

About a couple of minutes had to elapse before the cars started.

Hank looked around on the luxurious surroundings of the drawing-room car, and remarked—

"Isn't this too much for the money?"

"You'll find it very comfortable," replied Jack.

At this moment, Davis, the detective, entered the car, and looked round, as if in search of somebody.

Harkaway saw him, and thinking he wanted to speak to him, said—

"Are you looking for me, Davis?"

"Oh, there you are, Mr. Harkaway!" replied Davis. "Yes, I do want a word with you."

Jack got up and joined him in the centre of the car.

"Anything new?" he asked.

"I'm afraid there is danger ahead. I've been inquiring into the affairs of this man, Alfred Hunston, and finding out who his associates were."

"Well?"

"It appears this Columbia Mine is a very valuable one, and has been in the hands of a Ring in New York, who have been working it for their own profit."

"Is that so?"

"The title deeds which were given to your father in England are good ones, though he was swindled by false returns and unreliable information."

"Glad to hear it," replied Jack.

"The deeds, unfortunately, have never been recorded. If you can get them from Hunston, you can work this mine yourself, and make a fortune," said Davis.

"You bet, I mean to."

"But the Ring in this city won't let you, if they can help it."

"How do you know?"

"The telegraph's been at work."

"Already?"

"Yes. Hunston now knows that Leroy and his brother Alfred are captured."

"Then he'll be on the look out."

"Exactly. He expects your arrival, and you must keep your eyes open," replied Davis.

"Have you any idea what sort of shape the danger will take?" inquired Harkaway.

"I can't give you any definite information on that point, because I have not had time to push the matter, though I can hint at something."

"What's that?"

"I overheard one of the Ring say something."

"Stop a bit," said Jack. "Who are these Ring men?"

"They are seven in number, and speculate in the Street. That's Wall-street, you know, where all our stock and gold-gambling, buying, selling, &c., is done."

"Yes."

"Each man has money, is unscrupulous, and collectively they are not inclined to let this mine slip out of their hands."

"The villains!" said Jack.

"Hunston and his brother were to have shares in the profits. They have an agent, by name Sol Pike, at Granby, and you must beware of him."

"Sol Pike," repeated Jack, registering the name in his mind."

The bell rang for the cars to start.

"Train's off," said Jack.

"They run the cars to time on the New York Central," answered Davis.

"You've not given me the hint."

"No, but I will."

The train began to move.

"I heard one of the Ring say," continued Davis, "'If Mr. Harkaway can tumble to a blind man, a deaf man, and a stutterer, he'll be clever.'"

"What does that mean?" asked Jack.

"That's more than I can tell you. If I find out anything more, I'll telegraph. Ask the Depôt-master at St. Louis for a despatch."

"St. Louis? All right. Good-bye, and very many thanks, Davis," said Jack, shaking his hand.

"Good-bye. Wish you luck, Mr. Harkaway. You deserve it," replied Davis.

He got out of the car while it was in motion, jumped deftly on the platform, and waved his hand.

The long, commodious, and handsome cars rolled slowly out, the engine-bell clanging loudly.

"I must keep my wits about me," muttered Jack. "This mine appears a prize. It is all I have to depend upon, and, by George! I mean to have the title deeds, if I seize Hunston by the throat and strangle them out of him."

CHAPTER XXXV.
INCIDENTS OF THE JOURNEY.

HE paused. The expression of anger and fierce determination which had appeared on his face died away, and one of curiosity took its place.

"A blind man, a deaf man, and a stutterer," he continued. "That's a lick. What sort of a riddle is that to guess?"

His friend Hank did not seem at all at home in the drawing-room car.

He roused Jack from his reverie by touching him on the arm.

"Colonel," he said, "if it's all the same to you, I'll go into the smoking-car for a spell."

"All right," said Jack, who was not sorry to be left alone.

"These Pullman's machines are a heap too high for me, and you can't blow a cloud in them," continued Hank.

"Perhaps I'll join you," said Jack; "anyhow, come in again before we get to Albany, won't you?"

"I'll come and see you at Sing-Sing and Poughkeepsie," replied Hank "becos, you know, I'm kinder in charge of you."

"Very well, don't neglect me," said Jack, smiling at the idea of his wanting the paternal protection of the old hunter.

Hank strode off down the car, opened the door and stepped on to the next one, walking through the circus as he termed it, till he got to the smoking car, where he lighted his cigar and smoked tranquilly.

* * * * * *

Fatigued with the exertions of the day, Jack fell off to sleep, and did not wake until the train stopped at a station.

Most of the passengers were wrapped in slumber.

The lamps cast a heavy, sickly glare around, and shutting his eyes again, Jack indulged in a reverie.

He thought of all that had lately happened to him.

His escape from the asylum, and his still more recent good fortune in avoiding the death-trap in the office on Broadway.

It was impossible to deny that Hunston either had a master-mind, or was working with men who neglected nothing to insure the success of anything they took in hand.

Rousing himself, he got up, and saw a man standing close by.

"Where are we now?" he asked.

The man put his hand to his ear.

"I'm rather deaf," he replied.

"I was merely anxious to know how far we have travelled."

"You must speak a little louder."

"Have we passed Poughkeepsie?"

"How?"

Jack repeated his question, bawling into his ear.

"Perkipsey," replied the deaf man; "I guess we have. Are you a stranger in these parts?"

"Yes."

"From Europe?"

"Yes."

"I reckon you're a Dutchman?"

"Not much," replied Jack; "I'm English, and I suppose you're Yank?"

"Yee-a," replied the man.

All this time, Jack had to bawl in his ear.

"Will you take a drink?" said the man, pouring out some liquor from a flask into a tin cup.

"Thank you, no," replied Jack. "Excuse me, I'm much obliged, all the same. Drink it yourself, since you've had the trouble to pour it out."

"I won't drink alone," said the deaf man, who threw the liquor under the bed nearest to him.

Jack fancied this was suspicious, and walked away to the end of the car

He had been warned against a deaf man, and his idea was that this one wanted to drug him for some purpose.

Pushing back the door, he got outside the car, and saw a man holding on to the iron-work and smoking a cigar

Either by accident, or intentionally, he gave Jack a push.

If he had not been holding on to the brake, he must have fallen off and been dashed to pieces.

"What did you do that for?" asked Jack, looking up at him in the darkness.

"I be-beg your pup-pardon," said the man, who stuttered badly.

"So you ought to."

"It was an ac-ac-accident."

Jack glared at him, and passed into the next car,

through which he went to the smoking-car, which was at the extreme end of the train.

It was nearly full of people, amongst whom was Hank Smith, fast asleep, with the stump of a cigar in his mouth.

Taking a cigar out of his case, he lighted it, and seeing a place disengaged, sat down.

The next man to him was eating some bread and ham, which he cut with a knife.

He moved his arms about rather wildly, and the knife would have struck Jack in the side if he had not moved quickly.

" I say, you," he said ; " mind what you're up to with that pig-sticker."

" Excuse me," replied the man. " I'm blind, and my friend, who usually looks after me, has gone away for awhile."

" Then it's good enough for me to quit," answered Jack.

He rose and went towards the stove.

"I've met a blind man, a deaf man, and a stutterer," he said to himself. " I wonder if they are the three Davis warned me against ?"

All at once his eyes fell upon a coloured man sitting on the seat nearest the stove.

Leaning against him was a boy, around whose neck the man's arms stretched in an affectionate manner.

" Can I be mistaken ?" said Jack, half aloud.

His face became very grave as he touched the man sharply on the shoulder, causing both him and the boy to awake with a start.

"Monday !" exclaimed Harkaway.

" Golly, Mast' Jack ! That you ?" said Monday, whom his master had recognised.

" What does this mean ?"

" Don't pitch into Monday, father," said Young Jack. " It was all my fault. He wouldn't have done it if I hadn't pressed him."

" I didn't expect to find you here," said Jack. " Why have you come ?"

" To look after you, papa," said the boy, affectionately. " It was done out of love, and not mischief."

" That for certain," exclaimed Monday. " Um heart good, if um head bad."

" What will your mother say ?"

" We left a letter for mamma, telling her all about it, so she won't be frightened."

" I don't know what to do with you," said Jack, in perplexity."

" I'll mind the horse," replied Monday.

" And I'll look after the dog," said Young Jack.

" I've a good mind to put you both out at Albany."

" Oh, do let me stop," pleaded the boy, earnestly. " Don't put us off. I want awfully to see some fun."

" But I'm going a long way on business."

" That don't matter. There'll be something going on where you are. It's in the nature of things," cried Young Jack.

" What do you know about the nature of things, young man ?" said Harkaway, pinching his ear.

" It too bad, Mast' Jack, to go and leab um poor Monday," remarked the black. " Did he eber run 'way and leab you? As long's Monday got any blood in um veins, he pour it all out for you."

" I know it, my friend," replied Jack, feelingly. " But this is a breach of discipline. I gave orders that no one was to follow me, having particular reasons of my own for going alone, and these reasons have become strengthened since my start."

" We won't trouble you, father. Monday and I will only watch near you, and fight, if there is need."

" Fight !" repeated Jack. " A lot of good you'd do."

" I don't know about that," replied the boy, shaking his head. " Monday and I have been to a shooting-gallery, and I can gun some."

" Well," replied Jack, secretly proud of his young

son's spirit, " you may stop. I shall wire a message to your mother at Troy, and put her mind at rest about you, as far as I can, though I know she will be mad all the time you're away."

" Mamma makes too much of a fuss about me."

" Don't say that," corrected Harkaway. " She loves you, and that is sufficient to account for her anxiety."

" What I meant was, she needn't be so fidgetty about me. I'll knock the spots out of Hunston if he tries any games on with me again. Why don't you shoot that fellow, father ?"

" You may depend I'll give him no mercy if he trifles with me any more," said Harkaway, putting his lips firmly together.

" Shall um stop here, sar ?" asked Monday.

" Yes, till the morning. I will see if we can fix you more comfortably. Have you anything to eat ?"

" Lots of grub in a bag, papa," answered Young Jack.

" Well, go to sleep again, and be as good as you can," replied his father. " I'll hunt you up in the morning."

He kissed Young Jack on the forehead, and shaking hands with Monday, went up to Hank Smith, who still slumbered, and taking a seat by his side, finished his cigar in moody silence.

The discovery he had made was anything but satisfactory, because Monday and the boy were to a great extent a burden upon him.

He knew he was surrounded by danger, and had a difficult task before him, and the boy's presence was a source of weakness rather than strength.

While he was thinking, Hank woke up with a loud snort like that of a horse.

" What are you dreaming about, my friend ?" asked Jack.

" Hallo, captain ! is that you ?" replied Hank. " I was huntin' bars in my sleep, and thought a grizzly had treed me. I'd just dropped my rifle, old 'Kaintuck,' and things was beginnin' to look considerable bad. I feel a heap better to think it was only a dream."

" Are bears such dangerous animals to meet ?"

" You bet they air. There's something in the wind. I never dream of bars without bad luck. If you want to see raisin' Cain in the full sense o' the word, try and shoot at the bar's cubs, and then stan' and look at her through an eye-glass."

" I'd rather not," replied Jack, smiling.

" We're great on bars and buffaloes out West."

" It's a great country," said Jack, " and full of rocks."

" Wal, I tell you, colonel, we can show you some sights whar I've been in Arizona Texas, California, Washington Territory, Nebraska, and all round. Once I was a-huntin' this side of the Rocky Mountains, between the Snake and the Yellowstone Rivers, when I shot a bar nigh as big as a house."

" Come, Hank, that's too thin," said Jack.

" Wal, I mean a small house, of course ; but bar-huntin' aren't like eatin' pie. It's mighty rough work, anyhow. You bet," replied the old hunter, winding up with his favourite expression.

The train soon slackened speed again, and glided into Troy, where Jack got out to send his despatch to his wife.

It was about one o' clock in the morning, and he was looking about the imperfectly lighted place for the office, when he came across three men standing together.

They were all talking excitedly, and so much wrapt up in one another's conversation, that they did not notice his approach.

His excitement was wrought up to the highest

pitch when he recognised them as the blind man, the deaf man, and the stutterer.

The first had his eyes wide open, and could see very well.

The second did not experience any difficulty in hearing.

While the third spoke without any impediment in his speech.

"I tell you," said the blind man, "that Harkaway has had the tip given him in some way. He wouldn't let me stick my knife into his shoulder as I intended."

"Nor would he permit himself to be thrown off the cars by accident," remarked the stutterer.

"He evinced a decided dislike for poisoned wine," observed the deaf man.

"If he suspects us," continued the blind man, "our disguises are of no use. I was fully aware that Davis, the detective, was on the look-out for what he could discover, but I did not think he would know all our plans."

"I saw him enter the cars and speak to Harkaway," said the deaf man.

"That accounts for it all," said the stutterer. "However, we must keep up the disguise till the end of the journey."

They all seemed to agree to this proposition, and Jack slipped away.

His suspicions were confirmed.

The three men, who severally pretended to be blind, deaf, and to stutter, were in league with Hunston, and their object was to disable Harkaway from continuing his journey.

He re-entered the train, and on the following day kept as much in the company of Hank Smith, Monday, and Young Jack as he could.

It was a great relief to Harkaway when they reached St. Louis, and alighted to change carriages to get on the Atlantic and Pacific Railroad, along which they would travel to the nearest point to Granby, and then reach the latter place the best way they could.

The horse and dog were released from the confinement in which they had been placed for some days.

A small crowd collected round the animals.

The dog looked round for a master, and Jack patted him on the head.

"You're mine, now," he said. "Good dog. Good Rep. Ho! ho! now, down," he added, as the creature jumped up at him affectionately.

All at once he saw Hank, and made a rush for him, licking his hands and face, and showing signs of extreme delight.

It was clear that Hank was an old friend.

"Why," said Hank, "if this isn't the dog gonedst funny thing I ever did see."

"Do you know the dog?" asked Jack.

"I should think I did know the dorg. He was Frisco Bill's dorg, he was. Me and Bill used to run in the same track last Fall, down in Texas, and we had old Rep with us."

"Why did Bill part with him?"

"He didn't part with him of his own free will and accord," answered Hank. "He got his ha'r raised by the Arapahoes, and one ugly red-skin hit him once too often with his tomahawk. That's what the trouble was."

"Is he dead?"

"That's so, captain. Poor Frisco Bill died in my arms. He was the best friend a man ever had, and it makes my eyes water to think of him."

"How did the dog get to New York?"

"I took him. 'The dorg is yours,' said Bill, when he was a-dyin'. 'That, and my share of the skins, is all I've got to give you, Hank. Be kind to the dorg, for my sake.' Which I war, you bet. Look

at the beast now! Why, Rep, old cuss, whar ha' you bin to, you doggoned old varmint?"

"Did you sell him?" asked Jack.

"Not much. He war stole from me. I didn't think of such a thing, not being posted in the dark ways of cities, you see, captain. New York, I tell you, is not a place for men like me. It don't amount to chucks for a hunter. I'd ha' lost my head if it had been loose, and I'd stopped long enough."

Among the crowd were the three confederates.

"The dog was made a present to me by a friend of mine, who, I guess, bought it from the man who stole it," said Jack.

"That's right enough, colonel."

"But as you say your friend, Frisco Bill, gave him to you, why, take him back; though I feel real sorry to part with such a fine fellow."

"Tell you what I'll do with you, Mr. Harkaway," said Hank.

"What's that?"

"I'll accept half the dorg."

Jack laughed.

"We can't cut him in half, my friend."

"No; I don't mean that. We'll own him joint stock. He shall be our dorg. I am sot on that pup."

"Suppose we separate?"

"In that case, you shall own him half the year, and me the other half."

"Good enough, friend Hank," replied Jack, laughing at this comical arrangement.

The dog had got near the blind man, and smelt about his legs.

He gave him a vicious kick, which made the dog set up his back and growl savagely.

"Don't you do that again, stranger," said Hank.

"He's afraid of de-de-dog," said the stutterer.

"Did you ever see a big dog take a man by the threat, and tear his wind-pipe out?"

"No, I never did."

"Wal, ef you don't wan' to, jest let that pup alone, or he'll do it, you bet," said Hank, squirting his tobacco juice past the stutterer's nose.

"If the de-de-dog fe-flew at my fer-friend, I'd shoot him, and his me-m-master, too."

The blind man drew his knife, and began to brandish it about wildly.

"Keep the beast off!" he said, in well-simulated accents of terror. "I'm mortal skeared of dogs."

"Don't let us have any of that nonsense," said Jack. "Put up your bowie, or I'll knock you down."

The bystanders grew indignant at this threat.

"Hit a blind man?" said one. "No, hang me if I stand by and see that."

"Look here," said Jack; "these men are not what they seem."

"He's blind."

"No more than you. Look at him!"

Harkaway walked up to the blind man and dashed his fist within an inch of his face.

The man stepped back with such suddenness that he stumbled and fell.

"Ha! ha!" laughed Jack; "he's a heap blind, isn't he? He could not see me coming! Oh, no! I say, you deaf man, you've dropped a pile of bills out of your pocket."

The deaf man instantly turned round and looked for the bills, which he could not see, as it was an invention of Jack's.

"He's very deaf, isn't he?" laughed Jack.

"I'll give you something for this," said the stutterer, forgetting his assumed impediment.

"What!" replied Jack; "don't you stutter? Aren't you a pack of humbugs? Trail off. Step it. I've exposed you, and if you dare, any of you, to talk to me, I'll make short work of you, you pitiful counterfeits!"

The three slunk off together, looking quite crestfallen.

"Now," exclaimed Harkaway, "what's the next part of the performance?"

"I'm a-going to make a bee-line for a drink," said Hank, shrugging his huge shoulders, as if he felt he wanted something.

They saw nothing more of the three "counterfeits," as Jack had christened them.

The train started, and they continued their journey.

Jack was full of pleasant anticipations, for he had received two telegrams at St. Louis.

One from his wife.

The other from Davis.

Emily had merely said—

"Yours has reached me. Our child is in the hands of Providence. It will, no doubt, make him a fine manly fellow, to rough it with you. I need not ask you to be careful of my precious darling for my sake. God bless you both, and prosper you, dearest, in all your undertakings. We are all well and hopeful."

Davis was more laconic.

"Blind man, deaf man, and stutterer, bogus," he said. "They are three of the Ring who work the mine. Look out for a deal box. Can't say more at present. My regards."

The allusion to the deal box puzzled Jack considerably.

Davis got his information inch by inch, as it were, and though he could not say much, owing to he and his spies only being able to pick up a few words here and there, he could only throw out hints.

"A deal box," said Jack, to himself. "That's an uncommonly rum thing to look out for; but I'll be on the watch."

At last they came to their destination, and found they had to travel some distance by road to reach Granby, which is in the richest lead region of the United States.

All mining districts are very much alike. In the daytime, the men are all working underground, and the women populate the town, which looks like a colony of Amazons.

The village consisted chiefly of log-buildings, and here and there were mounds of red loam, gravel, and stone thrown up from the shafts.

In a valley hard by, rose the low, dull-looking chimneys of the smelting furnaces.

"How are you going up, captain?" inquired Hank.

"I shall ride Lightning," replied Jack. "What will you do?"

"Guess I'll tramp it. Shank's pony is good enough for me. What's Pompey say, and the youngster?"

"Name of Monday, sar, if it am all de same to you," said the black, with dignity.

"I'll call you 'Week,' my friend, if you like, and that will include all the days," said Hank.

"You're a very impirint sort of a person, sar. That for certain."

"Saddle the horse. Hurry up!" cried Jack.

Monday was not long in doing this, with the boy's assistance, for Young Jack was extremely handy at all matters connected with out-of-door life.

It was only when it came to hard study that he was slow.

"Darned if that boy can't slip on a bridle as well as I can," remarked the hunter, who saw him step on a rail, draw the horse to him by the mane, and put the bridle cleverly over his head.

"He's smart enough," replied Jack.

"You oughter be sorter proud of him, captain."

"So I am, when he does as he is told."

Young Jack bestowed a grateful look upon his father, as he always valued his praise most highly.

It was difficult to obtain, but when he did get it, he knew he had deserved it.

"Now we're landed, pop," said Young Jack. "I feel awfully jolly, and as light as if I was up in a balloon. 'Up in a balloon, boys, sailing round the moon.' I guess Hunston will soon be auchkerspiel, as the old Dutchman I lived with used to say."

"What's that, Tiny?" said his father.

He had got into the way of calling him by the name Kit had given him, though he did not merit it, being very well grown for his age.

"Played out, it means. We'll euchre him, pop. Give him the Right Bower, to let him know you've got the left one well guarded, and sick him 'most to death."

"Will you get up behind?" inquired Jack.

"I can walk with our coloured friend," said the boy. "I'm not proud—am I, Monday?"

"I'm Prince Matabella in my own country. What the use talking, sar?" replied Monday.

"This is a free country, and we don't recognise titles," answered Young Jack. "The sooner you see that fact in the proper light, the better. If you could dye your skin, it might improve you. Blacks have gone up since the war, and you're not one—you're Dutch or Irish."

"Oh! be jabers, Masther Jack, it's not going back on Ould Oirland yez are!" said a voice with a rich mellow brogue, close to him.

The boy started, and looked around, but could see no one but his own party.

"Arrah, now, ye spalpeen, wasn't yer father born in the County Cor-rk, and didn't yer mither come from Tipperary? It's rale mane for a Har-rkaway to say a wor-rd aginst the Imerald Isle, God bless it; and ye'll have no luck at all, at all."

The boy looked at his father, and saw him suddenly burst out laughing.

"It's you, pop," he said. "You've been ventriloquising. I couldn't make it out at first."

"Yes, Tiny, I did it," replied Jack. "I may want to exercise that gift of mine, and I wished to see how well I could do it."

Hank Smith was profoundly astonished.

"Do you mean to say it was you, captain, a-doin' that Irishman?" he said.

"Yes," replied Jack.

"Wal, may I never live to be scalped by a nasty Injun, if I guessed that! 'Where's the varmint hid?' I thought. That's right smart."

"Did you never hear it before?"

"Oncet, and only oncet," replied the hunter. "We were out on the peraries, when we met a band of hunters, and, to cut a long story short, one of them could ventrilise, don't you call it?"

"That's near enough."

"He amused us round the camp-fire, telling us how he'd saved his life 'mong the Injuns by using his powers. He never knowed any fancy name for it. It was his powers, and that was all he called it."

"I've no doubt," remarked Jack, "that the Indians were scared by it."

"You bet. They were powerful skeart."

"I tried it some years ago upon the savages of the Malay Islands," said Jack. "But I haven't time to tell you the story now."

"Hunky Dore we used to call the man with the power," continued the hunter, "and he related how he oncet come across an Injun by himsel', roasting an elk, and dancing round the fire like mad.

"He was a fine-looking fellow, about six foot five, and when Hunky saw he was alone, he said, throwing his voice into a tree, 'Why does my brother not ask his friends to eat with him?'

"The Injun stared mighty hard, and replied, beating his breast with his hand: 'Me big Injun! Me eat whole elk. Me big Injun!'

"'Go it, yer cripple, we're a-comin',' cried

Hunky, throwing his voice a half dozen places at once.

"The Injun guessed he'd make tracks, but Hunky drew a bead on him, and dropped him in his tracks. Then he tuk his ha'r, and sitting down before that elk, he eat considerable meat."

All laughed at the hunter's story. Harkaway sprang into the saddle, and the others started on foot, Monday having arranged with some one to express the baggage up to Granby, to the house of Sol Pike, the agent of the Columbia Mine.

Jack found that the horse was rather skittish, having got what English grooms call "bears on board." That is, he was well fed, and had had too little exercise.

"Ho! ho!" exclaimed Jack, holding him in with some difficulty.

"He looks as if he were going to make um bolt, sar," observed Monday.

"I don't care if he does," replied Harkaway. "The roads are dismally bad, and I'll soon take it out of him."

It was a fine day in June, but some recent thunder showers had made the roads abominable slusby, and those who know what American country roads are in remote places, will easily understand that a horse would not find them good going.

Suddenly Lightning reared, and tried to throw his rider, but Jack kept his seat.

"I mean to let him go," he said .but w ride back when he stops."

"All right, captain," replied Hank; "you're no country squash. You sit him like a Comanche."

Jack hit the horse with his fist between the ears, and brought him to his feet.

"By George!" he muttered, "one of us shall be master. You or I, and it shan't be you, if I can help it."

Lightning threw his ears back, and giving a defiant snort, started off like the wind.

"Johnny Gilpin's off," said Young Jack. "Hurrah! Look how he steps! Ain't he a beauty! My! what a pace he travels at!"

Horse and rider were soon out of sight.

Hank and Monday, with the boy between them, trudged along, choosing the driest spots, and helping the lad over the holes and puddles.

They might have been walking for half an hour, when they saw Lightning coming back.

But he was alone.

His rider was not with him.

Hank stopped abruptly, and held up his hands to stop the horse. which was going slowly, and showing signs of being tired.

He was easily caught.

The dog Republican went round the horse's legs, and began smelling in canine fashion.

"Something's fetched the dorg. What is it? Darn me, if it ain't blood!" said Hank.

He looked down at the horse's near hind leg, and saw patches of blood.

"Mast' Jack never fall off um horse," remarked Monday, with a grave shake of the head.

"Is that so?"

"That for certain. Him ride too well."

"I agree with Monday," said Young Jack. "My father has often boasted he could ride anything. He was a cavalry officer in England before he went to Naples."

"Then you bet he's been fetched with a shot,' said Hank.

"Come on, quick! Give um hold of um horse," said Monday. "I can't ride much, but I'll go after 'Mast Jack in double quick time."

"Hold on! We'd best keep together. There's two on us, and the dorg. He counts as one. That's three."

"And me," put in the boy.

"Oh! you're no 'count at all," said Hank.

"Well, I don't know. I've got a pistol Monday bought before we started. It's loaded, and if I don't give the first man Jesse up to the handle, say I'm Bucher, that's all!" exclaimed Young Jack.

"Well, step along. Lose no time. Go to the heel, Rep. Heel, boy. Keep your eyes open, all of you, and recollect an old hunter's advice."

"What's that?"

"Never throw a shot away, and don't shut your eyes when you fire. We'll show them what's the matter with Hannah, you bet!"

"All right, daddy; we're ready," replied Young Jack, who displayed a spirit as brave as that of his elders.

They all walked quickly along, with compressed lips and a slightly nervous air, which showed that they were anxious as to Jack's fate.

What had happened they could only guess at.

As they went along, Young Jack drew his pistol, and put the lock at half-cock.

"If I come across anyone who's been doing anything to my papa," he said, "I'll shoot him right away, if he's as big as—as—help me to a simile."

"Buffalo," suggested Hank, with a grunt.

"Good enough. If he's as big as a buffalo, and twice as ugly."

"I've got ducks that can quack as well as yours," said Hank.

"What do you mean?"

"Don't blow. If you do, you'll bust. I hate a youngster that blows."

"Wait till you see me shoot. I'm an elegant gunner—ain't I, Monday?"

"Yes, sir, That fo' certain."

"Well, perhaps you'll have a chance before long. I dreamt of bars, and I guess that's always a bad sign with me," replied Hank.

A dead silence fell upon all three of them, and they hastened their movements, the boy having to run to keep up with the others.

After walking about four miles, they came to a spot where Hank Smith pulled up.

The experienced eye of the hunter showed him that some disturbances of the ground had taken place there.

Rep also evinced a great interest in the locality.

He went sniffing about, here and there, and eventually stopped at a pool of discoloured water

"Blood!" ejaculated Hank.

He fell on his knees in the mud, and carefully examined the spot, crawling from one place to another.

The others watched him while he was at work.

"Here's where the horse stopped, boys!" he exclaimed, "and there has been a struggle, which proves that Mr. Harkaway was off his horse."

"Is he dead?" inquired Young Jack, whose face went white.

"How can I tell? It may be his blood, and it may be another's. What we've got to do is to push on to Granby, and see what we can."

The country round about was flat and uninteresting.

A view as far as the eye could reach was obtained and nothing met their gaze.

"Follow the road, boys. Follow the road straight up," continued Hank.

With heavy hearts, Monday and Young Jack made a fresh start.

Hank Smith led the horse, and the dog followed at his heels in a half-hearted manner, as if he knew that something had happened which he might have prevented had he been present.

Where was Jack?

That was the question which occupied the minds of the hunter, the black, and the boy.

CHAPTER XXXVI.
THE MYSTERY OF THE BOX.

HARKAWAY was a good horseman, and did not feel a bit afraid when Lightning ran away with him.

He let him go over the bad roads till he showed signs of exhaustion, and then he urged him on, making him jump over fences, and back again, till the horse was beaten, and gave in to the one he was in future to call his master.

When Jack saw that the horse was as docile as a lamb, he dismounted and patted him on the neck.

He was a little shaken by the jolting he had experienced, and somewhat out of breath from the swiftness of the run, while his legs, which were ungaitered, were chafed considerably by the friction of his pants between the animal's flanks and his legs.

While he was resting himself, four men, driving a cart, turned the corner.

In a moment, he recognised the three mysterious men of the journey.

He put his foot in the stirrup to jump on the horse's back.

But a stone, dexterously thrown, struck him on the forehead.

Falling to his knees half stunned, he clutched frantically at the mud in the road, striving to get up.

The horse ran away frightened, pursuing the same track that he had followed in coming up.

Jack's head was cut by the stone, and it was his blood which, by splashing on the horse, had startled Hank.

By an herculean effort of will, Jack threw off the dizziness that oppressed him.

He rose in his might, and looked at his enemies.

They were, as we have said, four in number.

At a glance he saw all.

The cart contained a long deal box, something in the shape of a coffin.

He remembered Davis's mysterious warning contained in the telegraphic despatch.

A cold sweat broke out all over him.

Were these men contemplating the crime of murder, and was this rude box to be the casket to hold his dead body?

Drawing his pistol, he fired, and wounded one in the leg; the others rushed upon him, and before he could discharge his pistol a second time, another stone had struck him a second time to the ground.

A film came over his eyes.

In his ears rang a dull roar, and he felt as if the pangs of hell had seized hold of him.

Then his senses left him, and all was oblivion.

The three men who remained uninjured picked him up, carried him to the track, lifted up the lid of box, and placed him inside.

They put the lid on again, and there were holes perforated in it to admit air, which, as he was lying face upwards, would enable him to breathe.

When this was accomplished, they turned to look at their injured companion.

"Are you hurt?" asked one.

"I've got a bullet in my leg, but I guess I can crawl home," was the reply.

"Will you ride in the cart?"

"No. It will only excite suspicion. I'll take my chance. Just bind a handkerchief round, won't you? It will stop the bleeding. I feel faint enough already. Curse the hand that sent that shot at me!"

The wound was soon bound up, and the cart, drawn by two horses, was directed into a side-road.

Hurt as he was, the fourth man hobbled along slowly, and watched his companions out of sight.

The cart travelled on until the outskirts of Granby were reached.

Those who guarded it were unusually reticent.

If they spoke, it was only to direct the horses and encourage them over the difficult ground, for the cart had left the main track, and had to make cut over the meadows.

The place at which they halted was the surface of a mine.

It was now late, and the miners had retired for the day.

Windlasses, to draw up the ore, huge piles of dirt and ore, were lying about, and the various implements used by the miners were to be seen on all sides.

The night-watchman heard them approach, and came out of his hut.

"Who goes there?" he cried.

"Express from Carsville," replied the leader, who was the one who had acted the part of blind man during the journey.

"What have you brought?"

"Dixon's patent pump for the mine."

"Dump it down anywhere."

"We've got to take it into the mine right away."

"Who says so? It can't be done at night," replied the watchman.

"We've got Mr. Pike's order. Here it is. You know his writing, I suppose?"

The man came closer, and looked at the piece of paper which was handed to him.

"That's Sol Pike's order," he observed; "and if the boss says it's to be done, why, you'd best do it.'

"I guess we'll wait a bit," said the leader, looking at his watch. "Mr. Pike promised to be here before dark."

"Then he's kept his word, for here he is," said the watchman.

Jack had recovered from his stupor, and could hear every word that passed.

He uttered a groan.

Immediately the leader picked up a bit of stick and poked it through one of the holes.

It touched his cheek dangerously near his eye, and pressed against his flesh so hard, that he deemed it prudent to be silent.

It was a significant hint.

Sol Pike, the local agent of the mine, was a tall, raw-boned specimen of a Western man.

He lounged up with his hands in his pockets smoking a cigar.

By his side was a man who had only one arm.

"Yes," cried the watchman, "here's Mr. Pike and Jack Harkaway with him."

Jack overhead this, and his surprise increased.

Were there two Harkaway's in the world?

Who could it be that had the hardihood to personate him?

Instantly the thought flashed across him that it was Hunston.

Nor was he wrong.

Hunston had had the audacity, on arriving at the mine with the stolen title deeds, to say that he was Harkaway.

Sol Pike knew different, but he was in the swindle, and readily fell in with the views of the Ring in New York, and agreed to treat Hunston as the real owner of the valuable property, out of which he had been for some time feathering his nest.

If Jack got the mine into his own hands, Sol Pike was shrewd enough to guess that he would quickly get his discharge.

It was too good a thing to let drop.

"Now, then," said Sol Pike to the watchman, "get some lights, and let us have this new pump down."

"Yee-a," replied the man.

He quickly procured lights, and the box was secured to a rope.

This was lowered away down a shaft, by the aid of a windlass, which was worked by two of the men.

Jack saw that he was caught in a trap.

What did his captors mean to do with him ?

Once in the solitude of the mine, seventy or eighty feet below the surface of the earth, he was, indeed, in their power.

At length, the deal-box touched the end of the shaft, and two men stepped into the descending bucket, clinging to the rope above.

It was necessary to use one hand and foot to ward off the rough walls.

When a depth of seventy feet was reached, they touched the bottom of the shaft, which was blasted through lime and flint rocks.

The two men were Sol Pike and Hunston.

Sol lighted a tallow candle.

This he stuck on a projecting ledge of rock.

"Get him out, quick," said Hunston.

Sol Pike grinned as he unfastened a hasp which allowed him to lift the lid.

"Get up !" he exclaimed, giving Jack a poke.

Harkaway was on his feet in a moment, but, being unarmed, he was entirely at the mercy of his persecutors.

"What are you going to do with me ?" he said.

"My good fellow," replied Hunston, with an insolent leer, "you will find all that out in good time."

"Anyhow," said Jack, "I'll have a cut in. Take that ! and that !"

He hit out with his powerful fists, and sent both Hunston and Sol Pike rolling against the rocky wall.

He would have made his escape after this if he could.

Unfortunately, the passages, or galleries, were dark, and he did not know where they led to.

The miners were absent, and in the deserted state of the mine he could not find anyone to take his part or guide him to a place of safety.

He stood grandly at bay, glaring at his adversaries.

Hunston and Sol Pike both rose to their feet, with the blood streaming from their faces.

"Shoot the skunk ! Shoot him like a dog !" exclaimed Hunston.

"Well," replied Sole Pike, "I don't know about that ; I've quarrelled considerable, but I've never killed my man yet. Spilled blood will show."

"It will be best to kill him out of hand."

"He's got friends," replied Sol. "There is a black servant and his son, and that hunter, Hank. I know that man—he's awful smart. If we were to kill Harkaway, and it got found out, we'd be lynched."

"Who by ?" inquired Hunston.

"Why, the miners and all the people round ; they're rough, but they're honest, and love fair play."

"Look here, Hunston," said Jack.

"Well."

"I suppose it's no use to ask you to make terms ?"

"If it's no use," replied Hunston, "why do you make the proposition ? Hang you ! isn't it through you my brother's in prison ?"

"He shouldn't have taken what did not belong to him."

Jack was standing with his fists clenched, as if he meant further mischief.

Sol Pike presented a pistol at him.

"Knuckle down," he exclaimed, "or I'll give you the lead right away. March after me, do you hear ? Mr Hunston, keep him up to the mark, won't you ?"

"Trust me," replied Hunston.

Sol Pike led the way up the mine, and Jack was constrained to follow him.

He knew that the desperate men who had him in charge would not hesitate to murder him if he proved at all ugly.

It was his idea that he ought to preserve his life at any price

Therefore he followed Sol as submissively as a child.

Sol carried a light ; so did Hunston.

They went through a labyrinth of passages, which were sometimes not more than two feet high.

In the day-time the miners were engaged in quarrying the metal, some blasting it from "pockets" in the rock, others lying flat on their backs, digging it with picks from the roof of a passage not a foot high.

In another place they were perched up in a gallery, breaking off the blocks and rolling them down.

The ore was carried on a wooden railway by cars, to the bottom of the shaft, whence it was hauled up to the furnaces.

A few feet above the floor was a stratum of flint, which made a hard and secure roof.

At best, the mine was a dark, unwholesome place, sometimes half full of water, and at others dangerous from foul air.

Sol Pike had been connected with mining all his life, and he had worked in this very mine himself before he became the agent.

Therefore, he knew all the turns and windings, which would have sorely perplexed any other person.

The passages they threaded seemed interminable to Jack.

He could see that they were entering a part of the mine that had been unused for a considerable period.

The ring of the pick was not heard in these silent caverns, and the busy hand of the miner was still.

"How much further are we going ?" inquired Hunston, impatiently.

"Well, I guess we're nearly home, now," replied Sol.

He held his candle up as he entered what resembled a dungeon, being a chamber hewed out of the ore, and forming a room about eight by ten, and about six feet high.

Attached to the wall, by an iron staple, was a long chain.

At the end of this was a padlock.

Sol Pike picked up the chain and fastened it round Harkaway's leg, locking it above the ankle, and taking away the key, which he put in his pocket.

On a ledge in the rock were a pitcher of water, a loaf of bread, and a packet of candles.

On the ground lay a pickaxe and a basket.

"You see your larder," said Sol Pike, with a diabolical chuckle. "Don't pitch in too hard ; you'll only have a loaf every other day."

"You make me a prisoner," said Jack, "in defiance of the law."

"Hang the law !" said Hunston.

"Perhaps the law will hang you some day."

Hunston grew savage at this taunt, and replied—

"Anyhow, you won't be there to see it."

"You can't tell that," retorted Jack.

"Here you are, and here you'll stay, a prisoner in your own mine. I've got the title deeds, and it will be pleasant for you to think that I'm bossing your property."

Jack gnashed his teeth with impotent rage.

"I've made you mad, have I ?" said Hunston, in the same provoking manner.

"I do feel mad to think you should have got the best of me," replied Jack.

"This is a fine place for a man to rot in," remarked Sol Pike, philosophically.

"How long would you give a man to live here ?" asked Hunston.

"Well, a strong man might keep up for two years, but a weak one would go under in six months. You see, the lead's unhealthy, and the damp gets into the bones. It brings on rheumatic fever; and when you've been accustomed to good living, bread and water pulls your strength down."

"All the better. This is the place I like to see my enemy in," replied Hunston.

"You're a contemptible hound to insult a fallen foe," said Jack.

"Am I? It's what I like."

"I despise you."

"That won't hurt me. I like to talk to you, and let you know I'm doing this. You've got my brother in gaol, but I've got you here, curse you!" said Hunston, savagely.

"It's rough on him," remarked the agent, "to think that he's here, and you're acting his part above ground."

"Yes. Do you know that I represent myself as Harkaway?" said Hunston.

"What good will that do you?"

"I own the property. Your father advanced money on the title deeds, and when he died he left you the papers. My brother Alfred stole them. I found we couldn't work the mine unless we worked in with some men in New York, who had been financing the mine for years. We now run it together, and I get my share of the profits."

"If you got out," said Pol Pike, "we should all have to quit."

"You think yourselves very clever, don't you?" replied Jack. "But you forget that I have friends."

"We know all about that," said Pike; "as soon as we leave you, we shall pay attention to Hank Smith, your son, and the black servant."

"Don't hurt the boy," said Jack, who was touched in a tender part.

"I'll see to him," replied Hunston; "the young cub escaped me once; this time I'll hold him fast enough."

"Do what you like with me, but for God's sake, Hunston, have pity on his mother, and send him back to her."

"Never!"

"You are like a demon in your hatred."

"To you I am. It's war to the knife between us, and one of us has to conquer. I'd rather it would be me than you," said Hunston.

"Well, it seems as if you had licked. I'm down. I shall soon be a dead man, for no one could live long in this dismal place. Still, I don't think a man ought to wage war against women and children."

"Bosh!" replied Hunston; "I've no scruples of that sort. The boy shall never see his mother again."

"I put my trust in Providence," said Jack; "and recollect, old fellow, that if ever we do meet again on equal ground, I shall go straight for you."

"If we ever do," sneered Hunston.

"I swear I'll kill you whenever I meet you," continued Jack.

"Swear away; your oaths don't amount to much," replied Hunston.

"See that pick and that basket?" said Sol Pike.

"What of that?" asked Jack.

"You'll have to work and fill that basket with lead ore every two hours. If I come along and find you haven't done your task, I'll cowhide you till your back's as raw as fresh meat."

"Well thought of," said Hunston. "Our slave of the mine mustn't be idle."

"Not much. I'm a good slave-driver."

Jack's blood boiled indignantly at these insults.

But he kept his passion down, and made no answer.

"Farewell," said Hunston; "we shall meet again, once on earth, and only once."

Jack looked at him inquiringly.

"When will that be?" he asked.

"When you are dead. I shall make a point of coming to look at your dead body, which I will spurn with my foot, and say, 'This carrion was once my enemy, over whom I've triumphed.'"

"I'm not dead yet," said Jack, trying to put a good face on it.

"I could kill you now, but I don't want to. I've had a chance of killing you more than once, but it suits my vindictive nature better to see you languish away."

"You're right, colonel," said Sol Pike; "let a man die by inches, without hope or comforts. If that won't give him his due, nothing will."

"You'll wish yourself dead every hour of the day," continued Hunston. "Deprived of liberty, away from friends, anxious about your wife and son, dirty, having none of the comforts of life, not even water to wash with, condemned to labour like a slave, your back cut up with the whip, which Sol won't spare—"

"Not I," said Sol. "I'll lay it on in heaps."

"You'll wish you'd never been born," concluded Hunston.

"Go on," said Jack. "I'm in your power, and can't help myself."

"Come along, squire," said Sol; "I'm getting hungry. We've got champagne and chickens waiting for us."

"I'm ready," said Hunston.

They left Jack one of the candles stuck in the wall, and walked as rapidly away as the irregular nature of the galleries would permit.

Harkaway was alone.

He moved to a heap of mouldy rye straw in a corner, and sat down.

The chain clanked with a dismal sound, which sent a chill to his heart.

"This is about the tightest fix I ever was in, and I've seen a few rough things in my life, but this beats all. It's the ugliest old fix that could have happened," he said to himself.

But, in the midst of his misery, and the natural horror engendered by his situation, he had one gleam of comfort.

His enemies had spared his life.

It was true that they had buried him alive, just as much as was a prisoner buried in the old days of the French Bastile.

But while there is life there is hope.

He could not believe that his lucky star had deserted him.

Hank Smith and Monday were not far off, and he knew that they would leave no stone unturned to find him.

No one had seen him go down into the mine.

The watchman merely knew that a patent pump, expressed from Carsville, had been lowered down the shaft by the agent.

Who would dream of looking for him underground?

The prospect of release was indeed a remote one, yet Jack clung to it as a drowning man to a straw.

CHAPTER XXXVII.
THE SLAVE OF THE MINE.

THE bleeding caused by the stones which struck his head when he was captured and put in the box had ceased. A dull, aching pain remained.

Taking a drink of discoloured water from the pitcher, Jack buttoned up his coat and tried to seek forgetfulness in sleep.

Fortunately, the drowsy god was propitious, and he was soon in the arms of Morpheus, traversing the land of Nod. How long he slept he did not know.

When he awoke, he felt refreshed, but a chill

had come over him, and he shook, as if with the ague.

"Chills and fever," he said. "Hunston was right. I shan't live long in this damp hole. All the more reason why I should try and get out of it as soon as possible."

The candle had burnt out, and he was enveloped in pitchy darkness.

Groping his way to the ledge on which his bread, water, and candles were standing, he struck a match and lighted another candle.

His watch had not been taken away from him.

He drew it from his vest-pocket and looked at the dial. The hands were motionless.

It had stopped.

"I've slept a considerable time," he muttered. "How cold I am! This place is like a well. I seem to feel the cold in my bones."

While he was lamenting the absence of warmth and dryness, a light appeared flickering along the gallery leading to his dungeon. Sol Pike appeared.

In one hand he held a whip, made of a long strip of cowhide, fastened by nails to a short, thick stick.

"How much work have you done?" he demanded, in a brutal tone.

"None," replied Jack, sullenly.

"What did I tell you?"

Jack made no answer.

"I'll have to hide you, my lad," continued the agent, setting down his lamp.

"If you touch me, you're a coward," said Jack.

"I'll chance that. Step to the end of your chain."

"I shan't stir an inch."

"Won't you? I think you will."

"Not I," said Jack, resolutely.

"I beg to differ," replied Pike, drawing a pistol, and adding, "If you don't obey orders, I shall settle you on the spot. Do you want a bullet through your head?"

"No; not likely."

"Step up, then, and hurry."

Jack saw that resistance was useless, and, with a sigh of rage, he stepped to the limit of the chain.

"Now strip to your pants."

Reluctantly Jack took off his clothes, and threw them down one by one, till he was naked to the waist.

"I thought that would fetch you," said Sol Pike, with a grin.

The veins on Jack's forehead were swollen almost to bursting, through the indignant blood which rushed into them.

They stood out like knotted cords, and he clenched his fists, and ground his teeth angrily together.

Sol Pike raised his whip, which flew through the air, and the cowhide descended with great force upon Jack's naked back.

It left a long, irregular, crimson stripe, from which the blood began to slowly trickle.

With a cry like that of a tiger, he sprang to the wall. Sol Pike followed him. He raised his whip again, but Jack, who had now room for action, sprang upon him.

His fingers tightened round the agent's throat, and so strangled him that his eyes started in their sockets, and his tongue lolled out of his mouth, black and swollen.

"Dog! wretch! scoundrel!" was all Jack could gasp; "strike me like a hound, will you? Hit me with a whip, eh? I'll let you know what sort of a man I am to trample on. My blood's up now."

While he held him with one hand, he pounded his face with the other till it streamed with blood.

"There!" he exclaimed, when he was tired of punishing him. "If I've killed you, it's your fault, not mine. If you've got any life left in you, live

to think of the licking I've given you. I guess you'll carry the mark to your grave."

Sol Pike, when released from Jack's strong grasp, fell heavily backward.

He lay perfectly still, but by placing his hand on his heart, Harkaway detected a slight pulsation.

"The cur ain't dead," he remarked.

Bending over him, he felt in his pockets, first of all securing the key of the chain which fastened his leg to the wall.

Letting himself loose, he cast the chains heavily against the wall.

"Badge of slavery," he exclaimed, "good-bye for ever. If I can't get out of this place, I'll die."

He next secured the agent's pistol. In ransacking his pockets, he found a written paper, which had been sent him by the Ring in New York.

Walking to the candle, he cast his eyes hurriedly over it, and made himself master of its contents It was a document warning the agent that he must be on his guard against a man of the name of Harkaway.

"Our agents in London," it went on, "have obtained half a million of dollars from an Englishman on the mortgage of the mine, and we deposited the tittle deeds as security.

"We have pretended that the vein of lead is worked out, and the mine cannot pay its expenses.

"Our agents have employed a man to steal the deeds, and bring them out here."

Here was a pause.

Then followed another date, and it went on—

"Since writing the above, the thief has arrived with the deeds.

"The man who advanced the money is dead, and has made his son his heir.

"This son is in New York, and on our track, as we believe.

"We have deemed it advisable to send a trusty party, by name Hunston, to you with the deeds.

"Please show him every attention.

"If Harkaway, who is the heir referred to, should start after Hunston, we will send three of our associates to stop him.

"Should their efforts prove insufficient, we rely upon you to wipe this man Harkaway out.

"Bear in mind that he is our mutual enemy, and that if he gets possession of the deeds he can work the mine, and our little game is gone up.

"You will suffer as well as us, because you will lose the handsome income you have been making.

"Once more, we rely upon you.   S. D. C."

Who the writer of this was, Jack could not form the remotest conjecture.

It, however, threw considerable light upon the conspiracy of which he was the victim.

The title deeds, which were his, and which would make the mine his property if he could find them, had left New York.

They were then in the town of Granby. Probably the agent had them in his house.

If not, Hunston, perhaps, carried them about his person.

If Jack could get the deeds, he could work the mine and make a handsome income for the support of himself and his wife, and the education of his child.

"I'll get the deeds," he cried, "and I'll make my home out here in Missouri. Mother can come and join us. I'll settle in the West."

He was, however, counting his chickens before they were hatched. At present, he was not out of the mine.

Seeing that the agent did not move, and thinking him done for, anyhow, for a few hours, he bestowed no more attention upon him.

Putting on his clothes, he stuck the revolver he had taken from Pike in his belt.

JACK CAST HIS EYES HURRIEDLY OVER THE DOCUMENT, AND MADE HIMSELF MASTER OF ITS CONTENTS.

Then he seized a candle, and prepared to start.

"What's the time?" he said to himself.

This was an important consideration, because in the daytime the miners were all at work.

At night they were on the surface of the earth, in their homes, or amusing themselves in the many drinking saloons with which Granby, like all mining towns, abound.

The agent had a watch, if a heavy gold chain hanging to the vest was any guide.

Jack took the liberty of looking at it. The time was noon.

He had, then, slept all night, and the best part of the morning.

Sol Pike, after breakfasting and attending to business, had descended the shaft for the pu, se

of indulging his vicious nature by ill-using his captive.

Grasping his pistol without showing it, so that he could shoot through his pocket if any one molested him, Jack sallied forth from the hateful dungeon.

The galleries were narrow and intricate, and a false turn might have made him lose his way.

It was a terrible thought that he might be lost in the mine. Innumerable were the passages leading to worked-out lodes.

More by good luck than any remembrance he had of the way he had come, he reached the busy part of the mine, in which the men returning from their dinner were commencing to work again.

Jack never thought of looking behind him. He only anticipated danger in front.

10

If he had looked o'er his shoulders he would have seen a sight calculated to make his pulse beat quicker.

He fancied that the agent was so badly hurt that he could not move, but in reality he had not severely injured him.

Sol Pike quickly recovered from the effects of his semi-strangulation.

The beating and punching he had received about the head had not deprived him of his senses.

Being of a crafty and fox-like nature, he had concluded to simulate insensibility. No sooner had Jack quitted the dungeon than Sol Pike got up.

He followed noiselessly in his tracks, creeping, gliding, and crawling like a serpent.

If he had been armed, he would have made an attack on Harkaway. The pistol was taken from him, and he knew he had a desperate man to deal with. So he bided his time, waiting till he could make sure of help.

His face was swollen and bleeding, his clothes torn, his collar and necktie ragged.

Altogether, he was a ghastly and forbidding object. Jack reached a portion of the mine where some men were driving a horse, drawing a truck which ran on rails. This was full of ore.

"Where is the nearest shaft, boys?" said Jack.

"There is one not far off. Go on to where you see the basket," replied the miner.

After replying, the man and his mates looked curiously at Jack.

"Say," continued the miner, "are you a stranger? I guess you don't work below here,"

"No," replied Jack. "I'm on a visit up above, and I'd come down to look around."

"And I guess you got lost?"

"Exactly."

Jack pushed by the truck, and was making for the shaft, when Sol Pike cried, at the top of his voice, in tones of tremulous excitement—

"Stop him, boys! Knock him down with a pick! Stop him!"

In an instant Harkaway turned round. He saw Sol Pike, and guessed that he had been pretending to be hurt.

"What!" he said. "Aren't you dead? You've been shamming, have you?"

"Five hundred dollars to the man who stops him!" vociferated Sol.

The miners hesitated how to act. Jack looked an ugly person to attack, and they did not know what he had done to rouse the ire of the agent.

"What's to do, boss?" inquired one.

"He's robbed me. Look at my face. He half killed me," replied Sol.

"You miserable fraud!" said Jack. "Back, for your life! I'll shoot if you advance another step!"

The scene was impressive and striking. Five miners stood by the truck, and others left off their work to see what was going on. The candles flared and flickered, giving out a ruddy, uncertain glare. All around were the dull surroundings of the dark and rugged mine.

Jack stood calm and defiant, though his pulse was going a good eighty to the minute, he produced his pistol, and exclaimed—

"Look here, boys! I've got six lives in this shooter, and I, when I fire, mean hitting. That's straight. I've done nothing to this man that he did not deserve."

"You've beat him about badly, sure enough," remarked one.

"Yes," said another. "I shouldn't have known him if I hadn't heard his voice."

"He's a robber," began Sol. "I—"

"Silence!" thundered Jack. "Listen here, boys."

The men looked at him with scowling faces. They knew Sol Pike, but they did not know him.

He was the agent for the mine, and could employ or discharge them at his pleasure.

"Wait till I tell you," continued Jack. "This mine is my property, and your Mr. Pike is acting with others who wish to deprive me of it."

"It's a darned lie," said Pike. "Let him show his papers."

"Yes, yes," chorused the men. "Show us the papers."

"I haven't got them."

An incredulous laugh ran round.

"It's too thin," said one.

"We don't want any bogus proprietors; we're paid our dollars every night; that's good enough for us. Put up your shooter, or we'll make you."

The men raised their picks threateningly, and advanced towards Jack. He ran for the shaft, the men after him like a pack of hounds in full cry.

"That's right," shouted Pike; "hit him over the head! Five hundred dollars to the man who first knocks him down. I'm a man of my word; you all know I never go from my promise. I've been amongst you for years, and you won't go back on me now, because a thief tells you a lie."

"Not us," replied the men.

They assumed a threatening attitude, and looked as if they could have lynched Harkaway, if they had him in their power.

One man got a little nearer than Jack thought safe.

"You will have it, will you?" he said.

The next moment he fired, and the man fell with a bullet through his knee, uttering groans of agony. His companions stood still, afraid to go any further, lest they should share his fate.

"That's one. I'm ready for the next!" exclaimed Jack.

"Cowards!" cried Sol Pike; "at him; bring him down, won't you? Holy smokers! isn't there one among you who has pluck enough to go for him? Freeze on him, I say."

"We've got wives and children," said one of the men, "and if we can't work they'll have to starve."

Jack had now reached the basket, he stepped in, and gave the signal to haul up. The basket began to move, and he slowly disappeared from the gaze of those below.

When Sol Pike saw that he had escaped, he raved and foamed at the mouth like a madman. There was another shaft close by, and seeing the value of time, he ran for it.

It was necessary for him to warn Hunston. Jack could not resist the temptation of giving a hearty cheer when he saw he was safe.

"Hurrah! hurrah! he cried. "Hip-hip-hip hurrah!"

This rang in Sol Pike's ears as the knell of all his hopes. He went to the second shaft as quickly as he could, and was in his turn drawn up. His house was not far off, standing on the slope of a hill.

Without stopping to try to arrest Jack's progress any more, he struck a bee-line for his residence. His only thought at that moment was to send Hunston away with the deeds of the mine.

Then Jack could do nothing but go to law for the treatment he had received in the mine.

Sol Pike could deny that he had confined him in a dungeon, and, being known to the people of the district, he felt certain that no jury or judge would believe him guilty of such an extraordinary charge.

Flying like the wind, he quickly traversed the ground intervening between the mine and his house. Hunston was in the sitting-room, drinking champagne with the men who formed part of the New York Ring.

The one Jack had wounded was lying on a lounge, with bandages round his leg. They were all merry at the thought of how they had euchred

Harkaway, and rendered him powerless to interfere with their schemes.

"I guess," said Hunston, "that we may reckon upon dividing a handsome sum in a few months out of this mine."

"That's so," replied the man sitting next to him. "Pass that bottle; there's plenty more where that came from."

Hunston was in the act of complying with his request when Sol Pike, blood-stained and flurried, dashed in at the open window.

"Why, Sol," said Hunston; "say, is that you?"

"Yes," replied the agent, panting with his recent exertion.

"What's happened?"

"Harkaway's escaped!"

"Der Teuffel!" said Hunston. "You don't mean to say you've been such a fool as to let him best you?"

"Curse him!" replied Pike. "He's done it, and will be here directly."

Every one looked blankly at his neighbour.

"You've got the deeds?" said Pike.

"Yes. Safe enough," answered Hunston, tapping the breast-pocket of his coat.

His tanned and weather-beaten face had turned the colour of coffee with cream in it.

"You'll have to quit," continued Pike. "Hurry up!"

"Where shall I go?" asked Hunston, in bewilderment.

"Get out of Missouri as quick as you can, and go into Texas."

"There's no railroad," replied Hunston, "and I don't want to go through the Indian Territory."

"Well, get down to Springfield or Carthage, and strike the Atlantic and Pacific road."

"That's better. I'll make tracks, and let you hear from me as soon as possible. Do your worst to Harkaway in the meantime, and I'll come back as soon as it is safe."

"That will do," said Pike.

Hunston was an old traveller, and it required no preparation for him to start. He shook hands with his friends, emptied his glass, and lighted a cigar.

"Which way do you expect this mad Britisher to come?" he asked.

"From the mine."

"Then I'll clear out the back way. Good-bye all. Drink to our next merry meeting, and may it be a speedy one."

He walked out of the house as unconcernedly as if nothing had happened, though, in reality, he was much alarmed and deeply grieved at Jack's escape.

His supply of money was amply sufficient for his wants, and he knew he could always get a letter of credit in any town he happened to stay in, by simply writing to his bankers in New York.

He had told Harkaway that they would only meet once again on earth. But he did not wish the meeting to take place just then. It would most likely have resulted in a way he would not have liked.

Jack was a determined man when aroused, and he would have shot Hunston down in his tracks as soon as he sighted him, let the consequences be what they might.

He had sustained great provocation, and after what he had suffered, it could scarcely have been called murder.

Hunston had not been gone ten minutes, before Harkaway entered the house, quite as unceremoniously as Sol Pike had done.

"Gentlemen," he said, "I have come sooner than you expected, to claim my rights. They tell me this is Mr. Pike's residence."

"Yes," replied Pike, "and I order you out of my house."

"I shall go when it suits me," answered Jack.

"Where is Hunston?"

"Where you won't find him."

Jack bit his lips.

The New York men were silent, in obedience to a sign the agent had made them.

"I demand my property," said Jack. "Give me the deeds of the mine, and I'll not prosecute any of you?"

"I know nothing about any deeds, and don't wish to have anything to say to you," replied Pike.

"You scoundrel!" said Jack. "Haven't you shut me up in a dungeon, and tried to kill me?"

"You must be dreaming," said Pike. "I never saw you before in my life. You get out, or I'll make you. It only requires a few words from me to bring a hundred men up from the mine."

"What then?"

"You'll see what then, if I do it. Quit!"

Jack looked sternly at the agent.

"Mr. Pike," he said, "our account is only half settled. I shall fight you to the last. If I go now, it is only to step back to take a better jump."

The agent laughed derisively.

"Get out!" he said. "You're as harmless as a dried snake. Hunston's got the deeds, and he's gone where you can't find him, as I told you before."

Jack made no further remark, but slowly quitted the apartment. He had hoped to surprise Hunston, but when he saw the agent, he knew that he had been too quick for him. The bird was flown.

Not knowing where Pike lived, he had to stop at the top of the shaft and inquire. While he was making his inquiries, Pike had reached his home, and sent Hunston away. It was unfortunate, but it could not be helped.

All Jack could do now was to go into the town of Granby and make a search for Hank Smith, Monday, and the boy. This he did without further delay. As he went along, he thought of the document he had found on Sol Pike.

He felt in his pocket for it, and to his great regret discovered that he had left it in the mine.

This was a misfortune, as it would have helped him to unmask the villainy of his enemies.

When near the entrance to the town, he saw a burly figure which he knew well. Running up gladly, he exclaimed—

"Hank! why, Hank Smith, don't you know me?"

The old hunter turned round, and, his eyes sparkling with pleasure, shook his hand.

"I'm real glad to see you," he replied. "What has occurred? Come into the shebang—they sell good old rye—and let's have a big talk."

Anxious to know where Monday and the boy were, Jack followed him into the saloon. They were quickly seated at a table, facing one another.

CHAPTER XXXVIII.

A COWARDLY ASSASSIN.

After Jack had told the hunter, in as few words as possible, what had happened, he inquired, in an anxious voice, after his son.

"I guess he's right enough," replied Hank. "Don't fret your gizzard, colonel, about him."

"But I want to know."

"I dessay you do. You'll have to wait while I think about them cussed thieves up at the mine. By thunder! who'd ha' thought of you being there?"

"Well, I'm out now, anyhow."

"When you was lost," said Hank, "and we come acrost the horse and seed the blood, we knew there was summat up, but what it war, beat us to guess."

"Of course you expected an attack on yourselves?" said Harkaway.

"That war the idea. So when we came up to the town I looked out for the first empty ranch."

"Ranch. What's that?"

"Why, a ranch is a farm, by rights; but we call a'most every place a ranch out here."

"Go on," said Jack, satisfied with this explanation.

"Well," continued Hank, "it war a poor-sized barn, and not very good at that; anyhow, we took possession right away."

"Did the owner say nothing to you?"

"A man come sneaking up. and says he, 'That's Sol Pike's ranch.' 'Tell Sol Pike,' says I, 'if he don't like it, to come and tell me so. I'm Hank Smith, and if that ain't as good as Sol Pike, I hope I may lose my scalp.' The cuss stared some, and at last he stepped it, whistling away like rain, he was that mad of me."

"Did Pike interfere with you?"

"Nary a bit. We put the horse in the barn, and the dog; then we fixed up some lumber for seats and a table. There was a heap of straw for beds, and hay for the horse."

"That was capital!" observed Jack, who knew that he must let Hank get at the end of a story his own way, and that it was no use hurrying him up.

"I reckon," replied the hunter.

"What did you do next?"

"We cut holes in the doors to look through, and your nigger kep' the fust watch. We war determined to shoot, mind you, if Sol Pike came on to us, but he didn't."

"That was a comfort."

"Wal, it warn't so much as you think," said Hank, who was in a contradictory mood. "If I could have given that scoundrel the lead, I should have been easier in my mind. I heer'd you talk of this Pike, and guessed he was at the fut of the trouble."

"You weren't far wrong."

"So it seems. Well, let me get on. I should have been through before now, if you hadn't kep' on interruptin' me."

"Very sorry, I'm sure," answered Jack.

"Don't matter a cent, captain. Tongue's cheap, and I've got plenty of it."

This was no news to Jack, but he held his peace.

"When we war fixed up, I started out on the scout, and brought in some victuals, such as beef, bread, and tea and sugar fixin's, though they were more for the boy than me."

"You seem to be known in this saloon?"

"Wal, I thought it prudent to establish friendly relations in a groggery. You hear talk in sich a place, and kinder find out what's going on."

"Very true," said Jack, smiling at the hunter's excuse for going after liquor.

"There is a hot crowd in Granby, but I guess I can drink square, without getting into a muss with anybody."

"Are Monday and the boy in the barn now?"

"Sure," replied Hank.

"Let's go to them."

"Monday's keeping camp while I'm on the scout, to find out news of you."

"I see. And what's Young Jack doing?"

"He walks up and down with a six-shooter and the dorg. He wanted to come scoutin' with me, but I thought it kinder risky."

"You were quite right to keep him in," answered Harkaway.

Hank finished his glass, and, throwing down some paper in payment, passed out, followed by Jack, who was glad to find that the "ranch" was not very far off.

It stood by itself. a little way back from the road, and was a substantial, frame-built barn.

As the two men approached, a shrill, clear voice rang out—

"Who goes there?"

"That's Young Jack," whispered Hank. "The nigger is having a rest, and the young one is keeping guard. He's bully on sentry-duty."

"Answer, or I fire!" continued the voice.

"Speak to him," said Harkaway.

"You bet. His orders is to shoot right away, if he doesn't know who's coming."

There was a click of the gun-lock, as if it was being placed on full-cock.

"Who goes there?" again said Young Jack.

"Friend," replied Hank.

"Give the password."

"Washington."

"What's the countersign?"

"General Grant."

"Pass, friend, and all's well," said Young Jack, in true military style.

"You see, colonel," said Hank, "that we are doing the thing up to the handle, and that Sol Pike don't catch us asleep."

"So I perceive," said Harkaway.

They neared the house, and when the boy saw his father, he threw open the door of the barn, and bounding out, jumped into his arms.

"Say, papa," he said, "where did he find you?"

"Not far off. I was captured by Hunston's friends, my boy, and kept in the mine; but I got out, and here I am."

"I *am* glad," said the boy. "I must fire a salute, or I'll bust up with delight."

He discharged all the barrels of his revolver, and danced about like a savage performing fetish.

The noise awoke Monday, who came running out.

"Mast' Jack!" he cried, "I'm real glad for to see you. Um heart beat forty-eleven to the dozen. That for sartin. How um been, sar?"

"I've had a narrow escape. Come inside, and I'll tell you all about it. What have you got to eat in your castle?"

"Plenty um cold beef, sar, and bread to any extent."

"We're minus mustard, pop, but I dare say you can make up without it," observed Young Jack.

Harkaway expressed himself perfectly satisfied, and made a hearty meal.

"Now," he said, "I'm going to sleep on that straw, for I've had no rest to speak of, except my first sleep in the mine."

"What um do in um mine, sar? Promise to tell that," said Monday.

"Hank will tell you. I'm too tired."

"Hank's been having a pretty good time, pop," said Young Jack.

"Has he?"

"I guess he has. Every night he goes to that saloon near by, and leaves us on guard, and he comes home as full as a tick."

"You dry up, you young imp!" said Hank.

Jack laughed, and, stooping down, caressed the dog, who came up and licked his hands affectionately.

"Rep knows me again," he remarked. "How's Lightning? I hope he wasn't hurt."

"The horse all right, sar. See him in um corner," answered Monday.

"Pop," said Young Jack, "I've got a conundrum, as the minstrels call it, to ask you. It's the worst that ever was made, bar none; but everything must have a beginning, and I'll promise to improve on it next time."

"Go ahead!" said Harkaway.

"Why is the roof of a house like a lame dog? Give it up?"

"Of course. It's the proper thing to do. You

should never rob a man of the pleasure of giving the answer when he asks you a riddle."

"Because it's a slope up."

"I don't see," said Harkaway.

"Well, you are dense, and it's hard on a fellow to have to explain his own joke. A lame dog's a slow pup, isn't he? Well, the roof of a house is a slope up. Twig?"

Hank Smith burst into a loud laugh.

"That's bully for you!" he exclaimed. "You're a pretty fast purp, you are, I'll bet."

"If I wasn't so thundering tired, I'd warm your jacket for that, Master Jack," said Harkaway, smiling. "Anyhow, you've made me feel sick, and it ought to be a warning to you."

"It shan't occur again. I apologise," said Young Jack.

His father threw himself on the straw, and was soon fast asleep.

Mind and body were fatigued, and stood in need of that recuperation which only sleep can give to tired mortals.

"Hank," said Young Jack, "you're not going out again, are you?"

"Well, no. I'm not partickler set on it," replied the hunter.

"We can't do anything till pop wakes and arranges our plans, so we'll keep guard over the castle."

"That don't take three."

"Tell you what—I don't know as there's much use in keeping sentry in the day-time," said Young Jack.

"P'raps there ain't," said Hank.

"Let's draw up our stools and have a cut-throat game of euchre."

"I'm agreeable."

"Bring out that greasy old pack of yours."

Hank reached in his extensive coat-pocket, and, after a time, produced a well-thumbed, worn, and greasy pack of cards, which he threw on the table.

"It's a euchre-deck," he said. "All out up to the eight spots. Come on, old table-varnish."

"What um mean, sar?" replied Monday, angrily.

"Sit down. You can't help your colour, can you?"

"Black man's good as white man, any day, sar."

"That, friend Monday, is entirely a matter of opinion."

"All men first made black, sar," said Monday. "One day a black man, who got um coward heart, saw um own shadow, and he got so mighty skeared that he turn white all at once. That's how it came about, sar."

"Ha! ha!" laughed Young Jack. "Our coloured prince had you there, Hank."

"Play your game," replied the hunter, who did not relish this chaff of Monday's.

Like all men who have been much on the prairies, he hated a red-skin, and had no kind of respect for a nigger, no matter where he came from.

That Monday was a Malay, and not a full-blooded African nigger in the skin, he did not stop to consider.

Nor would it have made any difference to him if he had.

The game at euchre went on steadily until about an hour had elapsed, when suddenly the dog began to growl.

"Down, Rep—soh! Good lad, quiet!" said Young Jack.

"There's the little joker, the right and left bowers, the ten spot of trumps, and an ace," cried Hank. "I guess you'll give me three."

"Not much, old Leather Stocking," replied Young Jack. "There are three trumps, and the queen to take your ten spot."

"Blow the luck!" replied the hunter.

Again the dog growled, and bared his gums ominously.

"What's got the purp?" asked Hank, anxiously.

"Rep, old man, what's the matter?" exclaimed Young Jack.

"There's some one about the shebank; I'll be dog-goned if there ain't!" continued Hank.

All at once the report of a gun was heard, and a cry proceeded from the corner in which Harkaway was lying.

"They've shot my father!" exclaimed Young Jack, springing up, and running to the door.

Hank and Monday followed him. Republican was tearing wildly at the door, with frantic efforts to get loose.

No sooner was the door thrown open than he ran full pelt at a man who was making off at the top of his speed.

"Down with him!" exclaimed Young Jack. "Stick to him! Loo, dog, loo! Go for him! Fetch him back!"

With huge bounds, the faithful hound cleared the space that intervened between him and the cowardly assassin who had fired the shot.

All this time they did not know whether Harkaway was dead or dying. Their first thought was to secure his would-be murderer.

Rep overtook him, and, flying at his throat, brought him to the ground.

Hank came up first, and pressing his thumbs under the dog's ears, where the jaw-bones meet, forced him to let go his hold.

He picked the man up, whose throat was fearfully mangled and torn.

"Sol Pike, by thunder!" he exclaimed.

The agent for the mine was trembling violently.

His rifle had fallen from his hand, and lay upon the ground.

Smoke was still rising from the muzzle, showing that it had been quite recently discharged.

"You cowardly sarpint!" said Hank Smith.

"I didn't do it," said Sol Pike, recovering himself a little.

"You lie!" roared Hank. "Look at your gun still a-smoking—ain't you a stinkin' varmint?"

"What have you got to say against me?"

"Agin you, you sneakin' reptile? All I have to say agin you would fill a book."

"It's my barn."

"What of that? Ha' you any right to come and shoot promiskus? Hold on to the purp, Snowball. I've got the shyster tight."

It was all that Monday could do to hold the infuriated animal, who, foaming at the mouth, and licking his chops, was making frantic efforts to get at Sol Pike.

Hearing the shot, a number of those who had been loafing around the saloon to which Hank was in the habit of going hurried up.

They were a wild set of fellows, having their own crude idea of justice. They believed a good deal more in Judge Lynch than they did in the sheriff and the courts.

Hank, during his potations, had spoken rather loudly about Harkaway, and how Sol Pike and others were trying to swindle him out of the mine.

The saloon-keeper, who was a Dutchman, by name Dippermann, had been listening to Jack's account of how he had been kidnapped and kept in the mine by Sol Pike and Hunston.

This was when Jack met Hank, and recounted his adventures during the time he had been missing.

Dippermann headed the crowd of miners and loafers.

"What's all this fuss about?" he asked.

"Oh! it's you, Johnny," replied Hank. "You've heard me talk of Mr. Harkaway? Jack, I call him, 'cos we're travellin' together round these parts."

" Ye-a," replied Dippermann.

" Wal, the Columber Mine's his, and Sol Pike, whom I've got here, has been and shot at him. Go to the ranch, boys, and see if he's got any life left."

Several men went to the barn, and others remained.

Young Jack was the first to run and investigate his father's condition.

The shot had taken effect, and Harkaway's condition seemed to be critical. He was insensible, and bleeding fast from a wound in the leg.

One man came back with the news, leaving Young Jack, with great presence of mind, tying part of his shirt round the wound, having sense enough to know that the only thing to be done before a doctor came was to stop the bleeding.

" Wal ?" ejaculated the hunter.

" I guess he's dead," was the cool reply, as the miner put a fresh chew in his mouth.

" Boys, listen here," said Hank. " This Sol Pike has been and shot Jack Harkaway. I reckon you've all heard of him. If not, I'll go bail for him."

" He's a Britisher," remarked a tall, thin Yankee in the crowd.

" What of that ? Ain't some of you Dutch, and some Irish, and the best part of you Peekes from California ?"

There was a laugh at this.

" You ain't goin' back on Jack 'cos he's a Britisher, are you ? But that ain't the question. We've beat the British enough to afford to be generous onct in awhile. The question is, ain't this sarpint got to be lynched ?"

Sol Pike had said nothing during this conversation, but when he heard the word "lynch," he grew very pale, and trembled violently.

He knew better than anyone else what a rough crowd there was to be met with in a Granby saloon after three o'clock in the day.

Dippermann had gone into the barn, and examined Harkaway, who was breathing heavily.

When he came out, he said—

" Boys, the Britisher is dying, sure enough."

There was a dark frown on the brow of each of those rough men at this announcement.

" The land adjoining ish mine," continued Dippermann, " and those trees are mine, too. Guess, boys, those trees are handy for lynching. If I saw you come on my land, I warnsh you off, so I go to mine saloon, and attend to my cushtomers."

The hint was sufficient, for a dozen hands were laid upon Sol Pike, and in no light manner.

" Who's got a rope ?" said one.

" Bill Jarvis and Montana Mike have secured a noose on that maple," said another.

In the West, men don't talk much—they act. Sol Pike saw that the tide of popular favour had gone against him.

Beads of perspiration trembled on his forehead, and his limbs shook under him. In a craven voice, trembling with terror, he said, in piteous, whining accents—

" For God's sake, boys, don't hang me !"

" Life for life !" was the stern reply.

This application of the Mosaic law, " An eye for an eye, a tooth for a tooth, and whosoever sheddeth man's blood, by man shall his blood be shed," found a ready acceptation among the miners of Granby.

Unheeding the agent's supplication, they dragged him to the nearest maple.

Over a stout branch of the tree, a rope with a noose at one end had been slung.

" String him up !" said the leader.

" Give me time to pray !" screamed Sol Pike; " you all know me "

" We know you for a hard, grinding villain," replied some one. " You never was the poor man's friend."

" I must make my peace with Heaven."

" String him up, boys !" again said the leader.

The injunction was promptly obeyed.

Half a dozen men put the noose round the agent's neck, half a dozen more bore on the other end of the rope, and up went the murderer in the air.

His face became as black as night, as the blood surged up into his head, and there stopped. He uttered incoherent cries, and then a dull gurgle was all that issued from his lips. His limbs, however, struggled spasmodically.

" Let him down three feet or more with a run, and bring him up short !" said the leader.

This was done.

Sol Pike was lowered with a jerk till his feet came within a dozen inches of the ground. The jerk broke his neck.

Then these rude executioners made the end of the rope taut round the branch of the tree, and their task was ended. It was horrible, but at the same time it was just.

The men all repaired to the saloon kept by Dippermann.

They all knew that when an inquiry came to be made into the matter, not one of their number would bear witness against the other.

Dippermann drove a thriving trade for the rest of the day.

When the men who worked in the Columbia Mine heard that Sol Pike had been lynched, they flocked down to Dippermann's in scores to get the news.

The story of Harkaway's persecution was told by ready lips to willing ears. No one was sorry for the agent.

In an hour or two the body was cut down by the authorities of the town to await an inquest.

The verdict of the jury was characteristic of the occurrence, and of the population.

They said—

" We find that Sol Pike, agent for the Columbia Mine, Granby, was discovered hanging by the neck from a tree, and between his neck and the tree was a rope, but how he or it came there, or who strung him up, we have no evidence to show, so that we find it was a case of accidental death."

Absurd as this verdict may be considered, it is literally true.

When Hank Smith had, with a grim smile of satisfaction, seen summary vengeance wreaked upon Sol Pike, the assassin, he went for a doctor, and brought him to the heap of bloody straw on which Harkaway was lying.

The doctor, whose surgical attainments fortunately were high, had no difficulty in discovering that the bullet had lodged in the thigh.

He promptly set to work to extract it, and after probing for it, made out its locality, and extracted it.

Binding up the wound, he said—

" All you have to do is to keep him quiet, and give him the things I shall send No important artery is severed, and his life is safe."

With this declaration, Hank, Young Jack, and Monday were content.

Pulling out a greasy leathern purse, Hank took out a twenty-dollar bill.

" Doc !" he exclaimed, " hold on to this shinplaister."

" But it is more than my fee."

" Don't care a continental for that. It's no more'n you deserve. Hold on, I say, and when you come agin you shall have some more physic of the same sort."

The doctor made no further demur.

During the night, Jack became feverish, but on the following day he was easier, and could converse with his friends.

In two days' time he was well enough to be removed to Dippermann's, where the whole party took rooms.

It was several weeks before he could leave his bed. But at length he got up, and moved about on crutches.

Hank Smith made inquiries about the mine, and found that the New York Ring had appointed another agent.

Without the deeds, which were in Hunston's possession, they could do nothing to dispossess the Ring of their prize.

It was now the middle of summer, and Jack was getting well fast. He had written to his friends in New York that he had been ill, but he did not tell them what had happened, for fear of alarming them.

No news could be gathered of Hunston. The month of August commenced, and Jack was able to walk without crutches. It was time to think of moving.

His inclination was to go after Hunston, but it was useless to chase a phantom. If he did not know where he was, he could not pursue him.

Perplexed and baffled, he knew not what to do. It seemed as if he would have to return to New York beaten, and give in, acknowledging Hunston and his friends the conquerors in the game.

But an incident occurred which put a new face on the aspect of affairs. Jack seemed destined to lead an active and adventurous life. A fresh career was opening out for him.

CHAPTER XXXIX.
AN UNEXPECTED ARRIVAL. AND AN EQUALLY UNEXPECTED COMMUNICATION.

"MR. HARKAWAY," said Hank, one evening, as the little party were assembled on the verandah at the back of the house in which they lived.

"What's that?" replied Jack.

"I guess I've had enough of this place. It's the back door to that country the parsons say the bad people go to."

"I'm not in love with it."

"I've stayed with you till you got well, and now I want to go hunting this Fall, and live fat. What are you going to do, if it isn't an impertinent question?"

Jack was lying in a hammock, swung on hooks in the roof of the verandah, and, looking down upon Hank, he replied—

"If you could advise me what to do, I should be much obliged to you."

"We've skunked Sol Pike," said Hank; "but you see, we're kinder euchered by this Hunston. Now, I never gave up a chase in my life."

"I don't want to give up anything," answered Jack.

"Same here, colonel. Ef I come across bartracks, I hunt that bar till I kill him. Wal, I guess Hunston's a sort o' human grizzly, and he's got to be hunted down."

"It's all very well to talk about it," said Jack, a little impatiently, "but how in thunder is it to be done?"

"Don't bile over, captain," replied Hank. "You can gas up without bustin'. I know how it is when the engine's started, but you can always regulate the speed by the throttle-valve."

"I beg pardon, friend Hank," said Jack; "I've been ill, and perhaps am a little irritable."

"That's so. Wal, you asked my advice, and I'm goin' to give it you, and you may bet your bottom dollar I ain't far off the mark."

"What is it?"

"Go after Hunston, and tree your coon."

"Very good advice," answered Jack, "if you could only find him. We've lost all traces of him. Where is he?"

Hank took off his hat and scratched his head.

"Guess you've got me in a hole this time, captain," he said. "I never thought of that."

"I once read a cookery-book," said Jack laughing, "and under the head of 'How to cook a hare' I found 'First catch your hare.' It's the same with us. Hunston's our coon. I'll back myself to tree him if I could find him, but you might as well look for a needle in a haystack as for a man on the Continent unless you have some clue to his whereabouts."

Hank was silent.

"I reckon I'll take a walk," he said, after a pause. He went outside and lighted his pipe, standing reflectively against the door-post.

"Pop," said Young Jack, "I guess friend Hank had to take a back seat."

"It is very annoying," replied Harkaway, "to think that Hunston has made off with the deeds of this mine. It keeps me out of my property."

"Go and take um mine, sar," said Monday.

"The lawyers would stop that. I want to prove my title," answered Harkaway.

Suddenly a voice was heard singing outside the saloon—

"Beer, beer, beautiful beer; there's nothing so wholesome as good lager beer."

"Hush!" said Jack, holding up his fingers. "I ought to know that voice."

"It's Mole, for a dollar!" said Young Jack.

"Be quiet, won't you," answered Harkaway.

They listened, and presently heard some one say—

"You man! You backwoodsman!"

"How?" replied Hank, who was the person addressed.

"Your face is familiar to me. I think you came to see us at New York. Have you a party of the name of Harkaway here?"

"You're Mole, aren't you?" replied Hank.

"Be civilised," replied the other; "and when you have occasion to address me, call me Professor Mole, of Oxford University, M.A., B.A., &c."

"You may be F. O. O. L. and A. S. S., for what I know or care," answered Hank.

"Conduct me to Mr. Harkaway," replied Mole.

"Conduct yourself. Do you think I'm your darkey?"

"My estimable border ruffian," said the professor, "will you relieve me from the painful necessity I shall soon be under of punching your classic head into a mummy?"

"What's that?"

"Indicate the exact position in the house which Mr. Harkaway occupies at this moment, or—"

"Go on, old hoss," said Hank.

"Or tremble. I am not to be trifled with, though my locks are becoming tinged with grey, and my arms lack that virile vigour which youth alone can bestow."

"Say, stranger, are you luny?" inquired Hank.

"Pardon me," said Mole, "if my language is a little high-flown, and above the comprehension of your mind. I have been quenching my thirst at various saloons during my search for my friend Harkaway, and your western bourbon is—is—what shall I call it?—ecstatic agony."

"The burbon is right enough, if you don't pile it on too high. But seeing you was new in these parts I guess they gave you kerosene. It's all the same when you're too full not to know the difference."

"Backwoodsman," said Mr. Mole, "there is an absence of that respect in your remarks which the presence of a distinguished man like myself ought to inspire. Why is this thus?"

"You had better switch off on Croton, or you'll have snakes in your boots," said Hank.

Harkaway had been listening to this conversation, and fearing that Hank might lose his temper with Mr. Mole, he said to the boy—

"Bring him in."

"I'll have him, if I have to carry him on a shutter," said Young Jack.

Harkaway was very anxious to know what brought Mole from New York.

He had written continually to his wife, telling her he was detained on business in Granby, and concealing from her the fact that he had been very nearly shot to death by Sol Pike.

"Mr. Mole, sar, him been on um burst," remarked Monday.

"It looks like it," answered Jack. "Wonder what brings him here?"

"Hope all well at home, sar."

"So do I."

"Here he is, pop! I've Bismarcked him!" cried Young Jack, in the passage.

Jack sprang out of his hammock, and was just in time to meet the professor on the threshold, and shake him heartily by the hand.

"My dear sir," said Jack, "I'm delighted to see you, and all the more pleased because your visit is so totally unexpected."

"I can reciprocate that sentiment," said Mr. Mole. "My heart rejoices exceedingly, but at the same time I could wish that your friend outside—hunter, trapper, wild man of the woods, or whatever he calls himself—were a little more respectful."

"It's his way," answered Jack.

"And a very unpleasant way it is, too. I should like to double discount that man, and then hang him out to dry."

"What is the news, Mr. Mole? I am anxious to know, as you may imagine."

"Certainly."

"What um done, sar? You not say 'Good-day' to Monday!" exclaimed the black.

"Oh! my faithful fellow," said Mr. Mole, "I overlooked you. How goes it?"

"Pretty fair, sar. Might be a heap worse."

Mr. Mole wiped his perspiring brow with a large bandana.

"I have done nothing but mop my face all day," he observed; "it's so jolly hot. It wouldn't be a bad idea to take off one's meat, and sit in one's bones."

"I can improve on that, sir," replied Jack. "Take the marrow out of the bones, and let the wind whistle right through."

"Ha! ha!" laughed Mr. Mole; "you are sure to cap anything. By-the-way, can you offer me any refreshment? My thirst is worse than that of Tantalus. Champagne will do, if it's well iced."

"You forget, sir, I'm a poor man now," replied Jack, "and can't afford luxuries."

"Oh! hang the expense, I'll pay. Harvey has given me plenty of money for travelling expenses."

"If I could only find Hunston, and get the title deeds of the mine, I should be fixed very differently."

"Is that all you want?" asked Mr. Mole, with a smile.

"Yes."

"Then I think I can help you."

"Is that so?"

"I have undertaken this journey for the express purpose of bringing you valuable information respecting the movements of that arch fiend Hunston."

"Bully for you!" said Young Jack.

Harkaway's countenance further displayed the joy he felt at hearing this good news.

"We have received a letter in New York, addressed to you, and your wife took the liberty of opening it in your absence."

"Who is it from?"

"Hunston."

"The dickens!" exclaimed Jack. "Hand it over, sir."

Mr. Mole gave Harkaway a letter, which he eagerly read.

It began: "From Hunston to Harkaway. In camp on the Big Cheyenne river, Dakotah. Having been badly wounded in an encounter with the Sioux Indians, lying, as I fear, at the point o death, I am desirous of seeing you without dela to make what reparation lies in my power for th many injuries I have done you during my li e. If you will hasten to me, and promise me your forgiveness, I will give you up the title deeds of the Columbia Mine, so that you can enjoy the property left you by your father.

"Proceed right away to Cheyenne City, on the Denver branch of the Union Pacific Railroad, and inquire at the Brevoort House for a man named Sublette, who will conduct you across the plains to where I am lying, too ill to move.

"If you grant me this favour, God will reward you for your kindness."

Jack read this aloud, and Hank Smith, who had re-entered the house, was much surprised at the contents of this extraordinary letter.

"It shows me that Hunston has a conscience," said Mr. Mole.

"What do you think of it, Hank?" asked Jack.

"I'm a-trying to remember that name," replied the hunter.

"Which?"

"Sublette. It seems kinder familiar to me. I once knew a chap of that name. Dakotah Dick we called him. He was a half-breed, and in with the Indians."

"It may not be the same."

"Prob'ly not."

"I'm inclined to believe the letter genuine," said Mr. Mole.

"Anyhow, it is worth something to us, because it gives us Hunston's locality," said Jack.

"There's treachery behind that, mark my words," said the hunter.

"I'm not easily scared," answered Jack; "and come what may, I'll go to the Cheyenne City and inquire for this fellow, Sublette. Where is Cheyenne?"

"It's in Wyoming, but close to Dakotah and Nebraska. The railroad's made it what it is. I can recollect the place when it didn't amount to chucks," said the hunter.

"Monday," said Jack, "get everything ready for a start to-morrow."

"You take me with you, sar?"

"Yes."

"And me, too, pop?"

"Aren't you afraid of the Indians?" asked Harkaway.

"Not much. I should like to perform on a few red-skins with my revolver."

"You little shrimp," said Jack, "I fancy you'd be safer if you went home with Mr. Mole."

"Pardon me," said the professor; "I am not going to allow myself to be shunted like a cattle-truck, or a freight-car. I'm in this thing, and want particularly to receive Hunston's last dying speech and confession."

"Very well. We will all go. I shall telegraph to-day to New York, and tell Harvey, Hilda, and my wife where we are going."

Mr. Mole went into the saloon, and presently returned with four bottles of champagne, which was soon bubbling in glasses.

"I'm going to treat on this," he said.

"Wal," said Hank, "here's fun."

"Success to Jack Harkaway!" cried Mr. Mole.

The toast was drunk with enthusiasm, and Jack replied in a neat little speech.

During the remainder of the day, extensive preparations were made for leaving these "diggings," and preparing for the journey.

Hank was delighted to be once more on the move.

Monday polished up the rifle Grim Death, and every one looked to his arms. The dog held his head higher, as if he knew his master was about to take the war-path, and even Lightning neighed joyously as Monday brushed down his sleek coat.

Jack was very grave, considering the news.

He scarcely believed in Hunston's letter, for he knew him to be a hard-hearted man, and did not think it likely that he would wish to make reparation, even if he were, as he said, at the point of death.

But he was determined to make an effort to secure the deeds of the mine, as it was necessary for him to have this property in order to obtain the means of subsistence.

During his illness at Granby, Harvey had been sending him money, and he did not like to be beholden to any one.

He wished to pay him back the money he had borrowed and start clear.

Early the next morning the little party got down to the railroad depot, and started on their journey to Cheyenne City.

CHAPTER XL.

A MEETING WITH SUBLETTE, AND OFF TO THE PLAINS.

WHAT Hunston had been doing up in that direction, or how he got there, or what induced him to go there, they could only dimly imagine.

If it was true that he had been wounded, and was dying, Jack could not feel for him.

Hank said there were plenty of Sioux on the Big Cheyenne River, and that they were treacherous and blood-thirsty.

So it was just possible that in an encounter with Indians, he might have been injured as he said.

. . . .

In due course of time, our party arrived at Cheyenne City, and went to the hotel known as the Brevoort House.

Here Jack inquired for the person named Sublette, who had been mentioned in Hunston's letter as the man to guide him to the place where Hunston was lying, sick unto death.

The keeper of the hotel was a German, and in reply to Jack's inquiries, he said—

"Sublette! I knows him. He is here one week. Then he go away."

"Where has he gone to?" asked Jack.

"He say he go to Bridger's Pass, on the Rocky Mountains. Not far from here. All on the railroad."

"Did he tell you when he would return?"

"He say to me, 'If man of the name of Harkaway come here, I should send a despatch.'"

"Very well," answered Jack; "that is my name, and as I want to see him, you can telegraph as soon as you like."

"Good enough, sir," said the Dutchman.

Jack engaged rooms for himself and party, and after a good dinner, sat down to enjoy a cigar and a chat with Hank about the Indians.

Young Jack and Monday went out together for a walk, but Mr. Mole, with the whisky-bottle by his side, listened to the hunter's yarns with as much interest as Harkaway did himself.

When Young Jack and Monday had been walking about for some time, they stopped before a tobacconist's.

Outside was a wooden figure of a painted Indian, holding up his hand threateningly.

This was the tobacco-dealer's sign.

"I say, Monday," said Young Jack, "wouldn't it be a lark to take this figure and put it close to old Mole?"

"Golly, sar! That um good idea!" replied Monday.

"Suppose we steal this figure and paint you up, too, and put feathers on your head? You'd pass muster as a red-skin."

"Anything for um bit of fun, Mast' Jack," answered Monday.

"Collar the figure, then, and look smart."

Monday looked round. There were few people about.

The tobacco-dealer was in his back-parlour, and there was not a policeman to be seen.

He stooped down, shouldered the effigy, and bore it off in triumph, carrying it to the hotel.

A few words to the people standing about explained the nature of the joke, and a dozen willing hands helped to dress Monday like a redskin.

They painted him, and did up his hair, gave him a belt and moccasins, furnished him with a tomahawk and a bow, and made him look very savage indeed.

The room in which Harkaway, Hank Smith, and Mr. Mole were sitting was separated from the adjoining apartment by folding-doors.

In the empty room they placed the wooden Indian, and Monday stood in a dark corner, ready to appear at a moment's notice.

A crowd of the hotel frequenters occupied positions which would enable them to see the fun.

When all was ready, Young Jack said to the landlord—

"I'll go up-stairs and set Mole on. First he shall be frightened at the wooden figure, and then Monday shall appear with a yell, and say he will have his scalp."

"I hope nothing bad will come of it," said the landlord.

"You go and eat saurkraut," answered Young Jack.

Just as he was about to go up-stairs, a new-comer appeared upon the scene.

He was a short, symmetrical, dark man, about thirty years of age. His face was full of character and of wonderfully perceptive faculties. He had long black hair, complexion like a Mexican, and eyes like an Indian.

"Ah!" cried the landlord. "Mr. Sublette, you have come back much before you were so unexpected."

It was Sublette, the famous half-breed, whom Hunston had appointed as a guide for Harkaway.

It was said that he had been a chief among the Crow tribe, and was the most famous Indian-fighter of the day, his body being scarred from wounds innumerable.

Rumour also had it that Sublette had been a Kansas border ruffian, a Nicaraguan fillibuster, a prisoner among the Mexicans, wearing a chain, working on the roads for more than a year, a surveyor on the Panama Railroad, and, in fact, a general utility man out West, though his most important character undoubtedly was that of a man of weight with the Indians, whom he boasted he could excite to war or keep in check as he pleased.

"What is this excitement?" he asked.

The landlord readily explained to him what Young Jack and Monday intended to do.

"Where is Mr. Harkaway?" he inquired.

"In No. 46."

"Did he ask for me?"

"Yes. He is anxious to see you."

Sublette ran quickly up-stairs, and knocked at the door of Harkaway's apartment.

"Come in," said Jack.

The half-breed raised his hat politely and said—

"My name is Sublette. You were expecting me, I am told. It is unfortunate that I should not have been here to meet you, but I didn't think you would arrive so soon, and I had business in the Rocky Mountains which I have been attending to."

"Pray take a seat," said Jack. "I am very pleased to see you. Allow me to introduce my friends, Professor Mole, and Mr Hank Smith, the well-known hunter."

"I guess we've met before," said the hunter. "Say, do you know me?"

Sublette looked keenly at him, and seemed to turn a shade paler beneath his swarthy skin.

"No," he answered, coolly; "we have never met before, to my knowledge."

"You lie, you half-breed thief!" cried Hank. "Weren't you with the Comanches in Texas when they murdered the whites in '64?"

Sublette's eyes flashed fire, he drew a knife from his belt, and advanced towards the hunter, threateningly.

"Take that back!" he exclaimed.

"I be doubly darned if I do," said Hank, stoutly.

"I'll allow no man to tell me I lie. Take it back, or—"

Jack hastily stepped up and interfered.

"Mr. Sublette," he said, "I am sure my friend did not mean to make any remark which you would deem offensive. He is misled by some peculiar likeness, or some erroneous reasoning."

"No I aren't," grunted Hank.

Sublette put his knife in his belt again, and turning to Harkaway, said, with a light laugh—

"Excuse me; I have wild blood in my veins, and am apt to be hasty. A moment's reflection has shown me that I was wrong to act so in your apartments. I should have despised such mean trash as that."

He pointed his finger scornfully at Hank, and sat down at the table.

"Will you take a little claret on ice?" said Jack, glad that the quarrel, which seemed imminent, was avoided.

"With your permission I will gladly do so, as I have just come off a long journey, and must confess to feeling a little thirsty, and somewhat parched."

Hank pulled away at his pipe in a surly manner, and talked to himself.

"I'll swear it's the same chap," he muttered. "Think I can be mistaken? Not much, sirree. That lobster was in the white massacree. I've heard of him. He's a sworn friend of the reds, darn his ugly skin!"

"Have you lately come from amongst the Indians, may I inquire?" asked Professor Mole.

"Well, not exactly," replied Sublette. "I heard that a band of Apaches had entered Dakotah, and I went in the interests of humanity to warn them that Captain Villard has a large force of soldiers at Fort Sully, and that the captain himself is in Cheyenne City now, picking up news."

"I don't think there is any danger from those untutored sons of the forest" replied Mole.

Sublette smiled, and showed his glistening teeth, white as ivory.

"You would change your opinion," he said, "if you fell into their hands."

"Not I. One white man is as good as ten redskins."

"That idea is often held by foolish young men, who come out here for the first time," replied Sublette. "But people who are the foremost in deriding the noble savage are the first to speak of his courage after they have met him in his native wilds."

"Rubbish, my good sir, rubbish!" said Mr.

Mole. "Show me the red-skin that would frighten me!"

At this moment, Young Jack drew back the folding-doors, and Mole, turning round at the sound, beheld a hideous, painted, grinning, ferocious, Indian, close to his elbow.

He uttered a cry, and tried to get up, but his legs failed him, and he sat still, shivering, however, with fright, and looking the picture of misery.

"Help!" he said; "shoot the villain! Shoot him!"

Just then, Monday, in his Indian get-up, appeared upon the scene, and advanced to Mr. Mole, with his tomahawk in his hand.

"Hiawatha, great brave," he said. "Want um white brether's scalp."

With a clever and dexterous movement, he pretended to pass his knife over Mole's head, and with a terrific whoop, lifted up his wig, leaving Mole in a state of mind more easily imagined than described.

Sublette approached, and slipped a pistol into Mole's hand.

"Shoot! shoot!" he whispered. "The savage will kill you!"

Monday was dancing a war-dance, and winking at Jack, who had recognised him, and was, with Hank, enjoying the joke.

The professor raised the pistol given him by Sublette, and fired.

Monday uttered a cry, gave a bound forward, and fell headlong to the floor.

"Good God! what have you done?" said Jack.

"My duty," replied Mr. Mole. "I have saved all our lives from that blood-thirsty savage!"

"Rubbish! You have killed Monday!"

"Monday! Impossible! Is that really Monday?" said Mole, alarmed.

Jack was by this time at Monday's side, and found that his faithful attendant was severely wounded.

The people in the hotel came up in a crowd, and the nature of the joke was explained, every one expressing the most profound sympathy for Monday.

Sublette had picked up his pistol when the professor let it fall, and replaced it in his belt.

He did not think it worth while to mention that the landlord had told him, when he first came in, that Mr. Harkaway's faithful servant, Monday, was about to play the part of a red-skin for a little fun.

But it is certain that, when the half-breed gave the pistol to Mole, he was perfectly well aware that if he fired at all he would fire at Harkaway's black servant.

Monday was put to bed, groaning deeply, and evidently suffering much pain, while a surgeon was procured, who pronounced him in considerable danger of his life.

When all had been done that was possible for the sufferer, Jack descended to the sitting-room again.

"My dear Harkaway," said Mr. Mole, "believe me, I am deeply grieved at this unfortunate occurrence."

"I am sure you are, sir," replied Jack; "but your grief does not do away with the stupid haste of your rash act."

"It is the fault of Young Jack, I am informed."

"Is that so?"

"Blame me, if I wouldn't welt that boy!" said Hank.

Young Jack had been sitting in a corner ever since the shot had laid Monday low.

"I'm here, father," said he, getting up.

"All this is your doing, they tell me," said Jack.

"I only did it for a bit of fun, and never thought it would end like this Monday agreed to dress up like an Indian, and he looked a regular Mulligan Guard, as he marched up to Mr. Mole and took his hair."

Harkaway paced the room thoughtfully,

"I'll tell you what I shall do with you," he said, at length.

"If I've deserved a hiding, give it me," said the boy; "I dare say I can stand it as well as I ought."

"You shall go back to New York," continued Jack.

At this sentence, the boy's countenance fell.

"I am very seriously annoyed," said Jack. "Monday is my right-hand man, and just when I want him most, this unlucky shot of Mr. Mole's lays him on what may be his death-bed, and all through you."

"I didn't mean it."

"No matter. You are the cause of it, and I desire that Mr. Mole take you back to New York, and look after your education. You know nothing, and your manners and conversation, instead of being those of a gentleman, are no better than a boot-black's."

Young Jack hung his head down in shame and annoyance.

"You won't send me back to New York, too, will you?" said the professor.

"Yes, I will," replied Jack. "You will be of no use to me. I am on the eve of making a dangerous journey. Is it not so, Mr. Sublette?"

"Oh," replied Sublette, "for the matter of that, travelling to Dakotah Territory is always more or less risky when the Sioux are about, and now the Apaches have crossed the frontier, we may have to fight before we reach Mr. Hunston, who is lying some distance from Cheyenne."

"Monday would have been of use to me," said Jack. "But I am really very much put out. You and the boy will oblige me by going back to-morrow. My wife will be pleased to see both of you."

"Do let me go, papa. Will you?" cried the boy.

"No," answered Jack. "You are wild and uncivilised enough already. I should be neglecting my duty if I did not try to make you a more respectable member of society."

Young Jack hung down his head.

"Go to bed. It is now past nine, and you ought to have been asleep an hour ago. Mr. Mole, oblige me by seeing Jack to his bedroom."

The professor gave his wig a hitch, which placed it in its proper position, and taking the boy by the hand, led him away in tears.

His disappointment was so keen that he could not help crying, and his tears were in some measure induced by the dangerous state in which, by his folly, Monday had been brought.

Getting into bed, he exclaimed—

"Will you hear me say my prayers, sir?"

"With pleasure, my boy," replied Mr. Mole.

Young Jack repeated the prayers his mother had taught him with considerable fervour, and added a special supplication to Heaven that Monday might not die through the effects of his unlucky practical joke.

"Don't go yet, sir. I want to talk to you," said the boy.

"Well, I will stay half-an-hour with you," said Mr. Mole.

"Do you think Monday will die, sir?"

"The doctor is doubtful. It was a most unfortunate shot on my part."

"Oh, it wasn't your fault at all. I will take all the blame, and I feel that I am rightly punished."

"That is a proper state of mind to get into.

When we commence our studies again, you must try and be a good boy, an apt scholar, and behave as befits a young gentleman."

"I will try," replied Young Jack, earnestly.

"I cannot say that I am sorry your father has come to the determination he has."

"Would you not have liked to go out and fight the Indians, sir?"

"To tell the truth," replied Mr. Mole, "I am getting old, and have seen many hardships lately. Teaching is more my forte than fighting. Besides, your father will, most likely, rejoin us shortly, when he has seen Hunston and received the title-deeds of his property, which that very wicked man has promised to give up."

"I don't believe in Hunston, sir," said Young Jack. "He is a bad egg, and this dying confession is some dodge of his to get papa into a trap."

"It is more than possible."

"It is a pity papa won't give up the chase."

"Harkaway is a very peculiar and determined man," replied Mr. Mole. "I have known him now since he was a child, and if he sets his mind on a thing, he will not give in while he has a breath in his body."

"Well, sir, I won't keep you any longer," said the boy. "Thank you for staying with me. If there is any change in Monday, let me know—I should like to see him before he dies."

"We will hope that he may recover."

Mr. Mole shook the boy's hand, and retired with the candle.

"There is a great deal of good in that boy," he muttered. "But boys are plants; they want caring for, pruning, and keeping clear of weeds, and he must be governed with a strong hand. 'Spare the rod and spoil the child,' was the truest saying that old Solomon ever uttered. I will be strict with him."

When he rejoined Harkaway, he found him alone. Hank Smith had gone to the bar, and Sublette had gone out on business.

"You will be ready to start early to-morrow morning, sir, I hope?" said Jack.

"Certainly," replied Mr. Mole. "What about Monday?"

"The doctor has just left me. He has extracted the ball, and says the poor fellow will live, though his recovery will be slow. I want you to leave some of the money Harvey furnished you with, so that the landlord of the hotel may care for him while I am absent."

"By all means. I have three thousand dollars. Will you not take some?"

"Thank you, no. I have enough for what I want," replied Jack, "and I hope soon to get the deeds from Hunston, and take possession of my property."

"Amen to that," said Mr. Mole.

"Do you approve of me sending my son back to New York?"

"Very much, indeed. He is at an age when boys learn quick, and if the precious hours of youth are wasted they can never be made up for. In after-life, one's pleasures and the work which the struggle for existence entails upon us absorb all our time."

"Yes," said Jack, "that is true, and the boy has been running wild too long. Make an educated young gentleman of him, Mr. Mole."

"I will do my best, sir."

"That I am sure of. I feel that sending him back with you is the most sensible thing I ever did in my life. In the first place, he is not old enough or strong enough to undertake the toils and privations of a life on the plains."

"No."

"Secondly, his life would have been in danger if

we met with Indians, and you must remember that there is always the chance of Hunston's dealing with us in bad faith."

"We have seen enough of his treachery," said Mr. Mole.

"We have, indeed, and I am on my guard. It is possible that I may not return to the confines of civilisation for several months. God knows what adventures I may meet with."

A servant entered the room with a telegram.

Jack took it, and tearing it open hastily, read its contents.

"Bad news?" queried Mr. Mole, as he saw Jack's face clouding over.

"Yes. I am sorry to say your perceptions have not deceived you. The despatch is from Mrs. Harvey."

"What does she say?"

"Dick has broken his leg."

"Indeed!"

"He was driving a fast trotter up Tenth Avenue, and when near High Bridge, the horse shied, threw him out, and broke his leg."

"Is that all?"

"No. Emily has caught the chills and fever, and is ill in bed. They want you to come back with the boy."

"In a day or two," said the professor, "they will see me. Shall I send an answer to that effect?"

"Do, please, without loss of time, and if Sublette has come back, send him in to me, won't you?"

Mr. Mole nodded, and was absent about ten minutes.

"I can't find Sublette," he said; "but there is a Dutchman outside who wants to see you."

"Call him in," said Jack.

A thick-set, sturdy looking German walked into the room, and without taking his hat off, or acknowledging Jack's presence in any way, said—

"I hear that you want to shuit yourself mit ein help."

"Well, yes, I do want an attendant. What have you been?"

"I bin tending bar."

"What is your name?"

"Mein name ish Hans Hasselbachboormorman-teurffelstrockhausenplatzbergenessengenfloomerflu-moxencarlsruheschoonerkint."

"Stop! stop!" cried Jack. "That's an awful name. Can't you give us a bit at a time?"

"They do call me Platzbergenessengerfloomer-flummoxencarlsruheschoonerkint for short."

"I am much obliged to you for the offer of your services," said Jack, "but Mr. Hans Hasselbach, &c., &c., &c., it would be too much exertion to pronounce your name every time I had occasion to speak to you. Therefore I am sorry we can't deal."

"Ah, vell," said the philosophic German, "there ish no bones broke. I shall wish you g suntheit"

He advanced to the table, and coolly poured out a glass of claret, which he drank, saying "Trinknalle" and adding, "Vell, I shay good-night, boss."

"Good-night," answered Jack.

Scarcely had he gone, before a little dapper man, looking every inch a Frenchman, made his appearance.

He was the pink of politeness, and bowed half a dozen times.

"What is your pleasure, my friend?" inquired Jack.

"I have hear that monsieur shall vant an attendant in his journey on the plains," was the reply, "and I have the great honour and satisfaction to offer myself as his valet de chambre."

"You should say valet de champ, as we are not likely to see anything but fields for some time."

"Ha! ce n'est pas mal. That is ver good," replied the Frenchman. "I admire ze choke ver moch. Monsieur is vat we call ze vit; he has beaucoup d'esprit."

"What is your name, mister?" asked Jack

"Varney Bonneau, at monsieur's service."

"Well, Mr. Bonneau, if you like to come with me, until my black servant gets well, I shall be glad to have you. Can you fight?"

"Zare!" replied the Frenchman, drawing himself up proudly. "vat is zis you ask of me? I am from La Belle France, vere ze men are born soldiers. Ha, it is not ze red-skin Indian would frighten ze soul of Varney Bonneau."

"I am glad to hear it. You can consider yourself engaged, and I suppose we shall not fall out over the question of payment."

"No, sare; I go with you for nothing, rather than stay is zis place. I have a secret vich I shall tell you."

"What is that?" asked Jack.

"I have been living for ze board in ze house of a widow woman's, and she do swear that she will marry me. I would rather prefer to be scalped by ze red-skin men than I would marry a widow womans."

Jack laughed.

"Get yourself ready to start early to-morrow," said he.

"Yeas, sare; I shall be ready quite at ze instant moment ven you vant me," replied Varney.

Hank Smith came in soon afterwards, and Jack informed him of his intention to let Mr. Mole return with the boy to New York.

The professor was apparently dozing in a chair.

"The boy's no good at all, if it comes to Injun fighting," said Hank; "and as for that old bummer in the chair, he'd scat like wild ducks at the first shot."

"I've engaged a French servant to come out with us," continued Jack.

"What sort of a chap?"

Jack described Varney Bonneau.

"Why, that's the fellow I saw talking to Sublette a few minutes back at the bar, you bet."

"You have a prejudice against Sublette," said Jack.

"He's a rank bad 'un, if ever there was one, and I don't like this Varney being so intimate with him. All the half-breeds are treacherous, and this fellow Sublette can do just what he's a mind to do with the reds."

"All the better for us."

"That depends upon circumstances. It may be his game to sell us; but howsomever, I'm a-goin' with you, and that's as flat as the bottom of a Mississippi steamboat."

"Have you heard any news?" inquired Jack.

"Yes. Captain Villard started this morning across the plains for Fort Sully."

"It is a pity we could not have gone with him," said Jack.

"I don't know that it would have made much difference. The captain's got troops up at the fort, but he rode down alone to Cheyenne City."

"Is that so? What was his reason?"

"He came to meet his nephew, Lylie Leland, a young fellow from Yale, who has gone up the country with him."

"When shall you be ready to start?" continued Jack.

"A'most any time. All time is alike to me. But I s'pose you've got to consult that sophisticated guide."

"I want to speak to him, certainly," answered Jack. "He came in just when Monday was shot, and went away again directly, so that I have had no opportunity of questioning him about Hunston

or where we have to go, or anything. In fact, I am regularly in the dark."

"It is quite unnecessary you should be so any longer. Mr. Harkaway," said a voice at his shoulder.

Jack turned round, and beheld the guide.

It was a peculiarity of Sublette's that he had a snake-like tread perhaps acquired on the plains and in the pathless forest, where the breaking of the smallest twig might have occasioned his death by revealing his position to a watchful enemy.

Oh, is it you, Mr. Sublette !" said Jack. " Be seated, if you please. I want to have a little conversation with you."

The guide took a chair facing him.

"How did you become acquainted with Mr. Hunston ?"

"In the simplest manner possible," replied Sublette, taking a cigar he was smoking from between his lips.

"Will you oblige me by relating the incident ?"

"With pleasure. I am, as you are doubtless aware, a guide and hunter by profession."

"I have heard so."

"While waiting about Cheyenne City, on the look-out for something to do, Mr. Hunston arrived at his hotel, and inquired for a guide. I was at his service."

"Where did he wish to go ?"

"He said he had six months' spare time on his hands, and would like to see some sport on the plains, up as far as the Yellowstone."

"Yes," said Jack.

11

"He engaged me," continued Sublette, "and we travelled as far as the White River, being fortunate enough to meet with antelope, buffalo, and grizzly bear, but being unfortunate enough, on the bank of the White River, to fall in with Sioux."

"Were you attacked?"

"I guess we were, and we had a rough time of it, after all," said Sublette. "We drove off the Indians, but Mr. Hunston received a wound which will cause his death."

"Are you sure of that?"

"Oh, perfectly. My only fear is that he will be dead before we can reach him. The bullet struck him in the lungs."

"That is dangerous," said Jack.

"I left him with a servant, who, like myself, is a half-breed, and he gave me the letter to post, which I forwarded on to you. instructing me to wait here until you should arrive."

"How far is White River from Cheyenne?"

"About seventy miles. We can do the distance comfortably in, say, two days," answered Sublette.

"We will start to-morrow, at ten o'clock."

"That is late. We travel with the sun's rise, and only rest when the sun sets," answered Sublette.

"It cannot be helped. I must see to Mr. Mole's departure with my son," replied Jack.

"As you please. It is not for me to dictate to you. Shall you ride?"

"Yes. I have my horse Lightning."

"I shall tramp it, my legs are good enough for me," said Hank.

"And I, too," said Sublette. "You will be the only cavalier of the party, Mr. Harkaway."

"Did you not say that hostile Apaches have been seen in Dakotah Territory?" inquired Jack.

"Yes," replied Sublette. "A strong band of Apaches have crossed the border, ostensibly to hunt buffalo, which have been heard of eastward of Fort Laramie in large numbers, but their real object is to stay and plunder wherever they have the chance."

"I knew an Indian who said he was an Apache chief," said Jack.

"His name?" asked Sublette, inquiringly.

"Par-a-wau."

"Ah!" cried the guide. "That is a mighty name in the Apache country. Par-a-wau is brave as a lion. I know him well, and heard he had been to some of the great cities with skins."

"Indeed," said Jack, pleased to hear this. "He is my friend."

"If Par-a-wau said he was your friend," answered the guide, "you may depend upon it, that if you should ever want his aid, and he could give it, you would not call in vain."

"Are the Sioux fiends quiet?" asked Hank.

"You know the Sioux as well as I do, if you are the great hunter you say you are," replied Sublette.

"I know they are a set of cowardly skunks, and you are never safe from 'em," said Hank. "But seeing as you were kinder born with 'em, I thought you might tell me something of the all-fired varmints' goin's on and movements gen'rally."

"I don't know that they are worse than usual"

"Oh! you know nothin'," replied Hank, sarcastically. "A purty innocent lamb you are, to be sure. You haven't heerd that the Sioux's on the warpath, and that Captain Villard is hastenin' back to Fort Sully, which used ter be called Fort Lookout, to bring his troops down, and drive the tarnal all-fired skunks back to their reservation?"

"This is news to me," said Sublette, calmly.

"Then you're the innocentest an' curiousest consarned cuss I ever cum across," replied Hank. "Did you ever live with the deaf and dumb? Makes you so blamed simple."

"My friend," said Sublette, who exercised an admirable self-control over himself, "what is the matter with you?"

"I don't like you," replied Hank, bluntly.

"I am very sorry that I do not meet with your approbation, but it is my misfortune, not my fault. You are prejudiced against me."

"Time will show whether I am right or wrong."

"We are to be fellow-travellers, and I offer you the hand of friendship."

"And I won't take it. Hang me if I shake hands with a man who is neither one thing nor t'other. You're as much Indian as you're white," replied Hank.

"Mr. Harkaway," said Sublette, "protect me from your friend, will you?"

"Hank is peculiar in his likes and dislikes," replied Jack. "What am I to do?"

"Do you join him in his suspicion? If you do, I will part company with you at once. I am independent of Hunston, and yourself, too."

"No, no," said Jack: "do not be hasty. I want to secure your services."

"In that case, ask Mr. Smith to be a little more guarded in his remarks."

"If that's what's the trouble, I won't snarl any more," answered Hank. "But mark me. I'll bite if there's any occasion for it."

Sublette turned his back upon him.

"Good-night, Mr. Harkaway," he said. "I shall go to bed now. At ten to-morrow I shall be at your service."

"He bowed politely, and quitted the apartment.

"The fellow seems to act in good faith," observed Jack, when he had left. "I wouldn't rile him up, if I were you, Hank."

"He's a darn'd sneaking thief, and you'll find it out before long," replied the hunter.

"I don't think so."

"He'd humbug a parson, he would; but I'll say no more. My knife's as sharp as his, and I can shoot straight, if it comes to that," said Hank.

Jack went to the window and threw it up, taking a look into the street.

The moon was shining brightly, and he hadn't been looking out long before he saw a dark figure gliding along the street.

He felt sure this was Sublette.

"By George!" he said, "there is our guide going up the street. He said he was going to bed. Shall we follow him, friend Hank, and see where he goes to?"

"I'm on, if you are," replied Hank.

"Step out, then. I don't feel like sleeping, and would like to have a little excitement."

They hastily put on their hats, and left the hotel, following rapidly in the direction taken by Sublette.

Mr. Mole got up as soon as they had vacated the room, and rubbing his eyes, said—

"I think I'll take a drink. It's been a long time between drinks. That old hunter thief called me an old bummer, and said he'd make me scat. I'd like to give him the contents of my revolver. Make me scatter, would he? Not much. What's this—claret? That's too thin. Eh! whisky? Good. I'll imbibe some of this old rye, and then go to bed. Thank Heaven, to-morrow will see me on my way to New York and civilisation."

Jack and the hunter kept close together, and followed Sublette until he stopped before the door of what was, to all outward appearance, a private house.

Keeping in the shadow, they observed him, in the pale moonlight, look carefully up and down.

No one was about.

Then he knocked with his knuckles upon the door,

giving three distinct raps, there being a pause between the first and second, but the second and third come quickly together, thus—

Rap—rap-rap.

The response from within was exactly the reverse, being two quick raps and one slow. Rap-rap—rap.

Then the door opened, and he was admitted.

"Wal, I swow," said the hunter. "There's some rampageous mystery up now."

"What sort of a house do you think it is?" asked Jack.

"It's some monte hell, I'll bet my bottom dollar!" answered Hank. "They play three-card monte up here till sometimes they'll stake their shirts and walk away next to naked. It's the fellow's last night here, and he means to go on a bit of a bust"

"I'd dearly like to go in," said Jack.

"Wal, we can try the trick as well as he, I guess. If you're sot on it, Colonel, I'm with you."

They walked on a little further, until they came to the house in question.

"Are you armed, Hank?" whispered Jack.

"Ye a," replied the hunter. "I've got my knife and a shooter."

"So have I. Stick close."

"Nary fear, you bet!"

Jack knocked at the door as he had heard Sublette do, and the return signal being made, the door swung back, revealing a well-lighted hall, in which were standing a full-blooded negro, and by his side the half-breed.

Sublette fixed his sharp eyes upon Jack, and raising a whistle to his lips, blew it shrilly.

The next moment Jack fancied he saw a man, with one arm only, appear for a moment at the further extremity of the passage, and vanish through a back door.

"Hank," he whispered, as they stood where they had entered, "did you see any one answer that whistle, and clear out down below?"

"Nary soul," answered the hunter.

"Then I must have been mistaken. But I could have sworn I saw a man with one arm, and the figure was wonderfully like Hunston."

"Like enough," said Hank. "I told you they were playing with us."

Any further remark Jack might have made was cut short by the advance of Sublette.

"Mr. Harkaway," he said, "I did not expect this It was my impression that it was inconsistent with any pretentions of gentility for one man to play the spy on another. You can scarcely say you came here by accident."

"No," replied Jack, who scorned to tell a lie; "you deceived me first by saying you were going to bed. I happened to be looking out of the window, saw you going up the street, and certainly did follow you."

"What are you going to do, now you are here?" asked the half-breed, his snake-like eyes twinkling maliciously."

"I want to see the circus."

"There's a little gambling going on below, if you e to go down."

'Won't you be our guide?" said Jack.

Sublette shrugged his shoulders, and answered—

"I am going down myself for a little excitement. you like to come with me, you can."

"Oh! we're quite independent, if it's all the same to you, mister." said Hank. "The boss and me's come to what I s'pose is a public place, and we can find our way without your help, and that's straight."

Sublette evidently did not wish to quarrel, either with Jack or the hunter, though he was very much annoyed.

Making no reply to Hank, he said—

"This way, if you please, Mr. Harkaway. Mind the steps."

"It's pison to him to be civil to us," whispered Hank, as they descended the stairs into the cellar where the gambling was going on. "Ain't he riled up! He's fit to bust wi' venom. The skunk's gone as white as his homely black face will let him."

When they reached the end of the staircase, Sublette threw open a door, and disclosed a plainly-furnished apartment, in which a dozen or more were playing three-card monte, more for the benefit of the proprietor of the den, than from any advantage which they gained, if the stern, furrowed faces Jack saw, and the deeply-muttered curses and oaths he heard, were any indication of the state of mind of the frequenters of the establishment.

Wines and liquors were displayed at a bar in one corner, which was presided over by a negro, who dispensed the drinks at the price of a quarter of a dollar each.

Cigars were fifty cents apiece, so that no inconsiderable portion of the proprietor's profit came from selling liquors and tobacco without a license.

"Holy smokers!" said a tall, rough-looking, ferocious man, with long, unkempt hair. "Lost again. I'll switch off no to something else, if I don't want to go home in my buff."

By "buff," he meant his skin, which was an allusion to the last resource of the desperate gambler staking his shirt against whatever it might be valued at.

A little, lithe, thin Mexican was gesticulating wildly, for he had been winning.

In his hand he held a black snake-whip, which he slashed through the air with a pistol-like crack and a keen stroke.

It happened to touch the rough-looking man, who seized it angrily, and snatching it from its owner, threw it at him.

"That's El Paso Tony," said Hank to Jack. "I knew him down in Texas. There'll be a row presently, you bet."

"Who is he?" asked Jack.

"He used to be a driver of the Wells Fergo Express. What he is now is more'n I can tell."

"Who's the other fellow?"

"I know him, too; he's a reg'lar border ruffian We used to call him Billy Shoot-dead. Look, he's goin' for him."

The Mexican turned fiercely upon Billy Shoot-dead, and said—

"What do you mean by touching my whip? Do you want to take the *jornanda del muerto* (journey of the dead)?"

"P'raps two can travel the same road," replied Billy Shoot-dead. "All I say is, keep your snake off me."

"Pick it up," said El Paso Tony.

"Not much," answered Billy Shoot-dead "I haven't come to be the help of a Greaser."

El Paso Tony grew furious at this remark, though "Greaser" is a common name for Mexicans, owing to their dirty, oily appearance.

"Call me a Greaser, will you? I guess I'm as good as a darned Yank, any day," replied the Mexican.

He drew a murderous-looking knife as he spoke, and would have rushed upon the American, had not the bystanders interfered.

"No carving, Tony," said one. "It's agin' the rules of this shanty. Put up your venison-slicer, and come and take a drink."

This request was an all-powerful agent in keeping the peace.

Half a dozen friends surrounded Billy Shoot-dead as soon as they saw him draw his revolver, at the sight of the Mexican's knife, and they drew him away to the bar.

Soon, all the men were drinking, and the quarrel was over.

Billy Shoot-dead held up his glass to El Paso Tony, saying—

"Here's fun," and Tony returned the compliment, saying—

"My regards."

"Who wants to have a throw with the dice?" said Billy Shoot-dead, looking at Jack. "What do you say, stranger?"

"I don't mind," answered Jack. "I'll go you a dollar a throw; but if I lose twenty dollars, I quit."

"Good enough," said Billy Shoot-dead. "You're from Europe, I guess?"

"Yes, I am."

"My! shouldn't I like to be a Britisher, and wear side-whiskers!"

"Do you know what we'd do with with you, my friend, if we had you in England?" said Jack, coolly.

"What's that?"

"Civilise you."

There was a laugh at this, and Billy Shoot-dead grew rather red in the face.

"How do you fight where you come from?" he asked.

"Do you want to know?"

"I guess I do, or I shouldn't have asked."

"Put up your fists," said Jack, "and I'll show you; but, look here, I bar shooting."

"That's good enough. I'm ready," replied Billy Shoot-dead.

In an instant, Jack was guarding with his right ready to hit with his left hand, and standing in a springing attitude on the ball of the foot, head thrown a little back, and body inclined an inch or so forward on the left side.

"Come on, my friend. Every time you hit me I'll give you a dollar," said Jack.

Billy Shoot-dead made a dash at Jack, who parried all his blows, remaining solely on the defensive.

It seemed impossible for Billy to get within his guard, and the spectators, who, with one or two exceptions, had quitted the monte-table to crowd round the combatants, applauded loudly every time Jack drove back his opponent.

"Well, I guess I'm licked," said Billy Shoot-dead, after another fruitless effort to touch Jack. "How do you do it?"

"It's science," said Jack, laughing.

"I couldn't get at you. If I had," said Billy, regarding his brawny, iron-like fist lovingly, "I'd have fetched you, you bet!"

"No doubt of it," replied Jack. "But you must recollect that if I had wanted to be ugly, I could have pounded you to a jelly, old boy."

"Well, I guess that's true. Let's see what you can do at throwing. I aren't a British prize-fighter, you know, and that makes all the difference."

"Nor am I," said Jack. "But I know how to keep a ruffian like you quiet."

"Don't you call me names," said Billy Shoot-dead, "or I'll make cold meat of you."

"You've got nary a bit of sense, neither one of you," said Hank Smith. "Say, boss, where's those dice? Let's have a chuck, right away, fair and square. What's the use o' snarling like a couple o' catamounts in a tree?"

The proprietor of the saloon promptly produced the dice, and placed them and the box containing them on the table.

"It's your chuck fust," said Billy Shoot-dead. "I'll give in to a Britisher, out of a kinder compliment, becos we've seen 'em give in to us Americans so often. Bowl away, stranger; they're all down in this alley."

"How much money have you got?" asked Jack, eyeing him curiously.

"Now, that's what I call bisniss," replied Billy Shoot-dead, putting his hands in his pockets, and not finding anything.

"Nary cent," he added, after a pause.

"If you've no money, what's the use of throwing?" said Jack.

"My credit's good. Hi! Paso Tony, am I good for twenty dollars?"

The Mexican was at his side in an instant, and although they had been nearly cutting one another's throats a short time before, he placed a fifty-dollar bill on the table.

"Owe it me as long as you like," he said.

Billy Shoot-dead turned triumphantly to Jack, and said—

"You wouldn't take my word! Didn't think it good enough, eh? Thought because I wasn't dressed up to your mark, and hadn't got no side-whiskers, I wasn't good for twenty dollars. Found your mistake out, have you?"

"He's good enough for a hundred," said Hank Smith, who had been an interested spectator of what was going on.

Billy Shoot-dead turned round.

"Say, Hank," he cried, "is that you, old hoss? I must ha' been blind not to see you before. Are you come ter watch this game of spekilation?"

"I guess that's my humble intention," replied Hank. "Give us your fin, old fish. It's years since we had a shot together."

"Hold hard!" said Billy, trying to steady himself, and speaking with drunken gravity. "The Britisher will excuse us while we take a drink for old acquaintance sake. Boy, bring drinks. Rye for me."

"Same here," said the hunter.

"Are you with this consarned cuss from a played-out territory?" continued Billy Shoot-dead, when the drink had been disposed of.

"Wal," replied Hank, "we're off to the plains together arly to-morrow."

"That so? Now, Cap'n, we'll toss. It's your fust show. Can't you cover this currency, and lump it altogether?"

"If you like," replied Jack, who placed a fifty-dollar bill by the side of the other.

He threw the dice, and had the luck to pitch two sixes and a five.

The spectators evinced great interest in the game.

"You're gone up, Billy," said one.

"Guess he's a gone coon," remarked another.

"Two sixes and a sink," said Billy Shoot-dead, having learnt the terms from the Canadian French when he was in Canada, the French calling six seize and five cinq. "I'll take three sizes to beat that. Here goes for it!"

He cast the dice, and, with a cry of disgust, turned up two aces and a four.

"Take the money," he said. "I'm whipped."

"Your luck's out, Billy," said El Paso Tony; "I won't back you any more."

"Tell you what I'll do with you, boss," said Billy Shoot-dead, addressing Jack.

"What's that?"

"I've got nary thing partickler on hand for a few months, and you're going on the plains."

"Well?"

"You'll want some one with you who onderstands the ropes, though you've got Hank, and he's a hunter born, and can smell an Indian more'n a mile off; still, I'll tell you what I'll do with you. I'll stake myself for three months."

"Against what?"

"Say, boys, what's Billy Shoot-dead worth?" said that eccentric individual.

"If I could buy you at my value, and sell you at your own, I should make money," said Sublette.

"Oh! you dry up," replied Billy; "we all know what you are."

"What am I?" asked Sublette.

"A darned spy. You're no better than an Indian, and I don't care to have any truck with you."

Sublette shrugged his shoulders in his habitual manner, when annoyed, and retired without saying another word.

"Have you got five hundred dollars, Cap'n?" continued Billy Shoot-dead.

"I have," replied Jack.

"Will you stake that agin me? If I lose, I'll come with you wherever you're goin', and I'll shed the last drop of my blood in yer service."

Jack looked inquiringly at Hank.

"Oh, it's right enough!" said the hunter. "What Billy Shoot-dead says he'll do, he will do. He's a blood-thirsty, quarrelsome, drunken varmint, but he'll keep his word if he dies for it."

"Thank you for nothing, you old bar-slayer," said Billy, with a good-humoured smile.

"If you were dead, Billy, I'd give yer five dollars for yer skin," said a bystander.

"What would you do with it?"

"See if it wouldn't make good boot-leather. It's tough enough."

"It would be no good for that until it's tanned, and there isn't a man among you who could tan me. Say, Cap'n, will you stake five hundred dollars agin me myself?"

"I don't care about it," replied Jack, hesitating.

"You won't have another chance like it so long as you live."

"If I win, won't it be like buying a white elephant? I shall have to keep you, feed you, and goodness only knows what use you will be," said Jack.

Billy Shoot-dead lowered his head, and whispered in Jack's ear—

"If you've got Sublette as a guide, as I hear you have, you'll want help. Not that I care. I'm only making the bet for devilment."

"Well, I'll take you," said Jack. "Throw first."

"Rattle 'em well up, Billy," said one of his supporters.

"Oh! dodrot the rattlin'. Here goes!" replied Billy Shoot-dead.

He threw a five, four, and a three.

"Tray, cater, sink," he said. "Beat that, Cap'n, and I've sold myself into the house of bondage. Cut along. Be spry. There aren't no nigger-sellin' now, and it's something new for a white to put himself in the market. Chuck, I say!"

Jack rattled the dice, and threw a six, a five, and a four.

"Beat, by Moses!" said Billy Shoot-dead. "When do you raise camp, Cap'n?"

"To-morrow, at ten o'clock," replied Jack.

"Where air you staying?"

"At the Brevoort House."

"I'll be on time," said Billy Shootdead, philosophically, and adding, "As you've got my bottom dollar, and won the finest man, bar none, in America inter the bargain, I s'pose you'll stand treat?"

"With pleasure," replied Jack, putting down the fifty-dollar bill he had won, and saying to the proprietor, "Let us drink this out, if you please, and be as quick as you like over it."

This act of generosity raised him very much in the opinion of the crowd, who drank to him, and generally made up their minds to have a good time; but Jack touched Hank's arm, and he and the hunter slipped away together.

When they were in the street, Jack said—

"I suppose I shall never see that fellow again?"

"Not see Billy Shoot-dead if he says he'll come?" replied Hank.

"No."

"Don't you make any mistake. Billy's a man of his word. He wouldn't have bet himself against your five hundred to-night if he hadn't been dead broke. His bank was bust, you see, and he was bound to do something. He'll come up to time, you bet."

"Is he a good man to have with you?"

"You couldn't have a better for rough work, and fightin', if it comes to that."

Jack began to feel as though he had done a good stroke of business, for he had his doubts about Sublette's honesty, and expected that there was danger ahead.

"Yer should freeze on him," replied the hunter. "He's true grit, is Billy Shoot-dead. When yer've come to him, yer've come to hard pan, as the miners say."

They reached the hotel soon after midnight, and found Mr. Mole had just left Monday's room.

"How is the patient, sir?" inquired Jack.

"He sleeps," replied Mr. Mole. "Where have you been, and what have you been doing?"

"I've won a man."

"How?"

"By throwing the dice. He staked himself against five hundred dollars, and I won him."

"For how long?"

"Six months, if I want him so long," answered Jack.

"It's a great country," remarked Mr. Mole.

"You bet!" replied Hank.

Soon afterwards, they retired for the night. Jack was up early, and engaged with Sublette in making purchases of several things which were considered necessary for the journey.

These were packed on a mule's back.

The train for the East touched at Cheyenne about eight o'clock, and Mr. Mole, with Young Jack, got on, in reply to the conductor's summons of "All aboard."

"Good-bye, papa," said Young Jack.

"Bye, my boy. Mr. Mole will mail me an account of your behaviour. Be as good as you can. Bye, sir, pleasant journey to both of you. Don't forget the letters I have given you for my wife and Harvey."

"No fear," replied the professor. "Success attend you, Harkaway!"

There was a waving of hands, and the cars rolled out of the depot, bearing Mr. Mole and Young Jack back to New York.

Harkaway turned sadly away, and repaired to the room in which Monday was lying.

The faithful black was in much pain, but his countenance lighted up when he saw his friend.

"Ah! Mast' Jack," he said. "So you seen um boy and Mr. Mole off, and now come to say good-bye to Monday."

"Yes, my dear fellow," said Jack.

"You be 'way long, sar?"

"There is no telling."

"You not 'spect be 'way more than a week or so?"

"No."

"It makes me kinder mad," said Monday, "to lie here while you go 'lone, Mast' Jack. That thing rough on Monday. I always 'spect Mr. Mole do some darn stupid thing with um pistol some these fine days."

"Your life is safe, Monday," said Jack, "and you ought to be thankful for that. Look how long I was sick at Granby."

"That true for you, sar."

"When any disaster happens to us, we ought always to think that it might have been a great deal worse."

"Well, I guess you's right, Mast' Jack; but I

aren't b someosopher like you. What you do without me? That's what puts me in such a debil ob a muss."

"Do the best I can," replied Jack, "and do what I have made a practice of doing all through my life, Monday."

"What that, sar?"

"Rely upon myself. The great secret of success in this world is self-reliance. I am not above taking the advice of a friend, or receiving his assistance; but a man should look to himself, rather than to others, when the hour of trial comes."

"Mist' Mole gone," said Monday, "me lie here sick. Can't move. I hear Missy Emily bad with the chills and fever. Young Jack gone home, and Mist' Harvey broke um leg. Why, you left all alone, sar? Something wrong about this, sar."

"Well," said Jack, smiling, "if anything should occur to keep me out on the plains, you must all of you make haste and get well, and come and join me."

"Good enough, sar," replied Monday. "You stop out 'mong the Indians, and me soon get well, and come and help you take um scalps."

"So you shall."

"Mast' Jack," said Monday, "they say these Indians have red skins, not like Malay. Have um all red hair?"

"No. Their hair's black."

"Very curious thing. Guess I'd like to 'natomise one of those 'Merican red-skins."

"Is there anything I can do for you?" asked Jack. "You will find the proprietor of this hotel kind and attentive. He has money to pay for your board, and the doctor has been paid in advance."

"That all um want, sar. God bless you, Mast' Jack!"

The large tears rolled down the honest fellow's cheeks, and Jack, after shaking his hand warmly, hastened from the room, as he, too, felt like crying.

Sublette was already organising in the yard attached to the hotel.

The mule was having his burdens attached to his back.

Varney Bonneau, Jack's French attendant, was assisting the guide.

Hank Smith was oiling a rifle, and looking to the stock of ammunition.

The clock struck the hour of ten.

"All ready," said Sublette.

"Where's the man I won?" said Jack. "I suppose he won't turn up. Just what I expected."

There was a noise at the entrance to the yard, and a loud voice exclaimed—

"By the hookey! I'm only just on time!"

The last stroke of the hour of ten died away as Billy Shoot-dead appeared on the scene.

"Mornin', Cap'n," said he.

"Glad to see you, Billy," said Jack. "Are you ready for a start?"

"That's me."

"Off we go, then," said Jack.

He sprang into the saddle, and Lightning neighed joyously, as if he were pleased at the prospect of the journey before him.

Rep barked and ran about wildly, as if he thought himself the most important item of the party.

Hank put himself by Jack's side, Sublette went on in front, Billy took the other side of Jack's horse, and Varney drove the mule, which brought up the rear.

Jack's rifle, Grim Death, was slung across his shoulder. In his belt he had two revolvers and a knife.

Whether Sublette was to be trusted or not, he had armed himself to the teeth, and so had Hank Smith, who was quite as wily as the guide.

They soon quitted the city of Cheyenne, and took to the road leading to the wild, unsettled country between the Rocky Mountains and the Missouri River, which is known as Dakotah Territory.

Visions of Indians, buffalo, antelopes, and many strange unknown sights and scenes, of which he had dimly heard or read of, floated before Jack's imagination.

Billy Shoot-dead roused him from his reverie, saying—

"Who'd ha' thought yesterday that I'd have been on the tramp now?"

"Better for you, Billy, than staying in the city," replied Jack.

"Mebbe. Don't say it isn't, though I must say I like to get on a tear sometimes."

"Do you know this country?"

"I guess I do. Two days ago, Captain Villard came to me and offered me a hundred dollars to come up to Fort Sully with him and his nephew, Mr Leland."

"Why didn't you go?"

"I was on a bust, you see, and my bank wasn't broke then," replied Billy Shoot-dead.

"Oh! that was it," said Jack, curiously.

"I'm an old frontiersman, and never do any work so long as I have got any money."

"Why did you come with me?"

"Why?" asked Billy Shoot-dead. "Because you won me fair and square. There's a thing I thinks more of nor money, and that's my word, boss."

Jack was interested in this man, whose ideas of morality were so peculiar; he would drink, gamble, swear, and fight, but he would not break his word on any account.

"Cheyenne is not what it was," said Billy Shoot-dead. "When it was the terminal station of the line, we had all the scum of the earth here. People called it 'hell on wheels,' but the Vigilance Committee hung a few dozen, and it's a bit better now."

They rapidly left Cheyenne City behind them, and found themselves in a gently undulating country, which seemed to be a perfect paradise for antelope, deer, or buffalo; but no game of any sort met their gaze.

"Shouldn't wonder, Colonel," said Hank, "if we war to meet with this Captain Villard."

"All the better. I hope we may," replied Jack.

The party progressed at the rate of about two and a half to three miles an hour, and though the heat of the sun was oppressive, no one murmured.

Jack Harkaway was now fairly started on his new adventure, and as he calmly smoked a cigar, he wondered how it would end.

"If we could only penetrate the future," he said to himself, "all the charms of life would be gone. The pleasure of living consists in the delicious uncertainty of human events. To-day I am in good health, and safe from my enemies. To-morrow I may be in the power of an Indian, who is triumphantly holding up my reeking scalp."

In spite of himself, he shuddered as his mind conjured up this picture.

Startling events, however, were about to happen. Treachery was at work.

Dangers, thick as leaves in Vallambrosa, were circling round him.

But what was about to happen cannot here be hinted at.

So we bring to a close the first portion of "Jack Harkaway in America," which we trust has fully realised the expectation formed of it by our many readers, and we promise them an exciting story, and a rare treat, at an early date, in

"JACK HARKAWAY OUT WEST AMONG THE INDIANS."

www.ingramcontent.com/pod-product-compliance
Lightning Source LLC
Chambersburg PA
CBHW081154170626
46813CB00009B/3189